REQUIEM FOR A KNAVE

Also by the author

The Wicked Cometh

REQUIEM FOR A KNAVE

Laura Carlin

HODDER

First published in Great Britain in 2020 by Hodder & Stoughton
An Hachette UK company

This paperback edition published in 2020

1

A CIP catalogue record for this title is available from the British Library

Paperback ISBN 978 1 473 66146 2
eBook ISBN 978 1 473 66146 2

Printed and bound in Great Britain by Clays Ltd, Elcograf S.p.A.

Hodder & Stoughton policy is to use papers that are natural,
renewable and recyclable products and made from wood grown in sustainable forests.
The logging and manufacturing processes are expected to conform
to the environmental regulations of the country of origin.

Hodder & Stoughton Ltd
Carmelite House
50 Victoria Embankment
London EC4Y 0DZ

www.hodder.co.uk

For my mother, Norma Underhill (1932 – 1998)

CHAPTER ONE

I wish to tell the legend of my life and hope its telling will not be unprofitable to any soul as one day might read it. Some folks will say it is extraordinary, some will say it cannot be true. But as God is my witness, this was the way of its happening.

Its history is begun by God's grace in a time long ago when I was a youth, ever walking forwards through a landscape of gladness and opportunity. Now I am old and my skin wears the marks of many years lived, but my mind is free of wrinkles and for the sum of my days I have laid down my thoughts on wafers of paper. Now, as I review my chronicles, I know the length of my days has given me deeper understanding, and at last I am compelled to order my thoughts and lay before you the story of my life ...

The start of my tale is on Saint Giles's day in the fortieth year of the reign of our king Edward. We lived in a house on the land at Crown Croft, some dozen miles from the town of Badeswell, in the shire of Derby. The house was built with timbers from the Whittaker woods, many generations ago. Originally a two-roomed cottage, it now boasted a house-place, a solar, three bedchambers, a cooking shed and a pentice for the pigs. We owned the house and all the land about, as far as sight would allow.

We had twelve acres arable and twelve acres mead, and our ploughland was rich and in good heart; lands quenched for a thousand years by the majestic River Crown. There was no rod of land without its crop and no stretch of mead without its beast. Over summer, our fields and strips would gather up every slant of light cast down by the sun. Not a morsel was wasted; every beam to become an ear of corn or a blade of barley. And each year by the will of God, the soil restored itself, content to yield its bounty. It was a land created by the Good Lord so far back in time, that time itself could not recall its beginnings. The pasture was so fertile that in antique times, they used to call it the 'Pure Land' or the 'White Acre': now it is called Whittaker; and I am Alwin of Whittaker.

We lived a good life back then; Mother, Grandfather and me. At eighteen summers I had thriven well; healthy and sun-washed I was. I recall a dose of chin-cough as a young boy, as many had hereabouts, but nothing worse than that. And from height to sole I was above middling; Mother called me tall; Grandfather called me adequate. But although I was above middle stature in height, I was wanting in breadth of shoulder and power of arm, and not even the merest flaxen down graced my cheeks and covered my lips. But despite my lean build, and my youthful appearance, Mother had bred me up to be active and strong. When other lads were still charged with stone-picking and weeding, I was already at the plough from morning till dusk and I never shirked my toil. No fat lay on my bones. Of skin and muscle I was built, nothing more, nothing less. Hale and trim I was, which even Grandfather could not deny.

We lived in a routine of comfortable monotony; church every Sunday, seed time and reaping, labour and rest, day and night. We brewed our own ale and spun our own butter. Mother weaved and baked. Grandfather and I shouldered the heavy work, and of that I took the larger share. Sweet and fair the days were, sweet and fair the life, and it was all such great liking to my heart.

That particular Saint Giles's day where I begin my tale, was one of those rare days that falls between the seasons, when the harvest is over but it is not yet time to lay up firewood for winter, when summer's labouring is done and the morning is slack, no birds on the wing – some already gone to their nests underground to hibernate for winter – no motion to the air. The harvesting of our barley, oats and maslin, begun on Lammas, was now done; a tenth of our crop to be paid to the church. Grandfather would be taking the cart to the tithe-barn in Badeswell later that day to pay our dues and would not be back until the following afternoon, and Mother was resting up.

I suppose most folks would take such an opportunity to lie abed till noon, stay long in sleeping, rest awhile before the hardship began again. But I awoke just as the sun was up-rising, a feeling of anxiety stealing sleep from me, which I could not account for. I experienced a desire deep inside me to wander the lanes, walk the uplands and glades, climb to the heights where the hill-streams rushed, and walk alongside the River Crown where the waters, gliding fleet and clear, would be studded with gems of sunlight.

I dressed, washed my face, hands and feet, and slid the shutter open in my bedchamber. I sat on the sill for some moments and watched the daylight expanding on the horizon, its glow casting rods of yellow light across the fine Whittaker lands, the shadows long and reaching out towards the house-place below. I always loved to watch the old house at sunrise; the timbers drinking in the hue of daybreak, taking on the colour of the day.

My room looked out onto a small garden where peonies and gromwell grew, where the scent of honeysuckle and lavender wound upwards through the window all summer long. There was a narrow herb-bed beyond – awash with tansy, rosemary, thyme and sage – which then flowed down to the meadow with its grasses tawny and sere from the summer sun, and went on to meet with the River Crown, where dabchicks and moorfowls oared themselves through the waters, and widgeon and coot were busy about the river's brink.

More than ever before, I felt as though I must be out there, I must walk along the September lanes and green glades, I must climb the hillsides raddled with the rising of the sun, tread the open pasture and feel the soil beneath my feet.

So, I stepped out into the morning, silver vapours drifting low above the meadow, and I fed forage and fodder to the oxen and milch cow. Then I made my way to the ewes and lambs; made sure they were all in good plight. But all the time there was a feeling of apprehension accompanying me, like a day that bodes rain but it never sets in, or a song you know but you cannot call the tune; always there but just out of reach.

It stayed with me all day: when I sharpened the coulter on the plough; when I repaired the furrow-board, and even when I walked through the far meadow, where three weeks since the whole field was tall and upright, stippled with purples and yellows, crimsons and blues, the entire meadow ornamented with wink-a-peeps and cornflowers. Mother always said it was where once a rainbow fell and left its colours in the grass. Now its grasses were withering on the stem, burdened by dew.

Despite my anxieties, I felt such an abiding love of the land on which I dwelt and also sensed more keenly the changing of the season and sadness of summer's end. But even with that melancholy feeling inside me, I had such a love of life that I knew I could have no complaint come the day the Good Lord called on me to quit it.

Strange and rare the day continued as I walked along the sheep-tracks and strolled through the woods, until at last I sat down and rested on a rock. Mother said the boulders thereabouts were as old as time itself, placed here and there by the hand of God to offer up a place for the weary to rest, a reward when toil and strife were done. From that vantage point, I could see for miles and look down on land and tracks that stretched away to the horizon. I had never spent a deal of thought upon the world that lived outside my own domain, and hardly a stranger crossed our doorsill from one year to the next, except for pedlars and tinkers. The ones that did stop by for ale and bread only told of the calamities that had befallen them, so it seemed to me the lands beyond the Whittaker woods were surely a fearful, brutal place.

I had not been there long before I saw Grandfather in the distance on the road to Badeswell, walking alongside the loaded cart, prodding the shoulder of the nearside ox with his goad. As he was intending to remain overnight in Badeswell and I would not see him until the next day, I might have troubled the air with a shout and had him turn to me, but I was disinclined to do so. For the whole of my life the man had been all grutch and grumble with me; it was always sour weather with him as far as I was concerned, and however much I pondered on the matter, there was never any good reason for him to be so, at least not as I could come to.

In the interests of equity, I cannot lie; he worked as hard as I did on the land and always acknowledged the contribution I made. But he was not a friend to me; he was cold and distant. Yes, he cultivated within me a rich knowledge of all farming matters, but he offered no tenderness to me, nor gentle kindness. In the deeps of my mind, I half suspected he might know of my deformity; but Mother always assured me the secret of it remained between just me and her.

You see, I was born in the year the Great Plague came on very violent in our county, when purple and blotch stained the skin of all England and corruption of the air was all about. Distemper spread its rage on the land and an abundance of folk did perish. Doomed souls were dying at a rate quicker than they could be laid to rest. Once the tokens of the disease showed themselves on their bodies, by a single turn of the sun and the moon, they would succumb to the pestilence and be dead. My mother's brother and their own mother fell in such a manner, and before the last heat of plague had cooled its wrath, it cast its eye in my direction and the violence fell on my tiny body.

A grain arrived in my groin with the stealth of black smoke and within a week it had grown to the size of a pigeon's egg, its malignant intent to destroy the organs that marked me out as a boy; the ones God gives to all sons of Adam. Once emasculated, then it would surely have carried me off to death. But it had not reckoned on my desire for life, nor my will to dwell on the Whittaker lands and be a fine son. It may have left me as an incomplete man, but it could not take my life.

Whenever I asked Mother if my deformity were the reason why Grandfather could never skim off the bitterness of his temper towards me, she told me no and said I must not take it to heart, and that a young man like me should not shoulder the burden of such sadness. Of course, she was right; especially at that time of year. Our harvest was as good as any. Our barley crop in August stood as tall and full-headed with grain as any I have ever witnessed. And soon I would be out there with my oxen again, the clink of the ploughshare biting into the ground, earthy scents rising about me. Why, any man should have been as glad as a pie.

But I was not glad and at first I could not place the feeling. It had been with me all day. In fact it had been shadowing me since Mother's health first declined; for her haleness fell away after springtime and by midsummer's day she was no better than middling. Since then, there had been a gradual decline in her soundness.

Daily she reported to me a list of her infirmities. She could no longer tend the geese, nor walk the pigs. I began to pay a penny a week for our neighbour's daughter, Alice of the cornfield, to tend to the fowls, but she could not come after Michaelmas. And at that time of year, Mother would usually be filling the storeroom with fruits, and drying lavender on the rafters, but she was not even able to fettle the homestead.

Now she said she must abide in bed and so she was mewed up in her bedchamber from daybreak till night. She bore the distemper with dignity, but it despised all physic and I began to wonder if there were venom in the pipes of her skin.

I convinced myself she would gain strength as soon as the harvest was in. And I treated her well; I always told her of the gains I had made during the day, told her what a fine son she had, just as I had been brought up to do. And I never cost her pain by vices or profanities.

When first she took ill, I asked Grandfather what might be ailing her and he told me women are the weaker of our species and they succumb to distemper more readily than men. He also told me women are made frailer still by the dog days. I had not heard of such a thing, so he went on to explain that from the onset of July to the middle of August, when the Dog Star rises and sets with the sun, it makes women more feeble than they naturally are. It makes the dogs unsettled, too, and can also bring pestilence, and make maladies more virulent.

But the dog days were over, so I was certain Mother should start to acquire more strength. In fact, I prayed to God that it would be so. Right there and then, as I sat upon that rock, inside my head I sent up a silent prayer to God, to ask that if Mother's flesh were made ill from the planets in the sky, then it was high time for the planets to move on and leave her be; let her go back to weaving hazel skeps for the bees; let her return to the vigour of her youth.

At the end of my prayer, I did not find solace. In point of fact, guilt burned hot inside me, and I recognised that the dread I had carried with me all day was neither apprehension nor anxiety; it was selfishness; it was fear. It grieved me sore to look at Mother and so I had run away, pretended to myself the land needed me more than she did.

I rose to my feet and turned, pressing forward in all haste. Then I was away through the woods, the breeze building in strength around me. I pushed on at a swift rate over meads and pasture, the grass greyed by the gathering clouds, the day fast changing to twilight. The skies had forgotten all remembrance of summer brightness, and the darkling hour came early that day.

As I neared our homestead, the winds continued to stir up, the air as cold as Janiveer, and before my eyes the glow of a storm slid above the horizon, the clouds the colour of mustard and pitch, the air swollen and heavy.

I was mightily relieved to put my hand to the latch on the door and close it safely behind me. For a moment, I stood, leaning my back against the timbers, breathing long and deep. The shutters were pulled to already, clean napery and plate had been placed in the cupboard, the floor litter was freshly rushed and herbed and the logs were burning orange in the hearth. In fact, the whole room was clean and all in fit order: the girl Alice must have seen to it.

I took up a knife with the intent of cutting some bread from the loaf that Alice had left on the table, but my own appetite had decayed of late, and Mother could no longer suffer victuals to come near her. I laid down the knife and looked about the room. Everything looked the same, but it was different. It was all so still, that is what it was. It was Mother's vigour and activity that was missing. She was always busy as a bird, ever glowing with rays of kindness. No chick was small enough for Mother not to care for, no lamb frail enough for Mother not to feed. Now, the house and the land all about seemed so still and quiet, as though holding its breath.

Softly, I ascended the narrow stairs and drew aside the curtain that gave on to Mother's bedchamber. There she lay as quiet as a daisy, overcome with fatigue, pale of skin, her hair unbound and let loose about her shoulders. I paused a few paces from her bed, looked at her face, and such sorrow it fetched to my heart to see her brought so low.

As to her exact age, I could not know; past the middle of life was all she would ever tell. But she must have been old – beyond the age of forty – because she could remember the years when the harvests failed and folks all around took their subsistence from leached acorns and groundsel.

It was a worn and sorrowful face she wore that evening, her youthfulness grown drawn with the passing of years and torment of her disease, her likeness softened and lengthened with pliant skin. Then her eyes opened slowly and from that tired, soft face, came tired, soft words: 'Alwin, lad? Is it you?'

Her voice was hoarse. The fevers scorched her so, and of late the slightest chills seeped into her chest and made her breath weak, her body at last yielding up to the malady. Those last two weeks, the distemper hollowed her eyes and puckered her skin as never before. It ravaged her frame from the inside, scoured her, discarded all that made her human and alive, until all that was left was an ashen husk of a woman.

'Mother,' I said, then I walked across the chamber to greet her. I knelt beside the bed, the candle on the table shivering as I moved.

With breath no louder than the rubbing of grass stalks, she began to speak.

'You are a handsome lad now, Alwin, and so tall and strong. You always grew like barley; stinted at first then a rush towards the sky come summer. And now look at you; my boy, my pride and joy.'

There was a thick silence after she stopped speaking, then in the distance a grumble of thunder sounded. I stood, with the intention of unbinding the rope and letting the shutter down on the window, but Mother said, 'Let it be, Alwin. A tempest is coming and there is nothing we can do to stop it. Time out of mind the rafters of this house have stood firm between a Whittaker and God's elements.

The storm will pass over and you will be safe, lad. But soon, my time and eternity will become one.'

'What are you saying, Mother?'

I knelt beside her again and took her hand, pale and cold as clay, into my own, red chaps on my fingers, grown rough through dint of exposure to the weather. She frowned, as though from far in the background of her recollection memories were coming forth, scant and obscure at first, then growing larger and clearer.

'There are secrets, Alwin,' she said. 'I have kept them for many years, but now they will not let me rest and—'

'Mother. You are gravely ill. Grandfather will not be home until tomorrow, so let me fetch Father Oswald—'

'No ... no. Father Oswald cannot help me now ... there's no time—'

'Mother. You must rest.'

At first her eyes made a gesture of acquiescence and a shallow sigh escaped her lips. Then she stared at me as though I were an obscure speck at the end of a very long path. Her head lay deep in her pillow, her clouded eye searching the rafters in the roof, and she seemed to be at peace.

Then, from the heavens above, the bark of a thunder-dint cut through the air and the skies burned bright with thunder-light. For many a heartbeat the clouds fought a battle, exchanged many flashes and rumbles. The disturbance roused Mother and, when the storm at last held its breath, her eyes opened wide, and she held my hand as tightly as her weakness would allow.

'Alwin. This night I shall die.'

'No, Mother. The dog days are over, you shall recover—'

'This night I shall die,' she persisted. 'And once I am dead, I cannot protect you. I am certain he purposes to ... harm you.'

'Mother. Lie easy now. The distemper is inside your head, you know not what you say—'

'Alwin. If he knows I am dead and he finds you still here tomorrow, he will not allow you to stay.'

'Who, Mother?'

'Your grandfather.'

At that moment, a thunderclap ruptured the air and rain began to fall so heavily that it blurred all other sounds, hissing as it fell, rapid and sharp. Over and again the clouds swelled then burst, and huge blots of rain fell hard and heavy.

All I could do was look at Mother; see the pity and sorrow in her eyes; know that what she spoke must be the truth, for she could talk but sparely, each word costing her a power of pain. The air was suddenly stagnant about us, a swollen sigh between thunderclaps.

'But why, Mother? What did I do?'

'You did nothing, my boy. All blame must lie with me ... and with your father.'

'But he died before I was born. How could—'

'Alwin, your father is not dead.' Her words came broken and fast, their meaning compressed and sudden. She coughed, her skin now withered with the furrowed lines of bodily distress. 'There is not enough time for me to explain. You must trust me, Alwin.'

As I looked at her ailing frame and pleading eyes, I thought back on the manner in which she had nurtured and directed me throughout my life. She had a story for every vice to deter my young mind, and the taint of her characters' misdemeanours was more than enough to set me on the right path. How frequently I had been grateful for her wisdom. So, ignoring the torrent of questions and doubts that flooded my mind, I took a deep breath and, believing her word as I had always done so before, I said, 'I trust you, Mother. What shall I do?'

That credence had a calming effect on her, her grip grew slack and she was easy again.

'The answers lie in a village faraway, Alwin,' she began in a whisper, the words clear and practised in her mind. 'In Walsingham, in the county of Norfolk.'

'You mean where the Holy House is, Mother?' I said. 'The shrine of Our Lady of Walsingham, of which Father Oswald has spoken? The place where the pilgrims go?'

I waited for Mother to answer, but the effort of speaking had robbed her of vitality and she could do no more than stare at me with vacant eyes, as though her mind had begun to sleep.

'Do you mean for me to go to Walsingham, Mother?' I tried. But she was too tired to reply. I sat in the silence and thought about the implications of such a journey; all I could do was think how many miles must lie between Crown Croft and the county of Norfolk.

The thought of Grandfather wishing me gone was somehow not entirely unexpected, as vile a thought as it was. And the word 'father' to me was no more important than the word 'tomorrow' or 'yesterday'; it was indefinable, distant and elusive. My mind was entirely dominated with the thought of a land wholly strange to the one upon which my soul had been nourished. And the prospect of leaving Mother, the house and the land I loved so well, caused me to blench and quiver.

With agony of mind and my voice uncertain, I blurted like a child: 'But what of our tillage season? The lambs must be weaned before the feast of Blessed Mary. And who will feed the oxen when I am gone?'

For the first time in my life, those silent words no man should ever speak broke forth from my eyes, and I wept long and hard into my upturned hands. Till that point, my thoughts and actions were like a character in one of Mother's stories; somehow a little flatter than reality and missing the raw feelings of a human being. Suddenly, I was immersed in the cold realisation of how matters truly stood and it grieved me sore.

Mother regained her lucidity, studied me for a moment, then said, 'We cannot stop the will of God, Alwin. I have laid up a store of silver coins for you. They are in a purse beneath my bed. And have my pearl ring. You will know what to do with it when the time comes. You must go to Father Oswald and—'

Her breath failed her and she fought to draw air in and expel it again. A shiver engulfed her. I pulled the coverlid over her, but it made no difference; pale beneath the shadow of death she was. I knew at last she was beyond all aid and cure, and time's fatal wrack was on her. For a while she fell to slumbering, but I believe she slept to no purpose.

Then in a broken whisper, she said, 'Alwin. I cannot help but recall your deformity, the one that did strike you as a babe. The image of it haunts me.'

'Forget about times past, Mother. Rest yourself, now. Let sleep come.'

At last, her features grew slack, as though she had been disburdened of a heavy weight and all her cares had been blunted. I abided with her all the night, but she barely moved again, so shrunken and infirm she had become, her whole frame depleted. Just once she spoke and the words did not make sense to me: 'I did bear false witness against you ... I lied,' she said. 'It was not the plague, dear boy ... I ... I brought it all about ... and great harm will grow from what I did ... forgive me—'

It stung to the quick of my heart to hear her so confused.

'You could never harm me, Mother,' I said, gentle, emphatic. 'Have no worries. I shall leave at sunrise and go to Walsingham. Have no cares.'

She looked at me in confusion and issued her last thoughts in a whisper: 'Forgive me—' was all she could reply. She spoke those last words with great compunction and then her voice was to be heard no more on this earth.

Her breath loitered briefly and her features foretold of her final deliverance. She looked at me one last time, then her eyes grew dark and her lids slowly closed, all toils softened, all pains relieved, her life's labours done. After all she had suffered, that final parting agony came and went in silence. And so, in the mid of night, she went out of this world, quick as a dream. Just as the season had slipped away, so had her life and at last she was gathered in the arms of Christ, her soul surrendered to God. I stayed with her, but nothing was left, everything was gone; her warmth, her voice, all stolen away in a moment, her name now only to be spoken in sad reminiscence.

The aspect of my world had changed forever and the ache of it did bind me sore. Much rain fell that night and the winds never ceased. But time was not one for waiting and it hastened away till morning, the clouds weeping their might on the roof until dawn. I outwore them all with my sorrow and at morning, with the blend of darkness and day, I prepared for my journey.

I looked out of the window. Summer had drawn her final breath and where before green foliage clung thick to every branch, and grasses stood tall and swaying, now the verdure was slack with dew, the leaves already beginning to yellow and curl. Since the crops were in, even the fields looked sad, all bereaved of their bounty, left to mourn the loss of those long summer days. The morn was bleak, the sky much darked even after sunrise, and mist hovered above the skin of the river, the waters below deathly black.

I wearily rigged myself out in my best outfit; Mother always said I cut such a fine dash in my tunic and chausses, but, of course, she was no longer there to say so. Such ruth it was that I must leave her alone after death, but Mother was so certain I should go before Grandfather returned. I determined to seek out Father Oswald immediately and have him attend to Mother's burial, that she would not lie alone for long. I packed a bag of wearing clothes and some provisions. Then I gathered up my knife, sword, candles, flask and bedsheet.

After that, I stood by the gleeds of the fire, just staring and thinking. I wondered if it might all be a misunderstanding. Perhaps the fever made Mother's mind rave. Perhaps she had slept and gained her strength. I climbed the steps, at once saw her cold, colourless shape, and knew for certain Mother had gone away for good and left the house all grey and drear in her wake.

'Dominus be with you, Mother,' I whispered, then I turned, collected up the bag of silver coins, the pearl ring and my parcel of belongings, and I took my sorrow with me and departed with it.

I tacked and saddled up the larger of our two palfrey-horses and filled two bags of oats for the mare's forage. Then, in silence, with no mother to bind me to careful regard, I left our lands and would not return for many a while. With no real care as to whether I travelled to Tartary or Persia or to the man on the moon, I rode one last time to the water's brink.

I stood tall in my stirrups and stared down at the mighty River Crown. The waters were in commotion; last night's storm had defaced the surface, the strong rains had goaded a roar from the old watercourse, and it raged as it frothed over boulders and rocks. I turned, drenched in my grief, and took one last look at the house as it sank gently into the mists, then I left, to begin a journey that would reshape my life, alter my world forever, change my very soul.

CHAPTER TWO

As the morning blanched around me, I rode along the river's verge, the waters rising and falling against the fraying banks. A wren issued a cast of notes into the silence, but no answer came, and the muteness rendered my situation even more lonesome. I took comfort to think of Mother in her youth, and in my mind's eye I saw her in such radiant tones as a character from the page of a priest's Psalter; clear and defined. But her image was stark against a vague background and she was alone in time, unmoored to any particular place or circumstance. Evermore in my life, that image would lend a fountain of tears to my eyes.

I followed as the river cut its course through the land and I made my way to the little settlement that bordered the Whittaker woods; the hamlet of Giolgrave. To reach it, I had to pass through a tract of land where the old plague village stood, a place Mother said once a cluster of farm cots and a smithy had thriven, the inhabitants of which were taken by the same pestilence that changed my own life. There the river first lapsed then lulled. The waters were wide and deep at that point and rarely spoke, which for me always provoked the image of haunted spectres, eternally trapped in their silent world.

Twenty-three folks perished in that one, dreadful night, so went the tale; cursed were they with the shilling in their armpit and no one to give them aid or cure. With no one to feed forage to the animals, the sheep and oxen were all left to starve, their bones picked clean by the rooks and corbies. How those ravens and crows grew in number, Mother said, the sky turning black with their feathered bodies, and all sounds stolen by their cawing and screeching. All that remained now were fallen bricks and scattered flagstones lying in the grass. Roofless walls and un-shuttered windows stood derelict and weed-choked. The goose-houses were empty, the hen-houses deserted, and all around was unworked land, scrub overgrown with rose-brier, where once fine pasture had prospered. I urged the mare into a trot and at last came to Giolgrave.

Beyond the east of the village stood the church, where each and every Sabbath for all the days of my youth, I had accompanied Mother and Grandfather, knelt my knees to the hassock, and offered up a prayer to God. As I neared the lychgate, a shape approached me along the lane and I recognised Father Oswald in an instant; an apparent infirmity of the haunch bones caused him to walk with a stoop, leaning always slightly to the left. I pulled rein and dismounted, dropping the straps over the mare's neck and letting her crop the grass.

Always pleased to see the dear cleric, I cherished the sight of the priest more than I had ever done so before. Simply the sight of his threadbare cassock, his worn leather sandals and the satchel he always carried with his books and papers, gave me a comforting sense of familiarity, a feeling of stability in a world that had changed so much for me and all in a single day. With his breviary in his hand, he raised it to greet me, then reading the look I wore on my features, he received me with questioning eyes and an enquiring expression.

'Father Oswald,' I began. My voice was reedy, my breath short. I fought to hold back the weeping that rose from within my chest;

I knew Father Oswald would reprove me if I wept. He told me when I was a boy that there was no worse a plague than a man who succumbed to tear-shed, and that such a weakness was a sign of ungodliness. I evaded his gaze and cleared my throat before beginning again with, 'Father Oswald. It is Mother. She … passed away last night.'

'Your mother is dead?'

I nodded and Father Oswald turned away from me. There was a shadow of incredulity in his voice and his stooped frame seemed to deplete for a moment before my eyes. He fronted me again, searched my features and I felt his scrutiny.

'There was no time,' I uttered in defence. 'I told her I must fetch you for the last rites, but she said there was no time.'

The priest recovered himself, ordered his faculties and said gently, 'Alwin, my lad. I am so sorry. I saw your mother two days since and she said she was gaining strength. I am so sorry, Alwin,' he repeated, his thoughts seemingly scattered. 'Did she talk to you before she died?' he asked, his question rushed, abrupt.

'Yes.'

That confirmation gave him a degree of relief and he ventured, more calmly, 'What did she say, Alwin?'

'That … my grandfather harbours an intent to cause me harm and that I must leave our croft and take the path to the east; to the county of Norfolk and the shrine of Our Lady at Walsingham.'

'Are you certain, Alwin?' he asked. 'She said you must go to Walsingham?'

I thought back to Mother's jumbled words, her muddled vagueness, and of course I could not be sure what she was trying to say. But I was always keen to prove myself to the world; make up for my deformity, so I replied, 'Yes, Father. I am certain that is what she meant.'

'And was that everything?' the priest said.

I pondered on that point, too; recalled Mother's sudden exposition of my father's vitality and the strange and troubling words that were to be her last. How vexed she was when she thought she had brought about the harm that came to me. I knew it was a sin to give false testimony, especially to a priest, but Mother was so confused at the end, her mind possessed by the malady.

'Yes, Father Oswald,' I replied at last, 'that was all she said.'

Those falsehoods stung me inside my ribs at first, but then the heat went away and so I judged I was right to withhold what I knew. Father Oswald seemed satisfied and he nodded, but behind his eyes he was clearly troubled. He turned away from me briefly, and when he faced me again his eyes had a sheen about them; just like when a troutling looks up at you through the flood-pools of the Crown.

'Alwin,' he began, his voice sounding different, frailer. 'Your mother spoke to me in the past of her concerns around your grandfather's treatment of you. I am not saying I agree with her foreboding, but I do know the man treated you hard. Why not come and stay with me, here in the village, just until—'

'But, Father Oswald, I did bind me to a promise. I shall leave the shire this day and journey to Walsingham.'

'Alwin, you have no experience of the road. You are just a willowy lad, you are so young, and there's such peril.'

'You cannot gainsay me, Father. I have to do it.'

He studied my face, then touching his right hand to the crucifix about his neck, he leaned towards me and folded his left arm about me. I hugged him to me and I confess to God here and now, a mort of tears fell from my eyes. I dried them as best I could before I faced him and said, 'Thank you for the comfort, Father.'

He collected himself and clapped me on the back, and I did the same to him.

'Listen, lad,' he said. 'You cannot journey on pilgrimage alone. And you cannot go without a letter of commendation from the abbot. Let me go to Crown Croft, see to the burial of your mother and make good the mass-penny, then I shall go to the abbot; obtain a mandate for you to become a pilgrim. Then I shall journey with you to Walsingham, Alwin. I am certain it is what your mother would have wished. But I have business to attend to before I can join you. So, let me write a letter of ingress for you, to present to the prioress of Winfeld. The priory is some fourteen miles from here, so you should be there before nightfall. Stay one night under her protection, then make your way to the township of Alfricstowe. Meet me at the tavern at the sign of the chequers, and we will go on together, Alwin. I cannot let you go on such a journey alone.

'According to the abbot,' he went on, 'when last I spoke to him, a group of pilgrims was scheduled to set off from that hostelry in two days' time; their destination Norfolk: Walsingham Parva and Bromholme. It will be the last pilgrimage to go from these parts before the season changes and the roads become too mired to travel. I do not know who the pilgrims are, but the abbot said they are a mix of gentlefolk and maidens. The roads of England and the foreign counties of this land are dangerous places, Alwin. Christ might have reduced the efficacy of demons, but they do still exist. By travelling in numbers, safety is improved for all concerned. So, I will meet you at The Chequers tomorrow at eventide.'

It was a relief to me that Father Oswald cared enough to see to Mother's burying and blessing. And I was mightily comforted that not only was he arranging hospitality for me that night, giving me a destination, a firm direction in which to set my steps; but also, he was pledging to go on with me to Walsingham.

Of course, Father Oswald had schooled me well in logic and trained me to think for myself, so I did not agree to his plans immediately. I questioned him on the exact location of the priory and asked if there was a more direct route to be taken. He gave me a list of waymarks and asserted the importance of keeping to the main highway, once I had left the familiar tracks. I listened to his advice and conceded to his will. As soon as the letter to the Winfeld prioress had been penned, and safely packed in my saddlebag, I took leave of Father Oswald and I sallied on the first leg of my journey.

Once more, I flowed eastwards alongside the river. Then, when the waterway shallowed, I forded it and made towards the moors. I held my course eastwards and left many acres of land behind me. Miles came and went, long and weary in their passing, the fragrance of the house fading from my cloak with each stride the mare took, until at last I came to an oak tree turned about by the violence of last night's winds, its head dashed to the earth, its roots flung high in the air.

That marked the place where the familiar cart-traces finished, and my knowledge of the paths and byways beyond the Whittaker lands ended. I did not pull rein or stop urging the mare forward with my heels, but still the horse halted. She became fresh with me, took a step or two backwards, fought for her head and gave a snort and a whicker. I sensed it too; a sudden coolness on the wind, a different flavour to the air.

Grandfather always taught me that a cudgel should be taken to a jibbing horse to beat out the demon from inside it. But I always found the opposite to be true. I used soft hands and a soft voice to coax the goodness from within, and thereby vanquish the devil that excited it. So that is what I did with the mare, Bracken. I slid down from the saddle, rubbed her neck and ran my fingers over her nose. With a loose leading rein, I walked before her, showed her the way.

We continued on in that like manner through a forest of ash trees and larch, until I remounted her when at last we came to the highway; a wide, flat road of smoothed mud, clay and cobblestones, the shrubs either side of it shorn away for many a breadth of yards. Father Oswald had explained to me that the roadside trees and herbs were cut back, to give clear passage for the traveller and ensure that parcels of robbers could not spring out from behind a tree or beyond a curve in surprise. But in truth, I felt exposed rather than protected, and wondered whether the brigands were better placed to plan their attack on a lonesome horseman riding the barren road, than if he were safeguarded by trees. Back at Crown Croft, I took little count of strangers, but there, alone on the road, I feared them for the strife they might bring to me.

By the time I rode past a waggoner – the first fellow I had seen since leaving Father Oswald – I was feeling anxious. I touched my left hip, to reassure myself my sword was still sitting in its leather scabbard. It was only a three-shilling blade with a pommel-topped hilt, but it was all I had. I gave good day to the waggoner and he confirmed I was on the right road to Winfeld. I made haste as I parted ways with him and pressed on as the sun started to fall lower in the sky, setting the hill-crests all aglow about me.

I stopped only briefly that day to let the mare Bracken drink from a brook, while I supped ale from my flask. A little further on, I rode past a sweep of barren land where wind-blasts had made the grass grow lean, then I came to an old clapper bridge that dipped its broken feet in the waters beneath it, just as Father Oswald had described to me. That was the place I was to turn and take the left-hand path, which ran through a sweep of forest and would lead me directly to the Winfeld Priory.

It was along that path, where rain-drenched leaves hung limp and dispirited and the birdcall was spare and thin, that thoughts entered my mind again about Mother's muddled words. At first, I supposed she had been telling some sort of story, just like she always did. Perhaps, to her, my father had never died in her heart and she had kept her love for him alive all those years. So, to shrive herself of that avowal, what with her being so close to death and deficient of words and time, she could only say he was alive; meaning, of course, to her and not in actuality. And as far as her believing she once harmed me; well that could never be true. Perhaps over the years, she might have meditated on whether she could have taken me away from the pestilence and better protected me somehow. From that tiny grain of guilt, her heart and mind had become diseased with her perceived culpability, to the point she believed she brought harm to me.

Alongside those musings, other occasional visions and fancies entered my head. What if my father were actually alive? Would he be a carter or a miller, or perhaps a man of quality? Why did he abandon Mother and me, and why does he not seek out his son? It was through those absurd and capricious speculations that a noise entered my ears, mellow at first then growing to a rumble.

Upon a sudden, a clamour broke out, a terrifying sound surging forward from behind me. All manner of noise threaded the forest about me. The ground shook and the sound of snapping wood rent the air. The mare beneath me reared and bucked, then galloped forward, as though the noise itself carried her away. I took mastery of her head some paces on and turned her about, only to face a body of soldiers, all mounted on horseback, all clad in quilted jerkins and with steel helmets. They thundered towards me and, on seeing me, drew rein; the lead man calling out orders for the whole detachment to halt. Fierce they looked with their pikestaffs and glaives, with their swords and fist-shields glinting in the filtered daylight.

I bowed my head in an act of passivity and did bid them ride by. But through the cluster of horseflesh and men-at-arms, there appeared a nobleman astride a magnificent black horse, its scarlet belly-band straining against the animal's broad flanks, a lyme-hound and a mastiff running close behind on the horse's heels.

The man sat tall in his saddle; the fine leather seat telling tales of his wealth. So rich he looked, with many a pan of brass to his name. How his horse shone; the furniture on it gleamed even brighter. He threw back the folds of his Flanders cape and loosed the clasp at his throat, cast off the garment and lay it across his horse's withers. How fine and rich he looked attired in his noble array; his cloak alone must have cost many a coin. A curtain of thick hair cascaded over his neck and shoulders, and his beard was as black as moleskin.

'God give you good day, young man,' he said, his words spoken deep and slow.

'May Our Lord give you good day, sir,' I replied, not so very deep, not so very slow.

'What do they call you?'

'I am Alwin, sir. Alwin of Whittaker.'

'And what do you do here, Alwin of Whittaker? On this maze of woodland paths, that threads itself from nowhere to somewhere and causes a fine detachment of militia men to lose their way?'

'I am on an errand, a pilgrimage, sir. I have journeyed since prime this morning and am to go to the Winfeld Priory, where I will be given hospitality for the night.'

'And do you know this land well enough to direct us to the settlement of Essover?'

'I do not, sir. I, too, am a stranger hereabouts.'

'What say you, then, to taking us as far as the priory, that we may seek direction from the incumbents of that house of God?'

'I shall gladly ride with you, sir,' I said.

I truly meant it. In every gesture, the nobleman carried dignity and there was honesty in his looks. He was obviously a man both wise and worthy and I considered him of great probity. How honoured I felt to be of service to him; a man whose eyes had witnessed a hundred battles and were set to hazard a hundred more.

He turned his horse's head and communed with his sergeant in a whisper, which I could not hear. The point was taken by common assent and, with no further tarrying, we plied our course onward through the woodland glades.

The lord took up his position at the head of the troop and the men fell in line behind him; some riding two abreast, most in single file. I brought up the rear and trotted alongside an old warrior, whose horse was listless and dull, the animal's jaw rather swollen and a sticky discharge issuing from its nostrils. The horse gave off an acrid smell, as though a distemper had crept beneath its skin, and his rider distilled a strong fragrance from his armpits, which I found to be offensive. My companion did not strike up in conversation and we rode on in silence, in contrast to his colleagues ahead of us who were in right and merry cheer.

Eventually the old soldier turned his face to me, his skin pitted and uneven like a gallnut, and in a low voice he said, 'You seem a good lad. The men here; they are not from these parts, they are not like you. I am from the town of Bishop's Lynn, some of the men are from as far away as the northern sea-coasts and our commander is from Walsingham. He is a powerful and wealthy lord and it is said he chambers great stores of coin. Some say his family has a hidden hoard of treasure that equals a king's. And all these men have lived a life on the road, lad, seen things, done things that a yeanling like you cannot imagine. Young cocks learn what the old cock crows; you remember that. Do not forget who you are, lad. Keep your wits about you.'

No sooner had he finished his one-sided talk, than I was called to the head of the detachment to advise on the direction at a fork in the path. Just as Father Oswald had instructed, I led us to the left and told the lord we could be no more than two miles from the priory. I fell back in line, but that time I doubled with a younger man with a lively cast to his cheeks and nose – as though his belt were drawn too tight – and a fine outcrop of whiskers on his chin. At first, he sang a merry lay, loud and clear as we rode forth, then at length we fell into some talk.

'Alwin, is it?' he said with a flick of his head towards me.

'Yes, sir.'

'No need for sir-saying to the likes of me. John of Stanton Magna, that is who I am, lad.'

'Pleased to make your acquaintance, John,' I said, then added, 'The old soldier tells me your lord and master is from Walsingham; to what family does he belong?'

'One of the most rich and powerful in the land, lad. Never forget that.'

My enquiry seemed to irk John Stanton for a moment or two, then his merry mood returned and he said, 'Left your good wife behind, have you?'

'Oh, I am not wed,' I said. 'I live with my grandfather and … my mother; she died but yesterday.'

'I am sorry to hear that,' he said and his tone was respectful, his eyes lowered. But in a moment, his voice was bright and jolly again as he said, 'All the more reason to find you a wife, to give comfort and to amuse you! The pleasure of love is a fine delicacy, Alwin; I do not mean of the heart, I mean of the flesh.'

'Leave the boy alone, John Stanton,' came a voice from behind. The old warrior from the back of the line had ridden alongside my new companion, and on we continued three abreast through a wide glade, stripped of shrub and tree.

'What harm can it do, Ilbert?' John asked his fellow soldier. 'The boy must be sixteen if he is a day—'

'I have eighteen summers,' I said, defensive, indignant.

'Well,' John went on, 'why the close-shaven lip and chin, lad? To grow a thicker crop on your face would suit you better; I would wager you might be handsome to any lady's eye. And by-the-by, you do not have a care that we talk like men, do you?'

'No,' I said.

'So, Alwin, tell our friend Ilbert here what you do think of women and their ways of amusing us.'

I had such little knowledge of the world and the folks that peopled it, that I did not truly understand what John meant by pleasures of the flesh and the heart; like they were two distinct and separate conditions. I could only suppose he wanted to know I had been brought up to be a man who knew the order of matters, so recalling what Father Oswald and Grandfather had taught me, I said, 'I know that women are considered to be very different creatures to men, their natural position in the world to be subordinate to us.'

That statement, that declaration, did not only invoke approval and mirth from John, but also the whole detachment. How glad and blithe it made me feel; that endorsement from fellow-men. Not from a priest or an old man, but from real men, true men.

'You are right in what you say, Alwin,' John said, laughter still to be heard in his voice, 'but the trouble is, women do not know it!'

There was a ripple of snorts and chuckles from the men, then Ilbert said, 'Do not be so quick to censure. We all like to indulge in the pleasures a woman has to offer, and that I do not deny. But they must be treated fair and right, for a lonesome bee does not make a mickle of honey. My wife is a comfort to me and I love her for the companionship she brings me. She understands me and in the years of our marriage, she has taken time to study me, learn my needs by heart; and I have done the same for her, that I may please her. I will not join in with your name-calling.'

'Your wife might be made of honey and cream, Ilbert. But some of us prefer them more sharply spiced.'

John's words once more brought merriment to all, with the exception of Ilbert, who pulled rein and returned to his position at the rear of the band and spoke no more on the subject.

'Take no notice of him,' John said to me after the old soldier had moved away. 'He likes to pretend he is a spotless man, Alwin. As though he has never sinned. He forgets I was with him when he put down more than a gallon of ale and visited the Flemish women in the London stews. Oh, yes; he was drawn to those harlots in their yellow hoods like a pike to maggots. Do not let him sway your opinion: some womenfolk are jangleresses, some are all grouch and groan, contrary and cruel, but all women are wicked at heart; so says Solomon. Never forget that, Alwin.'

As worldly a man as John Stanton was, I found he talked in riddles. I understood the basis of his argument, but some of the words I struggled to comprehend. Harlots I had heard from the bible, but yellow hoods, Flemish women and London stews were unknown to me. And as much as I respected his knowledge of the world, I could not hang a wicked deed on either Mother, Alice of the cornfield or any of the women in the whole town of Badeswell.

Pondering at my muteness, he said, 'You have been fostered up too lax, my lad. Your thoughts are all fresh, on account of you living a lonesome life with your late departed mother and your grandfather. When you have lived another score of years and seen more of the world, then you will know I am right, eh lads?'

His question was answered by assenting cries and hollers from all the merry band of militia men. One man shouted from the front that his wife was so loud she had the voice of three.

'Best place a staple through her jaws,' came the reply from another.

'It is not their volume you should worry about,' shouted the next, 'it is their slyness. My old father used to say that when cats practise physic, that is the day when you can trust a woman.'

A ripple of sniggers had already begun when, 'Hear this,' John called out, his voice louder than all the rest. 'A woman, a dog and a walnut tree; the more you beat them, the better they will be!'

At that, we all fell into fits of laughter. Even old Ilbert must surely have had a simper on his lips. I thought of Father Oswald and how, when next I met him, I could tell him what I had learned. Women, I had begun to deduce, were not that different from horses. Some, like Alice and dear Mother, were naturally pliant in their tempers and could be trained to serve menfolk with hardly an ill-deed about them; just like Bracken, the old mare. Others, it appeared, might yet need Grandfather's cudgel to drive out the demons from within them. How valuable that knowledge would be to me as I ventured out into the world. How grateful I was the soldiers crossed my path that day.

When I left Crown Croft that morning, sad farewells brimmed my heart and I wondered if sorrows would ever leave me. But however bruised I was inside, to talk and laugh with those sol-dier-men made me believe I may one day be mended. I would always be bereft of Mother's presence, and I would never be able to reverse the effects of my deformity, but I would never stop try-ing to be the man she wanted me to be.

It was amidst those thoughts of past and future that I began to sense the close of day fast descending about us. The trees in the distance became fainter, the air tasted of earth and leaf-mould, and mist swirled about our horses' fetlocks. With the colours of the day darkening from yellows to purples, the dew-quenched air had a sobering effect on the merriment of the cavalry-men.

We continued in quietude for half a mile further, then the noble-man sent an order for me to go to him. I threaded my way through the horses before me and, when I gained the front of the troop, the lord was a little way off the path, in muted talk with his sergeant. He signalled me forward with a gesture of his arm.

'Alwin,' he said. 'Evening descends fast in this county. Night will be on us in no time at all and will steal all sight from us. Know you well the prioress? Can you, with good grace and blessing, obtain shelter for me and my men?'

'Oh, I do not know the prioress at all, sir,' I said apologetically.

'Then how can you expect a guarantee of hospitality?'

'I have a letter, sir. Our village priest, Father Oswald, knows the good lady and has written a letter of ingress.'

I rummaged in my saddlebag and presented my document to the lord. He took it, studied it, then turned the head of his horse away from me and resumed conference with his auxiliary. He placed the missive in the hands of the sergeant and sent him off to a clearing further ahead.

Turning again to me, he said, 'The light is dim beneath these trees, Alwin, and my eyes do fail me. My man can better read the paper up yonder and report its contents back to me.'

I nodded and leaned in my saddle to follow the sergeant's path with my eye, but he misheard his lord's order, passed through the first clearing and went beyond and deeper into the woods. Some time he took, too, to seek enough light to read by. But on his return, the dispatch was safely reverted to my hands and the nobleman was assured by his officer that the letter was honest and true, just as I had described.

'What do you know of fellowship, Alwin?' the lord asked me, as he turned his horse back onto the path.

'I have lived a lonesome life, sir. But many a friendly conversation I have had with my mother and our neighbours and—'

'Fellowship is not conversation, lad; it is loyalty. And loyalty is as powerful as the sun; it dispels darkness and gives us light, places us all under its obligation, makes us all devoted to its unifying rays. But treat it without respect and your skin will be burned to a cinder. So, what say you to showing deference and constancy to these good men? How feel you about joining our fellowship, just for one night, and using your persuasion to gain harbourage and hospitality at the priory for all of us together?'

'Without a doubt, sir. Gladly will I do it.' And it was true what I said at the time and I was keen to obey his bidding; I had no doubts, no hesitations or misgivings. It was all as clear as grass-dew to me back then.

At last, we came to the Winfeld Priory, the candles from within the three arched windows sending a flickering, nervous light through the trees as we approached. Though twice the size of our own village church of the All Saints, the priory looked timid that night, flanked either side by oaks, surrounded by a forest of ash trees, elms and sycamores. Three storeys high it was, its panoply of stones nothing less than monoliths, the slates on its roof worn casque-tight like a helmet; but defenceless and exposed it seemed to me as it sat all alone in the midst of that wooded tract.

We broke out from under the canopy of trees and advanced past the west wing. How the winds did whip up against us, a sudden rain shower abounding slantwise in our faces. The good noble-man and I dismounted and walked on together to the oaken door, already bolted shut against the oncoming of darkness. Three times we rapped against that wooden portal before latches were lifted, locks were un-sprung, and an old woman presented herself to us, wimpled and wary of eye.

I removed my hood and said, 'God give you good day, lady. I am Alwin of Whittaker and do request an audience with the prioress.'

'I am she, young man,' the woman answered, a question in her eyes.

I made my obeisance to her and said, 'Then I would ask with good grace that I and my fellow travellers be lodged here this night.'

'All of you?' she asked, studying the men and horses behind us, suddenly vexed; her voice rising to a higher key. 'It would be highly irregular and—'

'I have a letter,' I replied, 'from Father Oswald of Giolgrave.'

I handed her the folded document and her fingers trembled as she took it. She stepped back behind the door to gain a better light in which to read. Troubled by the script, she put her hand to her pursed lips, as though in thought.

'And this alteration,' she asked. 'His inclusion of all of you, that is Father Oswald's bidding?'

The question was directed to me, but I could not answer. I suddenly realised that the nobleman's sergeant must have taken it upon himself to add further script to the letter, written a falsehood in order to secure overnight accommodation. I looked over my shoulder at the soldiers and their horses, standing as they were in a crescent shape, no individual discernible through the evening gloom. I looked down at the ground, felt my breath becoming tight. The sergeant would surely deny his amendment and the nobleman would take offence at my accusation, if I raised it. But how could I gainsay the prioress? Then, whilst perjury and panic set deluge to my mind, I hit on the answer.

'I do not believe you are in a position to question Father Oswald,' I said, the words pushed through my lips by the anguish of the moment, invoked by the sentiments I had learned from the militia men and persuaded by their judgement. 'The good man has communicated his wish to you, lady, and expects it to be granted, as any man has a right to presume. And would you go against the teachings of God? Are you not obliged to extend hospitality to passing pilgrims?'

The poor prioress knew at that point she was defeated; that a man's favour must always be obeyed by a woman and there was nothing she could say to contradict it. She looked at me long and hard, as though she could sense the uncertainty inside me, see the serpentine falsehood that snaked within. Her features remained gracious and steadfast, but her eyes made a brief, beseeching appeal to me, before she meekly said, 'As you like,' her manner now indifferent and cold, then to the nobleman, 'Have your men bait and straw the horses, then yea, sir, welcome.'

So, we took access under the colour of Father Oswald's note and were admitted into that haven of tranquillity, that spotless realm of innocence and divine sanctity. We all removed our hoods and hats as we crossed the threshold, surrendered our swords and armoury to our hostess, and washed our feet in a pail of water, as tradition dictated, thus to convey formally our intent to bide throughout the night.

The good nobleman was shown to a private chamber and the rest of us were invited to sleep in either the buttery, the pantry or the guesthouse. Apart from those rooms and the refectory, we were not sanctioned to stray further and all the nuns were at prayer in their cells, with the exception of two that were to serve refreshment to us in the form of a late supper.

The old prioress led us into the refectory at the close of vespers and the room was warm with a hearty fire in the grate, the sconces flamed with candles, linsey-woolsey rugs on the floor and red sendal curtains hung across the windows. Once seated on our benches, together we said the paternoster in praise of the Trinity and the prioress said, 'Lord Jesus Christ, son of God, have mercy upon me.'

We were received with generous benevolence. Lavers and napkins were brought before us and we were invited to wash our hands before we were served with a bowl of hot sheep's feet, pot-herbs and bread. Once the prioress and her two young nuns had served up the dishes and brought to table four green-glazed ewers filled with ale and perry, the good women left the refectory and went about their prayer and worship in another part of the convent.

The men were now all in good cheer, and we toasted our good health. Blithe talk was plentiful and a chorus of men's voices amplified and rose about me. Ilbert and John Stanton made peace between themselves and now offered up hearty boasts of the dangerous roads they had travelled, the foes and adversities they had faced together. And through hearing those tales of companionship and loyalty, I began to understand the value of fellowship, just as the nobleman had explained to me.

If only matters had stayed constant, perhaps my tale would have ended there, with a crowded table, ruddy faces and a roaring fire, a fine feast, jugs of ale and merry cries of wassail. But as I have learned since, sometimes good fortune is a deceiver and happy acquaintance withers on the vine. If I lived for one hundred winters, I could never forget what played out later that night, and as much as I strive to quell and quench those fearful recollections, such grievous sadness must and will be told and will ever cause cold water to fill the pipes beneath my skin and drip in drops down the small of my back.

CHAPTER THREE

It was a jovial and good-natured suppertime that began that night at the Winfeld Priory; the men were in fine voice and good spirits. Their manners were unvarnished but respectful and each time the nuns brought bread or meat to the table, the men's conversation dropped to a whisper so as not to offend the maidens, and no one spat on the hearth when the good women were in our presence.

Tales of yesteryear and happy recollections of past deeds were told with fondness, from lips that carried smiles and eyes that held a glint of sunshine. The nobleman, seated at the head of the company, charmed our ears with his jests and drollery until we all trembled with mirth; all puffed up like the cock of the roost he was. And the more ale we took, the funnier he became and the better the witticisms he delivered.

Each time the nuns entered the room to clear away a jug or remove a trencher, the nobleman cried out, 'Fetch us a pot of ale, a foaming one at that!' or 'Liquor of the vine, my hostess, bring liquor of the vine!' So, a ewer of ale or a runlet of wine was brought, the barrel broached, then tumblers decanted and passed round to each and every one of us, that we might all drink enough to stretch our bellies.

With my mind already tainted with ale, I took up a wine cup, then I drank morat and mead. Such supplies of liquor I had never seen before and how easily one drink followed another. Once, the old prioress made an attempt to countermand the nobleman's requests, but I do not believe he quite had full command of his faculties. He tried to stand, but unsteady on his legs, he tugged at the old nun's habit and pulled the wimple from her head, revealing a grey, close-shaved scalp, which the lord said looked like the rear-end of a badger.

I knew the nobleman had behaved indiscreetly, but the jest made such good cheer that we each and all laughed our fill, brazen and heedless. In my heart, I did not like his manner, but everything he said was so funny and the more we all laughed, the more we drank; the more we drank, the more we laughed. The lord raised such enjoyment that we followed his lead and we drank, drank, drank, till we all drank deep into drunkenness.

I cannot pinpoint the exact moment the ambience changed, because I supped far more than my measure, and my own reasoning became trackless. But in the blink of an eye, mischief began to unfold and, what before had been comical, at once became tragic.

It began with the nobleman; of that I am certain. He led the way, being instrumental in conjuring lewd thoughts in the men's minds by speaking bawdy jests. And that degeneration in gentility spread like black smoke among the soldiers and roused them all into a frenzied mood. They chanted immoral songs and became unruly. I conformed myself at first and went along with them, but I knew it was wrong. Then I began to feel ill and I stopped drinking, quit my singing.

The liquor I consumed had a strange and deteriorating effect on me, which I had not noticed at first. A physical impairment ensued, the likes of which I had never known before or since. The room became unstable about me and my eyes and ears played me false. But the men around me were unaffected and continued to drink greedily.

Such vulgar words spilled from their lips. The air seethed hot with their curses and oaths, and as cross language abounded, quarrels broke out. The clamour went on for some time, then suddenly, a hush fell about the room.

Whether the old prioress was unable to return to the scene of her humiliation and was lying prostrate in her cell having given orders to her subordinates to quieten the men, or whether the two novice nuns had taken it on themselves to bring order to the refectory, I shall never know. But the two maids entered the room, walking side by side, as close as ever they could. The nobleman saw them immediately and he nodded an order to John Stanton. The soldier walked furtively to guard the door and I do not believe the maidens even noticed him, or indeed perceived they were now trapped.

They approached the lord, faithful in their respect. But even beneath the pull of liquor, I could see the evil look in his eye and knew that the sense of his own power had tinted his character, coloured his temperament with a dark and arrogant hue. Before he permitted the holy maids to speak, he raised a complaint, blunt and severe.

'I have had better ale at a huckster's brewhouse and this food is no better than horse-bread.'

To me, his manner was very hard and the poor girls, dumb-struck, had no answer to give him. They stood compressed against one another and looked about the room at the rigid faces that stared back at them. The shorter of the two looked over her shoulder, saw John Stanton at the door and then fronted the lord, appealing to him with her eyes. All was silent, but discomposed, a thread of awkwardness stitching the moments together. Even the tables and benches looked ill at ease, as though they were appealing for Mother Nature to take them back to the woods and copses from where they had come.

'Do not look so worried, fair damosels,' the nobleman began at last, his voice easy.

At that, I thought the evening might still be saved. The nobleman would show his breeding, I was certain, and satisfy the gentleness the situation commanded. But my hopes decayed to ashes in an instant.

'Answer me this,' he continued, brazen with his speech. 'Why would such pretty maidens as you wed yourselves to the book and the bell? Such a waste.'

At that, the two women bowed their heads and began to retreat, fear in their eyes at his over-free speech. But the lord rose and, taking each sister by the wrist, he said, 'No need for coyness; I know you are saving yourselves, awaiting the touch of a man's hand. Well, I believe you are ripe for the plucking and there are pleasures to be taken here this night.'

Both girls fought to free their hands, but the lord used his strength against them. His grip tightened and, in the tussle, a cup of wine was spilled.

'Of course,' he declared. 'Wine to kindle your desires. And music, perhaps?'

At that, three soldiers to my left began to sing, the lyrics indecent, the melody grating. Like a creeping, seeping odour, mischief tainted the whole company.

Casting the taller of the sisters into the arms of his drunken sergeant, the nobleman focussed his attentions on the smaller novice. The girl was trembling, her features stiff, as time and terror stood against her. Tears came down her cheeks and she could only stare at her captor with disbelief.

'See, lads?' the lord said. 'See the manner in which she gazes at me? I will wager she will flit from daytime looks to midnight whispers in the blink of an eye, and she seems like the sort to be easily pleased. Throw her a crumb of flattery and see how she will hunger for a man's touch.'

That vile, deliberate incitation was nothing less than incendiary. The men responded with raucous hollering and through the din the old soldier, Ilbert, rose to his feet. With determination he staggered his way towards his commanding officer. Fists were banged on tables, jugs were smashed and shouts filled the air; a few of the men had drunk less than the rest and sat quietly, looking rather ashamed of both themselves and the rumpus about them, but most of the others had lost all sense of propriety and were no better than rogues. Ilbert's voice still cut through the uproar, resolute as he was. He raised his eyes to meet those of his captain, lifted his upturned hands before him and called to all the company: 'It is surely time to stop all this!'

His plea punctured the air, diffused the ruction in an instant. Three or four of the men called out their support for Ilbert and I truly believed the immorality had been brought to book, but they were soon shouted down by the others and, in their drunken state, they had not the courage to fight for right. So, in the end, it was only a pause, a mere hesitation; the wickedness had only just begun.

The blow that felled Ilbert was delivered from behind. It knocked him squarely on the head. Such a crack! A shattering of crockery and bone as the jug was flung at his skull. Blood flowed readily from the wound even before the old warrior began to topple forwards. He neither crumpled nor folded; felled like an oak tree he was, his head dashed to the ground and his feet upturned as he slumped over the bench.

At that, all sanity deserted the men and I was living in a different realm, borne on a spirit of madness. Whether fellowship drew them together in some diabolical bond, or ale and wine displaced their morals and drew something from them, diseased and malevolent, which somehow was absent from Ilbert, his handful of supporters and me, I cannot wonder.

I tried to stand, but the floor moved beneath me to such a pitch that I slid to the ground, beneath the table, prostrate, helpless.

From above me and around me, I could still hear disjointed screams from the sisters, and shouts from the men as they menaced them with cruel torments.

'She likes my suggestions very well,' said one voice.

'That venomous bitch has spurned my advances,' declared another.

From then on, I experienced uneasiness in my head and stomach. Spasms came and went in my guts, and how my head throbbed! All I could do was put my mind to breathing and steadying myself, but although I was on my knees with my head held low, the room still spun and the sickness still rose. Sweats broke out, my skin prickled and the noises outside my head became distant. Then just as I was dizzier than a player in Hoodman Blind, my belly began to spew. Over and again the heaving came, my heart-ticking loud in my ears as I spat out the bitter effusions, until with dry tongue and empty retching, I lay down and lost the light.

In the fullness of time, I came back to myself. The candles and fire had burned lower, lending a dull, reddish blush to the room. I shivered and wiped my fingers over my face, dried my lips with the back of my hand. Apart from snores, snuffles and heavy breaths, there were no other sounds about me.

I crawled from beneath the table and stood upright, slowly, my head feeling woolly and my throat tasting sour. Ilbert lay just where he had fallen, the blood on the back of his head now black and lustreless, no signs of life. Other men were still in the refectory, too. One leaned forward, his head on the table, a loud wheezing noise coming from his gaping mouth. Two others had fallen asleep on the floor and one was curled up in the corner of the room, a rasping snore in his throat.

With eyes bleared and balance unsteady, I made my way through the doorway. Initially, the priory was silent and I believed the other soldiers and their shameful lord had gone away into the night. But a noise caught my attention; faint at first, then growing louder as I followed its source; a discordant wail, a tuneless lament.

The passageways and corridors were dark and I could only navigate them slowly, sometimes laying my hands to the walls to feel my way, sometimes stopping to blink my eyes and squint through the dimness. I took so many turns that my sense of direction was lost to me and I could not remember the way to the buttery, the guesthouse or even the entrance. Then, turning a corner, I saw a light and heard the source of the noise; harsh sobs distressing the air. Drawn by the light – God's first and greatest contrivance – that shone at the end of the corridor, I walked towards that flickering beam; but God was not there.

A crowd of soldiers, perhaps six or seven, stood shoulder to shoulder around the last of the nuns' cells. They jostled one another in the narrow entrance, their bodies mobile as they tried to gain better advantage to see the spectacle within. I approached them unobtrusively and, being tall and on the tips of my toes, I sought sight of the curiosity that fascinated them. But before I could acquire a clear vision, John Stanton turned about and called out to me, 'You can wait your turn, lad, like the rest of us.'

As he shouted those words, the other militia men turned about and fronted me, thereby leaving a narrow gap that revealed the object of their inducement. I wished at that moment with all my heart that God might have spared my eyes and taken all sight away from me. The horror was so vast that nothing else existed.

That fine commander of the detachment; the lord; the genteel nobleman, was standing over the wooden bed in the centre of the room. On the bed, he had pinned down the smaller of the two sisters, his hands pressing down on each of her shoulders. The girl's habit was roughly pushed above her knees, revealing her slender legs, her skin the colour of milk. She could have been no older than Alice of the cornfield: fifteen? Sixteen? Wholly subdued she was, as though her sobs had garnered such little response from the men that she had been forced to accept her situation in despondent silence. My arrival stimulated a grain of hope within her and she cried out, her sobs then conjoining into one long lament.

I pushed my way into the room and said to the lord in disbelief, 'What are you doing? You must surely have lost your senses! Have a care, sir. Have mercy!'

'Do not meddle, boy,' he seethed back at me. 'Hold your tongue!'

At that moment there was such darkness in the nobleman's eyes. All of his anger was entirely in those eyes, his other features redundant. I looked about the room, appealing with my own eyes to the other men, but they too seemed entranced by some strangeness. Had the liquor infected them, but somehow not impaired me? Or were they already diseased with thoughts of debauchery before they came here?

'If you are not here for pleasure,' John said, 'then get you gone, lad.'

'No, wait, John,' the lord intervened, slanting an eye at me. 'Make him watch; make a man of him; he will thank me when it is over.'

I turned but could go no more than two paces before rough hands were laid on me, applied to the crown of my head, and my face skewed around to witness the awful scene that began to unfold. The exchange of words and the tussle brought the realisation of her fate closer to the girl; where before she had taken the nobleman's wrath in great patience, now in her final fears, she thrashed her arms and switched her head from side to side. And for that she received a violent strike for her trouble.

Subdued, motionless and with a runnel of red spilling from the corner of her mouth, she was slack as a rag as the nobleman despoiled her of the clothing from her upper body, which raised jeers of encouragement from the soldiers, and provoked a grotesque and unnatural ripple of energy, a wave of dark expectation, that bewitched all souls in that room, with the exception of me and the poor novice-girl. As the tension increased, and surely impelled by the venom of the Fiend, all the men laughed, just as they had done so in the refectory. Their hearing must have become impaired as well as their reason; they could not discern that all jollity had gone from the world and that their laughs had become just howls; the baying of wolves.

Unsettled by the distress, the girl fought back, tried to free herself. At first, she defended herself stoutly, unwilling to yield, but with the power of lust running so strongly within him and frustration growing as he laboured to take her, he subdued her with his mastery and she was overcome. With carnal craving blotting all sense of consequence, he fell on her and did such villainy. A deeper shade of evil I had never witnessed before. The shriek of her woe pierced the core of my heart, then she fell to praying and weeping and sobbing.

What compelled him to assault her, I will never understand for it is surely beyond the range of my senses. Tear-swollen and bereft of clear sight, I tried to turn away to relieve my eye, but hands held my head fast, and with passive will I was forced to watch that monster possess her. The shame and the filth of it all! The stoutest heart would surely bleed at such a sight!

But on he went with the endless slaking of his lust, no care to abridge his base deed, a mighty fancy he would never be judged and punished. At last, his violence finished and I could only be thankful the girl's suffering was over. But as John Stanton released the grip he had on me, he did not leave the cell; none of the soldiers did. And I began to comprehend the full horror of their intentions; the nobleman was just the first, and fellowship dictated that his subordinates would follow: the young cocks had learned what the old cock did crow; just as poor Ilbert had tried to warn me. I backed away, scrambled to get to my feet, but the lord took me roughly by the arms.

'You have defiled her,' I cried out with disgust. 'You have corrupted her and—'

'She was already corrupt,' he said, coolly. 'She is corrupt because she is a seducer of men.'

'But she gave you nothing to set your anger against,' I said. 'She gave you no reason to—'

'Nonsense,' he said, now stern in his manner. 'We all saw her approach me in the refectory; we all saw the way she eyed me. You look at me as though I moulded the enterprise myself, Alwin, but you saw how she trifled with me. It was she that beguiled me. It was she that summoned up my lust. My only sin is that I was weakened by the wine we were served. And who served us? I could not fight her guiles, was that not so? With sadness, I confess here and now, that I was tempted into lechery and I succumbed to her trickery. The Devil was inside her. She tempted me and, in the process, dishonoured herself. Now she laments in her regret. Plain and simple. She enticed me and I could not resist; she maddened my blood; she is a sorceress, Alwin. But if your concerns are around the lie you told to gain us access, or the manner in which you disrespected the pulpit-bawler's wimple I dislodged, then worry not; I will make the appropriate payments to the saints. I have enough wealth to pay for all our pardons.'

'But even if you are convinced she bewitched you,' I said with desperation, 'you have recovered well enough. If you truly believe this girl has the Devil inside her, then can you not now save your men from her seductions and prevent another ill-done deed?'

At that, the nobleman laughed and, availing myself of his distracted state, I took the opportunity to wriggle free of his grasp. The time for words was over; I might as well have talked to the north wind for all the good it had done. I swung my right arm back and then brought it forwards, towards his chin, landing a blow with my clenched fist that knocked him backwards. My intent was to cause an affray, a distraction that would stop a repeat of the atrocity I had just witnessed, break the strand of diabolical camaraderie that threaded from one man to the next.

I gnashed my teeth and roared, pulled my balled fist back ready to throw it forward again. I made a pounce at the lord, but that time he was ready and I took a heavy blow to my cheekbone. Other men joined in and an untidy exchange of pummelling ensued as the brawling intensified; I received many cuffs and clouts, but stood my ground well, spreading the nose of one man, which discharged a satisfying quantity of blood, and setting a flow of gore from the mouth of another after dislodging his tooth.

But, of course, I was no match for those hardened fighting men however much liquor they had consumed and, as though summoned by the drumming of a tabor, they came at me as one body and I could not stop them from their intent. At the brink of defeat, I was hewn by a strike just below my left eye and I fell to the floor and knew no more.

When at last I regained my faculties, I had lost my awareness of time. For all I knew, whole days and nights might have been stolen away while I had slept, but the memory of past events stayed with me, bold and clear in my mind.

I was alone in the corridor outside the nuns' cells, a weak light seeping through the darkness. I rose to my feet, my head disordered and my chin stiff and smarting. My midriff was tender and my ribs ached cruelly, but worst of all were my hands; skin scuffed from my knuckles, joints throbbing with sharp pangs.

I shuffled my way towards the light that emanated from the nearby cell. In my fuddled head, I was hoping to convince myself matters had not truly happened in the manner I recalled. What I wished to see most was an empty cell, unvisited by vexations, calm in its holy tranquillity. Perhaps the grotesque theft of chastity I thought I had witnessed was in fact conjured by the wine I had consumed; nothing more than hideous delirium. But as I neared the open doorway, one look within turned my stomach over inside me and presented me with a vision that would be engrafted on my mind forever.

I fell to my knees and dispelled a series of empty retches. I could only look at the poor girl for a moment. The sight rendered me sick and chill. Her eyes were open, but all lucency was lost. Those brave orbs had stared at her aggressors until the very moment the blade had been drawn across her throat, and they lingered still on some heavenly sight far and away from the barbarous treachery that had befallen her. No excuses could ever divert the pity of such a scene.

Such a feeling of horror, of abject revulsion, consumed me that my senses became deficient and a rawness took possession of me; a fusion of anger and guilt and futility and utter incomprehension. Why? Why? Dogs are beaten, horses are whipped; man holds dominion over all creatures, but why treat a woman worse than all the rest? I balled my fist and punched the wall, but I stifled all cries of pain, and my suffering was nothing to that of the poor girl whose remnant lay dead before me.

I might have stayed in that awful moment for all eternity, trying to unravel the conundrum, searching for an answer to a riddle that could never be found. But the sound of voices provoked me into movement. I passed by the other cells, turning my head first one way then the other, and each little room had been transformed from sanctity to sepulchre as basely as the first, each housing defiled female forms, ravaged and murdered with uniform consistency. I walked on, beyond the limit of my emotions, feeling nothing but feelings of failings.

As a boy, I spent many a morning swimming in the deeps of the River Crown, the waters gently toiling about me. Lithe and strong as I was, the current could never take me far. But one morning, the waters were brimming with heavy rainfall and I was washed out of my depth. For the first time in my life, I was tossed and chafed by waters that hitherto had been kind and cooperative. A heavy weight bore down on me as the river took me under and shut the air off from my chest. Frantic as my arms thrashed, the river would not be appeased and there came a point when everything seemed lost and all my efforts were forgotten. In that final moment before at last I managed to take hold of a tree branch and haul myself out of the torrent, a strange composure infused my mind; an acceptance that my life from before might never be revived; submission to a state of darkness from which I might never escape. And that same sense of hopelessness returned to me as I walked past the holy sisters' broken bodies and made my way out of that sacred house of hell; the air pressed from my chest as though a weight of water lay on it.

I dared not seek out my sword for fear of discovery, so I crept through the dimness until at last I came to the entrance hall. I lifted the latches and drew back the bolts, noiseless and cautious as I made my escape. Fearing the sound of the closing door behind me, I left it swinging on its hinges and I pressed forward to the stables.

The moon was bright as I saddled and tacked Bracken and led her out into the courtyard, but the lunar light soon dimmed when the moon turned her eye away from me, and the night thickened about me as I mounted and trotted on.

In spite of my silent exit, the cold night air must have wormed its way through the doorway, snaked over the threshold and crept like fog into the convent, alerting the militia men, for no sooner had I gained the forest path than shouts and oaths sounded from behind me.

I quickly dismounted, pulled Bracken's head and guided her beneath the canopy of trees, certain we would be invisible in the blackness of night. But the moon, she was unforgiving, and she stared down at me between the clouds. In her icy glare she caught me fast and, exposed and haunted by my fears, I took to the saddle again and urged Bracken on into a gallop.

The soldiers were quick and were not for surrendering their chase. Bracken kept up a good pace, trustful and loyal to my guiding hands, responsive to my seat and legs, but she could not out-run the militia men's horses. I only had one chance of escape. With stealth, I slipped my feet from the stirrups, let go of the reins and slid down from the saddle, hitting the forest floor with a thud. Bracken slowed for the slightest of moments at feeling the weight leave her back, but the soldiers were close behind and the motion of their horses seemed to awaken some primal reaction in her, drove her forward as though they were born to run as one entity. She would surely gallop as long as they galloped and would not stop until exhaustion consumed her, and the sight of her leaving me, never to be seen again, wrung my heart dry.

In a moment she was gone from me, the pursuing soldiers thundered past and I was alone. Part of me wanted to lie down, close my eyes, have the world stop. But I knew the soldiers would soon realise they were chasing a rider-less horse and would turn back to search for me. In time, some force, some energy as strong as a river current, made me rise up and run for my life. Life, with all its twisting twines of pains and laments; its yarn still pulled me onwards.

On foot and beneath the cover of night and forest, I took narrow trails that wove threadlike through the woods, too compacted for horse and rider, and thus I evaded discovery and escaped the militia men. I ran and ran, and when the sound of my pursuers became fainter, I slowed to a dogtrot. On I walked with no more sense of direction than a roving bee until, as the night folded darker about me, I stopped, sank to the ground and lay down in a hollow, hardly daring to trouble the air with my breath.

With moss for a pillow and rain for a blanket, I cowered beneath a trellis of leafless boughs and spent the dark hours starting in and out of fitful sleep. Eventually, with just the wind for a watcher, dawn began to blanch the night and, with my palms and knee bones badged with mud, at last I breathed the raw air of daybreak.

The sun rose shyly that morning, barely amending the sky from black to blue, scarce bright enough to kindle the horizon. I watched it for some moments from the earthy cavity into which I had crept the night before, the trees hovering about me, their boles sunk deep in mist. Huddled and compacted, I unfolded myself with stiffness, but could not stand up for some time. There was an ache in my stomach and its contents griped and burned, and my head was most tender. Dizziness came to me on rising and stooping, and continual throbs harried my brows. Eventually, I was able to walk towards the sun's hesitant light, knowing I must track eastwards, press on and meet Father Oswald at The Chequers before nightfall.

I picked and ate a little hedge-bank fruit as I went along and quenched my thirst at a brook. The water seemed to restore the balance in my body and I was able to walk more vigorously and make good ground from then on. But however well the water washed the fermentation away from my insides, my mind was plagued with the horrors I had witnessed and I could not put the scenes out of my head. From my wounded thoughts, doubts bled thick and persistent and I could not stop the flow of them.

If God made man superior to woman, then why punish her so? Why cannot man use kindness and patience to correct her, just as man expects those virtues to be used by God to correct him? In the wholeness of truth, I could not see any wickedness in Mother,

Alice or any of the nuns. Was I blind to their wiles? Do some men have the power to see the Devil in others, or do those others have the misfortune to reflect the Devil in some men? The uncertainties trudged on within me as I crested hills and forded streams, and the further I travelled, the larger those scruples grew, until I realised that by doubting, I would one day be obliged to decide: what sort of man was I?

It was just before eventide that I hailed a man who was driving a waggonful of sacked and bound cornmeal and I was relieved to learn he was travelling to the township of Alfricstowe. I paid him a silver penny, we went on our way together and he agreed to take me to my destination. Despite the turmoil in my mind and the woes that vexed me, I could not help but drowse as I sat up high on that waggon, and I did not wake until the waggoner shook my shoulder and pointed his arm, past a pond and market cross, to where The Chequers stood.

It could not have been long before curfew when I entered the tavern, because the lights were flamed and the fire was orange in the hearth. The place was crowded; people's heads all pushed together like apples in a loft-room. Such a swell of conversation rose about me that I felt it in the bones of my skull as well as through my ears. On the far side, one man strummed on a gittern and another blew his lips to a shawm and between them they made a merry sound. But I did not feel merry and the contrast between my cast of mind and the cheeriness only served to aggravate me.

How I longed to relieve my discontent with tear-shed, but, of course, no man could do such a thing amongst his peers, so I held it inside my ribs and felt it turn to frustration and anger. I was nursing quite a rage by the time I was descried by God's own delegate; my own, dear Father Oswald. He welcomed me with glad cries and approached me with hasty feet, but his features dropped when he saw the bruises around my lip and eye. He quickly cast his eye about my person; noted the ripped sleeve of my tunic and the mud on my knee-pans.

'Alwin! Whatever has happened to you?' he gasped, then, 'Who has done you this offence?'

The questions ran through the tavern like a blade, pared all conversation and even cropped the music. Father Oswald, sensing my awkwardness, took me by the arm and guided me to a table and bench set beneath a shuttered window. Many of the townsfolk stared their eyes at me for a good while, but then gradually the hubbub and music-craft returned and Father Oswald said more quietly, 'These good folks around this table are to be our companions, Alwin, when we set out for Norfolk tomorrow. You sit with them here, while I go and fetch you some wine. Then, if you are good and ready, you must tell me all that has happened to you since last we met.'

The cleric touched his hand to my shoulder as he stood and I was left to nod my salutations to the company about me. A man and his matronly wife sat on my left and two maidens perched on the end of the bench to my right. At first, I did not see the last of our group, for she stood a little apart.

Eventually, she stepped forward, her lilac kirtle splitting the air with its colour, half in shadow and half bathed in firelight. She nodded her head and her hair took the colours from the fire: first chestnut, then golden, then aflame with russet, like sunrise and sunset all blent into one. I looked at her only briefly, but saw she was blue of eye; irises whose colour mocked the blooms of borage.

Her expression was impassive, she announced her presence with silence and her eyes alone rendered me uneasy. I could not tell for certain whether I viewed her with a different aspect or whether she herself was variant; all I knew was that I found in her no resemblance to what I was accustomed.

Father Oswald returned, set a measure of hippocras in my hand, bade me take sup, then gently asked again, 'Pray tell us what happened to you, Alwin.'

'It was nothing,' I said, the words scalding my temper again. 'It was a moment of misfortune, but I ...' My voice lost a measure of its breadth and my eyes felt hot. Up until that moment, I had never intended to tell a falsehood, but the recollection of my night at the priory was so awful, so abhorrent to me, that the shame impelled me to erase it from my history. '... I never reached the Winfeld Priory, Father Oswald,' I said.

With one timid word upon another, I unfurled an abridged version of reality. I described my journey, just as it had been, until the point I reached the forest glade. Then I introduced disunity between my story and actuality; I said a body of soldiers had ambushed me, tried to despoil me of the bag of silver coins I wore about my person, and had stolen my horse. After spending a night beneath the stars, I had made my way to the township and was tired and dishevelled as a result.

As I spoke the words, my heart danced behind my ribs, but knowing that the prioress and nuns had all been sent to their Maker and could never gainsay me, I saw no harm in cleansing bygone troubles from my sorry retrospection. Father Oswald and all my new companions took pity on my adversity and offered up words of comfort and condolence. Then as my tale was spread among the patrons of the tavern, strangers brought me cups of wine and clapped me on the back. My mind began to be easy, started to distance itself from the visions that pained it, and I experienced a burgeoning sense of safety I had not felt since last I wandered the Whittaker woods.

Then, just before the bells were to be rung to send us all abed, a man burst in through the tavern's door, breathless and wide-eyed. He was in such high feather and said he brought news of an unspeakable act that had occurred at the Priory of Winfeld. He told of soldiers and defilement, of godlessness and villainy.

My heart beat heavily and I cast my eyes downwards, fearful everyone would see through me. I waited for the townsfolk to respond, wondering if they would suspect my involvement, but of course there was no reason to. One and all agreed how fortunate I was to have survived the soldiers' ensnarement; how blessed I was to have been prevented from reaching the convent.

The chatter went on and the details grew more frightful until, at last, a question was put to the messenger: how had he come by the news? At that, he disclosed that the holy sisters had all been barbarously murdered, with the exception of the old prioress, and she had raised the alarm.

The blood in the pipes beneath my skin all drained away and a shiver prickled over my scalp. I could hardly breathe. I tried to keep my composure and, darting my eye to view the people around me, I could see they had not connected me with the priory. The incident which befell me was a separate matter to the atrocity at the convent; that fact had been established and nobody saw reason to question it. Nobody except for one; the maiden in the lilac kirtle.

She did not simply look at me, but looked inside me, something raw and untamed behind her eyes. She fathomed me in an instant. Nothing eluded her, I was certain; from the flush of my cheek to the thrumming of my heart. I had somehow aroused her suspicion and, by so doing, had rendered myself greatly vulnerable.

CHAPTER FOUR

Talk of destruction and slaughter went on long into the evening and echoes of the truth were intertwined with wild flights of fancy. Fears and fury were described in imaginative detail; blood had been cast high on the walls and spilled in such quantity that the leaves on the oaks thereabouts had all apparently turned scarlet. But however much the proclaimer augmented his despatch, I knew the outrage I had witnessed carried such grief as more than mouth of man could ever tell. The messenger revelled in the attention he received and embellished his story each time it was repeated, but his words never told of hope's deceit or trust's betrayal, never captured that final disbelief, that cruel disappointment at man's inhumanity that lingered in the fair maid's eyes as her spotless soul journeyed on to its immortal rest.

Inside I flinched each time the talebearer's stories expanded, and the disparity between truth and fiction intensified my own recollection of reality. Once again, remembrance gave vent to angry blood beneath my skin and I was frustrated by the lack of condemnation afforded to the perpetrators. The lord, his sergeant and John Stanton were never mentioned individually; all focus was put on a vivid reimagining of the horrors that had taken place, in a ghoulish and prurient manner. The soldiers' anonymity and godlessness were accepted as though they were a plague, deadly and invisible, and could never be controlled or brought to justice. It was as though a tempest had been blown into the priory by some force of nature, applied its destruction and moved on.

With the prate of the townsfolk still rising and eddying around me, I leaned in to Father Oswald and said, 'There must be something we can do, Father. Can we not raise a hue and cry? The soldiers must surely be held accountable.'

'The moon is too dim tonight, Alwin, the roads too dark and dangerous for travel. The soldiers will be long gone by now, but at daybreak, I will go to the town constable and have him employ the services of the tithing men. I shall ride out with them and go to the priory; and I will not rest until they have heard of this at the shire moot.'

'And will you talk to the prioress?' I said, my heart giving off a violent kick.

'If her health will allow; then, yes.'

'Then I shall come with you,' I declared in haste, at once desperate to know what she remembered, but also fearful she would recognise me.

'No, Alwin. You have been through enough. You are tired and bruised. Best you bide here in the town. I have your letter of commendation from the abbot, just as I promised. I shall keep it safe in my satchel with all my private papers. But there are jobs for you to do to get us ready for the pilgrimage; provisions to be bought, horses to be hired. I will leave as dawn breaks and return by dusk. And Alwin—'

'Yes?'

'I know, as God is my witness, you never reached the priory. But if you had done so, I also know you could never have been party to such barbarism.'

I suppose Father Oswald intended to give comfort to me. But because I had lied to him, the guilt within my mind changed his words from solace to suspicion. Had he guessed already I was there? Was he going to the prioress to confirm his doubts? If the moment had lingered for a heartbeat longer, then I might have confessed the truth to him, wiped away the guilt that plagued my conscience. But in those ensuing seconds, as ever, my ego painted images of shame and embarrassment; to prove my innocence to Father Oswald, my secret deformity would have to be revealed to him and I could not bear to witness the disappointment in the priest's eyes. Then, of a sudden, Father Oswald said, 'Alwin! You are bleeding.'

I followed the line of his gaze and touched my hands to the top of my thigh. A small, dark patch had bled through my leggings.

'I must go to my sleeping quarters at once, Father,' I said. 'I shall tend to my wounds and dress them and—'

I left the tavern in haste and made my way to the shelter at the side of the cooking shed; just like the place where travelling men took their slumber in the town of Badeswell. I found a palliasse of straw in the far corner, filled the water pail from the trough and washed myself down as best I could. With the blood cleaned away, I looked for a mark on my body; a scratch or a cut. But there were only bruises, and the absence of any abrasion or incision rendered my misery even greater than previously, as it meant the site of my plague-wound was set to haemorrhaging, just as it had done so twice before.

I had not told a soul of its happening; not even Mother. But the thought of it becoming steadily worse and impairing my health, was of deep concern to me. I padded my groin with compressed hay, just as I had done so last time, and I hoped its meagre flow would be short-lived as before and be staunched by morning.

I fell into a deep and dreamless sleep as soon as my head touched the straw mattress and I next awoke at dawn, disorientated at first, believing I was in my own bedchamber in the house at Crown Croft.

But the noises of the morning were different. The chanticleer's crow was narrower, more grating than our own cockerel. Outside, water pails were being filled, and shutters were being creaked open. The clamour of dogs cut through the air, and closer to hand there were deep, sonorous snores all about me from the other men in the shelter. I rose, washed my face and hands, smoothed down my hair and cleaned my mouth with a hazel twig. Then I stepped out into the morning, a blue chill having settled on the day.

Some townsfolk were already astir; a butcher was at the shambles setting up his stall with quantities of swine flesh, and a pelterer was scouring furs by the pond. Above the rooftops, the moon was still just visible, sitting high in the azure, her face ashen, and I wondered how she had the heart to watch the world each day with her knowledge of what had gone before.

'Telling your troubles to the moon, lad?' came Father Oswald's voice from behind me.

'I think she's witnessed enough already,' I said, 'without me adding to them.'

'You could always return to Giolgrave tomorrow, Alwin. Your mother would not think the less of you, I am sure.'

'No, Father. A promise is a debt and I intend to repay.'

'Well, I must be getting ready,' the priest said. 'We leave within the hour for Winfeld. Let me introduce you properly to the company of pilgrims before I go, though. It was all so hasty last night, with all the commotion, I had no time to tell you their names.'

With that, the cleric led me back into the sleeping shelter and had me shake hands with the man whom last night had sat on my left. The man pulled his hodden grey cloak about his shoulders as he rose from his mattress and, standing to his feet, he searched my face with his eyes, then offering up his hand he gave me good day. His palm was cold and clammy and I noted that his fingernails were bitten low to the quick.

'William Tanner,' the man said, bowing his head, his face old and rough as though made from clay and fashioned with an axe.

'Alwin Whittaker,' I replied, trying not to stare at the large wen he had grown on the side of his nose. 'God keeps you well, sir?' I added.

'Aye, lad,' he said, then, 'You travelled much?'

'No, sir. All my life, until yesterday, I have not travelled more than a dozen miles from the place I was born. Neither did my mother before me, so the county of Norfolk and the shrine of Our Lady in Walsingham might be as far away as the moon for all I know.'

I thought my confessed inexperience would engender sympathy from Master Tanner, have him speak kind words to me. But his face puckered into a frown and he said, 'It might have served better if you had been older, lad. Broader and stronger. I spoke to a fellow yesterday, see. A swain from the north. I could tell he was a foreigner straight away; you know, dishonest-looking. Said he was a miller, visiting his cousin. Told me of the dog-headed people gathering in great numbers in the far north of our country, and in the east. Know you of them, lad?'

'No, sir,' I said.

'Tall and mighty he said they were, with human bodies, human minds, but with the head of a dog; gnashing teeth and a deadly bite.'

'And might they cross our path, Master Tanner?' I said.

'Who knows. Who can guess the mind of a demon? We can but pray to God for deliverance and be thankful that God protects the innocent.'

With that, he bowed his head and returned to his palliasse. Father Oswald then walked with me back towards the tavern.

'Are there really dog-headed people, Father?' I said, after walking a few yards.

'I cannot say, Alwin. I have never seen any with my own eyes, but then neither have I seen the Devil. But with pure minds and true hearts, God will protect us, so you have nothing to fear.'

We walked on in silence, then in time we crossed paths with the dame and three maids who formed the remainder of our group; they having slept in a room at the inn. The dame was more than average stout, and as we approached, she talked in an animated, jolly manner to the two younger maids; the third was left trailing behind them. Pleasantries were exchanged and I learned Dame Goody Tanner was wife to William, and the two young maids, Matilda and Adela, were from neighbouring villages and, like me, were travelling on their first pilgrimage. Both girls were hoping to wed within the year; Adela – who looked no older than a goose-girl – was on her way to Walsingham to seek out the blessing of Our Lady, to set her on the path to good motherhood, and Matilda was in behopes of purchasing a lady-girdle blessed by the Virgin Mother. The last member of our newly formed clan was the woman in lilac.

She approached me casually, as though I lacked importance. I smiled and bowed my head, did my utmost to behave pretty towards her, but she was unmoved. Her lips curved slightly upwards, her eyes were impassive, and my effort availed me nothing. I dared not look at her for more than a moment, because she somehow ignited the flesh beneath my skin, like when a careless hand strokes a nettlebed.

I cast her age at one-and-twenty and decided she had the sort of face as would draw your eye in a crowd. For the first time in my life, bashfulness robbed me of speech. Father Oswald told her my name and spoke hers to me: Rosamund Blackmere. I held the shape of her name in my head, felt the rhythm of the syllables like they were strummed on a gittern. Was that what it felt like to be bewitched? I took a sudden step backwards, the heat of her too hot for me to bear, knocking Father Oswald's arm as I did so.

'Steady, lad,' he said, a jokiness to his tone. 'You young men are all so graceless!'

I composed myself and believed the hex was broken, but a fullness of heart remained with me, a straw-tickling pleasure that persisted beneath my ribcage, which I both revered and feared in equal measure.

Within the hour, Father Oswald had ridden away to the priory with the constable and the tithing men. I wished God and Saint Martin would speed him well and watched as the dust-cloud settled in their horses' wake. Then, in an attitude of charitable kinship, I joined my new companions and we began walking as a group, making our way to the hackney-man to hire horses. We walked together along streets that were narrow and humming with motion, thronged and loud, noisome and smoky with cookhouse fires. We passed a man locked up in wooden stocks where he was closely kept and ill-fed, and then we followed the sounds to a lively quarter where stalls and trestles were dressed with provisions.

On reaching the market square, there were lanes to the right and left, but we took the master-street, where vendors and merchants plied their trades in separate quarters of the thoroughfare. Benches loaded with apples, pears and nuts were set up alongside a man peddling tanned hides and fleeces, and many women were at a stall that sold lampreys and Aberdeen fish.

The mercers had set themselves a little apart and were trading their leather gloves, purses and needle-cases to a sparse crowd and at a high price. Most buildings we passed were made of wood and cob; structures crowded together with tanned plaster walls and unkempt thatch, but I could only marvel at the merchants' houses; three storeys high with slate tiles on the roof, they were twice the size of any house in Badeswell. As we walked along, our group fragmented. William, Goody and I led at the front, Matilda and Adela with their arms hooked together walked a little way behind us and Rosamund strolled alone at the rear.

As we ambled past a series of booths that gave on to the market square, Dame Goody, winsome as before, said to me, 'Do not look so glum, lad. Forget about the soldiers and the brawl. Take it not to grief. Matters will be cheerier today. They say the sun shines brighter after a sharp shower and I believe it is so.' Then with a smile in her eyes, she touched my arm and said, 'And even sad dogs must sometimes wag their tails.'

'Thank you for your kind words,' I said.

'And a young buck like you,' she went on with jollity in her voice, 'should be thrilled at the chance of meeting the maidens in our band of travellers.'

There was a giggle from behind us and I felt the blood rise to my cheeks.

'The maids Matilda and Adela; well, I can happily vouch they both have gracious and submissive tempers and are always keen to serve their masters.'

'And what of Rosamund?' I said. It was the first time I had spoken her name and, to hear myself speak it made me tremble a little inside, and in so doing, Rosamund – the name and the person – at once became part of my own history.

There was a moment of pause and the smithy's hammer dropped a series of clangs, which wrangled in the air, then Dame Goody looked at me with kind but cautious eyes and said in low tones, 'My sister's husband was born in the same village as Rosamund Black-mere. The girl's mother was a Wise Woman and the girl herself; well, she knows of charms and herbs. And by an intricate tangle of kinship, they say she is imbued with noble blood. Some say she can even read the written word! But the day she was born, the corn developed a blight and the ewes slipped their lambs. The odour of witchcraft coils about her if you ask me and you would be well served to keep your distance, my lad. To be wed to a creature like her would never work. It would be like fire and cream; sure to curdle in time. I would sooner chop my bones for the pot than be acquainted with that one. I bid you take consideration of my counsel.'

That warning and the reference to sorcery caused me a deal of vexation, but a strange battle had begun to be fought in my head and my heart; the latter beginning to win through. Already, against my better judgement, the worries in my mind concerning Rosamund Blackmere were gently becoming unremembered and, by the time we reached the hackney-man's stables, the apprehension I should have harboured against her was much diluted and had changed its form from fear to fascination that danced moth-like behind my ribs.

There was a congregation of townsfolk at that end of the district, hovering and swarming over the benches and wares, a body of hoods and hats moving all around. We paused and in time, Matilda and Adela caught up with us; Adela kept up a cheerful chatter with her fluent tongue and Matilda looked all about her with eyes wide with wonder. Then, without a word, Matilda scampered off and returned with a milking stool.

'I have borrowed it,' she said shyly. 'For you, Dame Goody! That you might rest your legs while we wait for the hackney-man.'

'God bless you, child!' Dame Tanner exclaimed, taking the girl's hand in her own as she sat down. Matilda blushed deeply at that, and although she must surely have had seventeen summers behind her, aspects of childish innocence yet lingered in her countenance and made her seem much younger.

'Have you ever wondered,' Adela then began, addressing the group, sudden and thoughtful, 'why a milking stool has but three legs?'

The question put us all in pause. Goody and William frowned, Matilda scratched the top of her head and I searched my mind for logic and reason to explain the riddle away.

'Because if it had only two; it would fall over!' Adela said, her voice choked with giggles.

And with that, Goody erupted into fits of laughter, Matilda bent herself double with mirth, even William could not help but chuckle to himself, and I laughed with such glee that the bones in my face began to ache. Goody could not resist having Adela tell the quip again, that she may learn the telling of it; and the words once more had us dissolved in jollity. But each time the riddle was retold, it lost a little of its sheen and in a while it had worn out its favour.

So, we stood in a little knot around the seated Dame Goody and we waited the attentions of the hackney-man.

'Ah! How pleasant to rest up my legs,' the good dame said. 'They become so sore and fatigued.'

''Tis a pity, dear wife,' William retorted, 'that your tongue does not tire as swiftly as your knees; that you may sit in silence.'

'And a pity, husband,' she came back with, 'that your ears do not heed my tongue when it tells you to hold your ale better.'

William threw a hard glance at his wife, then strolled away from us, returning moments later with a handful of pears. He offered the fruits to us, and Adela, Matilda and Goody all took one.

'I know your ruse, husband,' Goody said as she bit into the pear. 'And it will take more than a ripe pear to silence my mouth.'

'Take more than a ripe pear tree, if you ask me,' he mumbled. And with that he moved away from the group and continued hovering a foot or two to our left, both unified and separate, like the shadow of a shadow.

Goody went on to list out loud a number of William's ill habits, but her husband no longer responded, and I supposed over the years of their marriage, Goody must have wound her affections around William's heart so tightly that he suffered her gentle prejudices against him without complaint. The public airing of their private bickering continued in spats over the next few minutes, then I turned my attentions back to the hackney-man, who was busy parading an old rouncy before a parcel of youths.

The nag looked lame in its hind quarters and held its head low and dispirited. Its sorrel coat was lustreless, but the colour reminded me of the old mare, Bracken, and once again I sensed the bitter after-taste of loss. From that fleeting retrospection came thoughts of death, then images of Mother; and vibrations of her passing echoed loudly in my heart, amplified further by the guilt of my recent laughter. I swallowed the self-reproach and sorrow down, clenched my fists and stepped briskly away towards the stream that bordered the street. In so doing, I clashed elbows with a passer-by and, looking up, saw I had run into Rosamund.

'I did not see you, Damosel Blackmere,' I said, unapologetic, sour and disagreeable, desperate to disguise the weakness of my emotions.

She looked at me abstractedly, apparently bemused, and the initial relief afforded by my abruptness was short-lived and at once became regret. I walked on towards the stream as though I were unaffected, stood alongside a group of youths who were on the gad and watched them busy at the casting of stones. By the time I returned to the hackney-man's, Dame Goody, William Tanner and the two maids had reserved their mounts and wandered away towards the crockman's stall.

I stood and leaned against the spears of the fence that marked out the palfreyman's paddock, and Rosamund was but a few paces from me, but I said nothing. With stealth I cast my eye in her direction from time to time. Momentarily, my thoughts took her up and wandered away with her to a realm of conjecture; was Goody Tanner right to scorn her as a witch? Behind her comeliness, was there wickedness that was fetched to the Devil's fire when backs were turned? Or was that spark of intrigue she generated within me born of a purer integrity? As I looked away, the wind got up and blew a streak of dust along the ground between us. The air was confused that day; the summer sun was all but gone and autumn ambers were still to blush through; bright skies but a chill breeze.

The hackney-man led a bay saddle horse from his stable and walked it towards Rosamund. The animal, compact at fourteen hands, had a fair constitution and looked well fed, but he did not walk as smoothly as he might and although he lifted his knees well, the heel of his foot did not come first to the ground. He would serve well enough, but I suspected the hackney-man was not hiring out his best pony.

'Do you have another the maiden may choose, sir?' I asked, walking a little closer to Rosamund, availing myself of a reason to approach her, trying to catch her eye as I addressed the man.

'This one will do well enough,' she said, speaking only to the horse-hirer.

The man looked at me, awaiting my final decision and I said, 'Just as the lady wishes.'

The horse was led away and Rosamund produced a coin from her purse, ready to pay the reckoning. I started to leave; I would come back later to hire my own horse. Perhaps Goody Tanner was right all along and I should keep clear of Damosel Blackmere.

'Master Whittaker,' she called after me. I turned and at last she put her eyes towards mine, and I was saturated in her gaze. But her mouth did not speak kind words to me.

'Why would you suppose I did not notice the weakness of that pony's step?' she said, cool and flat, a hint of amusement behind her eyes. 'In an instant, I could see the animal was well fed and in good plight; that his coat was smooth, and his eyes alert. His forelegs showed no signs of ever having had splints, so compared to the sore back of William Tanner's mount and the dull eyes of all the other nags this man has for hire, I believe I chose well. So,

why,' she asked, with both a frown and a smile, 'would you suppose me incapable?'

'I … I did not suppose anything,' I stuttered, momentarily
devoid of poise.

'And would you have stepped in to advise William Tanner?' she
posed, again with that same look of ridicule behind her eyes.

'Of course not,' I said, assertive and sure. 'A man seeks advice
when he is ready to do so and should not be subordinate to another
man's unsolicited opinions.'

'But a woman is naturally subordinate to a man and should
therefore be grateful for his wisdom, whether solicited or not?'

'Yes! Why would matters be otherwise? And why should you
not be grateful for the subordination man bestows on you? It
makes you better at being … female. And besides, the male has
a greater strength of body and therefore earns his superiority and
his right of authority.'

'So, a tall and muscular labourer should hold dominion over a
small and frail king?'

'Well,' I began, but I could say no more. It felt as though she
had trapped me with her words, just for the fun of it. I do not
believe she saw me as her master at all.

'Your argument is indeed weak, sir,' she grinned, 'but nevertheless it has tied you in a knot.'

Her words were delivered with gentle mockery, but they
were also sharp and they stung me. I took a step back; I was
unaccustomed to receiving such barbs and was confounded
by her derision. Her manner quite punctured my confidence,
and in spite of being taught for my whole life that hurry was
the mark of a fool, still I said the first words that entered
my head.

'God did not create women to issue such caustic rhetoric!' I
said, contemptuous and proud.

'Would you have God expunge my soul to render me more pleasing to you?' she asked, a coy, taunting tone to her voice, a smile burgeoning on her lips.

'No, but—'

'Ought I to be more docile?' she tried, the sarcasm in her voice barely disguised at all.

'Well, yes ... but—' I stuttered.

'To gratify your insecure senses? To convince the world you are masterful?'

In all my life, by Heaven's will or hand, I had never before been so overcome with such intolerable embarrassment. And there was such confidence that she carried within her, as though the rules of life had not yet tamed her. Silence lay between us, jagged of edge, sharp of thorn, and through the pain and annoyance of my situation, I realised it was the honesty of her words that cut me deeper than anything else. Just a few days before, I had well known the order of the world and my place in it. But since the events at the Winfeld Priory, now I half doubted, only half believed, and my world was a place of contradictions.

Time passed quicker than I perceived, and in a moment a small crowd of vendors and youths had gathered, perhaps in the hope of seeing the power of a man and the submission of a woman. I suppose I should have taken a hand to her, as tradition dictated, but in my mind's eye I recalled the nobleman's violence and the holy sister's terror, and from those images I began to experience an inner strength; an expansion of morality and fairness that took all aggression away from me, until a satisfying calmness infused me and I realised that meekness could perhaps become a new strength.

I looked at Rosamund and hoped that through her perception of my magnanimity, she would sense the beginning of change in me; but she only gave me a look of astonishment, as though by not striking her I had somehow done something unexpected. By that time, there were mumblings in the crowd:

'What sort of man would let himself be spoken to like that?'

'He might be a coward … if he had the courage!'

'Perhaps if he grew whiskers and looked more like a man than a boy—'

The townsfolk were reluctant to disperse and, in my agony, I could see no end to the matter. How easy it would have been for me to pacify the spectators, capitulate to their consensus. I might have publicly denigrated Rosamund or cast aspersions on her father's name, raising jeers and whoops from the onlookers, as surely as if I had knocked Rosamund into the dust with a blow hard enough to fell an ox. But I resisted what was expected of me. I held fast; the image of the holy sisters checking my learned bias, and I let the crowd melt away one by one, watched as they each rolled their eyes, tutted and went about their business, until Rosamund and I were left standing alone.

Rosamund was difficult to read; but there was surprise and admiration in her eyes, of that I am certain; a look that said she had always half-anticipated scorn from me and that those expectations had now been rebuffed. She turned from me, walked away; and how strange and confused I felt at our parting.

I lingered alone in that quarter of town for many a while. I hired a nag with splints and dull eyes, together with a sumpter horse for the bundles and bags. I bought new wearing clothes; a tunic and a travelling cloak. Then, as Father Oswald had suggested, I bought provisions for the journey. I tried to keep myself busy, but many a weary hour did pass.

At noon-spell, hunger brought sharp sauce to my belly and made it grumble and pinch, so I bought my midday meal from a public cook-shop and ate it while watching a maker of spigots and combs at his employment. Then I sat by the edge of the pond and watched the townsfolk going about their business. It was not the buildings' stone, wood and plaster, or the citizens' mobile forms that I watched, but instead their gentler, shimmering images reflected in the waters of the pond.

As I strolled back towards the tavern the streets were still, the townscape fading from my sight as eventide began to descend. What was restless but an hour since had become calm, the voices of the townsfolk now barely a murmur, the clatter of barter and trade just a memory. Then, from the head of the master-street, came the sound of a disturbance, growing louder by the heart-beat. The noise drew immediate attention, doors were flung open and the streets once again became busy with people. Heads were shaken, shoulders were shrugged and questions were asked, then as though one entity, the crowd moved, active and fluid; a trickle at first, then a flood of movement that washed me along with it and carried me towards the source of the sound.

Some yards further along, the impetus stopped and a circle of the citizenry gathered in a cluster, casting their eyes on a spectacle just beyond my sight. Slowly, I threaded my way through the onlookers and at last viewed the scene. A man was lying on the ground, apparently in severe pain, tearing the shift from his back and voicing his distress with cries and oaths. The ladder to his right lay broken in two pieces and I supposed he had fallen from its height. Torches were held in the air to better inspect him, but no one approached him and at first I could not understand why.

I took a step forward, but a woman grasped my elbow and whispered, 'The Devil's inside him, lad! Look at his arm.'

Peering through the half-light, I eyed the man's shoulder and where the surface of his bones should meet and glide beneath his skin, the head of his long bone had been thrown out and back-wards upon the rear of his shoulder-blade. His shoulder had lost all its roundness and was quite flat, his left arm suddenly grown disproportionately longer; the Devil must indeed have entered his body, perhaps was also the cause of his fall from the ladder. Or perhaps having seen his accident, Lucifer was simply exploiting the man's distressed and weak state to use him as a host. Whatever the preceding events, the man was surely lost. For more than a moment, he writhed and wept as he wrestled with the Fiend, and the townspeople and I could only watch in horror.

Then a shape broke out from the crowd: a woman; Rosamund Blackmere. Slow and steady she approached him, then sat herself down beside him, her legs parallel to his body and stretched out towards his head. At that, gasps were voiced from many in the crowd and a ripple of speculation flowed outward in a circle of sound.

Rosamund proceeded to ignore all about her, her sight concentrated on the man, his wailing subsiding to a series of whimpers on seeing her take pity on him. Of a sudden, she gently placed her heel in the man's armpit at the head of the bone, then firmly holding his arm above the elbow, she steadily pulled with her arms and pushed with her heel. At times, she stopped and manipulated his elbow, flexed it upwards and inwards, lay it on his chest; all the time provoking cries of suffering from his lips. Then in a moment, it was over; the shoulder-joint was returned to its natural place of repose and the man was silent as he got to his feet and looked about him.

'Have not a care, good people,' Rosamund said. 'The Devil has not visited himself upon us this night; this man's long bone was displaced by his fall and I have returned it to its natural seat, that is all.'

And with that, she turned about and was swallowed by the crowd. A stunned silence fell over us all after that, until one or two of the bystanders finally approached the man, calling him by his name, and asking how he fared. How I marvelled at Rosamund's skill and knowledge, her courage at coming forth and repairing the man.

I stood for some moments, awestruck and fascinated, but then the woman whom had first whispered to me on my approach, again touched my arm and said, 'We must trust no one who consorts with the Devil.' Then speaking louder, addressing the crowd, she repeated, 'We can trust no one who converses with the Fiend.'

'But,' I said, 'she explained to us his shoulder was dislodged by the fall, and even if it were the Devil, then she surely saved this man from Hell.'

One or two of the townsfolk mumbled an assent, but most shook their heads and one man called out, 'It might seem as though she banished the Devil, but what if she summoned him here in the first place, eh?'

That caused a swell in the chatter, and from then on there was dissension and strife amongst them, and accusations and suspicions abounded from menfolk and women alike. At least two dozen tongues assailed Rosamund, but no one invoked imputations against the injured man himself, no one suggested he had called the Devil to him; all aspersions were cast in Rosamund's direction, and I began to sense feelings of sympathy towards her. Then Goody's words of witchcraft and sorcery rang loud in my ears and my burgeoning benevolence withered away, replaced instead by doubts and suspicions, and just as before, I was left with a conflict of opinions regarding Rosamund Blackmere.

In time the crowd dispersed and as the sun slid lower on the horizon, I returned to The Chequers bathed in the purpling shades of dusk and, on entering the hostelry, I passed a storyteller and a troubadour with his guitar, and then I strode on beyond the men playing a game of tip-cat, eventually making my way to the far corner of the tavern. There, on the same bench as the previous night, sat William and Goody Tanner, Matilda and Adela, and set back in the shadows with darkness thrown across her features, was Rosamund.

'Well, do not stand there like a sack of chaff, lad,' Goody cried as soon as she saw me, her eyes glinting with kindness, her voice jolly as ever. 'Sit you down here, Alwin, next to Matilda.'

I bowed my head to all the company and took my seat. Matilda glanced at me, quick and shy and touched her fingers to her rams-horn plaits, then she sat quietly watching me, her burgeoning maturity stopped in its progress every now and then by her childish giggle or the youthfulness in her eyes. Then, of a sudden, she jumped to her feet and declared, 'I shall fetch us all some wine!'

'Let the innkeeper attend to us, child,' Goody said, good-heartedly.

But Matilda would not be gainsaid and she scurried away, to return moments later with a ewer filled with wine, together with six drinking vessels, which she proceeded to place before all the company. She poured us each a portion, taking care not to spill a drop, and at last she took her seat and smiled a broad smile.

'Of course,' Goody began at length, 'this is not my first journey as a pilgrim. I will have you know, I have touched a fragment of the True Cross, and when I was a girl, I went to see the fingerbone of Doubting Thomas.'

She spoke the words with solemnity and when she had finished, a sort of reverent silence ensued. Then, with a glow of mischief about her eyes, she said, 'But I found out afterwards it was only pigs' bones!'

She fell into mirth at the recollection and provoked laughter from us all, then with her cheeks flushed up, she turned to me and said, 'Before you arrived, Alwin, we were holding conference about marriage, were we not, girls?' She paused, grinned and glanced at Matilda and Adela, then went on, 'My advice to them was that a woman should be led by a man and a man should be led by his fancy, then all is right with the world.'

Adela shuffled in her seat beside Matilda and a giggle escaped from her lips, before she said, 'The only man I shall fancy,' her voice suddenly bright and piping and a twinkle in her eye, 'is Mr Do-As-You-Please.'

At that, Goody shrieked and erupted in another fit of mirth. Matilda and Adela threw their arms about one another in unbridled hilarity and laughed until tears stood in their eyes. Old William could only reach for the jubbe of wine, fill his horn cup and take a long draught, his face brittle and glazed. I dared not observe Rosamund and so, like William, I supped a deep pull of my own wine until the merriment subsided.

'Whatever would make you say such a thing, Adela?' Goody eventually asked, injecting contrived decorum into her tones.

'Well, men can be so ... difficult sometimes, with their profanities and vices and ... what with the terrors at the priory.'

'It is true that non-conforming habits are sometimes visited on our menfolk,' Goody acceded, slanting her eye at William as she spoke, then resuming with, 'But is it not part of their nature? Should we be obliged to unsex our lords and husbands and have us all be women? How then should we be wedded and protected if we cannot place our temperance alongside their fallibility. Just as my mother said before me; as long as men sin and women forgive, then our species will continue to thrive.'

'But does it not adulterate man's own character to subjugate women in such a way?' The voice was Rosamund's and she cast it low from her lips as she spoke through the dimness, the gravity of the thinker manifest in the thoughts that were spoken. 'Should a man choose a blind horse to ride it at a gallop, that it may be obedient and seek no other pleasure than to obey its rider's command? Surely it is better that both horse and rider see clearly and complement each other's assets. Can a better man not reflect on his own shortcomings in life and find a woman with whom he can unite and, by use of her virtues, strengthen his own being?'

The question seemed to hang in the air as though supported by its own truth and, succinct and powerful, it lingered long after it had been asked, and in time became its own silent answer. Rosamund did not wait for a response from any of us, she simply rose and left, the candlelight dipping and flaring by turn in her wake, and I could only admire her ease of deportment and independence of mind.

'There's such unfamiliar lore on the tip of that girl's tongue,' Goody said, eyeing us all one at a time. 'What a mort of opinions she has! And do you not think her cleverness suspicious?' she asked. 'I do not know what meat she is made of, but it is not roasted to my taste, however much she spices her words. Spun from the same twine as the Devil, that one,' she concluded. 'Common report supposes—'

But I never heard what common report supposed, because outside through the town, there came a tumult and din. The beating of hooves tabored hard on the ground outside and voices rose loud on the air. A sudden hush fell over the tavern, as thoughts of renegade soldiers widened all eyes and slackened all jaws. Some men armed themselves with jugs and stools, others backed slowly away from the inn's entrance, until at last, dear Father Oswald passed through the doorway alone and entered the hostelry, thus bringing relief and quenching the alarm. He must have ridden hard to reach the town before nightfall and his face was ruddy and drawn, his cassock and satchel of papers both flecked with mud-spatters. He was followed in by six other men; the tithing men and constable, and each man at once set to talking.

From the drifts of conversation that blew in my direction, I learned the old prioress was in a state of delirium still and had offered up very little information. The carnage was as grim as the first messenger had described and the manner in which the nuns had been defiled and murdered was beyond their understanding. You would suppose the tales they brought would have been delivered in the same manner as the night before; morbid fascination with the details; growing exaggeration to hold their audience's wonder. But, of course, last night's messenger was re-telling what he had been told. Those men standing in the tavern that night, had, like me, seen matters with their own eyes and awoken sorrows in their hearts that would never go, learned distress that dehumanised part of their souls and carried sadness in their eyes that only Heaven could heal. At last, one of the tithing men broke down in a fit of sobs, took himself away and no one upbraided him for his weakness.

The customers at the tavern parted company early that evening, the hollowness of humstrums and merrymaking too vulgar to lay alongside tales of the Winfeld Priory. As drinking cups were laid down and benches vacated, it was a weary and haggard Father Oswald who threaded his way towards me.

'Alwin,' he said, his eyes downcast and dull, 'before we retire to the sleeping shelter, I must talk with you. Will you walk with me?'

'Of course,' I said. My words did not waver, but my belly turned in on itself and my heartbeat raised its voice in my ears.

We left the tavern and walked on in silence through air that was still, beneath gables that were fading from sight. As evening deepened its shades, we walked to the corner of an alley where the lights from an un-shuttered window cast an amber beam onto the street. Father Oswald turned to me, his eyes searching mine in the dimness.

'The prioress was afflicted with great pain, Alwin,' he said. 'Her thoughts were muddled and she laboured to speak them with any clarity.'

I sighed inwardly, relieved my duplicity might at last be cast to oblivion, but the priest was not done.

'Horror past compare she witnessed that night,' he went on. 'She had not the words on her tongue. It was so unlike anything she had ever seen before and was beyond her reckoning. But she had possession of the note, Alwin; the letter of ingress I wrote for you.'

'They ... they must have stolen it,' I said. 'The soldiers must have found it in my saddlebag and ...'

'The prioress remembers that a young man presented the letter to her; a lad who was lean and tall, no whiskers yet grown on his lip or chin. She suspected he was not a soldier; she worried he was being put under duress—'

My heart was beating wildly by then and beads of sweat damped my face. I found it hard to swallow and the spit all but dried on my tongue. If I admitted I was there, then I could not defend myself against allegations of ravishment and massacre – certainly not without surrendering the truth about my deformity. But if I could never tell a soul about the pity I had witnessed, then my sanity would surely be lost. It was a fathomless abyss where demons dwelled and how they grew in number about me!

'How fortunate I was to have been despoiled of horse and harness,' I eventually said glibly, slyly. 'How propitious were the winds that did blow me from that place.'

Father Oswald held his eye on me for many a while, whether in condemnation or in Christian understanding, I could not tell.

'Then I say it again, Alwin,' he said in earnest. 'Although you were never there; if you had been, I know you could never have acted in concert with those tyrants. I would swear it to all the lords and gentles of England.'

The cleric left me then. He pressed me to walk with him to the shelter, but I declined; said I wished to breathe the night air until the curfew bell rang. The darkness was quiet and the quietness was dark about me, and my errant mind began to sift through sundry images; a review of times gone by, both melancholy and halcyon in their textures. Then I thought of William Tanner and his talk of dog-heads, I recalled my fears of the world beyond the Whittaker woods and I wished with all my heart I could return to Crown Croft. But of course, the Crown Croft I loved so well, with Mother brisk about the homestead, was gone. The fearful and brutal world beyond the Whittaker woods had become my new habitation and to survive, I knew I had to walk on through that new wilderness and try to forget past events.

There were answers I had to seek out to make sense of myself, and dogged by sorrows and guilt from the past was not the way to put my best foot forward. I decided I would not speak of the priory again, to Father Oswald or any other; I would apply the balm of effacement to the matter and respectfully lay it to rest.

I turned about with a sense of hopefulness, a feeling of new beginnings. But in the gloom to my left, something moved, as though a breath of moonlight had coloured the air; but the moon was obscured by clouds and gave out no light. The air moved again, tinged with lilac, and Rosamund walked out of the twilight. How long she had been there and what secrets she thought she might have heard, I could not know. Her look was oblique and she examined me with a penetrating eye. Before, I had begun to intrigue her but now she despised me, I was certain.

'I wish for there to be no further impact between us,' I said stiffly, bowing my head.

She raised her eyes, scrutinised me for a moment, then said, 'I cannot turn my thoughts from the nuns at the Winfeld Priory, Master Whittaker. I cannot deliver my mind from the evils that I imagine took place there, and the deaths the holy sisters suffered before their final breath. How cruel those soldiers were; how cruel all men can be.'

'You ought not to be so rash in your imputations,' I said, defensive. 'All men are not the same. I could not influence the soldiers who attacked me. And for the failings of one detachment of militia men, you despise all men that follow?'

Her eyes searched from side to side, before she regained her footing and, steadying her gaze on me, she said, 'All I do know, is that any man who was there that night; let him be damned!'

'But what if such a man were there that did not comply, that tried with all his endeavours to bring an end to the atrocity?' There was desperation in my voice, I could not disguise it, and I knew I was betraying myself to utter such words, but I needed some sort of forgiveness.

Rosamund turned away, then said coldly, 'Indifference to others' suffering is the greatest sin and to allow the preventable is the same as to consent.'

I could not say why she held such dominion over me; for I did not know. But I knew at that moment I was truly damned and it would take a miracle from the hand of God to change Rosamund's opinion of me and to save me from Hell and the Devil's whip.

CHAPTER FIVE

For fear of sleep and the dreams it might have brought, I stole a good few hours from the night and remained awake in the shelter while all around me lay in slumber. Before we bedded down, I ate a supper of bread and cheese. But afterwards, I felt griping pains and the food lay heavy on my belly; perhaps I ate too hastily, or perhaps all my worry and anxiety stopped the flow of viands through my body. Whatever the reason, the cheese disrupted my sleep and fed my mind with ill thoughts. Cheese digests everything but itself, Mother used to say. How I wished it might devour all the world's suffering and evil!

I arose while it was still black outside and I dressed in my new apparel; in the dark, just as Mother had taught me. At sunrise, I washed my hands and face and went about the town. It was much quieter than before. It was not market day, and the nature of the district was different; vendors whom yesterday shouted with hard voices, drove barter and trade, had lost their passions and avarice and now wandered with a look of serenity about them. I gave good morning to everyone I passed and made my way to the hackney-man's paddock.

My horse was soon saddled and tacked and I trotted him off to gain a sense of the softness in his mouth and the rhythm of his gait. I took the sumpter horse, too, and headed back towards the tavern.

As I rode along the master-street, my eyes were drawn to a woman buying a loaf of bread at a baxter's stall. She paid the reckoning, tucked the loaf in her bag, then turned and strolled through the shadows in a contrariwise direction to my own. She walked softly, with a little give to the knees, making her step quiet and graceful. Then the clouds rearranged themselves, the sun sent out a bright, downward ray upon her, and I realised the woman was Rosamund. I looked briefly at her face and wished the awkwardness between us could be gone and wondered how I might speed it. As though she sensed my presence, she flashed her eyes towards me, then she paused fleetingly and bent her steps in my direction.

At once I compressed my lips and prepared myself for conflict, the tension already tasting sour in my throat. My pony seemed to sympathise with my anxiety and began to prance and caper. I cast another casual eye at Rosamund as I slackened and tightened the reins, and supposed she might look at me in the same, accusatory manner as before, but she approached me with urgency and a look of would-be accord in her eyes.

She laid her bag on the ground, then reached up and took hold of my pony's bridle straps and I believed she was about to say something important to me, but before she could speak, Matilda and Adela came running towards us.

'Master Whittaker,' Adela cried. 'Master Whittaker!' she repeated, arriving breathless with Matilda following on her heels.

'What is the matter?' I said, to either and both of the maids.

'It is Dame Goody,' they said in unison.

'Goody cannot mount her horse,' Adela went on, regaining a measure of decorum. 'And Master Tanner does chide her for her gluttony.' She paused and a giggle escaped her lips, before she added, 'He told her that although she is the laziest woman he has ever known, her stomach never seems to get tired!'

At that, Matilda and Adela both fell into a bout of sniggering, before Matilda added, 'And Goody told William that his flatulence could turn the sails on a post-mill.'

It was several moments before the two maids could control their hilarity at recalling Goody's insult and by the time peace returned to our little district of the town, Rosamund had silently left us and was making her way to the palfrey-man's paddock. I watched her for some moments, but time and distance showed partiality to her and not me, and soon her image turned the bend in the street and was lost to my sight, and I could not help but sense that I had been deprived of an opportunity.

I slid down from my saddle and walked back to the tavern with the two maids; and in time, with the help of four pairs of arms and a very patient pony, Goody was eventually seated in the saddle, her short legs swinging free of the stirrups, the reins loose in her hands and her voice telling the pony how well behaved it was going to be.

Rosamund arrived next, then William mounted his pony and began curbing the animal with great cruelty, and Matilda threaded her horse's reins through the hitching ring and began gathering stems of late-flowering yarrow from down by the stream. She delivered one white bloom to Goody, one to Adela and one to Rosamund, before saying discreetly to her last recipient, 'I am compelled to admire your hair, Damosel Blackmere, for it shines with such brilliancy, the like of which I have not seen before.'

Rosamund bowed her head with good grace and smiled, then Matilda moved on, untwisting one of Goody's stirrups as she passed and brushing away a stray tendril of bramble that had caught on the tail of William's horse. Neither Goody nor William appeared to notice those little anonymous acts of kindness, but Matilda was unconcerned with their indifference, and seemed simply pleased with the pleasantness of pleasing.

Finally, two hours after prime, we were all in our saddles and Father Oswald arrived. His unremitting labours of the previous day had left the man exhausted and his over-sleeping had resulted in a tardy haggle with the hackney-man. The poor cleric's choice of animal was so narrow, he arrived along the master-street riding an infirm-looking mule, which provoked a roar of laughter from all those around. When the hoots and the heaving of sides had diminished, we were ready to set off, and I was relieved to be riding away and leaving past events behind me.

But we had not travelled long – still approaching the east gate – when Father Oswald pulled rein.

'Damosel Matilda!' he called. 'Dear maid, your horse is lame.'

The whole company halted and looked at the maid's pony. Matilda clucked at the horse and had it move forward, but I could not see a deficiency in its stride, however hard I looked. Apart from the grass stains that coloured its hind fetlocks, I could see no issue with the animal. Father Oswald, still uncertain, dismounted his mule and walked closer, his stoop more exaggerated as he bent low to inspect the beast.

'I am not sure this animal is fit for the journey, Matilda,' he said.

There was a general sigh and groan from us all, and Goody threw a sideways glance towards Rosamund, in which I read both suspicion and scorn.

'Are you certain, Father Oswald?' William asked.

By then, the priest had opened the pony's mouth and was examining its nippers and grinders. In my mind, I had no doubts he was right; he had always shown discernment in horse-flesh, rode as though he were born a nobleman. Many a time I had viewed his knowledge with a jealous eye and, although frustrated at our delay, I knew his judgement would be right.

'I will walk the horse back, Father, and exchange it,' I said.

Father Oswald, who remained silent, deep in thought, ignoring both William and me, finally took up the horse's hind left foot and said, 'Ah!'

Still holding the pony's leg, the cleric took a knife from his belt and carefully picked around the frog of the hoof, eventually winkling out what looked like a walnut. Father Oswald scrutinised the object, pressed it gently between his finger and thumb and then passed it to me. The article was heavy, dense; made of metal. Its edges were notched and sharp and it was akin to no other artefact I had ever seen. If God could have created an instrument with which to cause certain lameness in a horse, then that was surely it. I handed it to William and then it was circulated among the group, with the exception of Rosamund; she had ridden a little way off and was staring at the lie of the land. No one voiced their opinion of the strange device; no comment was raised whether oblique or direct. But I believe all of us were thinking of one and the same thing; infidels, witchcraft and Rosamund Blackmere.

'Alwin,' Father Oswald eventually said. 'The pony's foot will be sore, but if you lead him on a loose rein, walk instead of ride for a while, then he will soon recover well enough for the journey. Perhaps you might take him through a puddle or a brook; cool his hoof. Matilda can ride your horse in the meantime, Alwin, if you have no objection.'

I agreed, bowed my head to Matilda and the exchange was completed. Father Oswald, seeing how Matilda was shaken by the matter, ran his hands over her new pony and declared the beast fit and strong. Not to be outdone, William dismounted and followed the priest's actions, ran his own gnarled hands from feather to fetlock, from pastern to poll and, independent of Father Oswald's conclusion, he too declared the horse to be in good plight.

At last we set off, with William at the front and Goody leading the sumpter horse, the two young maids behind them, Father

Oswald alongside me, and Rosamund at the rear. We followed the lych-ways and woodland paths of antique times through hushed lands whose curve and swell had been worn flat by age and the elements, and I mourned the loss of my native uplands and peaks. How low the land. How wide the sky; vast with its mares' tails and hens'-claws.

After three miles of travelling, we left the pastureland behind us and traversed a tract of moorland. The ground became spongy and soft where last year's heather and ferns had died off, so I took to saddle and stirrup and we all moved on at a faster pace. The pony was steady, but I fell to the back of the group, just in case he became fresh, and in time I was trailing several yards behind the others.

In truth, I was the architect of my own design; I deliberately placed myself in a situation where my chances of talking to Rosamund were increased. If Father Oswald had questioned me on that point, I would surely have denied it; but now I declare it to be the truth. So, I rode on in silence, listening for Rosamund behind me, a flutter present in my inmost heart, which I could not wholly account for.

At midday she came to me. I heard faint sounds travelling on the surface of the air behind me; the gentle tread of her pony and soft breaths emitted from the horse's nose. Reason had me sit tall in my saddle and set my features with a look of resilience; Folly had my cheeks glow and my palms become damp.

'Alwin,' she said, her lips exhaling softness in her tone. 'I do not wish to war with you.'

Still smarting from her unfavourable verdict the night before, and disappointed by our confusing meeting in the morning, I turned to her but said nothing and, for the first time, her eyes sought me out and dwelt on me. She was more docile and submissive than I had yet seen her, and the transformation unnerved me.

'I have come on pilgrimage under false pretences,' she went on. 'You must surely have guessed that by now, what with the loud complainers in our group and the aspersions they peddle like stock-fish and turnips?'

I continued on in my sulky muteness and turned my head away from her, pretended I was indifferent.

'There is a man, Alwin,' she continued. 'He did a very great wrong to my family name and I ... I will find him and take him to task. He will pay for his actions.'

So, that was her ruse. She had bewitched some poor soul, given herself to him and he had fled when he knew the sarcasm and condemnation of her tongue; and who could blame him?

'How could I possibly help you?' I said, my tone weary. For a moment, I continued to demonstrate my apathy, but in the end, my heart's bias demanded otherwise and I looked her in the eye.

'Because the man I seek is a soldier,' she said. 'You were set upon by—'

'Weapons were brandished!' I snapped. 'Punches were thrown in a rain of blows! I might have been killed. I do not wish to discuss it further.'

'I am trying to offer you some sort of salvation, Alwin. The truth will out and the world will discover exactly who was there that night. Tell me who they were. Tell me their names, and the Devil may one day spare that part of your heart that disburdens the truth to me.' She aimed her dart of supremacy at me, but she was wide of her mark.

'I did nothing,' I said. 'I am innocent. And one day I will prove it to you. Not all men are tricksters, Rosamund.'

'And not all women are content to be servants of men. Forced submission only breeds contempt, Alwin.'

At that moment, sense and reason told me that in Rosamund Blackmere there was little to venerate and much to scorn, but whatever I thought about her, I could not deny she owned a well-stored mind and was as wise as Pallas; what a compound of complexities she was. But despite all she said, and how sagely she said it, I still had inclination to demonstrate my loftiness, remove all possibility she might ever be able to denounce me.

'Pray tell me, Damosel Blackmere,' I said, haughty and cold, 'can you sketch with words the man whom you seek, that I may know him if his path should cross with my own?'

By then, she had moved ahead of me and so cast the reply over her shoulder.

'He is tall, strong; the commander of his troop. He is a nobleman who does not always like to give his name. And he rides a black stallion with a scarlet belly band.'

The revelation drove air from my chest and forced heat to my face, her words menacing my mind, reproving my conscience. If only matters were different, I could have told her all I knew; the soldiers' names I had learned, their descriptions, the nobleman's home near Walsingham. We could have shared our knowledge and gone on together. If only I had not lied about my presence at the priory; if only I had treated Rosamund with more respect and gained her trust.

Father Oswald, whether through chance or Divine Providence, happened to look back at the exact moment Rosamund rode away from me, just as my face was contorting with the perplexities she had provoked. He turned his mule about, the animal fighting for its head.

'Alwin?' he hailed. 'Is all well?'

I kicked my horse on into a hand-gallop, steered alongside the cleric and we rode on together.

'Aye, Father. All is well,' I said wearily.

'Most women have guiles, Alwin,' he observed, 'so, have a care when you talk with Rosamund Bla—'

'Do most women really have guiles, Father?' I asked, heedless of interrupting him, so burning were the questions on my tongue, so lost in my beliefs. 'Are they all wicked, as Solomon said? Even Mother? Even the mother of Jesu? The Lady Mary? Was she wicked at heart, Father?'

My words put him in pause, and I never heard his reply, as a sudden hurly broke out ahead of us. Just as Rosamund was passing the two young maids, Matilda's horse kicked its heels in the air. As though a demon had suddenly leapt on the animal's croup, the horse bolted forwards, throwing its head skyward and gnashing at its bit. Matilda sat firm in her seat to begin with, but soon she lost the rhythm and began to bump along, her feet slipping out of the stirrups. She shrieked and the horse galloped faster. In an instant, both Father Oswald and I urged our steeds onwards, but the priest's old mule was not for running. With Rosamund, Adela, William and Goody only able to stare wide-eyed and try to take mastery of their own mounts, I alone sped forward in pursuit.

Within moments, I began to catch up with Matilda. Her arms flailed wildly and she lost all governance of her steed. As I drew alongside, she slipped forward over the animal's left shoulder, her right hand grasping a tuft of hair from the horse's mane, her left arm entangled with the reins. Once adjacent, I leaned to my right and grappled with the bridle, seized it firmly and pulled the pony's head down towards its counter and barrel. With the weight of Matilda's enfeebled body also lurching towards the ground, our combined heaviness was too much for the pony to withstand. Within twelve strides we were slowing; twelve more and we stopped. I dismounted and tied my horse to a tree branch.

Matilda was unresponsive at first and then, as she raised her head from the horse's neck and untangled her fingers from its mane, she became agitated. At once troubled and restless, she set a cry with loud voice, and tears flowed full and fast from her eyes. I unbound the leather rein from her arm; the strap had torn through her outer-sleeve, ripped through the arm of her linen shift and left a bright red weal on her skin. She slipped down from the saddle into my arms and I set her on the ground, then fastened her horse to the tree.

Through soft sobs Matilda used her newly freed hand to touch it to her pony's neck.

'There, there,' she wept to the animal. 'No cause for fright, my lamb.'

Her lament began to diminish, until she saw blood on the horse's left flank, where during the violent dash the stirrup had chafed the animal's skin. That sight brought a fresh deluge of tears.

'Oh, look what I have done!' she sobbed. 'The poor creature! And what of our companions, Master Whittaker? Are they all well?'

She lowered her head and sat down on a nearby clump of tussock-grass.

'None of this is your fault,' I said, gentle and kind. 'Your horse simply shied. Perhaps a bee bit him or the sight of a hawk caught his eye or—'

All the while I had been aiding Matilda to dismount and recover from the incident, her pony had still been fidgeting its hind legs, continually lifting its gaskins and hocks as though it stood on hot ashes. I stroked its nearside flank, spoke gentle words and leaned askew to survey its hindmost quarters. There, just above the hoof, was a pea-green stain akin to the grassy pigment I had observed earlier on the other animal. I looked across at the other horse, but the stain had been washed away when I rode through the stream to cool its hoof. Just as I was cogitating on those matters, a rider approached along the track; Rosamund.

She drew rein, climbed down from the saddle, ignored me, and went on to talk to Matilda, briefly stopping on her way to glance at Matilda's pony as it stood restless and stamping. The two women spoke in low tones, outside the compass of my ears, and Rosamund placed her arm about the maiden in an act of comfort.

At length, as the remainder of our group came trotting over the brow of a small hill towards us, Rosamund walked over to me and whispered in my ear.

'Do you see the green tint?' she asked.

'Yes,' I breathed.

'It is a compound of herbs. Once applied, it seeps slowly into the skin of the horse and burns like fire. The animal believes that flames are chasing it from behind and instinct dictates that it bolts. A practised hand can measure the quantity of the elixir so exactly the animal will flit at a time of the herbalist's own choosing.'

'You are saying this was deliberate?'

'I am.'

'But who would want to do such a thing?'

'Well, only two men touched the horse's flesh before we set off; and only one man suggested Matilda ride that particular pony.'

'Father Oswald?' I said, incredulous. 'How could such an idea take lodging in your head? And how can I even know you speak the truth about the herbal elixir?'

'You see how the horse still twitches and jerks? Untether him, Alwin, and walk him down there, where the bog-myrtle grows; have his feet be washed and cooled in the marsh. Then see how quickly he recovers.'

Mother used to say truth can only be seen by those who believe in it. I knew for certain Father Oswald could not have brought about such a matter, in spite of his way with horses. But still, the green pigment and the manner in which the pony suddenly took flight without reason; they were both undeniable facts. Logic dictated to me that the suspicions Rosamund harboured would only be supported if, as she said, the horse's excitation would end when the herbs were cleansed from its legs.

So, before the others could reach us, I untied the pony and led it through the mud and morass. By the time William and Goody arrived, the horse was calmly cropping the grass, its hind legs steady and still. I could tell Rosamund was eyeing me, whether with triumph or further scrutiny, I knew not, but I did not return her gaze. Inside, turmoil and anxiety held me fast, spun silk-like about my mind and glued my thoughts to suspicion, Father Oswald and to Rosamund. I knew I was the master of her, because it was my birthright as a man, but at that moment as to which of us was the spider and which was the web; I do not believe I could fully discern.

When Goody finally, in a matronly and ungainly fashion, dismounted from her horse, she went to Matilda, threw her arms about the girl and spoke kind words of great pleasance. The gentle dame then turned her attentions on me, took my hands in hers and bent as low as her frame would allow in a curtsey.

'You will become famous in our age, Alwin! What a story to tell when I return to my village. How heroic—'

'Dame Tanner,' I interrupted. 'It was all over in a moment; no bravery at all on my part. And I am certain one obliging deed should not lead to talk of heroes.'

'Brave and modest,' she giggled, casting her eyes towards Matilda, who in turn looked shyly at me. The maiden's eyes were pretty, I could not deny. But they lacked depth of expression; compliant and simple they were, like a calf's or a fawn's. They were not like Rosamund's at all; a place where a heart could become lost in the expanse of possibility they promised.

Finally, Father Oswald and Adela descended from their saddles, and our little company was again reunited. Talk erupted in profusion, with discussions and descriptions readily volunteered from one and all. But as the outcome was merely a torn sleeve, a bruised arm and a delay in our trek, the mood was tinged more with blitheness and relief, rather than dejection. Matilda, in spite of her trauma, fussed over Goody with gentle words and a soft heart, fearing the dame's constitution might have been compromised by the fright of it all. And Adela, whimsical and brazen, suggested that if it had been up to Father Oswald and his antiquated mule to chase down Matilda and her shying pony, then the pursuit would still be afoot.

The spot where we stopped was just beyond a clearing where deer had stepped outside the woods in the gloaming and grazed the shrubs to the ground. Matilda insisted on carefully unpacking our supplies from the sumpter horse, offering the choicest of provisions to Dame Goody, and we ate our midday meal sitting on the flat turf, as though the bolting animal were a minor inconvenience and we had always planned to take our refreshments at that particular glade.

Goody talked most of the talk and ate most of the meat, and Matilda, sympathising with all given views as she went, packed away our leftovers and shook crumbs from the empty clouts. Although Goody dominated the conversation and Matilda, in comparison, was but a timid maiden, I felt certain the girl had unriddled a basic truth; if we wish to be liked, then we must make ourselves likeable. I watched our happy-tempered group and I picked over my pie and pears, but in the end put them by, for the day's vexations had quite stolen my appetite.

We resumed the journey in good time and at first the company's disposition was in unity; a universal gratitude that Matilda was none the worse for wear; an acceptance that an accident had happened of its own volition, but all was well in the end. The sky was clouded as we headed east, but the clouds were white and, far and away on the horizon, a little patch of blue had broken through.

I supposed at first I was the only one tangled in a web of distrust and anxiety, but as we rode forth, we all stayed closer together than before and no one spoke, everyone lost in their own conjectures. Then, like when a brown trout flicks its fin and stirs mud from the riverbed, sending a shaft of brown water far downstream; so, William Tanner broached his thoughts about Rosamund and cast his muddy opinions on the wind.

'Why, it is all witchcraft if you ask me,' he began. 'The maid Matilda's horse was placid enough until the damosel Blackmere brushed past it. Of that, no one can deny!'

'Rightly said, husband,' his wife replied, all merriment gone from her voice.

'And despite that orb of intellect she carries on her shoulders,' William went on, 'she seems decidedly slack at scripture. Well, the bible has a name for her; a witch that peeps and mutters; so says Isaiah. I say we should cast her out, continue without her.'

'We cannot do that, William,' Father Oswald said, judicious in his tone. 'It is not Christian even to speak of such a plan.'

'Then,' William answered, 'instead of allowing her to follow behind us brewing potions and casting spells, we should have her ride out in front, that we may keep ear and eye upon her.'

There was a mumble of discussion that echoed through the group, and with no one speaking out to countermand the suggestion, the motion was deemed to be carried. With our band of pilgrims riding at close quarters, Rosamund heard the proposal, comprehended the assent, and urged her horse forward past all the company, each one eyeing her as she rode by, and on she went to the front without looking back.

With the order of our line changed, it was me who brought up the rear, took Rosamund's place, perhaps in more ways than one. At that moment I no longer felt an affinity with William, Goody, the two maidens or even Father Oswald. There was a larger number of people about me than ever before in my life, but I felt so alone. The summer had started so well; Mother had not yet lost all her health and our bees had gathered in huge numbers: swarm of bees in June, worth a silver spoon. Then, of a sudden, troubles had thronged about me in their multitude and, in my confusion, I could not discern whom to trust or how I might resolve the relentless riddle that now usurped all other questions in my head: Why had I become so uncomfortable in my own skin?

I sought out conversation with no one as we journeyed on and spoke not a word until Father Oswald, now leading the sumpter horse, halted a little further up the line and then guided his mule alongside me.

'Matilda seems to have recovered well, Alwin,' he said.

I nodded but said nothing.

'She seems a fair maiden to me,' he went on. 'No doubt she will find a rustic or a churl and live in wedded bliss with a clutch of happy progeny about her. Her language is too plain for you, though, Alwin. I do not blame her; most women are not educated, after all, and a vast number of them suffer from ignorance of the mind.'

Thinking of Rosamund, not Matilda, I replied: 'Perhaps it is not ignorance of the mind that afflicts most women, Father, in some it is surely elegance of the soul.'

The cleric jerked his head about and looked at me, his brows arched with incredulity. But I had done with both talk and explanations for that day, so I kicked my horse on and rode some paces to the left of the others, took to the higher ground and found some space in which to think. That is the formation in which we continued until, as the sky quietened its glare and the daylight slipped lower on the horizon, we came to the out parts of a village.

A narrow lane ribboned its way between two hedges of wych-elm and rose-brier, the track broken up here and there with buildings; a low church with a small bellcote; an inn, and an assortment of cottages and houses, all timber-framed and willow-thatched.

It reminded me of Giolgrave and a pang of sadness tightened my throat.

In bygone times, I would have admired the dell in which the village dwelt and smiled blithely at the skies that arched above it. The sun was just retiring and the few wisps of cloud that remained were no more than streaks of vapour that curled their smoky path upwards, absorbing pinks and ambers as they went. But on that day, my eyes would not hold communion with my heart and I felt nothing but qualms and confusion as we entered the courtyard of the inn.

Weary and dull I was as we watered and fed forage to the horses, and I was relieved to pay my penny to the innkeeper and take myself to my room. But no sooner had I sat down on the bed, when there was a gentle knock on the door, and Matilda, her face bright and merry with the freshness of youth, presented herself to me. With her customary childish aspect, she stood for a moment shifting her weight from one foot to the other then, shaking off her ephemeral shyness, she said, 'I have brought you a cup of ale, Master Whittaker. And I did wish to say my gratitude for ... for saving me today.'

I contemplated her with fondness and smiled at her. She handed me the mazer, blushed deeply, then turned and left, and the gesture touched me with its kindness.

That night, because the inn was small, only the men would take lodging there. The women all sought harbourage at a private dwelling house at the far edge of the village by the river, and had been granted accommodation by the proprietor, as all good Christian gentlefolk were obliged to do. We all walked with the women to inspect their lodgings, Matilda and Adela running on ahead in excitement, then the company arranged to meet for supper at the inn. But I did not feel in a condition to join them at feasting, so I took to my room and retired to bed early. Father

Oswald followed me up the stair and entered the room next to mine and, in spite of my shortness with him before, it gave me comfort to know he was there.

I hung my outerwear on the wall-hanger and lay down on the bed in my shirt and braies. Thoughts jostled inside my head, gathering one upon another; some offered comfort and others brought pain. My journey had begun with such a number of difficulties and there were so many miles yet to travel, but travel them I must, because I knew a thing once learned could never be forgotten, and that my heart would not find peace until it found the answers it craved. So, with heavy eyes and a freighted mind, I fell into slumber feeling tired and winter-gloomy.

It was the air that roused me first. It changed its taste and temperature, all in a moment. From cool, dew-laden emptiness, it filled its space with an acrid flavour, bitter and warm at the same time. Then outside, the noises of the night changed, and sent a gentle shock upon the air towards my ears; the sudden rushing of wind through the trees, sounding like the roar of a river. I awoke with a start, all dream-shapes dislodged from my mind, and I slid open the window-shutter.

I rubbed the sleep from my eyes and stared out along the village lane. The sun had risen early and the far horizon was shot with crimson rays. But something was wrong; apart from the burgeoning sunrise, everywhere else was still swathed in the blackness of night. No cocks crowed and no other birds welcomed the morn. The day was as flat and dark as midnight. I stood and pondered for a moment with a sense of ill-ease, then a terrible discovery took shape in my mind; we arrived in the village on the west road and the sun should rise in the east, so why on that day was the sun coming up in the north?

Just then, a dog set to barking and the church bell rang out a peal of chimes. I wondered if Hell had started to ascend or if dog-heads were waging an attack. I felt my way through the gloom and banged on Father Oswald's door, then William's, but there was no answer. Running as I pulled on my leather boots, and still in my shirt and braies, I called out to the innkeeper and his wife, but was met with a curtain of silence.

Both drawn and repelled by the haunting light and choking air, I ran down the lane through swirls of mist that eddied around me, my arms held out before me, my eyes squinting. The trees and buildings all around, which should have been invisible in the night, were engraved on the horizon, like strokes of charcoal on the face of the sun. Twice I tripped, once I fell to the ground, but on I ran, arriving breathless at the house at the end of the track.

In those last few yards, a terrible golden light flapped about me, expanded and flowered out into the night sky, the bitter air became concentrated, and heat tingled against my skin. Turning that final corner, and standing alongside a group of others, some wailing, some weeping, the rest standing stiff, I looked at a ghastly scene, a dreadful sight; a vision that spoke in deafening tones, so loud were its colours.

When I had last descried that building, it was a handsome dwelling house with ivied walls, a welcoming abode for Dame Goody and the three maidens. Now it was a wall of fire. Within a heartbeat, I heard Father Oswald's voice from behind me. He called for water-pails and for more hands to help carry them. I blinked my eyes, hot and dry, and searched the faces about me: Father Oswald, Goody, Adela, the master and dame of the dwelling house, the innkeeper and his wife and sundry villagers. But there were no more.

'Where are Matilda and Rosamund?' I shouted. 'Where are they?'

'I would wager the damosel Blackmere is long gone by now,' chimed William's voice from behind me, the man seeming to appear from nowhere. 'She's cast her magic spell, conjured an inferno from the underworld and fled into the night. Let any man gainsay me if they dare.'

'What are you talking about?' I quizzed, but William stepped back into the misted air and was lost to my sight. 'Goody?' I said, turning about and fronting the dame. 'If Rosamund is gone, then where is Matilda?'

At that, the smoke stole my breath and I started to choke. Goody, her cloak drawn over her mouth, gestured with her arm towards the house. Through the Hellish peal of snapping and cracking, a splitting sound rent the air. Flames played around the upper windows for a moment or two, then burst up through the top of the house. A ripple ran through the thatch, then how the rafters trembled. There were flashes of red and yellow and then, with a roar, fire poured out, devouring the building from the top down, flames now torching high in the sky and smoke fuming upwards.

In the few moments that had passed since my arrival, more villagers had burst forth from their cottages with pails and shovels. I joined them and, forming a line from the river, we passed water-filled buckets from hand to hand and threw the contents onto the edifice. But the fire had taken hold and the water just hissed, impotent, and rose as steam. Huge tongues of flame licked from floor to rafter and gave off a deep swell of sound as they grew in power. In such anger it raged; nothing I had seen before could compare; all other concerns became deceptions when measured against the purity of that heat, and the light reflected in every surface it could find; the pond, the river, the water-pails. The river itself was just a scarlet ribbon. The whole earth seemed to be ablaze and we were losing the battle against it. Time bore hard edges in those intervening heartbeats, my heart convulsed with anxiety and I despaired of Matilda's life.

'I must try to find her,' I shouted through the sobs and wails.

As I declared it, I had not the pluck to do it, but time was burning itself away. A murmur of doubt blew hot through the crowd, but I made no scruple it was the right and proper action for a man to take. I lifted the next water-pail and poured its burden over my head, soaked my shoulders, midriff and legs. I walked rigidly towards the doorway, my sight obscured by a curtain of black vapour, my insides burning with fright, and I walked headlong into the smother. At the last moment before I crossed the threshold, Father Oswald called my name and begged me to stop, but some spirit in my feet carried me forward.

The parlour was not yet aflame, the blaze having begun in the upper chambers of the house. Instead it was alive with smoke, which closed around me, dense and abundant. I drew my arm across my mouth to stave off the noxious air and blindly took three steps forward, catching my shin against a hard surface.

With breath enfeebled within my chest, I called out Matilda's name, then spluttered. I heaved and choked, then tried to call again. I inched towards the orange glow and flames fell down from above me. Then something soft touched my arm, a dark wraith appeared before me and I wondered if Death had come to find me out. I raised my hand in an attitude of defence, but instead of it being swallowed by the Reaper, it made contact with a human form. In an instinctive motion, I drew Matilda towards me and placed my arm around her waist, then turning about as the fire crackled and spat above us, I led us out into the night.

We both collapsed to our knees when we had walked clear of the danger and, powdered with smuts and smoke, our own mothers would not have known us. I tried in vain to stand, but the smoke robbed me of all bodily strength. I drew a breath, but all I could do was splutter. All and some gathered about us and Goody was the first to speak.

'Matilda! Matilda!' she cried over and again, circling the figure that knelt at my side, which was still attired in its night-time chemise and cap.

Water was fetched and, still hunched on our knees, we both quenched our scorched throats, rinsed the fume from our heads. In time, the crowd pulled back and a lantern was put before us, its beam first falling on my face, then resting on the shivering shape at my side: Rosamund Blackmere.

In a single heartbeat I suffered vexation and shock; from William's allusion I had, of course, assumed Rosamund was not in the building. But suddenly to see her before me, it laid bare the lowness and audacity of William's lies. And how close Rosamund had come to dying. How relieved I was that a life had not been lost. Then, gradually, clarity intruded the smoke-filled chambers of my mind and I realised that one of our party was still absent: Matilda. Goody must have reached the same realisation. She spun about on her heels, her face orange in the firelight, and she shouted Matilda's name in a haunting, hopeless lamentation.

Still troubled with hot lungs, I scrambled to my feet, spluttering and rasping. But even if I had been able to muster the strength to re-enter the building, the flames would have burned me alive, for their hunger was inappeasable and they devoured every morsel their tongues could reach. Matilda was lost to us and there was nothing that could be done, and the discovery of that knowledge hung about me, dark and acrid, stinging my eyes. Stunned into muteness, everyone remained silent for the longest time until at last the hex was broken.

'She is the sorceress that has brought this about,' William shouted from behind me, jabbing his finger in Rosamund's direction. 'She is the one that has cursed us. Daughter of a witch and an incubus, that one. She rides a she-wolf through the night and sucks the breath from newborn infants. We should send her back inside and damn her to Hell!'

At the close of her husband's speech, Goody dissolved in a fit of weeping, which provoked a likewise reaction from the other women thereabout. The men threw curses and oaths at Rosamund, suggesting in their rage that she had not only murdered Matilda, but also bewitched me; forced me to act in unity with an enchantress. Eventually, one by one, the congregation fell apart and Rosamund and I were left divided from the others to watch the building's final suffering.

A quarter turn to our left and the sun showed its face on the eastern horizon, but its creeping light could barely compare to the inferno I had just witnessed. The fire's rage fell away as quickly as it had risen, leaving charred rafters that stretched and shrank, occasionally falling in on themselves. I stared at the house; where before it had been alive with motion, it now lay still, black and desiccated, the ashes of its former self. The church bell no longer clinked, the villagers were mute and through soundless silence I nursed sad pangs in my heart.

At length, Rosamund tried to speak, but her mouth was still afflicted by the smoke. She swallowed with difficulty and whispered with a rasp in her voice, 'Matilda ... Matilda ...'

'You should not speak her name,' I wheezed. 'The others will think you are casting a spell ...'

'She was already dead, Alwin,' she went on regardless.

'What do you mean? How do you know?'

'They would not share a bedchamber with me.'

'Who?'

'Any of them. Matilda was supposed to share with me, but Goody was so worried about the girl's constitution after the horse bolting, that she put the maiden to bed early, in her own bedchamber. She clucked over those two girls like a mother hen and

I was left alone in my room. Then a caller came, an hour after quarter night.'

'Who?'

'Alwin, I can only tell you what I saw—'

'Who was it?' I asked with impatience.

Rosamund paused, whether to stave off the moment of her revelation or to savour it, I could not guess, then she said, 'It was Father Oswald.'

'Impossible!' I cried.

'He called Goody and Adela down to him, then, leaving them in talk with the proprietor and his wife, he ascended the stairs. I opened my door just enough to observe him entering Matilda's room ...'

'He would never do such a thing!' I protested.

'... then, with no talk between them as far I could hear, he left soon after. I awoke in the night to the snapping of flames and, after my cries of alarm were unanswered, I burst out of my room, calling to the others to get out. The door to the maidens' bedchamber was open. Goody and Adela had already left but Matilda lay asleep on her bed. I rushed in through the smoke and tried to rouse her, but there were marks on her neck and she was not breathing.'

'How could you see?'

'Because the flames were burning the window frame and shutter, and they lit up her face.'

'You think the fire started inside the bedchamber, or just outside it?'

'I am not trying to provide answers, Alwin, I am merely telling you the facts.'

Although the fire had burnt out and the air about us was becoming cooler with the dews of morning, thoughts scorched inside my head at Rosamund's words and lay like a hot iron on my heart. Her previous allusions to Father Oswald still lurked poisonous in my mind and, since the moment she had voiced them, I had tried to dilute them. But why was he not in his room when I banged on the door and called his name? Where exactly was he when the fire began?

The questions caused me such ache and fret and I felt so alone. Mother once said that everything is possible for him that believes and I wondered at that moment, despite what my head was telling me, if I should believe the whispers in my soul that breathed of trust and openness. Perhaps I might have acted on them, let Rosamund know I could never have doubted Father Oswald, told her how it was at the priory and said that we had a common goal over and above the visiting of a shrine; the destination of the nobleman's seat in Walsingham, where answers would be found and peace finally attained for both of us. My mind led me one way then the other, fussy in its temper, doubtful in its cause, then it was sharply pulled up in its tracks.

'Alwin!' came the cry.

It was Father Oswald. Despite myself, I flinched as he spoke my name and looked him hard in the eye, as though I might see into him, through him, at last seek out the truth.

'What a tragedy, Alwin,' he went on. 'In all my days, I have never witnessed such a thing. And for a life to be lost in such a violent manner. But how brave you were, my lad. I trust you have suffered no lasting ills?'

'No, Father.'

'How we will travel on together,' he continued, 'after such a calamity, I know not. William and Goody have become forthright accusers of the damosel Blackmere, rigorous in their censure, and I cannot see how we might attain harmony between them.'

I turned to view Rosamund's reaction, but she had gone. I spun about, searched with my eyes through the morning blur, but she had left as quiet as a ghost and was nowhere to be seen.

CHAPTER SIX

The ruins of the house took on an ever more hideous form as the daylight expanded and cast its grey tint over it. The clouds were tainted with last night's smoke and hung low and heavy above, weeping occasional bouts of rain that fell on the blackened timbers, drawing final gasps of smoke upwards. We stood and watched, waited for the building to settle and cool, that we may search its final dilapidation. Each time a beam collapsed or a cloud of ash was sent up, I hoped the house would be gentle with Matilda's remains, but instead the sounds of destruction were brittle and harsh.

In time, we returned to filling water-pails and carried them sombrely from river to house, poured their contents with respect over the spoilage, drove out the final hisses and spits. Then with pot-hooks, billhooks and pitchforks, we began to pull out the seared furniture; it was no more than charcoal and it splintered to parings at the mildest of touches. From time to time, the master of the house came along and inspected the progress, took his turn in the labour, but was soon overcome with sadness, began to yammer in lament and could not continue.

A strange fog curled about the place and clung to the house's skeletal frame, a mingling of smoke, mist and rain; and the building's carcass, wreathed in that haze, seemed to move of its own accord, drifted away from us little by little as we diminished and dismantled it.

At last, we found her blackened body. All tools were put by and a sheet was brought in which to wrap her. Fleetingly, I looked at her, and all that was human had been burned away. Shrunken and weak as eggshell her body was, no semblance of its former incarnation. The sunshine of her benevolent disposition never again to rise and ray the living world, her gentle charms choked and stifled. Such contrast to her living form. Neither man nor woman she seemed to me; her face unfinished, empty sockets from where her fawn-like eyes had once looked out.

That evening, what was left of her body was laid in the church, until it could be fetched by her kith and kin. A washerwoman from the next village was sent for and, with hot water and black soap decanted from a barrel, she washed all our tainted clothing and set it all to dry on the tree branches thereabouts.

In my room at the inn, I took a pail of water and I scrubbed at my skin, until it was red and tender. I laboured for many a while to rid myself of that smoke and smudge, but I could never quite banish the odour. To this day, when the wind is set from the north and the season is sliding into its autumn garb, sometimes a caustic fragrance enters my nostrils and, for a heartbeat, I relive the horrors of that tragedy.

It was a fitful sleep that wrote my history that night; dipped me in and out of ink-black terrors and paper dreams. No comfort did my mind-wanderings bring me, no relief for my idle brain, and I awoke in the morning feeling dull about the head, and with a cough that bruised my ribs. It was in a dreamlike state, a continuance of my dullness of mind, that I attended a mass for the maid, Matilda.

The ceremony was attended by a concourse of villagers from the neighbourhood and we all showed our respect for her memory. Already, I missed her little kindnesses and I wished she were alive again. As a boy, I had been taught to scorn the external embodiment of internal emotions. But as the widows, mothers and daughters in that church released the woes from their breasts with their sobbing and wailing, I took comfort from it and wished I might have had the liberty to join them. It was a wordless elegy beyond the constraints of music, that might have been sung from the beginning of time.

It was not until the ritual was completed and the congregation then broke apart, that I realised Rosamund was not there. I did not blame her; William's words were harsh beyond compare and were as persuasive as they were hostile; and as to my own opinion of Rosamund, I knew not where it fell. But when we returned to the inn and there was still no sign of her, I sought out Father Oswald.

'Father, have you seen Rosamund?' I asked.

He hesitated for a moment then said, 'She is not here, Alwin.'

'I know,' I said. 'William's bias is set against her and will take time to—'

'I mean she is gone, for good.'

'How so?'

'A woman from the village came to me this morning and told me she had seen the witch that walked out of the burning house making her way towards a woodland path that no stranger would ever dare to tread and no local would use without just cause, because it leads to a Wise Woman; a practiser of folk-herbs. I suppose one black heart must sense another and the Devil fetches them together that they may ply their dark craft.'

'You truly believe Rosamund Blackmere is a witch?' I said with consternation.

'Her tongue speaks of heresy and we are better without her. I told that to the woman this morning and counselled her to forget Rosamund Blackmere ever existed. And you should do the same, Alwin.'

I bowed my head in reverence then left Father Oswald and returned to my room. I did not join the company for the rest of the day, and kept myself to my own thoughts. More than two score miles I had travelled since leaving Crown Croft, but it was not the acreage beneath my feet that was teaching me about the world; it was the new and fertile ground within my mind. Where before I had derived all my learning from Mother, Grandfather and Father Oswald, and never doubted any of it, suddenly I was learning to think differently, learning to think like Rosamund. But thoughts gave on to opinions and in turn led to confusion, and as I strolled through the images inside my head, I wished I had discovered more from the damosel Blackmere. It was with that feeling of unfinished beginnings and hindered progress that I finally fell into a puddle of vague and muddy dreams that lasted long after sunrise.

When I did finally rouse myself from sleep, I made my way downstairs and saw Goody and Adela standing outside the inn. Adela was greatly changed; a sad shadow beneath her eyes and the recollection of jest long forgotten. Bereft of her sweet companion, she cut a sorry figure, as though part of her own self had died along with poor Matilda. My inclination was to turn about and return to my room, but on seeing me, the gentle matron Goody cried, 'Alwin! How fare ye, lad?'

'I am well, Mistress, thank you. I trust God finds you both ... as well as might be expected?'

'Well,' Goody said, 'the death of a young woman, and her not even being wed; it will not be forgotten easily by me, that is for sure. And poor Adela, here.' She slid her arm about Adela's shoulders and drew her closer. 'This poor creature will not be left alone and who can blame her? I told her the witch was far away now, and she cannot harm us any more, but the poor girl will not be said. It is such a pity Father Oswald is not here to pray with her—'

'What do you mean?' I said.

'He is gone away, sir,' the dame replied.

'I do not understand,' I said.

'I did counsel him to wake you, lad. But he said you must be left to regain your strength, what with all that has happened.'

'And where has he gone? How long will he be?'

'Well,' Goody said, 'a messenger came from an abbey some ten miles north of here. The abbot has learned of the Winfeld Priory and the fire; and of the witch who conjured their doing.'

'But Rosamund had nothing to do with the priory,' I said.

'What a strange thing to say,' she countered. 'How could you possibly know? You were not even there.'

Goody looked at me with what seemed to be hard-favoured eyes, and where before her face had always been benign and maternal, I began to imagine her features taking on a different cast and reducing themselves to a frowning accuser.

'Of … of course I was not there,' I stuttered, blinking my eyes to dispel the image of Goody's censorious expression. 'But the messenger at the tavern never told of a witch; he only spoke of soldiers.'

'Either way,' she said, her voice at once sounding hard and fluty to me, 'winds have blown the ill news to the abbot and he seeks an audience with Father Oswald.'

I sighed and lowered my head. 'When did he leave?'

'He left at terce and will return tomorrow,' she said, all bright and jolly again. 'Then we shall confer and decide if it is fitting that we continue on to Walsingham. Although as much as anyone I wish to tread that hallowed ground and offer my prayer to Our Lady, I do wonder if it would not be better for all of us to wait and go another time.'

'But I made a promise,' I said, indignant. 'I will not turn back.'

'I believe you will not, Alwin,' she said, her tones now gentle and warm again in my ears, 'because you are a fine and brave young man. But do not be too bold; lean your mind to the prudent side, and talk to your priest when he returns. At least allow him that respect.'

With that, I stepped back a pace, bowed my head, and left the two women. Reluctant to spend more time in the darkened bed-chamber at the inn, I decided to walk the length of the village and beyond. Just as the taint of smoke was still in the air, so my doubts of Father Oswald's integrity still blew dark and dense in my mind as I strolled the lanes. Not only could I not account for Rosam-und's mistake in seeing him at the dwelling house, but also I could not come at a reason why he would leave without telling me. The further I walked, the more I suspected him of some sort of con-cealment or betrayal. But the more I doubted him, the more I lost trust in my own judgement. In the end, I decided that if I had to believe in someone; it must surely be Father Oswald. I had known him my whole life and my mother trusted him like no other; recent events might have swayed my eyes and ears, but faith was what governed my heart and I must be true to both it and the priest.

I held on to that thought as I roamed the farmland and sheep-tracks of the surrounding vicinity and began to feel more akin to the version of myself that had dwelled so long on the Whittaker lands. After two or so miles, I rested, then having ascended a small hill, I climbed the branches of a tree to gain a better prospect of the landscape.

Looking back towards the village, far in the distance was a post-mill, and a mile beyond the settlement was a lake, some quar-ter mile in diameter. Such an expanse of water I had never seen the likes of before. There were always pools alongside the River Crown after it had bloated itself with storm-water, but nothing to compare to that lake. Dappled with sunlight and drinking in the colour of the sky, it spangled itself between a grove of sycamores and oaks that were still garnished in their summer foliage and the whole scene was pleasing to my eye.

I stayed there for a while, looking at the mere, staring at the forest paths that threaded web-like away from the village and deep into the trees. I thought of Rosamund and, although she was lost to my sight, she still held a firm place in my memory, and somehow her absence rendered me doubly alone.

I considered Father Oswald's words; his counsel to imagine she never existed, but his warning only conjured fascination in my mind and in the end, I forgot to forget her. With freedom to observe, I looked out across the forest of trees, selected a spot with my eye and had myself believe she was there, but I was unable to deceive myself for long, and was forced to console my mind with memories and regrets.

An hour or so after midday, I retraced my steps to the inn, expecting to find William, Goody and Adela all safely together. But as I approached from the top end of the lane, Adela was walking towards me, quite alone.

'Damosel Adela,' I said as we converged. 'Is all well?'

'Yes, sir,' she said and curtseyed a gentle greeting, bowed her round face with its up-turned nose. 'Dame Goody and Master William have taken her horse to the farrier in the next village.'

'And left you all alone?'

'She said you would be back soon—'

'If I had have known,' I said, 'I would have returned all the sooner. Come, let us return to the inn and wait for Goody and William.'

We took our seats on a bench in the parlour of the inn. Adela was quiet, her eyes red and watery. Twice, she made an attempt to speak, but instead of words breaking forth upon her tongue, her thoughts and frets were expressed in a stream of tears, which trickled from their source and readily flowed down her nose and chin.

I studied her briefly and called to mind the image of Rosamund when she was comforting Matilda, after the horse had bolted. How natural it was for the two women to divide and share the anxiety; how simply Matilda's woes were chided by the curve of another's arm, the warmth of another's embrace, heartfelt, sexless and pure. That same gesture was called for now, but of course could not be given, because I was at a disadvantage; I was a man, and if I reached for Adela and proffered physical solace, her chastity and my reputation would be called into question.

I began to wonder exactly when the line had been drawn; that moment in time when our innate status as human beings had been rent asunder, when neutral affinities had been cast out and replaced with manly men and wicked women. I could not help but question whether anyone truly benefitted from such a schism and wondered if God's laws might not one day be rewritten. But for now, I could only offer up cold words of logic and reason to Adela, instead of the comfort the situation called for.

'Matilda feels no pain any more, Adela. So, you must stint your sadness,' I began. 'She left this world a spotless maiden and now her soul is with the Virgin Mary. We must not be selfish and weep for what we have witnessed, nor question that God chose to take her away from her mortal life. We must hold her graces in remembrance and try to stem our flow of tears.'

Adela dried the final swell of water from her eyes and nodded her assent. But she was not composed enough to speak. To distract her from further melancholy thoughts, I began to talk about Crown Croft, the meads and pastures, the river's happy flow, the breeze that sung through the Whittaker woods. But all the while I was speaking, my own thoughts returned to Rosamund and the final disclosure she voiced about Father Oswald's visit to the dwelling house. Respectful of Adela's sensitivity, and explaining that discourse on painful events was a means of healing them, I gradually steered my voice towards the night of the fire. I told her how I was awoken by smoke on the air and by church bells and dog barks. Then with gentleness I finally asked her what she had witnessed on that night; but how her answer might exonerate both Rosamund and Father Oswald, I did not know.

'We left the inn after supper,' she began, her voice still hoarse, 'and we were welcomed into our place of harbourage by the master of the house, Master Oakshott. His wife did take us to our rooms, but Goody did not wish Matilda to share with Damosel Blackmere, on account of the discord between William and Rosamund, just before we left the inn.'

'What discord?' I asked.

'William had been upbraiding Rosamund about her lack of scripture-learning and saying how she should acquire a better temper that might be more easily managed. Rosamund had such strange ideas; that a woman should have her own thoughts and that few men should be trusted. She asked William what the greatest miracle of the bible was, like it was a test of his faith and, of course, William answered it was the Resurrection. Then when Rosamund asked him why he thought Christ the Saviour had revealed such a wondrous act to women instead of men, William had no reply. So Rosamund told him: she said it was because the miracle was meant for the simplicity of benevolent faith. Most men would have corrupted it, she said, been seduced by the power it might have yielded. Well, Goody never spoke to Rosamund again, not until after the fire. As soon as we were shown to our rooms, Goody told Matilda she must share with us and have no more to do with Rosamund. If it had been up to Goody, I think she might have sent Rosamund away there and then in the darkness of night, but I suppose she was heeding Father Oswald's words and being a good Christian.'

'And then did you all take yourselves to bed?' I said.

'Yes. Matilda was exhausted; her arm gave her much discomfort and she suffered from a megrim. She was slow to put on her chemise and night-cap and then, just as she lay her head on the pillow,

Goody said she heard a noise. She went downstairs to consult with the master of the house, then came back in no more than a moment and said Father Oswald had come.'

Until that moment, I had supposed an explanation was possible; a mistake from a tired eye, perhaps even a dream. But on hearing Father Oswald's name, my soul contracted a little and, by a small degree, I was no longer the person I had been but a moment before.

'Goody said we should go down to talk with him,' Adela went on, 'but Matilda must stay and rest.'

'And Matilda was ... awake when you left?'

'Yes, sir.'

'What reason did Father Oswald give for his visit? What could be so important?'

'I cannot say, because when we reached the solar-room, he brushed past us in haste and went directly to Matilda. Goody said he must have his reasons and we should not question him.'

'Did you see him leave?'

'Yes, sir. He left in much hurry.'

'And Matilda?'

'She was fast asleep when we returned and Goody said we should not wake her.'

To this day, I still cannot discern the difference between the pain inflicted by bereavement and the distress experienced following betrayal: the former is acute and burns like a brand on the soul, but gently heals as time passes on and eventually leaves fond remembrance in its wake; but the latter is crueller than death. It lingers and expands until nothing of the betrayer is left but the deed itself.

As Adela innocently confirmed my deepest fears, I could only grit my teeth and clench my fist with my heart inside it. Puzzles environed me from every quarter and, with absent respondents and answers I did not wish to hear, I was confounded by the confusion of it all.

'My constitution is a little out of sorts, damosel,' I stuttered. 'I find that I must return to my room, please excuse me.'

Like a man pursued, I ran up the steps and threw open the door to my chamber. Once inside, I slammed the door closed with such force that it sent a spray of dust and splinters into the air when it met with the frame. Still consumed with a passion of wrath, I kicked out at the wall, then punched at the plaster and cob, catching my hand against a wooden strut and drawing fresh blood from my scabbed knuckle. But the pain inside me was still worse than my hand, so I cast another clout at the wall.

In time, my temper cooled and I sat, vacant and dispirited, on the stool at the side of the bed. I knew I must wait until Father Oswald returned, report to him the facts and demand he explain himself to my satisfaction. But how I might accuse him of such impiety and iniquity, and continue to have our relationship flourish, I did not know. Many moments passed by and it was during those cogitations that there was a knock on my door. I waited for a moment, then bade the petitioner to enter, and over the threshold stepped Dame Goody.

'Adela said you were a little despondent,' she said. 'And who can blame you for such a mood? We all feel it; man, woman, beast or bird. When a witch conjures her magic, it steals away all cheer of heart. Why, even the trees seem dismal to me today.'

As amiable as Goody was, I was in no mood for her company, but like an upturned pail, she poured forth a torrent of words and went on in a sing-song manner, regaling murmurous tales about her walk to the farrier's, the weak ale served at the inn, the aches in her knee-bones and all manner of trifles that entered her head. With no thought or reason to the words that gushed from her lips, her monologue was endless. In the end, I could stand it no longer; a full quarter hour she had prated.

'Enough!' I said, glaring mastery from my eyes.

She blenched at my tone, shrank back, lowered her head and said meekly, 'I beg of your pardon, sir. I talk a lot to alleviate the pains in my stomach, from which I suffer. I mean no offence by it.'

I eyed her, expecting to see the subjugated temper and mellow disposition of which she had spoken on so many occasions. But for an instant, there was a scowl in her eye; a mixture of defiance and contempt, and I found it most unnerving. The flash of disdain was over in a heartbeat; so quickly done that I doubted I had seen it at all, and Goody's expression returned to its usual benign state.

'I must ask you to leave,' I said, firm and gentle. 'I have matters to consider, then I shall seek out Damosel Adela and reassure her I am no longer despondent.'

'You just missed her, Alwin,' she said. Her voice was impassive, her features blank, but in my mind I imagined a poisonous look of triumph behind her eyes as she spoke those words. Was I beginning to learn about women better than before? Was I at last seeing the slyness inside Goody Tanner, the wickedness that Father Oswald believed really did dwell within some women?

'Explain yourself,' I demanded, dominant, unafraid.

'Why, she's gone to meet Father Oswald.'

'But you said he was not returning until tomorrow.'

'Well, what do I know? A villager came with a message: Adela is to meet the priest at the lake, and that is where she went.'

'You knew all this and yet you filled the air with your babble?'

Still heated from the steam of my anger, I pushed past her. She tottered on her legs, then issued a series of shrieks and gasps as she righted herself. I ran out of the door at the rear of the inn and sprinted into the yard. An ostler was there, lifting the saddle from Goody's horse, and the fellow stared at me blankly as I knocked him aside in my haste. I took up the horse's reins and, leaping onto the animal's bare back, I set my heels to the horse's flanks and urged it forward with my voice.

The horse lost traction as I reined sharply to the right, then it regained its footing as we took to the lane. Such a clatter we made as we galloped along the dry road, sending clouds of dust in our wake. At the end of the track, stones had been laid to fill up the holes and I was forced to slow pace over the uneven surface. The lane eventually dwindled into a grass trail and the pony stumbled on through a pathless grove before I was compelled to dismount for fear of being unseated by the overhanging branches. I ran on at a smart pace through dingles and dells, leading the horse behind me along tracks overgrown with vetches and made thorny with briers.

At last, the trees receded and the ground became softer, wetter, the shafts of grass more reed-like, until all in a moment the scene changed and a wide expanse of water was laid out before me. Each step I advanced broadened the view until I stood at the brink of the mere. I tied up the horse and walked along the water's edge, searching the shores for Adela and Father Oswald.

When I had seen the lake before, its surface had glinted in the sun and the water was the colour of the sky. But in contrast, daylight was now beginning to fade from the already grey clouds and the mere was robed in blacks and greens. A lip-chapping wind gusted across its surface, drew water from my eyes and tumbled my hair. I peered across the water and, on the far side, there were two shapes; a man in dark robes with a deep cowl about his head, and a maiden with skirts blowing wildly about her legs.

'Father Oswald!' I shouted. 'Adela!'

With air-swayed branches creaking above me, my distorted voice was carried away by the wind and the figures did not respond. I stepped back from the water and looked about me; the lake was oval in shape and I was standing on the shores of the narrower end, at the farthest point away from Adela and the priest. I called out once more, but to no avail and was obliged to make my way on foot through the reeds and grasses that fringed the water.

At a quarter of the way round, and with the wind now blowing diagonally across from my right, I shouted again. Adela turned about to face me and I raised my arms, waved to her and called out. With her gaze fixed upon me, I advanced, still calling and waving, and in so doing, I lost my footing and fell to the ground. There was a splitting sound as fallen branches and wilting reeds gave way beneath me. But there was another noise too, a composite; a shriek and a splash and a plunge all found my ears at the same time.

I scrambled to my feet and scanned the spot where I had last seen Adela and Father Oswald, but there was no one there. Then, some yards away from me, the surface of the lake began to fizz and ferment, the waters disturbed. Arms thrashed and hands clawed at both the lake and the mist that rose above it. Just once, Adela's face ascended, then sank as quickly as it had risen, the frothed-up water bubbling and winking as it swallowed her.

It was instinct, not a conscious decision, that impelled me to wade out through the thin, watery light and into the black depths. As wind-waves broke and shattered about me, the coldness stole my breath, and my lungs laboured to inhale and exhale. It was a sharp cold, a burning cold and it stung my skin wherever it touched. Within two strides, the lake was waist-high and I struggled to walk forwards, as though beyond the flower of my age. I looked out across the dimpled surface, towards the site I had last seen Adela and there, beyond the water, safe on the shore, was Father Oswald, his face obscured by his hood. Perhaps he went to raise the alarm; perhaps he could not see me for the mists. Whatever the explanation, he turned about, walked away and blended his shape with the shadow of the trees.

I pressed on at all hazards and only three paces further in, the lake-bed was beyond my reach. With pinching anxiety, I leaned forward into the darkening flood, the water yielding to the shape of my body, and I swam onwards to the race of brown, spuming waters where I had last seen Adela; but she was not there.

I swam in a circle around the place where the puckering waters had drunk her in, finning my way through the ripples. I called out her name, then filled my chest with air and plunged down into the shifting greens and greys. The water was tight about my head, pressed its iciness about my skull, and the weight of it pushed me down and down. I scurried my arms and stared blindly through the murk until at last I pushed up from the lake's base, my foot sliding from the upturned face of a stone, fingers of vegetation curling about my ankle-bone.

I reached the pale pane of the water's surface, gasping, and I looked about me, then stared down at the water and saw my own face through trembling rings of scattered light. Ignoring reason and time, I submerged myself over and again, continually wrapping myself in sheets of water. I swam to the innermost deeps, then out to the bleakest extremities, until my own skin seemed to be fashioned from the waters of the mere.

I swam and dived, over and again, tearing in and out of the water's skin, panting and thrashing, a sort of insanity taking possession of me. Breathless and choking, I descended one last time and, whether through fatigue or carelessness, I became entrapped in the arms of a fallen tree that had sunk to the very bottom of the lake and now lay with its branches outstretched in an attitude of beseeching. Deep into the left of my belly the shaft of wood sank itself as I wriggled to free my body from its clutches. Even through the water's chill, I still felt the branch penetrate my flesh and drive itself hard inside me, cutting more keenly than the barb of an arrow.

The pain drove all air from my lungs and, in a most lamentable condition, I fought my way to the surface, kicking my legs, paddling my arms, fearful of being overcome by asphyxia. It was in a virtual state of suspended animation that I finally broke the water's façade and drifted my way to the shore.

The lapse of an age passed by before I felt mud beneath my knees. I inched my way over the dirt and grass with lifeless arms and a frailty that rendered my legs useless, all the time shivering from my throat to my ankles. At last, as exhaustion set upon me and with want of air in my chest, I knew I was spent and would be obliged to give up. The lake had stolen Adela's existence, she had begun her eternal sleep and was no more than a recollection; a memory as flat and cold as the water that had taken her.

With the weather growing worse about me, I could do no more than lie among the vetches and reeds as they staggered against the wind, knowing I was far outside the compass of villagers or travellers and might never be found. Also, some of the lake had swum inside my head, and the sound of my own breathing and heartbeat dominated all other noises, as though I were still caught fast in the waters and would always be so.

Sometimes I drifted away from wakefulness and the day seemed to dwine in the blink of an eye. Briefly, I saw the cloud-stifled sun expiring on the horizon, then in a moment the twilight hour fell about me and darkness lay all around, the stars glaring down from their ocean of black sky, blinking and twitching above me.

I was unable to judge the passing of time and could only venerate its transit and hope it might touch me gently as it went. The puncture in my midriff caused a pain both broad and severe, and the water that had invaded the opening in my skin was beginning to burn the divided flesh beneath and cause sickness in my belly.

Angry blew the winds and darkly frowned the night, but I was helpless to rescue myself. By turns I was languid then fretful and tremors consumed me every once in a while, agitating the whole of my body and bringing sweats to my face and forehead.

Long after the passing of goblins' hour, I lay in the mud with my eyes tight shut, deaf to all sound and blind to all light. It was the sense of movement that roused me. The winds had dropped to an easy sigh and the grasses had silenced themselves. It was the snapping of twigs and a rustling in the undergrowth that caught my attention first. Then came the snorting of a horse and I smelled the hay-scented breath that issued from its nostrils.

I turned my head, my eyes stretched wide, and a Will-o'-the-wisp light played its beam from side to side. Looking up, a figure stood before me, hooded and robed in black. Illumined by a lantern's quivering ray, a hand came out of the darkness towards me; whether to give salvation or to push me down into a watery grave, I did not know. I could only watch and wait.

CHAPTER SEVEN

The lantern light shone in my face, blanching the night, then it passed down the length of my body and back up again. Someone wiped mud from my mouth and a hand touched the point above my hip; the aperture to my wound where a special soreness had set in, and I flinched and let out a gasp.

'Hush,' came a whisper. 'Come, rise you up now.'

Too weak either to countermand the suggestion or identify its petitioner, I drew in a breath and, with conviction, pushed myself up onto my knees, but was soon overcome with weariness. With the lake dripping from my skin, and a burning heat from the pit of my stomach to the top of my left thigh, I had no appetite for speech or movement and could only slump back down into the mist. The lantern was placed on the ground at my side and my benefactor moved away. Then I sensed a horse moving nearer, felt the ground tremble a little each time a hoof was thrown down, until at last it was standing as close as ever it might.

'You must find the strength to climb on the horse's back, Alwin,' whispered the voice again.

With particles of the lake still swimming about my head, I could not tell from where the utterance was voiced or indeed who spoke the words; it could have been man, woman, demon or saint. The sound was disembodied, with neither pitch nor tone to it, as though a spectre had risen from the lake and was guiding me to safety from beyond its grave.

I reached upwards and felt the horse's shoulder; its skin twitched where I laid my hand on it, but it stood in perfect calmness. I struggled to my knees, sensed hands reaching beneath my arms and labouring to support me. With tenderness, I was raised to my feet. I let out an involuntary moan as I straightened myself, for my ripped skin stung so. With a cupped hand placed beneath my knee and my own fingers clutching at the horse's mane, at last I heaved myself onto the animal's back.

I supposed it was Goody's horse; there was no saddle in which to sit or stirrups for my feet. I tried to hold myself upright, but all strength had been stolen from my middle and I could only sink forwards, rest my head against the pony's neck. Slowly, we moved onwards and I glanced behind at the lake; a sea of blackness enveloped in the night.

At the far side, there was a faint twinkling of lights, too low to be stars. And across the face of the mere, above its constellated skin, a dull sound was carried on the breeze, which for a moment I thought sounded like my own name. But we were travelling away from the water and the sights and sounds it conjured were soon lost to me.

Occasionally, branches and vegetation brushed my legs and arms, and the pony balked and shied. Each time I was jarred, the distemper in my stomach intensified and distressed my mind. I could no longer focus my eyes on anything, which made me believe I was falling, tumbling to the ground, but I remained on the pony's back and the world went on spinning about me.

On we ventured along untrodden tracks and densely wooded paths, endlessly threading our way through foliage and undergrowth, until at last we came to a clearing, vaguely illumined by moonlight. In the centre of the glade amidst overgrown shrubs, wild and free in their development, stood a cottage built of planking and thatch, set like a jewel in the heart of the forest, a curl of turf-smoke rising from the roof and a flickering light within.

The pony stopped, dipped his head and I began to slide down his shoulder. An arm was thrown about my waist and I leaned on it for support, my knees weak beneath me. With my mind walking slower than my legs, it came to pass that we entered the cottage, the inside of which was seasoned with wholesome smells. I was seated on a mattress, the scent of tansy and lavender rising from the bedstraw as I was gently encouraged to lie prostrate.

From that moment on, motes of light began to freckle behind my eyes, I fell into a sort of half-sleep, and time and reality converted themselves into a confusing and fluid substance. My thoughts bloomed random and primitive; I trembled, my tongue was dry and all I could picture was a jug of ale; pain darted about my belly and I wished I might call forth the warmth of an August day to soothe me; my scalp and chest were infused with acrid heat and I longed only for the Crown's waters. On I lingered until a deeper darkness took hold of me, stole away my physical senses and left me ghosted and fragile.

I lost all the colours of life and dreamed my thoughts in greys and blacks. In the genuine world, I had been able to move on and away from tragedy, escape the true impact of bereavement and emotional shock. But there, destitute of mobility, I was forced to confront all the feelings I had tried to out-run.

Clasped in moonlight, Mother's face came to me and how it summoned feelings of despair! How broken and bruised I felt without her. Then Mother's face fell away into a lake of stars and Adela rose up before me, robed in fire, with Matilda at her side. After some time, and unbound from their cloister wall, manifold holy sisters daunted my spirit with their passage through my dream. Desolate was the vale they wandered and silent was the sound of their feet, leaving only a whisper of farewells behind them for comfort.

After that, I was left to rave and rage alone; I thrashed my arms, switched my head from side to side and felt the blood washing restlessly against the shores of my heart. With the stain of bodily ills upon me, my head was hollow and my teeth were soft, and tainted air wrought gravel in my lungs and pulsated hot against my skin.

At times, soft hands came out of the darkness, touched a drinking-vessel to my lips and fed potions to my mouth, which in turn tasted of sulphur, salt, honey and herbs. On each occasion, the elixir first disturbed my senses, then gendered heat in my bones, and finally brought me calmness. Once in a while, there was pain above my hip and I cried out into the night, then kind words would tumble out of the moonlight and a poultice would be placed on my belly. Once, I even dreamed arms cradled me and absorbed all my shivers and fears.

How long I fell under the calamity of sickness and how many nights passed perilous about me, I could not say, but at last my eyelids trembled open, scant light pressed between them, and I looked about me. The room was a cauldron of darkness, the only source of light being moonlight that pierced the shutter-laths and fell speckled on the floor.

Over time, the night faded to blue and all I could do was watch as daytime hues brought depth and mellowness to the room. The light was sparse, but I liked the opaqueness, the burgeoning identity; where before there was flatness, gradually colour and perspective were introduced. Purged of all substance, I felt empty and light and could only observe in silence as spangled dust-specks danced about me and a low-burning candle wagged its flame.

For an age, I stared at the bare roof-trees above me in the eaves, and could only breathe and blink my eyes, so spare of fortitude I was. Then I sensed movement at my feet and there, sitting on a stool with her body slumped forward on the bed, was Rosamund.

She sat upright, rubbed her back and stretched her arms to the side. By then, the sun was fully risen and it cast its yellow pleasure through a gap in the shutter. Rosamund got to her feet, stood between the sun and me and at once she placed me in her shadow. She looked wiser and more learned than I had yet seen her and there was a gentleness in her eyes that had been absent before.

'What ails me?' I asked, wanting to trust in her knowledge.

'Some distemper crept in through your wound and fermented your blood,' she said while straightening my blanket.

'And am I well now?' I asked, at last capturing the vagrancy of her gaze.

'The high fever is passed,' she said, 'but we must guard against fresh attack. You must lie abed until your strength is advanced.'

'Where am I?'

'This cottage belongs to my mother's sister, Maud, she is a Wise Woman and is away practising her knowledge on the wife of a local lord. We are lodged deep in sylvan thickets here, Alwin, far from the common path. The villagers hereabout revere this place and also fear it. No one will come by, we are quite safe.'

'How long have I been here?'

'The moon is three days older since you slept.'

'And you warded and watched me day and night?'

She blushed a little at that question and I, too, felt warmth rising upwards from my chest.

'But how did you find me?' I said, still shy in my thoughts but rash in my speech.

My boldness put her in pause, then she replied, 'I ... I decided to seek you out, to quiz you further on matters regarding ... the nobleman.'

Her disclosure somehow pained me. I do not know quite what I expected her to say, but her answer left me feeling emptier than a moment before. She, too, seemed uncomfortable with her words, looked briefly away, then continued with, 'I went to the inn at dusk, asked the ostler to give a message to you, and he said you had galloped off towards the lake and had not returned, so—'

'So you searched for me?' I said.

A smile flickered briefly in her eyes, then she said, 'Hush now, there will be time for talk when better health returns to your body, but for now you must lie meekly and take rest.'

'But Rosamund,' I said, suddenly experiencing a lowering of my vitality, my eyes widening and a shortness of breath bringing imbalance to my senses. 'Adela! Adela was swallowed by the lake … I could not … he pushed her—'

'Bide quiet, Alwin, you must rest. There will be time for questions and answers when your health is more robust. But for now, you must be easy.'

With that, she touched her fingers to my shoulder, slid her hand lower and gently squeezed my arm, a soft smile on her lips, a promise of greater warmth behind her eyes. Then, she turned away and set about her day's industry.

Firstly, she opened the shutters and let loose a haze of sunlight that cast fingers of bright warmth about the room, sloped its light from rafter to reed. Next, she threw a faggot of leaves on the embers of the fire and conjured an orange flame, on which she placed dry logs, then a brand-iron with a cauldron on top. Into the vessel, she poured stock-fish, herbs and farina and stirred it with a pot-stick. A gentle breeze blew the sycamore outside the window, sending alternate waves of shade and sunlight rippling over the room, and it ushered in an enchantment of birdsong, such as you might only hear in high summer, and the air blew sweet and fair about me.

With a mellowness in her movements and her eye, she cared for my needs with kindness and was attendant upon me with an equal flow of sympathy and cheer. In all ways, she was obliging and knew not only what my body needed, but also exactly when the requirement was craved. Water was fetched in a pail from the stream and decanted into a mazer before even a thirst had intruded itself upon me; food was served at the precise moment my belly voiced its grumble; and a rag soaked in cool water was placed on my forehead long before fevers could begin their shivers. With manners and niceties, she supplied me with good store and all my wants were satisfied.

At times, she concocted a more particular brew; she mingled mulberries, hemlock and ivy, together with some plants I did not know, and had me inhale it. Later she took mustard seed and meadow rue, rubbed them together in a vessel with the white of an egg to make the salve thick, then using a feather, she smeared the potion across my forehead and temples. In time, a blush of warmth flowered about my head and all the pain went away.

When I first awoke, my body was not in a condition to eat, but after beginning with water and bean pottage in small quantities served up at considerable intervals, Rosamund trained my hunger to increase its demands, and after a period of three days, my stomach was no longer tired and could eat a fair portion.

It was on that third day I became more aware of my surroundings. For the first time since I arrived at the cottage, there was strength enough in my mid-belly to allow me to sit upright for more than a moment. It was as I shuffled myself into a seated position, I became aware of my clothing; I was no longer arrayed in either tunic, chausses, shirt or braies. Instead, I was dressed in a linen shift, tight beneath my arms and barely covering my knees. On a table at the far side of the room, my own garments, freshly washed, mended and dried, were laid in fold.

Initially, I was untroubled by the matter, but over time I considered the subject more narrowly and it came to me that Rosamund must surely have noticed my deformity. The concept caused me abundant vexation and I came to understand better the change in her attitude towards me; she cared for me out of duty, but behind her eyes she pitied me.

At length, Rosamund returned from her woodland walk, a basket of herbs in her hands, a gentle smile on her features. But I could not look her full in the eye, as I was fearful of the false compassion it would reflect. Instead, I pushed the coverlet away, swung my legs around and made to stand. Rosamund dropped her basket and rushed towards me, placed her hand on my arm in a reflex. I shook it off and tried to raise myself to my feet, but there was still weakness in my limbs and I was compelled to sit again.

'Alwin, you must take matters slowly,' she said, issuing her command with cool authority as though she were my superior.

'I will take matters how I please,' I said, putting her in her place, flying my stare towards her.

My words and the manner in which they were delivered stung her, because she stepped back briskly and could only stare at me. I glanced at her then looked away; I could not fully read her expression. I suspected there was a glow of contempt in her eyes, but not as it had been at the town. Surprise and confusion were there also, but more than anything else, it was pity that radiated from her, I was certain.

'Are your symptoms worsening?' she ventured, a conflict of understanding shaping a frown on her brow.

But I was not for talking. I shook my head, frowned and climbed back into bed. She started to pull the covers over me, but I snatched them from her and saw to my own comfort. She observed me for a moment, then went about her household drudgery and we did not commune with one another again that day.

The following morning when I awoke, Rosamund was still sound asleep on the bench beneath the window. I pulled the shutter-rope and let a sprinkling of daylight into the room; just enough to see by. She did not stir, so I rose, washed at the water-pail and dressed myself in my own raiment. It was as I cut a portion from the cake of wheaten bread, that she roused herself.

'I am glad your fortitude is returning,' she said, her tone docile, respectful.

I turned towards her and bowed my head in an act of gratitude for her nursing and physicking, but I said nothing. There was something about her that was different. She spoke the words as though she meant them, but beneath her voice, behind her eyes, there was that grain of knowledge I was certain she would use against me.

The shadow of a feud had risen up between us and for some reason it caused me distress. All my life, my deformity had remained a solemn secret between just Mother and me. Upon a sudden, my imperfection had been laid bare; and to of all people, a practiser of the black arts.

I kept my own company for the remainder of the day and channelled all my vitality towards gaining better strength. I fetched my own servings from the pot and kept myself active. I brushed down the horses with straw, cleaned mud from the tack and whittled at sticks with my knife. Advantages were obtained from my physical movement, but I could not deny the distemper had weakened me and continued to subject me to a propensity for fatigue.

With only a fragment of daylight left and just before twilight set in, I was obliged to return to the inside of the cottage and sit on the bed. Rosamund had brewed a gentle linctus made with queene-apple jelly and she offered it to me, but I declined to take it. As the sun sank lower and the horizon deepened its shade, Rosamund lighted two candles and added a log to the hearth and it burned with ample flare.

In that tense orange glow, we sat in silence, the wind occasionally whispering through the thatch, the wood on the fire splaying and crackling. A better person would have spent the evening thanking Rosamund for finding them and saving their life, told her how grateful they were for the hospitality with which she had entertained them. They would have laid to rest suspicion of witchcraft and instead, venerated her for the wisdom and bravery she had demonstrated whilst placing her own life in jeopardy.

But instead I could only think of my own humiliation and exposure, and as shadows crept along the clay floor to warm themselves at the hearth, I sat coldly on the bed beringed in a halo of darkness and I turned matters silently in my mind.

I thought back to the first time I met Rosamund, recalled the fire in her eyes; that wildness and cunning I had seen in no other's. Her steps were so certain, she could not be swayed from her own opinion and her contrariness only served to make me listen to her more closely and examine my own reasoning. But since she had discovered my secret, our intellectual rivalry had ended and she no longer saw me worthy of her persuasion. Sexless and impotent as I was, she saw me as less than a human being, simply as a creature that required physicking, just as Mother used to nurse orphaned chicks and lambs. How strange to be the subject of someone else's judgement, of a Wise Woman's judgement! The thought troubled me, but a greater problem vexed me also; I knew there was a rupture between Rosamund Blackmere and me, and I suspected it might never be repaired.

My thoughts rolled on in that like manner for nigh well an hour. The sweating candle burned lower and the blood-shot flames in the hearth consumed all their fuel, the force of the fire all spent, until the cottage was infused in a dim half-light that seemed closer to Hell than Heaven.

At last, Rosamund's features lengthened, she gave a deep sigh and rose from her bench.

'I know you have discovered my secret,' I declared, my tone already wrathful and defensive, not even the merest hint of civility.

Rosamund approached me, that same blend of compassion and superior knowing in her eye.

'Sit you down,' I said. I stood to my full height and began to pace about the room. I waited until she had returned to her seat, then I stopped and clasped my hands behind my back, a stern attitude of authority etched on my face. 'I shall tell you how it came about; for it was no fault of my own,' I began, careful not to catch her eye as I spoke, afeard I would not have the heart to continue. 'I cannot abide concealment but have been obliged to live a life different to the one Nature intended. Some are born with afflictions, some are subjected to bodily calamities by the will of God; none of us is perfect and not one of us should seek pity from fellow humans for the way God has formed us, or offer false compassion where it is not wanted.'

With that, I cast off my caution and told her how my deformity had come about; how the plague had almost stolen my life and, in its wrath, left its mark on my body in such a cruel manner.

'But it could not steal my strength,' I went on. 'I can drive a team of oxen better than any ploughman, my step can cover thirty miles in a day and my body is in vigorous condition. To the eyes of the world, I have not been compromised as a man and I seek neither the world's pity nor yours, damosel. You should remember your place and respect me as your master.'

In my naivety, I supposed the matter would be laid to rest; Rosamund would bow her head in a courteous manner and our natural positions of overlord and subordinate would return. In my mind, I predicted Rosamund might perhaps even issue a wry remark about the weak state in which she had found me at the lake, remind me of her generosity in taking me in. I braced myself for the return of her former character, but matters did not come about in the way I foresaw.

Instead, through the scant light, scarlet burned high on her cheeks and I saw only despondency in her features. The pity from before had deepened and expanded into a vastness of sorrow, which I could not look at for more than a heartbeat. And that is how the day ended. We each put ourselves to bed in a separate and silent manner and I received no more of her company that day.

I closed my eyes and the slow, black hours began. But instead of sleep being sent through the darkness to comfort me, fresh worries clouded my mind and, drop by drop, a new and disconcerting prospect rained down on me and brought me great torment: Rosamund must have noticed the degeneration of my plague-wound. With her knowledge of charms, herbs and the human form, she realised the site had begun to haemorrhage, and the look in her eye that first spoke of pity, now saw the onset of my death. My hearty boasts of physical wellness contrasted with the reality of my ailing body, struck a chord in her heart and lent her that terrible look of condolence.

All night that look was a thorn in my pillow and, as time made its way to the morning hour, thoughts of my own death squeezed at my heart. By the time the sun rose and Rosamund opened the shutters, I cherished a great deal of self-pity that swelled like a tide within me. Rosamund called my name, a note of compassion in her voice, but I counterfeited unconsciousness and made her believe I was still asleep.

She took her basket, as was her usual habit, and left the cottage to roam for berries, nuts and herbs. More than ever before, I keenly felt the absence of her attentions and the morning passed long and slow without her. Before, she had always returned well before noon, but on that day, she was delayed. I wondered if she could not face me; could not bear to be the one who finally voiced the fact of my ebbing life.

With daylight dying, I sat in the gloom and stared at leaf-shadows as they were swayed by vesper winds. I had no appetite and my vitality was very low; to stoke the fire was such a burden that I let it burn down to its gleeds and did not care I had done so.

For a while I sat on the bed, took up my knife and busied myself paring my nails. Then I began to wonder if Rosamund had abandoned me, and that strain of thought gave rise to feelings of anger and resentment. I paced about the cottage and spoke aloud to myself, told myself I should have expected no less from a sorceress. Why, she was probably on her way to the village to declaim me publicly, buying herself good favour by surrendering a mutable man. I was still in that high state of anxiety when Rosamund quietly opened the door, walked to the table and set her basket down on its surface. Then she cast brushwood and logs into the hearth and sent up a spray of embers and ash.

'You bothered to return, then?' I hissed, bold, menacing.

'You should not doubt me, Alwin,' she said, no malice to her voice, only gentleness. 'But you are not yet well.'

'Not yet well?' I said, stealing her words and using them to my own advantage. 'Do you think me so infirm that I do not notice the look in your eye? I may be a poor witling, a simple franklin farmer, but I can see that you readily withhold what you know. And when we first met, I saw the manner in which you silently condemned me as a debaucher of nuns. What say you of that now?'

'I am sorry, Alwin, my prejudice against men whispered doubts to me,' she said, her under-lip quivering, her features vivid with grace and wearing the emotion of remorse with great beauty. 'I was wrong and ...'

'Do not colour your words with tear-shed; it will gender no shrift from me,' I snapped, subsumed by my anger. 'I offered you a truce to our grievance, enjoined you to my trust, but oh no; you could not give me honesty in return, could you? Well, perhaps I do not trust you, either. And why should I? You are a witch; I knew it from the first moment I set my eyes on you. There was something about you I could not account for; my flesh always quivers beneath your touch and your presence always robs me of my poise; what can that be if not beguilement by a heathen? I know it; even Goody Tanner knows it!'

'Goody Tanner does not know a pickling pan from a pig's trough!'

'Oh, I had quite forgotten; you are so superior to everyone else. With your herbs and your charms and your ridiculous notions! You purport to own a store of intellect, damosel, but you forget your place and your station in life. You fail to recall I am your master.'

That sudden proclamation of authority rendered her unable to brave my wrath and with teardrops dewing her cheeks, she turned away from me.

'Do not turn your back on me,' I shouted. 'Do you think me not man enough to hear the truth about my own condition?'

'Alwin,' she said, fronting me, soft in her tone. 'It is not the right time to tell you. Leave it be, until you are stronger. Pray do not ask me more.'

'So, you do have knowledge of how my plague-wound will develop?'

I searched her eyes for contradiction, but she lowered her gaze, looked at the floor.

'Is it some sort of revenge,' I asked, 'that you withhold what you know? Are you already acquainted with the bleeding that comes to me with the waxing moon?'

'Yes,' she said.

'So, I suppose you know when ... when death will—'

The breeze that had blown through the rafters all day suddenly stopped. Nature drew her breath in pause and my own life paused with her. At speaking out loud those words of my own demise, it rushed the concept from thought to reality in the blink of an eye. I came to understand that I would never again return to Crown Croft, never walk the long mead where the summer breeze whispers through the barley-sheaves, nor sit beneath the Whittaker oaks with their broad heads and wide arms, nor touch my fingers to the Crown's riverbed, pebbled and cressed in all its rippling splendour.

With the irk of my anger spent, there was nothing left but weeping. I sank to my knees and, naked of all my inhibitions, I let the tears flow, as I had no strength left to stop them.

She in her goodness came to me; after all I had said, she took me to grace and still came to me. She clasped me in a silent embrace, cradled me in her arms and pillowed my head on her shoulder, gave me something for my heart to hold onto. The tears took breath from my lungs, I laboured in my language, unable to express myself, and I could not speak words without a little convulsion in-between them.

'I ... I do not want my life to end, Rosamund,' I sobbed, my heart quite broken by discontent. 'Pray ... tell me how long I have left? Swear by your saint and tell me ... when will death come for me?'

She lifted my head from her shoulder, raised her hands and wiped the tears from my face with her fingers. Then, looking at me pure-eyed and faithful, gentle words took flight from her tongue and she said, 'Alwin, you are not dying ... you are a woman.'

CHAPTER EIGHT

When Rosamund spoke those words to me, I cried out in consternation, denied the possibility of such a notion and voiced my dissent with a deal of violent language. One by one, I threw my grievances at her, as an archer lets fly his darts. But as the words were issuing from my lips, in the margins of my mind I was slowly surrendering to the belief in what she had said, and the revelation brought me anguish.

I considered the want of breadth in my arm, the whiskers that never came to my lip and chin, the final words Mother had spoken about my deformity. Incidental behaviours that had meant nothing to me before jostled their way to the front of my thoughts; dressing in the dark, never baring my chest, hardly ever wandering beyond the Whittaker lands. In the end, I quit my speech and sat dumbfounded. Rosamund rose, helped me to my feet and then sat beside me on the bed, a look of kindness blooming in her eyes.

'So, I am not dying?' I said at length, my voice compromised by tear-shed and phlegm.

Her gaze still rested on my eyes and, gently shaking her head, she said, 'No.'

At that, I took some ease, but unable to dislodge that persistent feeling of impending sickness, I said with anxiety, 'But ... but what about the ... bleeding?'

'The menses are a female disease, Alwin,' she smiled. 'Imposed propriety withdraws the subject from public discussion, so they carry dread and mystery for those who do not succumb to them. But you have nothing to fear. Nature would not burden us with an obligation we were not strong enough to bear.'

'And all women suffer from them?'

'Yes, when they grow from a girl into a woman, until the day they become old. And yours will come again with every cycle of the moon.'

'But how can such a thing be tolerated? When they visited themselves upon me, they brought such pain to my belly and my back, they sent fever to my head and dulled my thoughts; I could barely sleep.'

'The symptoms may ease, Alwin. And you will learn to live with them, for you must.'

'But why be cursed by such an affliction?'

'Because the body must rid itself of the female seed, clean itself, make itself ready for childbirth.'

'I do not have the body to carry a child! Look at me! I do not have the … strength to be female. There must be some other explanation. And besides; I do not want to be a woman.'

At once, my mind was filled with thoughts of weaving skeps for bees, baking bread, spending hours at spindle and spool, and carding wool at midnight. All my life I had been so active; I could out-ride and out-run any of the youths from Giolgrave; none of our neighbours nor Grandfather could plough as many rods as I; and to spend a late summer day scything a strip of barley was one of the greatest pleasures I had ever known.

Upon a sudden, my thoughts about life took on a new colour, for never before had I truly considered what it might feel like to be compromised by the disparity between a woman's lot and a man's, and the idea caused me acute distress. How narrow a woman's world must be; how weak and inert her duties made her. And how I might fit into that world, I dared not think.

With my feelings so subverted, a multitude of dreads swarmed about me, then by hazard of fancy, I struck on a particular thought that plagued my heart with a harsher sting than all the rest: the world was no longer mine to forge into a habitation of my own approval; it was someone else's: and where before stood mandate and expectation; now stood inhibition and doubt.

At once, certitude fell away from me and I felt akin to Jude's wandering stars, for whom darkness is reserved forever. I turned to look at Rosamund, my eye already tinged with pity for the road she must tread in life, pity for my own future. She was studying me.

'Your body conformed itself to the demands made upon it,' she said, still inspecting me with a frown on her brows, as though still not wholly certain of her own theory. She rose then stooped to light a wax-light and, returning to her seat beside me, she held the candle in her hands and scrutinised me, the flame posing and swaying, suddenly uncertain of its purpose.

'Was there ever a time you remember being a girl?' she asked, her voice soft.

'No,' I said. 'My only early recollections about maids and dames were that they were weaker than me; that I had a duty, an expectation to be stronger, braver. Mother always made sure I was worked harder than other boys. I thought she was edifying me, but she was changing me. But look at what I have become, Rosamund; could a woman really look like this?'

I pulled up my tunic and shift, had Rosamund scrutinise the muscle on my torso and abdomen. Where women had soft tissue on their bones, my frame was padded with undulating muscle. On my chest, there was the merest hint of breast, but it had no real softness to it; it was hard like the top of my arms. And on my stomach, two lines of four protruded out from the skin beneath, like rows of pebbles.

'You have been bred up to have remarkable dexterity in all aspects of physical labour and you are an extraordinary specimen, Alwin,' Rosamund said, a little colour rising to her cheeks, clearly visible to me in the half-light.

'But what about my mind?' I said. 'How could my thoughts have been manipulated without me knowing?'

'You are not alone in that, Alwin. Remember how I treated you when first we met? I could not see you were a person; I only saw you as an oblique representative of the man who wronged my family, or the men who assaulted the nuns – just as you only saw me as an example of a witch.'

'But why do we live like this?' I said. 'How can such a state have come to exist?'

'We are all governed by tradition and are forced to invent an artificial character to survive, and we have all come to accept our gaol. I have experienced great trouble in conforming myself to the world and thought I knew my own mind, but I can see now I was burdened with wrongful prejudice and I subjected you to false blame, for which I feel deep regret.'

'It is nothing compared to the manner in which I treated you, Rosamund,' I said, turning and seeking out her eyes. 'I wronged you very much. I almost took my hand to you! It was as though I were playing the part of an oppressive tyrant. I believed it was somehow expected of me. I weakened you, Rosamund. I weakened us both.'

'Your beliefs induced within you a false character, Alwin. It was not you; we are all tinctured by the manner of our upbringing, by the sights and sounds of our life, and we all suffer a great deal from presumption and pride.'

'It is true. I was schooled to think that most women were fools, incapable of being educated: what a fool to think such thoughts! And how did I not see what now seems so obvious?' I said.

'You did not see the need for change because the world you lived in suited you best. And we are all blinded by dogmatics and have become too afraid to trust our own thoughts. We have all been manipulated by the acceptance of tradition, our minds already tainted by the time we learn to speak. It is not our parents' fault, nor our grandparents'; who as a babe has the knowledge and strength to take on every human that existed before them?'

'You are right, Rosamund. It is ignorance and tradition that begets prejudice and subjugation.'

'And fear that drives them onward,' she added.

'But why does it never change?' I said.

'Because women are brought up to be physically weaker than men. Menses and childbirth weaken our constitution further and ...'

'But if women were bred up stronger,' I said, 'would we not all benefit? I do not believe disparity suits either sex, and with such false inequality, harmony can surely never truly prevail. But ... but Rosamund?'

'Say what you must.'

'I am not entirely certain the disparity is unique in its disfavour to women.'

'What do you mean?'

'I ... I was at the priory and witnessed that most lamentable tragedy,' I said, hurrying the words in the hope they might pass from my lips without leaving their mark on my mind. But even that brief reference called forth clamorous beats from the base of my heart.

'Oh, Alwin,' Rosamund whispered. 'Pray do not speak more of it.' She reached out her hand and laid it on my arm. My skin was hot beneath her touch; a concentrated heat that disorganised my mind and provoked a flutter behind my ribs, but it also gave me comfort and fortitude. And oh, how I cherished it.

'Not all the soldiers were brutal, Rosamund,' I went on at length. 'Some of them disapproved, some of them were good men, but they had taken much liquor and I believe each man supposed he was alone in his thoughts, dared not be the one to countermand all others and risk his own death. And there was a man named Ilbert. He tried to warn me, and he would not join in with the prejudice that was voiced. Some of the men were so savage in their bias, but only Ilbert had the courage to speak out.

'He said he loved his wife and that the bawdy songs and drinking must end. He paid for his fidelity with his life, Rosamund. But do you not see? Manly men and wicked women; that is the concept tradition would have us believe. But it is not a war between the sexes; it is a battle between good and evil, as it has always been.

'Men do have a greater physical strength than women,' I went on, 'and when they succumb to the call of the Fiend, they cause more damage and, as any coward would do, they vent their wrath and torture on a weaker vessel. But women in their own fashion can cause harm, too. Goody Tanner was quick to censure you in public, Rosamund; she knew many tales against you and might have had you hanged as a witch. She told me that on the day you were born the ewes slipped their lambs and the corn developed a blight.'

'But I was born on the feast day of Saint Nicholas,' Rosamund said. 'What lambs are born on 6 December?' she laughed. 'What corn is blighted in winter?'

'Goody may not have had strength in her arm or been able to brandish a sword,' I said, 'but her tongue was as sharp and adroit as any blade, and using tradition as a disguise, I suppose an evil soul can cause damage, whether it is male or female.'

With that, Rosamund looked at me and, between us, I believe we had hit upon some great truth. But with the satisfaction of understanding, there also came recollection of my own surrender to the dictates of custom, and shame blushed a taint on my cheek, as it also did on Rosamund's.

After that, I succumbed to an intense feeling of exhaustion and I experienced a sudden and irresistible inclination to sleep. My mind seemed overcome with stupor, bloated with a surfeit of endless questions and uncertainties, which foamed and fermented themselves to such a degree that I could not order my thoughts, could not begin to discover who I really was.

Rosamund sensed the limits I had reached, both in my mind and body, and she fetched a woollen blanket and had me lie down on the mattress beneath it. Then she lay down beside me and placed her hand on my shoulder, as though she knew I was a stricken deer, isolated from the herd, and needed soft hands to mend me.

So, there we stayed as the last drops of sunlight poured from western skies and the fragrance of evening mists curled through the windows. Dream after dream entered my mind that night and walked about my thoughts, bringing fierce mental conflict with them. Several times I awoke in confusion, a question on my lips but no power to voice it, or a cry issuing from my throat but no ordered thought to translate it. Each time I fretted, gentle hands were placed on my head and gentle words were whispered in my ear, and at last, the night fractured its blackness and daylight slowly filtered through the gaps.

I awoke with a suspicion, perhaps even an expectation, of change within me. I wondered if I might immediately begin to feel unburdened by tradition's laws of manly virtues; freed of the duress to be dauntless and valiant; liberated from the desire to impose my authority over the world, as I had been bred up to do. But although in my mind I had developed a broader understanding of my own self, I did not instantly feel that different. And there were aspects of my life I was extremely reluctant to relinquish; my independence; my aspirations; the respect I received from other men. So many advantages would be lost to me, so much potential would be stifled if I simply accepted the lot of a woman's world.

And so began a complex, internal dialogue, which would continue for the whole of the rest of my life: is it deceitful for a woman to assume the guise that fits her best and let the world believe what it will of her? Is it sinful for any and all humans to seek equality with their neighbour and offer reciprocal parity in return, irrespective of their sex or their intellect or haleness? With those thoughts dancing around my mind, I came to understand that hitherto, I had talked with received opinion, not one that was wholly my own; I realised in future, I must think with new thoughts, just like Rosamund, and not only learn the art of individuality, but also feel comfortable in its garb. Rosamund must have sensed the change in my demeanour, because her look had lost its gesture of pity and was now founded in affinity instead.

In time, the morning's fresh air further stimulated my wakefulness and Rosamund and I rose together at prime. Rosamund laid out bread, cheese and cups of ale for us to stave off our hungers, then we washed our hands and faces together at the water-pail and Rosamund chanted such a sweet melody as she did so; 'Angelus ad Virginem'. Then she took up a linen clout, handed me her basket and bade me join her on her morning walk.

The sun was risen above the treetops when we set out and gilt with its treasure it shone above us, gently steaming the morning as we wove through branches and boles, further penetrating the forest with each step we took. Every once in a while, Rosamund would find a store of swollen hedge-fruit heavy on the bough, and would have us pick it and lay it in the basket. Filberts grew aplenty, plump in their shells, and hips and sloes glowed bright and ripe on their stalks.

As I held the basket, and Rosamund loaded it with her harvest, I discreetly studied her. Each time she selected root-bark or a leaf or berry, she would tell me all its curative powers; which species of disease it would conquer and how its preparation should be undertaken. Her knowledge of herbs and berries far outreached my own and her navigation of the woodland paths was surely a feat beyond human endeavour. Once, she turned to me and the sun rayed its colour on her face. How soft on the eye she looked; and there for the first time, I saw her clearly, untrammelled by prejudice or customary contempt.

As the morning passed, we only spoke of immediate matters and did not touch on either old subjects or future hopes. Then, when the basket and clout could be filled no more, Rosamund led us deeper into the wilderness of trees and, with chequered sunbeams flashing through the canopy above us, she threaded a path through a series of wooded alures, which brought us out into a wide glade yellowed by the sun.

The air was warm – a breath of June in September – and birds swam splashless through the sky, the woods fairly ringing with their song; a ribbon of music that endlessly plaited itself through the forest. Steeped in the shade of a sycamore, she had me sit beside her on the trunk of a fallen larch that overhung a stream, the waters below us trembling with the wriggling fish beneath.

Happily we sat as time flowed about us; two pebbles in the stream of life, until at last, Rosamund said gently, 'If you will allow me, Alwin, I wish to tell you about my sister.'

'I would gladly listen to your tale,' I said. I meant it with all my heart, and so she began.

'Eleanor is her name, tender is her blossom, and she has but thirteen summers behind her. Her temper is always placid, but she has such a curious mind, and I shall love her as much as any other, for the sum of my life.

'In the springtime of yesteryear,' she went on, 'she took to wandering farther from home than she had ever done so before. At first it was to pick posy-knots from a brake where primmies and violets grew, and she would return home with blooms in her basket and flowers in her hair. But then, when the buds had finished their blow, still she wandered.

'I followed her, Alwin. I know I was wrong, but I could not think what else to do. Mile upon mile she walked, real purpose to her gait, and at last she met with a man; a nobleman arrayed in rich cloth, astride a black stallion with a scarlet belly band. He lifted her onto the saddle and rode away with her.

'When she came home that night, I told her what I had done and quizzed her on the matter, but she looked me in the eye and gainsaid me, told me I had mistaken her for another. She made sport of me, Alwin, and evaded further accusation by ridiculing such a notion. It was as though she had been schooled, as though her mind had been washed clean of what it knew before of morals, and false ideas had been planted and nurtured in their place. What enticements he had promised her, I shall never know, but he changed her, Alwin, manipulated her for his own benefit, without a care for the impact on her.

'I tried again to dog her footsteps in secret, as I had done so before, but she had been well trained and was wise to me. In time, she developed a sickness and we both knew she was with child. Right up until the day of birthing, she believed he would come for her and make her his wife, just as he had promised. But he never came. I do not believe he ever intended to. An unsigned letter arrived from him, not long before the baby was due, demanding his family's midwife attend Eleanor's lying-in, but my sister never replied, for by then her birth-pangs had come early. I pressed her to surrender his identity, but she would only say he was a nobleman, a fighting man and that he would come for her and their child.

'She complained of grinding pains in her belly, flashes of heat and chill on her skin, and she spewed in great quantity. Her frame was still too young to withstand the rigours placed on it and she became very distressed and could not prevent the temptation to deliver the infant in haste. The feet and breech presented themselves first and I suspected the infant had its navel-cord tight around its neck. The pulsations of the cord began to cease, but I could not bring the child's head to the air. I could not gain any purchase on the arms and shoulders.

'At last, I was obliged to use much force to extract the infant, but that only brought on a rapid flow of blood. When at last the head was freed, I gently placed my finger in his mouth, to permit air into his chest, but the babe died without drawing a breath. My sister never heard her baby's longed-for cry; his sweet voice never greeted our ears. Eleanor's own dear face became that of a child again and, fatally exhausted, with her last words she simply asked me for forgiveness.

'She blamed herself, you see, and said she had suffered from a lapse of virtue and had tempted her lover to come to her. She could only have been twelve years in age when she conceived. He debauched a child, Alwin; my sister; a matchless maid, and he tutored her to believe it was all her fault. He filled her belly with an infant and let her deliver it as a base-born sideslip, allowing her to believe she was immoral to have done so. What sort of man could do such a thing?'

I thought about Rosamund's question and clearly in my mind's eye I saw the nobleman's face and, deeper within his frame, I saw the two ghosts that dwelt inside him; that self-aggrandising, smooth-tongued lord, and his devilish and depraved counterpart. Like a man and his darker reflection, he was both divided and united; two men posing as one, and I could not but hope that one day I would see him again and rend his body in two; send both his souls to Hell.

'Rosamund,' I began, hesitant, uncertain. 'I ... I have met the man who did this to your sister.'

'How so?' she said, a frown at once darkening her features.

'He is the commander of the militia men who debauched the nuns at Winfeld. When you described him to me as we were leaving the town, I should have told you straight away, I should have helped you. But I judged you with the thoughts of a bigoted man looking down on the falsified image of a woman; I did not think freely ... or wisely. I can only pray that you forgive me.'

'Alwin, there is nothing to forgive. We cannot change the past. But are you certain it was him?'

'How flattering his tongue was and what evil lived behind his eyes; I am not mistaken and I shall never forget him. Just as you described to me, he was tall and strong of muscle and he rode a black stallion with a scarlet belly band.'

'And know you his name?'

'No. I asked one of the soldiers, but he was evasive. What a fool I was not to have been more persistent. But two other names I learned: Ilbert was one and the other was John of Stanton Magna. And Ilbert said his commander was from Walsingham, of that I am certain.'

Rosamund meditated on my words for more than a while, then said, 'This gives us more reason to continue on to Walsingham, Alwin, when your full health returns.'

'I would like it very much if we could journey on together,' I said. 'But what will you do when we find him?'

My question put her in pause and her eyes changed from borage to nightshade, then she said, 'I have made him a special tincture of smallage, henbane, hemlock and belladonna. First, he will be stupefied, then experience convulsions and delirium, before anxiety and madness will enter his mind. Then the belladonna will call up visions of beautiful women who will float through his disturbed imagination. But, of course, he will not be able to touch them and that will drive his derangement to a higher level, from where he will die in agony.'

When Rosamund spoke those words, there was no sense of pleasure on her lips or vindication behind her eyes. She even shivered a little as she listed the maladies and disorders that would intrude themselves upon him. I suppose, as an executioner wields his axe or a hangman ties his rope, Rosamund was intent on delivering justice. But the respect with which I had grown to esteem her made me wonder if she were instead demeaning herself, seeking some sort of wild revenge, which in its finality would only leave regret in its wake.

After that, we both fell silent, bygone times calling sadness to my mind. How painful truth turned out to be; how joyful and simple to live in ignorance. Such a short time since, and Rosamund knew not of her sister's corruption, and I was just a young man, a franklin farmer, who sowed and ploughed and kept his beasts in good plight. But all the while, a second reality was in existence, untouching and unknown. But once revealed, it could not be un-learnt and had already become a terrible weight that slowed life down and tinged the future with echoes of its sorrow. And with its sadness, it brought me much confusion and I wondered if I might ever be able to unspool it. At the heart of it all, I saw Mother's face and could not come at a reason she would wish to change me so.

At length, I asked Rosamund, 'Why would my mother lie to me?'

I did not ask the question in hope of an answer. What answer could there be? I spoke the words out loud, simply to proclaim their existence in the world, to test my own feelings and voice my sense of betrayal to another.

'I do not believe she lied to you, Alwin,' Rosamund said, gentle in her tones. 'She was just unable to tell you the truth.'

'But why? What possible reason could she ever give to explain why she corrupted me?'

'She did not corrupt you, Alwin; she protected you. You were her most precious jewel. All she did was hide your true identity, devoid of suspicion.'

'Hide it from whom?'

'Your grandfather, your father, perhaps others. It may be impossible to find out; you must prepare yourself for that, Alwin. Just remember how much she loved you, that she asked for your forgiveness and believed you would find the answers in Walsingham.'

'I ... I can never be certain that is exactly what she meant, Rosamund,' I confessed.

'What do you mean?'

'Mother was gravely ill. Her mind, it wandered and stumbled. She did say the answers lay in Walsingham, but she did not specifically send me there. I harboured so many doubts about myself, you see. I was so very frightened that night. I somehow clung to the strength that I believed dwelt inside me. I felt the need to exaggerate that strength, prove how brave I was and that I was a worthy son to her. I suppose I interpreted her words with a bias towards my own needs. I was selfish, foolish.'

'Or perhaps your mother knew how close she was to dying and was forced to be economical with her speech,' Rosamund said warmly, 'safe in the knowledge she could rely on your intuition to untangle her message and do what you thought was right and proper.'

'Was I right to set out on this journey, Rosamund?' I asked, searching her eyes as I spoke.

'The whole of life is a journey, Alwin. The rightness or wrongness of its purpose is beyond the limits of anyone's intellect.'

We sat in silence for some moments thereafter, then as the sun oared her circuit towards the western skies, Rosamund rose and I stepped into the rippling channel beneath us and steadied her as she climbed down from our perch, and she led the way back through the woods. Where before the morning sun had mellowed the autumn chill, the noon-spell hour brought cooler winds that stole leaves from the boughs and sent them tumbling about us, like so many unanswered questions.

Stepping along that woodland path, how easily my mind raised ghosts about me. The gusting wind became the sound of rushing water, the crackling leaves conjured themselves into orange flames, and I could neither dispel images of poor Adela and Matilda nor suppress recollections of how roughly the elements had treated the blossom of their girlhood in the final moments of their lives. The swiftness and violence of their deaths still tormented me and would always do so. Yet I had liked the maids very much, so I determined there and then to ensure I would always be slow to forget them, however much the sadness of their deaths shadowed the goodness of their lives.

I was mightily relieved when at last we crossed the cottage's threshold and closed the door behind us. I had come to view the little cottage as some sort of sanctuary; a place where an unwritten law of truce was upheld, where the force of ill-thoughts could be quelled, and both tomorrows and yesterdays existed only in another realm.

Just as before, weariness beset me long before the close of eventide and I was obliged to lie down and rest. With strength beyond that of my own, Rosamund raised a hearty blaze in the hearth and cooked a pot of pease-pudding and bran for our supper. Then as the eventide tones fell away to night, I made no appeal and Rosamund made no offer, but in silence, she lay by my side and took the sting from my night-time dreams and smoothed the creases from my midnight fears, just as though we were sisters.

The following days my mood improved; my strength prospered and I was better able to understand my new mind. In the mornings, Rosamund and I walked in the woods and it was there we spoke of our thoughts and fears. I told Rosamund again about Adela and how at first, I was certain she was with Father Oswald at the lake but had since reviewed my recollection with a new and critical eye and had refined my opinion to know it was a person in a priest's cassock, no more, no less; and may or may not have been Father Oswald.

In turn, Rosamund confirmed she had not clearly seen Father Oswald's face before the fire, and in hindsight could not swear to his identity. She also cautioned me to remember that Adela had believed the last visitor to Matilda was indeed Father Oswald, and that I must not erase all doubts about the priest, nor carry unconscious bias in my heart.

During those woodland mornings, we felt free to propound and suggest; were Goody, Father Oswald and William working in unity against us? Could the strange incidents that had befallen Matilda and Adela been accidental in nature after all? Was it Rosamund's knowledge of herbs and charms that had saved her? Were all matters in life linked with an invisible chain or were all things separate? Could the nobleman's evil act at the priory have set off a sequence of subsequent calamities? The questions seemed endless and the answers so dissatisfying, but it helped to ask and discuss them, then leave the words behind us on the forest floor amongst the dying ferns and ghosted leaves.

When we returned daily to the cottage, as soon as the door was closed behind us, we lived in another world and insulated ourselves against the mysteries and perplexities of the other realm that existed far beyond the margin of the woods. As each day passed, we became more at ease in each other's company and I could not help but smile when she was by my side, the warmth of her countenance always leaving its reflection in my own features. My strength returned and I made myself useful chopping wood, repairing pans and tending to the horses. Rosamund was never still, and she brought such homeliness to the little house, created a sense of settled tranquillity about the place that I came to hold so dear.

In the early mornings, with her voice carrying a smile in it, she bade me take my ease, and so I would sit on a stool and watch her baking loaves. I always loved the smell of the yeast, clean and fresh, with that enticing promise of goodness yet to come. I watched as she took all the component parts and merged them together in an earthenware bowl, caressed them and kneaded them; fused them into something new. Her hands, so steady and knowing, pressed and squeezed the dough and I found myself studying them; the colour of her skin, the shape of her slender fingers, the neatness of her nails. All the while, I could smell the faint trace of wheatgerm, hear the whisper of the dough as she drew her hands over and around, sending tiny gasps of flour into the air with the rhythm of her knuckles. She shaped and pulled the dough with the heel of her hand, her fingers working with firm assurance, and I could have watched her until the end of time. So, there I passed my mornings by the hearth, the soft heat frothing about me, kneading my skin, rising and encircling me like a crust, and the sight of Rosamund yielded great pleasure within me.

It was during those mornings that my life's conflicts had most effect on me. I supposed, as Rosamund suggested, my frame and flesh had conformed themselves into living the life of a man. Now, whether at repose or in vigour, my body still obeyed the instructions from my newly balanced mind and I experienced no difference from my life before. My reason demanded wood to be chopped or knives to be sharpened, and my muscles and limbs obeyed just as they had always done so.

It was in matters regarding Rosamund where I found most confusion. Some echo of my past learning as a man had left its mark beneath my flesh and I could not shake it off. I could not look at her without admiring her comeliness; jimp as a broom-stale she was, so handsome of face and form, and surely the seemliest of all things.

When we walked in the woods and our arms brushed, the place where we touched grew warm and sent a gentle ripple to the core of my heart; when we exchanged glances for more than a moment,

I always felt a flush of heat rising from my chest; and when I watched Rosamund making her wheaten loaves, a sudden heat rose up inside me, made my heart kick and my skin prickle, and it came to pass in my mind that I must be standing at the smithy's furnace, so hot the fire burned inside me.

The slightest look from her kindled heat beneath my skin, passion attempted new war within me and made me cherish a yearning for that which could never come. Father Oswald and Mother had taught me that there were two types of love: religious love and marital love, but there in the cottage with Rosamund, I began to suspect there might be a third; the love between two kindred souls. I suppressed the strange feelings as best as I could and Rosamund showed no sign she had noticed my struggle.

From then on, I was more particular in my actions. I took care not to walk as close as we had done so before and tried to evade her eyes as subtly as I could. Two or three times during our morning walks, I thought I might ask her why the flutters and shivers behind my ribs persisted, but when it came to the moment of asking, I had not the courage.

I was managing the oddity tolerably well, but then one morning we were obliged to remain indoors by stress of the weather. Busy and smart came the rain, vanquishing our habit of strolling through the trees. Rosamund baked her bread, as was her custom, but I took pains to occupy myself in carving a pot-stick from a hazel branch and averted my eyes from her all the morning.

After we had eaten our midday meal, Rosamund said she thought I was almost free of all malady and the wound had healed well. She said the final part of my remedy was to soak my body in a bath of medicinal herbs, which was a necessity in banishing the last remnants of poison from my flesh.

She had me fetch a wooden vat from outside the cottage, then she scrubbed it and placed a cushion of lamb's fur in it and then lay a sheet inside the tub, to line it for my comfort. She set about boiling roots and herbs, some fresh and some dried, in a cauldron over a vigorous fire. Hollyhock, mallow, fennel, scabious and flax all went into the pot and she also stirred in withy leaves and green oats. Sweet green herbs and lavender flowers she hung about the room, and through a fragrant mist, she had me disrobe and sit myself down in the vat.

She cooled the infusion with cold water and poured it over me one jug at a time. How soothing it was. But how unusual became the feeling on my skin. Rosamund took a basin of hot herbs and began to wash my shoulders and back, and her tenderness made me wilt. Outside, the rain suddenly abated and the afternoon breeze set sighs among the branches, sending a gust of perfume through the lavender stalks, bathing us both in its sweet fragrance. The cloud-rags blanched white, swam apart to reveal a river of blue sky and the air became solid with sunlight and smiled its warmth on my skin.

Sweet and benign Rosamund's manner was and gentle was her touch. It brought such liking to me and it should have been no more than a cleansing of my skin, but when she laid down the herbs and touched my flesh with her own fingertips, myriad pleasures arrived unsought, my breath became suspended and I thought I might pass away into a faint. As though a thread were strung between my skin and heart, I trembled within and with-out, as her fingers stroked their gentleness upon my neck, then slid themselves lower towards the mounds on my chest.

I supposed Rosamund had no knowledge of her effect on me. I tried desperately to think with my woman's mind, but the prickles on my skin and the tingles inside me spoke quite another language to me. At last, I could take no more of the bliss that was growing within me and in my confusion, I cried out, flung my arms wide and staggered to my feet.

What manner of creature was I, with a woman's body but still the desires of a man? The question left me in bewilderment and I could neither face Rosamund, nor tell her what my flesh had felt beneath her touch. Mired in disarranged feelings of ignorance and shame, I stooped to snatch up the foot-sheet and used it to dry myself roughly, then I dressed in my shirt and braies and sat shivering on the bed.

'Alwin,' she said in time, on bended knee, mopping the pools of water I had left in my wake. 'What is it?'

'I ... I cannot ... I do not quite know my self,' I said, holding my head in my hands, the words faltering on my lips. 'Some of my thoughts and words belong to the person I was before; I do not know what to think or what to say. I cannot reconcile my thoughts about ...'

'About what?' she pressed, with mild eyes and soft features, rising and stepping closer to me.

I shook my head, looked down at the floor, my face feeling flushed and awkward. I conjectured, but could not suffer to speak my thoughts, so I closed my eyes in the hope Rosamund would sense my discomfort, but still she advanced. I held my breath and compressed my lips, but she would not leave it be.

'I cannot abide wrongs and rancours,' I said, a surge in the heart-blood beneath my ribs. 'Let it lie, Rosamund! Let it lie.'

'Alwin, you must trust me,' she said in a whisper. 'Tell me what feelings you do not understand.'

I do not know how long I sat there in silence, but I turned the matter this way and that in my mind, at last admitting the truth. Finally, I spoke from the very core of my heart, I dragged and pulled the words from the privacy of my mind and laid them before her: 'I have begun to wish for you ... in carnality.'

CHAPTER NINE

When I was a boy of no more than six years, Father Oswald took me to the church in Giolgrave one summer evening and he promised I could ring the vesper bell. He sat me down next to the rope that hung from the bellcote and asked me to wait a while, until such time as he would return and give me the signal to ring in the mass.

I was filled with excitement at the responsibility and could barely wait until the bell's soft music was sent across the valley, all under the power of my own will. Father Oswald was delayed for the longest of ages, and in my young mind, the sound of the bell's laughter swimming through the skies was too marvellous and true to be withheld any longer. With no thought for consequences or reprimands, I tugged at the rope and tolled the bell with all my might; it was as though the clarity of the chime were held inside me and the honesty of its resonance could be contained no longer. At first, I was delighted at dispatching the peal, but as soon as the first note sang its way through the village, I realised it told tales of my guilt and could never be called back; I had condemned myself to unknown repercussions and could never reverse time's advancement.

That same feeling returned to me when I voiced my confusion about Rosamund; that fear I had brought my feelings forward too hastily. As soon as the words left my lips, I sat trembling, the deep murmurous after-hum of a recently struck bell ringing in my ears. It had seemed so right to say the words, to discharge my honest thoughts to her, but as soon as they were said, I realised there was no going back; and how Rosamund would react and how I would explain myself, I did not know.

I rose to my feet with some sort of notion that my height and strength might yet exude some sort of mastery and thereby end the difficulty. Perhaps I was clinging to the last vestiges of traditional masculinity in my body and mind. Perhaps I was simply too afraid to speak.

Rosamund came closer to me, until she was standing before me, and an urgent stirring shifted beneath my skin. My features petitioned for a soft answer and with lovely eyes she smiled on me, and the only prayer I carried in my heart was that God might place her in my arms. We stood there for a while and a while, the air sweet and fair about her, and it was there and then those first scattered seeds of true love began to take root in the deepest chambers of my heart.

We both moved closer. Our hands touched, her fingers soft and inquisitive. She took my hand in hers, and I gazed at her with joy-teeming pleasure. Then with charm in her eyes, she offered up a kiss, and my shy lips smoothed her budding mouth. I took the kiss warmly; and warmly did reply. That feeling! That shimmer of dew. It left me breathless, intoxicated.

Our lips briefly parted and Rosamund smiled; the sort of smile that answered yes to all my questions, then a ripple of happiness broke over her, and with my arms about her waist, I pulled her closer and stooped my lips to hers, and something potent and wonderful drew into puckers inside me.

I felt as though springtime were growing from within me; stirring, aching to yield up a treasure of precious things, dormant for so long, now ready to surrender its inner self and let bloom what was once held back. With her body pressed close to mine, something rapid and feverish beat inwardly that tugged at my belly; a gentle storm that rained its voiceless chant within me.

For an age we stood there, exploring with our lips, kissing away our inhibitions, caressing with our hands. Then Rosamund broke our bodies apart and with a smile in her eyes, she sat down on the bed and began to unbuckle her belt, untie her kirtle. She unpinned her sleeves, unthreaded her shift, discarded her woollen stockings and bared all the curves of her flesh to me. Then she divested me of my shirt and braies.

We lay down beside each other, my naked limbs met hers, her warm flesh taut against my own and her soft breasts yielding against me. With the abruptness of shyness, I set lip to the skin of her neck and she let out a murmur, then her lips found my own, and trembling, I held the taste of her kiss in my mouth. Quivering, breathless, I enfolded her in my arms, pressed her into me, gathered the shape of her to me and passed my hands over the curves of her flesh.

Endlessly we kissed and with each heart-pulse, a tremble ran through my frame, rising and surging. Something was building; a surfeit of fierce pleasure threatened to flourish inside me. Then Rosamund slowed the frenzy of our lips and tongues, and slid her hand between us, set her fingers to stroking my belly, and her touch fetched fire to my flesh.

Where her fingertips brushed my skin, heat spread outwards, tender and keen, then she touched her fingers lower and a thrill of passion ran through me. I put my hand to the slope of her hip, then let my own fingers fall slowly down between her naked-soft thighs. She let out a sigh and arched her back a little, then descended her fingers further and sent a feeling blushing upwards that made my heart leap and my insides feel quick; she drew such pleasure from me.

With rapture rising, I was tense with the desire to surrender, but impelled by a yearning to linger and possess, a delicious anxiety spreading itself inside me. Our lips found each other again and, through kisses and caresses more urgent than before, she gently held me in some sort of stasis, as though time between the hours were suspended.

A wild and persistent euphoria then swelled and dilated, ever expanding. At last, a potent-soft tempest broke inside me; a sublime unity of possession and surrender; the sum of both our souls rising within me.

Readily I yielded and could only let out a sigh from my throat and a long, soft moan from my mouth, then Rosamund grew tense against me, her own ecstasy reaching a crisis point, her limbs growing stiff about me. I kissed away her sighs and held her wildness tight against me until I felt her slacken, and the echoes of her pleasure resonated deep inside me – that final tremble of a parting storm. It was more than carnal; it was soft communion, sacred delight, and I had never been so complete, so alive, and I knew evermore that love was not an object to be desired, but an affinity to be earned.

There and then I gave her possession of my heart, unburdened with anything but love, for before that moment I had never felt such perfect bliss, and I could feel her love inside me; a gleed in the chambers of my heart, ever to glow, never to be extinguished.

They say time glides away and is lost to us at the moment of its passing, but although time may steal years from us, it can erase neither the pleasures nor the memories of the blissful happenings we are fortunate enough to experience, and the following hours and days that Rosamund and I spent together in our world in the woods were the greatest gift time ever gave a living soul.

There we lived in complete contentment, lost in our own seclusion, isolated but together and outside the fold of mistress and master, of lord and priest. There in the cottage, we had no cares for days gone by, no thought for future tomorrows; the light of

Heaven had placed us there, unborn and immortal, unbegotten and created anew.

Many times we sampled sensual pleasure and tasted the savour of each other, quite forgetting daytime routines. We could not sleep for long, so we ran our course with the moon and the sun and took liberal sip from the midnight cup. Morning passed and we could not stint from embracing; whole days were lost to us, borne away on the wings of our passion. I could not swear that time passed more slowly, but it plied its course both deeper and wider than it had yet done before for the sum of my life.

Sometimes, when the evening star rose, a delirious peace rendered us inert and we lay mingled on the bed for many a while, motionless and sated. Then a glint of starlight in Rosamund's eyes would strum a heartstring behind my ribs, passions would rise and we were helpless to fight it, until only the attainment of pure abandonment could release us.

I cannot be certain what spell of time passed as we laughed and loved in our sylvan dell, because my life existed outside the gauging of earth's spinning; days were not for toil, and nights were not for slumber. I suppose we must have dwelt in the cottage for no more than a fortnight, perhaps only ten days, but because we lived in the eternal now, time was not for measuring; it was simply for savouring. And each moment was unique and incomparable, every heartbeat replete with the giving and receiving of love that heated my heart and amended my soul.

With the expansion of our physical honesty, there also came a new freedom in my mind and I talked to Rosamund of my life on Crown Croft, how I loved the turning of the seasons and the glory of Nature; how I marvelled that Nature herself was ever young and though She slept in winter, every spring She returned and the world was made sweet and fair again. I told Rosamund precious thoughts I had confessed to no other; that however much I listened to Father Oswald, I could not help but believe that Heaven was not a place beyond the cold, blue sky where we go when our flesh dies, but instead was the living world all about us, pressed close to us, visible to all who chose to see it, and Heaven after death is just a memory of what beauty we once witnessed on earth. I told her of hidden cow-paths, where even Mother and Grandfather never walked, of the secret places where violets and periwinkles were always the first to push out their buds and where cowslips paved the way like links on a golden chain.

In turn, Rosamund talked to me about her life before. Her mother died during the birthing of Eleanor, she said, and her father in his grief then took to tankard and trencher, drank and ate to such excess that he eventually died of a surfeit, leaving Eleanor and Rosamund to the mercy of their uncle and his wife, with whom they lived until Eleanor died and Rosamund left for Walsingham.

'So is that where you shall return to, after ... when all this—'

'I cannot return to my uncle's,' she said, 'because his wife has a spite against me.'

'How so?' I asked.

'She despised my mother for her knowledge of folk-herbs and she scorns me for the same reason, as so many people do. So, my choice in life is either to find my own husband or to live as an outcast as Maud does, here in the woods.'

'Then you shall return with me to Crown Croft and we shall live there together, always,' I said, emphatic, final.

At that, we set aside talk of the future and the past and we returned to our blissful present of simply living and loving, as though the better land of Heaven were indeed this side of the firmament.

One morning we rose with flushed faces and tousled hair, washed ourselves, then set logs to the fire and raised a vigorous blaze, but there was a chillness in the air that had been absent before and the sky's white clouds were shot through with twists of grey. A northerly wind, keen and driving, started to blow, winnowed the thatch and rattled the shutters. Where before the air had been temperate: a lenient breath fragranced with the echoes of summer; on that particular morning it held the threat of winter in its grasp. A pinch of night-time frost wilted the dog-wheat and heart's-ease that grew outside the cottage's door and a slant of rain began to fall not long after daybreak.

The harrying winds made the trees shed their leaves in abundance, scattering them brazenly on the forest floor, leaving their branches naked and exposed. With the shedding of their garb, they had inadvertently opened up a portal to the outside world, and what before was an impenetrable dell, at once became less hidden, less safe. From then on, the world beyond the woods seemed closer than ever, the suspension of the present fell fast like a plummet and the future stood ominous and threatening before us.

I did my best to convince both Rosamund and myself that nothing had changed. We exchanged tender touches and croodled all the morning, but however much I resisted, thoughts of Mother, Father Oswald and pictures of my past sketched themselves inside my mind and brought recollections that were most sorrowful. Once or twice, I caught the look in Rosamund's eye that had me believe she too harboured melancholy thoughts, of her sister and the noble lord, but neither of us spoke up and the images persisted.

In that state of pendent inactivity, we might have remained suspended for an age. But not long into the afternoon, the horses began to be uneasy and a dog's bark echoed through the trees. I rose and went to the window, searched the glade with my eyes. At first there was nothing to see, then through the undergrowth and leaf litter, a black-and-tan terrier appeared, running and sniffing, then charging through the leaves towards the cottage. Some few paces behind the little dog walked a woman, a cloak about her shoulders, and her un-braided, silver-streaked hair blowing wildly about her head. Nimble in her step, she carried a willow basket in one hand and a brace of hares and a limp, brown hen in the other.

By then, Rosamund was at my side and as soon as she set eyes on the woman, she said, 'It is Maud.'

The woman opened the door and stepped lightly over the threshold, neither stiffness nor stoutness on the swerve of her bone. The terrier followed soon after, his trundle-tail wagging heartily and his fine, sharp muzzle charged with enmity towards vermin, whether imagined or real.

'Ah! Rosamund!' the woman said. She set down the capon, hares and her basket, then when she had peeled the burrel cloak from her shoulders, the two women embraced.

Maud then turned to me; her oval face was comely, her age not yet defined on her skin and she carried that same spark of freedom and self-possession I had admired when first I met Rosamund.

'Alwin Whittaker,' I said, bowing my head. It was the first time I had spoken my name out loud since arriving at the cottage and somehow it tasted different in my mouth. Before, it had been a cloak that hung about me, a sort of concealment that was always with me, but set apart. Now it represented a new beginning, a garment of skin that had become part of my wholeness, and I spoke its syllables in a freer, lighter tone.

'Alwin,' Rosamund said to Maud, 'did suffer a wound to the belly and I staved off the fevers with golden tincture of hemlock and vervain. Then I macerated valerian root and applied a poultice, just as you have taught me to do.'

Maud stepped closer to me and I lifted up my tunic and shift, that she might examine my midriff and the lesion made sound by Rosamund's healing touch. Like Rosamund, Maud's grey eyes were prominent when measured against her other features and lent her an air of wisdom.

'Fine work, Rosamund,' she said, then turning to me: 'Your life might have ebbed, Alwin, but for Rosamund's knowledge of herbs.' She looked at me thoughtfully, then in a good-natured tone she said, 'You are very fortunate, Alwin.'

When she finished examining me, I wondered if she suspected I was a woman and the thought sent a quiver, a sort of tiny shock, running through me. I wondered if, with a lifetime labouring in knowledge, it might have been suggested to her by the shape of my hips or the lie of my ribs. But unlike the new comfort of my name, I still did not feel wholly at ease thinking of myself as a woman. I could not help but wonder if tradition had dictated us to plant our flag with either one of the two sexes, when in fact there might be a third or even a fourth species; like there were dog-heads or Amazons. I was still pondering on that point when Maud sat down at the table and drew out a book, an inkhorn and a quill from her basket.

At first, still under the dominion of bigots and tradition, I believed she must have stolen them and I felt a ripple of disapproval run through my mind. Then, with Rosamund at her side, the two women talked of balsams, aromatics, tinctures and liniments. Every once in a while, Maud scratched the nib across a page and recorded notes, as meticulous and neatly as a cleric. How strange that if they had been men, they would have been respected for the knowledge they carried and given opportunities to share it; but there they were, outcasts, shut out from good hearts, with every man's hand against them. How different Wise Women were when compared to the way Father Oswald described them; they were not witches with black hearts who practised heresy and magic; they wore their wisdom like fine gemstones and were as learned as any scholar. How strange the world beyond the Whittaker woods!

At length, Maud turned her discussion with Rosamund to that of the lady she had been called to visit.

'An unusual distemper to strike a woman so tender in years,' she began. 'I suspect she is already at the turn of life and her belly is quite diseased. I gave her comfort with viscous syrup, had her take henbane smoke and raspberry leaf and made a mustard poultice for her. But the planets are against her, and her humours would not be balanced by the blood-letting.'

'She had also been vexed in her mind,' Maud went on. 'Just before I arrived, some lord and his men demanded hospitality at the manor house; pleaded kinship, the lady said. But they were liquored up and rowdy, so the lady's husband did send them on to the next township, but not before a scuffle had left their steward with a black eye and their stables set to flame. I was glad to be on my way, I can tell you, for fear the ruffians might come back.

'I would have returned to you sooner,' she went on, 'if not for the travellers I was called to apply remedies for in the village. Most years my services are requested once or twice a month, what with merchants and pedlars plying their course to the east in search of trade, but this year it is pilgrims that direct their steps to the east in great numbers; more than ever before, and it seems as though I must attend them every week!'

A strange feeling came over me on hearing talk of pilgrims. Where before the real world of flesh and blood had existed there within the walls of the cottage, and that other realm of reality beyond the fringe of the forest was mere truant fancy; all of a sudden, actuality turned itself about. Rosamund grazed her eyes upon me for a moment, a distant, dreamy look about her, as though she too sought reassurance I was there and not a figment of her mind. Then she spoke and her words seemed to pull me from one place to another. One moment I was living in a world of sunshine, birdsong and warmth. The next, I was standing on a cold clay floor, in a draughty wooden lodge that crouched itself in a copse of bare trees.

'Who were the people you attended to?' Rosamund asked Maud, briefly darting a glance at me.

'As I said, they were pilgrims: a man and his wife, and a priest,' Maud replied, and with those few short words, a change was heralded in, and there was nothing I could do to prevent it.

'What ailed them?' I asked.

'The woman was quite well, apart from her corpulence and busy tongue. She said an attack of fevers and gooseflesh, sudden and well-marked, had come upon the two men from nowhere and that God exempted her from the malady on account of her worshipfulness.'

'And what did you think about it, Maud?' Rosamund said.

'I believe both men had somehow submerged themselves in cold water and taken in poison from the lake.'

'You mean they both fell in?' Rosamund said.

'Whether by hazard or intention; yes.'

'And how fare the men, now?' I asked.

'They are recovered well enough, and all three travellers did leave yestermorning to resume their pilgrimage to Walsingham.'

'What road did they take?' I said.

'There really is only one route; the road that follows the old spirit tracks, where cairns and cromlechs were built by our ancestors, and churches now stand where pagan temples once were. It is an ancient and well-trod route and I know of no other.'

With that, I knew we would be forced to follow time's example and move forwards to another place, set our feet to fresh paths and ply our course to mutability. With a silent confluence of understanding, Rosamund and I had no need to discuss our plans to leave; they seemed set so clearly before us that words were unnecessary.

While Maud cooked up a pot of stewed hare, Rosamund washed our shifts and undergarments and hung them on the tree branches to dry in the wind, and I cleaned the saddles and tack with lavender oil and barley water. At sunrise the following day, we said our thanks and farewells to Maud and took our departure.

I left the cottage with sadness, for beneath its roof I had received more bliss than ever I could have wished. So warm and cosy had we been inside its four walls that I would not have cared if a tempest had started up outside. It would only have enhanced the sense of our serenity and had us hold the elements in further contempt, so safe and blessed I felt. In the naivety of my youth, I did not consider how quickly those precious moments would come and go, holding fast to you, then being blown away like ears of dog-wheat that catch on your legs and a heartbeat later are borne on the breeze to another world, another time. And if I had been able to guess the future, I would not have had the courage to leave the cottage at all.

But on the morning of the feast day of Saint Theodore, we set about our journey, determined to head east to Walsingham, the aspiration of wisdom and discretion my weapon of war. Rosamund led the way through the swaying oaks and larches, following the ribbon of stream that wound about the forest floor, and I rode behind. Fully recovered from the gash in my belly and the fevers that followed, and invigorated by fleshly pleasures, never before had my body felt in such fine case. But inside my heart and mind, matters were not in good plight. I experienced a depression in spirits, but at the same time felt restless in my thoughts. In turns, my heartbeat was impatient, then seemed to pause for an age, before a contraction would start it again, and all the while there was a tightening in my neck, as though something caustic were rising, and with anxiety so large in my throat, I could barely swallow.

We travelled on in silence but could have gone no further than half a mile, when I pulled rein on the banks of the stream, dismounted and humbled myself before Rosamund. With fevered air blowing all about us and trees creaking against the wind, she slid down from her saddle and we came together in gentle collision. She took me in her arms, but all my words silted on my tongue and would not flow.

'Tell me what is on your mind, Alwin,' Rosamund whispered.

'I ... I have lost sight of who I am, Rosamund,' I said at length. 'I am a woman dressed in men's raiment; I am two people, but I am no one. I acted a part, I know, but it was a part I knew so well. It seemed so simple to me, so natural. Now, I am to step out of the shadows and I do not know how to ... to be.'

'Sometimes in life,' she began, 'you live in fear of a happening, but you brave it through and the happening is nothing compared to the fear itself. It does not matter who you are, Alwin; it matters how you live. You cannot hide from yourself.'

'But,' I said, 'it is as though I have been brought up as a dog and someone has called me out as a cat. I do not know whether to bark or mewl.'

'You are made this way and can be nothing else. You must grin and abide it and learn to govern your own character, steer it for your own pleasures. And why would you want to be anything different? You are the perfect version of who you are. You are unique and beautiful, you are complex and varied, and I swear on the arch of Heaven's cope that I shall never love another.'

As she spoke, the beauty of her soul was brought forth in her eyes and I gathered up the look she gave me and hold it still to this day in my heart. We stood in tight embrace for many a while and then I struck on a thought. I untied the purse of coins from my belt and fished my fingers inside until I caught hold of the pearl ring. Mother had said I would know what to do when the time came; and the moment had arrived, I felt certain. I held the ring in my hand and my fingers trembled around it and doubts encircled my mind.

'But can we still be sweetings, Rosamund,' I said, 'out there in that realm of reality? Will you not be discomfited if we are mocked and scorned?'

With lip and eye both smiling, she simply said, 'Faithful love carries no shame, Alwin.'

I took up her right hand, slid the ring on her fourth finger and said, 'I love you with a hundred hearts, Rosamund Blackmere.'

To speak from my heart, took the splinter right out and where before I had deliberated on how I might begin my new life, I realised it had already begun.

We rode on side by side and where the landscape allowed, we joined hands. At first, the day dawned brightly, the weather was benign and a weak sun marbled the skies, then wintry gusts blew in from the east and we were obliged to ride on beneath shadowless clouds through the hiss of slanting rain. The sky drew a token of colour from the ground beneath it, and vapours tinged with greys and browns went sailing over the horizon, harried by the easterly breeze, and the weather, being intemperate, urged us on at a tight pace and we covered many a mile.

For hours at a time, we saw nothing but sheep-tracks and meadows, heaths and holts. We followed a brook until it was no more than a rusty thread stitched into a patchwork of mead, until eventually we arrived at a township.

Half the size of Alfricstowe, it sat in a shallow dell alongside a stream where footfalls had poached the little watercourse into nothing but mud. Sparse trees grew alongside its banks, their branches already rubbed bare by the northerly winds, and swine roamed the town's out parts, feeding themselves on beech-mast and chestnuts. We followed a goose-girl as she drove her gaggle through the west gate, and market men and vendors were busy trading at their booths and stalls. Despite the low cloud and chill air, there was the distant hum of revelry, and as we rode along the master-street, the day resounded with a din.

In my ignorance of mind, I had supposed we lagged behind Father Oswald, Goody and William, them having set off a day before us. All throughout the day, I had wrestled with the tortures of meeting Father Oswald face to face and confronting him with the doubts I harboured. But I had convinced myself time would abide and give me room to resolve the conflict of reason that dwelled within me. It was Rosamund who took note first; she saw Father Oswald at a distance leading his mule into the inn's yard. She touched her hand to my arm and pulled rein, and we both sat perfectly still. Our future fate was upon us already and the reversion of easy days was far away.

CHAPTER TEN

I watched Father Oswald as he led his mule beneath the inn's archway and to the courtyard beyond. He walked slowly, with a greater stoop than was usual, his head sloping downwards in an attitude of dejection. He paused just once and touched his hand to his worn and mud-flecked satchel, then continued on until I could see him no more, and I could not help but look at him with fond eyes, in spite of the corruption I suspected he harboured in his soul. Although visitors were always sparse on the doorsill at Crown Croft, the cleric never stinted on his time with us and eagerly frequented our homestead, whatever the season or weather. He always applied his mind to piety and virtue, and laboured hard in his duty as a priest. My childhood days were littered with his words of kindness and acts of Christian love; he schooled me in scripture, logic and rhetoric; he taught me how to be a scribe of Latin, French and English; he showed me how to ride; he read me psalms and proverbs and told me what a fine young man I was.

In spite of the malady in his haunch-bones, he was handsome enough and well-made and I only ever saw benevolence in his eyes and would struggle to name the qualities in which he was wanting. Seeing him there at the inn, after all I had experienced, I wanted nothing more than to run to him, clasp him to me and have him say words that would make amends; tell him all I had learned about life and myself since last we met; tell him who I really was. But alongside those feelings of favour, I could also sense a deep-brooding distrust in the chambers of my mind and could not rebuke the suspicions that rose in wave upon wave whenever I meditated on Matilda and Adela. At last, Rosamund sensed my tangled thoughts, and she broke the thread of my reverie by touching her hand to mine.

'Alwin,' she said. She dismounted and gathered up her pony's reins in her hands, then looking up at me, she went on, 'Sometimes we are all guilty of thinking about future prospects, both good and ill. But to assume reality will in any way reflect what we have presupposed is reckless. I must admit I thought we could simply confront Father Oswald, Goody and William with our suspicions. But now we are here, I sense the danger to be too great. What do you feel about it, Alwin?'

I slid down from my saddle and walked alongside Rosamund as we turned our horses about and retreated down the master-street. Then I glanced briefly over my shoulder, stopped, and fronted her.

'I know you are right,' I said. 'But we cannot walk away. We cannot fear our destinies.'

She smiled at me, as though I had spoken a significant truth, a very high thing that was much to her liking.

'Then we must bide,' she said, resuming our walk, 'and invent a stratagem to suit our purpose. We have an advantage over them: they do not know we are here or that we are working together.'

'But what can we do to avoid a hostile attitude if we do come face to face with them?' I said.

She meditated on my words for a moment as we walked, her eyes bright and thoughtful.

'We could perhaps retrace our steps,' she said quite suddenly, 'and gain intelligence from the monks at the abbey Father Oswald was called to visit?'

'We would lose too much time,' I said, 'and there's no reason for the abbot to speak to us.'

'Perhaps,' she tried again, 'the abbot has had a scribe record ...'

'That is it, Rosamund!' I said, stopping and placing my hand on her shoulder. 'Father Oswald always carries a satchel with his papers in it. He writes a sort of calendar and makes a record of his actions. It might hold vital information. I must find a way of distracting him, create enough time for me to read the papers in his bag.'

I spoke the words plainly with only the merest of hesitation on my tongue, but inside, my heart was beating like a shrewmouse's.

'Alwin,' Rosamund said, her eyes gentle. 'Is it not better if I ...'

'No, Rosamund. It must be done and I shall be the one to do it. Let us wait until the daylight begins to ebb and the shadows grow blacker about us. Then at dusk, when the inn is crowded with townsfolk, I shall take his satchel by stealth, read his chronicles, then return them to him before he knows they are gone.'

My tone was brimming with decisiveness, but I could also feel the sting of folly behind my words. I had always tried to apply reason and logic to the steps I took in life, but since leaving Crown Croft I had begun to rely more on my feelings, as though my heart had become stronger than my mind and was lending greater credence to sympathies. Initially, I inwardly chastised myself for growing weak in my brain, but as time went by, I began to see it as a strength; I was reading life's complexities better than before and was surely wiser today than yesterday. As we walked back through the town, I gradually quelled all sense of sin and blot and, as we tied our horses to the hitching post, I had already begun to edify my conscience over stealing the satchel, with thoughts of justification.

To blend ourselves with regular townsfolk, we visited the stall of a man selling wooden-wares, then we talked a while with a youth pushing a handcart charged with pears. Finally, the sure and certain stroke of time passed and, as the evening's blue tints infused the air, we collected our horses and took ourselves to the inn.

The inn's shutters were not yet closed and the sound of merrymaking, chant and instrument surged in waves from within the hostelry; first hollers, then laughter crested with the piping tones of a shawm, followed by a lull infused with mumbled conversation and the occasional plucks of a harpist. As we passed by the open windows, each leading our horse on a short rein, we both searched the parlour with our eyes. I scoured the scene, brushed a sweeping glance from flagstone to rafter, every trestle and bench; studied each form and visage. Myriad faces I observed before at length, my heart gave a kick behind my ribs; seated on a bench beside the central hearth were Goody and William, their complexions ruddy and cups of ale in their hands. But Father Oswald was not there.

'Where can he be?' I whispered to Rosamund.

She pondered for a moment, then said, 'Perhaps he has left the town and sought harbourage at a holy place.'

I drew in a sigh and nodded my head in agreement. Deferment of my planned deceit offered me the briefest of comforts, but the disappointment of not being able to discover at least some small grain of information was hard to stomach indeed. We stood for a while in silence, thinking how we might best proceed. Rosamund's horse fidgeted, played its mouth on the bit, and mine dipped its head and nosed the ground. Then from inside the inn there happened a commotion.

Both the man piping on his shawm and the harper stopped their melody in an instant, and the hubbub of conversation bluntly halted. One man's voice rose above all the rest, his words slurred and nonsensical. Other deep-throated voices joined in and then the inn's door burst open and two men dragged a third out of the parlour-room by the scruff of his canvas tunic, throwing him roughly to the ground.

Both our horses started back, Rosamund's throwing its head into the air and pulling the reins from her hands. She caught the straps and gently pulled the horse's head down, patted its neck and spoke gentle words to it. A scuffle ensued among the three men, then one of the two victors turned about and re-entered the inn; but the other, dressed in a bull-hide barm-cloth stained with ale slops, lingered with a threatening look until the third man lifted himself out of the mud and staggered away into the gloom, muttering oaths beneath his breath as he parted.

'Are you the innkeeper, sir?' I asked at length, when the defeated rogue had quite gone away and the man in the apron had calmed his look.

He squinted through the half-light, taking my measure, pushing up his worn and frayed fore-sleeves as though he might take a swipe at me. I stood, apprehensive and stiff, worried he might be able to see me for who I was; a woman in tunic and chausses. But I believe in the end he was still quelling the anger wrought by the sot he had just turned out, and after a while he said, 'Aye, lad. Why do you ask?'

'I am looking for a pilgrim priest, sir. My … wife and I are supposed to meet him here. He came with two other travellers and …'

'Oh, I remember the pair, they are inside. Come in and …'

'It is only the priest I seek, sir,' I said. 'Know you where he is?'

In my haste of thought, my tone had become more severe than I intended and the innkeeper eyed me with mistrust.

'He took sup,' he said stiffly, 'and went directly to his sleeping quarters.' He jerked his head towards the yard behind the inn and, giving me one further look with narrow eyes, he returned through the door and went about his business.

'My heart knows neither peace nor comfort when I do not speak the truth,' I said to Rosamund when we were alone.

'It is right that you doubt,' she said with wisdom in her eyes. 'But it is only by doubting that we come at the truth.'

Her words and her look blushed warmly inside me, seemed to hold all perils at bay and with her at my side, I felt stronger, better. We took a further moment to allow the horses to calm down, then we made our way through the arch in the centre of the building, to the courtyard at the rear of the inn.

At first, I was hopeful my foray into the world of deception would be short-lived, because the inn was small and access to the sleeping quarters was made easier by an external stair that ran from the courtyard to the upper floor. When we first arrived, the yard was devoid of man or beast, the horses were stabled and the ostler was absent, and all those signs gave me reassurance.

The light faded quickly, the shadows blackened and a low mist did sodden the air, rendered everything greasy to the touch. Two cressets had been flamed and gave off a meagre glow, and a lantern was hung on a nail outside one of the stable doors, but the light was more deficient than I had expected and I did not know whether that boded ill or good.

Outside the courtyard on the master-street, passengers and travellers still made their way to the inn and a burst of orange light flashed each time the hostelry's door was opened and closed, but no one entered the yard and, as each moment passed, I grew in daring. With Rosamund standing between the two horses, the reins from each animal grasped in her hands, I took up the lantern, hastened upon the appointed task and made my way towards the wooden steps.

The moment I placed my hand on the rail, in the tail of my eye I caught sight of a shape shifting in the shadows. I stopped and turned about and, seeing it was just a dog – a rather ragged looking lurcher – I turned back to my task. The dog however, whom I assumed had been sleeping behind the steps, was not so keen to return to the status quo. Instead, it hurtled about the yard, nosing through the loose straw, chasing its own tail.

In a heartbeat, our horses took fright, throwing their heads back, widening their eyes and stamping their feet. With just one bridle to hold, Rosamund would have had the strength to calm the animal down, but with two ponies simultaneously shying and rearing, she could not control the both of them. One continued to rear and the other dropped its head between its knees, arched its back like a barrel, distended its flanks and proceeded to buck, as though a wolf had pounced on its back and was gnashing at its withers.

I had no choice but to drop the lantern, shoo the dog from the yard and take up the reins of the bucking pony. In time, Rosamund's horse returned to its former placid state, but mine simply would not settle. An age passed and still the animal was fresh, and with time advancing and opportunity diminishing, I came to realise our plan was born of folly. I looked across at Rosamund; she was leaning slightly forward, the reins in her right hand, her left hand placed flat on her belly.

'Are you hurt?' I asked.

'No. It is just a strain,' she said breathlessly, 'but I cannot hold both horses, Alwin.'

'Then come. Let us take ourselves away from this place. We will think of another plan and ...'

'No, Alwin. I am recovered well enough. But you must hold the ponies. Let me look for the documents; we cannot squander this opportunity.'

I breathed an agonising sigh, shook my head and frowned. But I had no real reason to gainsay her, so in the end, I nodded and, with dark misgivings, I said softly, 'Be careful, Rosamund.'

She gave a half smile, then once I had taken up the reins of both ponies, she turned, picked up the lantern and began to climb the stairs. Her foot slipped on the first step and she curled her fingers around the rail to steady herself, then one step at a time, she crept up those creaking stairs with only darkness visible above her.

At the top of the steps, she lifted the lantern and illumined a gallery that led on to a number of doorways. The first two doors were partially open and when she pushed each of them wider, she turned to face me, shook her head, and I assumed the rooms were empty. The third door was closed and latched. Rosamund took a moment to compose herself, then reached out her hand and pushed it open. It stuttered on its hinges and gave a faint whine as she pushed her weight against it. Gingerly, she lifted the lantern higher and cast a pale beam through the doorway, then she stepped inside the room and both she and the light were lost to me.

Several moments went by, tense and drawn in their passing. I walked the horses around the courtyard and then had them halt. I barely moved and I could only breathe in short and shallow gasps; the thought of Rosamund being discovered lay close upon me. I waited and watched, then at last Rosamund appeared from the room. She pushed the lantern out before her, raised the satchel with her left hand with an air of triumph, then knelt on the gallery boards and concentrated the quivering light on the papers, which she withdrew one by one from Father Oswald's bag.

I watched her scan each wafer of paper with her eyes and how sorely I regretted standing there, surely about to bring mischief down on our heads. I could even hear Father Oswald's voice from days of yore inside my mind, telling me that even our Lord Almighty had not the power to make a deed undone.

In time the documents were read and placed back and the satchel was tucked quietly inside the doorway of Father Oswald's room. With a surge of relief rushing through the pipes beneath my skin, Rosamund finally began to descend the steps.

She raised the lantern, but its light barely illumined the shadows. She looked over the stair-rail and down into the courtyard towards me; I led the horses to the base of the steps, ready for us to ride away. I was so glad the distasteful business was over, and such was the alleviation of my anxieties, that I was far less cautious than I might have been.

With the lantern returned to the hook from which it was fetched and Rosamund safely mounted on her horse, I let down my guard and did not see the man who was entering the inn's yard. He had no lantern of his own and seemed to appear from nowhere out of the darkness. Rosamund, thinking I must be right behind her, had her pony trot beneath the archway and out onto the street, but before I could step my foot into the stirrup, the man was standing next to me, as close as he might be without touching.

He swayed, unsteady on his feet, and reached his left hand out for me, but missed. He staggered and thrust his arm out again, grasping my shoulder to steady himself, but his half-lidded eyes were unable to focus on me, and they wandered this way and that with a life of their own. He seemed confused, then opened his mouth and laughed, and his breath was foul with liquor. I brushed his hand away from me, took a quarter turn that I might stand in the light of the cresset, point the way to his room and let him be gone, but in an instant, I wished I had not stepped into that light.

In a heartbeat, I saw the tear on the sleeve of the man's canvas tunic where the innkeeper had thrown him to the ground, then as his face grew clearer in the half-light, I noticed his raddled skin and the tufts of whisker on his chin; not only was it a face I loathed, but also one I hoped I might never see again: it was the face of John Stanton.

I believe at the same moment I recognised him, he discovered the recollection of me. With his heavy face turned towards me, he frowned and his eyes regained their forward fix. At that, I pushed John Stanton aside and managed to mount my pony. Somewhat sobered by our encounter, John collected himself, unlocked his jaw and cast forth such a shout.

'Alwin! Alwin of Whittaker,' he bellowed, sending his voice brittle on the air about the courtyard.

I kicked hard against my pony's flanks and urged it forward to follow where Rosamund had guided her horse only moments before. But John Stanton was quick to dog my steps and, before I could steer the pony out beneath the archway, the soldier lunged his arm through the darkness and caught my foot with his hand. I thrust out my leg with violence to shake off his grasp, but he would not let go. With my horse turning in circles, rearing and trampling, at last I freed myself, John Stanton fell to the ground and, with his head still befuddled with ale, he could only lie prostrate in the mud.

'My lord and master,' he rasped, 'is on the road back to town as we speak. You had best watch your step, Alwin of Whittaker!'

I must confess, I struggled to cast out the fear those words imbued within me and, stricken with fright, my body seemed to communicate my anxiety to my horse and it took more than a moment to calm him; he fidgeted, backed away from the inn's entrance and fought for his head. It was as I was taming him down to obedience, that I heard a sound wholly unexpected, which touched deep memories in my heart and stopped me in my tracks.

'Alwin?' came the tentative call, the voice high above me, falling down from the darkness, then again, 'Alwin!'

I turned my eyes to the source, and there on the gallery was Father Oswald. He held a solitary candle in his hand and the flame barely lit his face. Perhaps if I had seen his eyes or studied his features, I could have judged once and for all whether he was for good or ill. But just his voice was not enough for me to decide. At first, I thought his tones conveyed disbelief, then perhaps betrayed the lightening of a burden. But I could not be sure and in the space of a heartbeat, I suspected the stress of his voice was accusatory; a timidity that told tales of deception and discovery.

In the end, it was Rosamund's voice that called me to my senses; she had brought her pony to stand beneath the inn's archway and was calling my name with urgency. At last I took control of my horse and set him to a fine gallop that carried me out and away from the inn.

Side by side, Rosamund and I charged through the twilight and on towards the east gate. The reeves and burgesses of that township surely had no intent to keep the streets sweet, for they were mired in mud and filth, and littered with debris from the day's trade and barter. Twice my horse shied at discarded pigs' carcasses and Rosamund was forced to have her pony leap a broken barrel. Some of the townsfolk shouted at us and shook their fists; one man dropped a sack of apples in his fright and the fruits were trampled to a pulp as we passed, but most folks heard us coming, pushed their handcarts out of our way and backed themselves into the shadows to let us pass unhindered.

As the light from the flamed braziers faded behind us, we finally left the town and slowed our pace to a trot. It took some moments before my breath steadied itself and for an age, we both travelled on unable to speak, our mouths agape with air passing loudly from our chests.

'Do you suppose they will send watchmen after us to seek reparation for those apples?' I said, pulling at the reins to slow to a walk.

'No,' Rosamund said, quite certain. 'That was just an accident. We are not citizens and we have not threatened any of the townsfolk with violence, so they will not have a care to trouble themselves.'

'You are right,' I said. 'I am sure Father Oswald will not wish to court attention either, even if he does suspect we tampered with his documents. But we are not safe on the road at night, Rosamund. We must seek hospitality at the first homestead we find. John Stanton did warn me that …'

'Hush, Alwin,' she said. 'Listen.'

I harkened and, in the distance, there was the sound of a horseman approaching; perhaps two, or more. The light was fading fast; it was at that singular heartbeat when the treetops are black but the sky still holds a tint of blueness, when day and night pass so close they brush elbows as they go by. I looked about us, for a place to where we might retreat until the travellers had passed, but the trees to our left were too far away and the thickets to our right, that led down to the stream, were not easily navigable.

'There is no time to hide or return to the town,' I said.

From then on, John Stanton's words and the possibility of coming face to face with the nobleman rendered my tongue a useless organ, and I could do nothing but sit in silence and urge my horse forward. I was certain it was the best and safest action to take; why unnecessarily alarm Rosamund when the chances were that those travellers were simply merchants or perhaps pilgrims? They say the greater part of trouble lies in your imagination, so why have Rosamund imagine what might never pass? Perhaps it was sense; perhaps it was cowardice. Whatever the justification; Rosamund, in her innocence, clucked to her pony and on we went.

The skies were clear that night, the stars already flamed with a white gleam, the moon a disc of doubt that hovered just above the horizon giving off a clew of pale light that coloured all the world in tones of grey. Five score yards we travelled and no more through that cold, half-light, before two horsemen rounded a bend and approached us head-on.

I pulled my hood over my head and, as we converged on the riders, Rosamund and I drew rein and had our horses move aside. It was not until the travellers were almost upon us that I knew I had seen the lead horse before; its black coat glistening, the furniture on its back holding silver threads of moonlight and casting them back into the night, as though the horse himself were made of metal.

The horse's rider was barely visible against the background of trees, his rich array muted by the darkness, the blood-red colour of his Flanders cape, his sparkish clothes beneath it, and his mount's scarlet belly band, all transformed to drabs and greys beneath the scant starlight. The horse looked weary and I noted the patches of broken skin on its flanks where the nobleman's rowel-spurs had dug deep into the animal's flesh. The sergeant followed on behind, his horse on a slack rein, the animal's nostrils wide and steamy, as though it had travelled a significant distance at some speed.

As soon as I recognised the nobleman, the cold night air seeped beneath my flesh and touched the core of me. My skin prickled, my heart thumped hard, and I seemed to lose all power of strength in my body and senses; it was as though the night were a bank of earth that was sliding down on me, holding me fast.

The moment I caught the vagrancy of Rosamund's gaze, I could tell she knew we were face to face with the man who had defiled her sister, and I suspected she also knew I was overcome with doubts in my ability to end his life. So many times since Winfeld, inside my mind I had rehearsed the moment. I would draw my knife from my belt, look with steely unforgiveness in the man's eye and sink the blade deep into his black heart. But there, outside the safety of my dreamscape, where the opportunity was so real and decisive, so final, I could not muster the boldness to do it, and was forced to blench from my purpose.

At first, the lord and his man paid little heed to us and I believed, in their weary state and at such a late hour, they wished to ride past and on to the town. I kept my head down, passive, anonymous and benign, shrunk myself low into the saddle so they would not recognise me. They glanced at us briefly as they passed and the sergeant nodded his head, and I thought the danger must be ended, then out of the darkness, Rosamund spoke.

'Sir?' she said, pulling her reins to the left that she may face the nobleman. 'Do I know you, sir?' she asked, her bold tone causing me great anxiety.

The nobleman pulled rein, turned his head and looked slantwise at his petitioner through the half-light. I wondered what thoughts chased around his mind when he heard that voice. How similar were Rosamund's tones when compared to her sister's? How common were their familial features? It certainly held some strange effect on the man for an instant, as a sudden contraction of spirit seemed to put out his eyes and, as though a spectre hovered before him, he blinked his lids quickly and shook his head to dispel whatever vision he thought he saw. Then collecting himself, he turned his horse about and fronted Rosamund.

'I am certain I would not forget such a face as yours,' he said, that honey-tongued insincerity returning to his voice.

I coughed, kicked my pony's flanks and held my reins low and tight, made the horse give a little rear and paw the ground. I was in such a disorder of my spirits.

'Heed not my brother, sir,' Rosamund said. 'We are keen to reach our destination up yonder before the thick of night. I shall detain you no longer. I was mistaken; I thought I had visited you as a child at your family seat in Walsingham.'

That put the nobleman in pause and he scrutinised Rosamund more closely, squinted his eyes through the darkness. Then a sly look fell over his features.

'Indeed, lady. I can recall the very visit,' he said, the lies drifting fog-like from his cloven lips.

'The time and place I can recall with clarity,' Rosamund went on coolly, 'and I could never forget such a fine young man as you were, but it is your name I have sadly lost to my memory, sir.'

'Roger de Marsh,' he said, bowing his head as though he were a gentleman.

'Of course; de Marsh,' Rosamund repeated, nodding her head.

'And you are?' he asked and, in his tone, he talked archly.

But for ill or good, Providence dictated that Rosamund would never answer that question, because behind us, in the direction of the town gates, came the plaining of dogs and the cries of men's voices.

'There is a commotion in the town, sir,' Rosamund said. 'Your services may be needed there, and we must be on our way. I shall be in the vicinity for a number of days; perhaps we shall cross paths again? I should very much like to cast light on fond reminiscences. Adieu, until we meet again, Roger de Marsh.'

And that is how Rosamund defended us both against a murderous tyrant, with neither a poniard on her belt nor a sword in her hand. Where I had been brought up always to use brawn, so Rosamund – subjugated by feminine bodily development as she was – defeated him with her brain. She had played up to his self-interest, allowed him to sup full of her flattery and stolen from him a vital piece of information without him even suspecting the theft had taken place.

In the blink of an eye, we turned our horses back onto the road and galloped away into the night. I called out to Rosamund that we must head for the woods, so we both pulled a left rein and rode hard until we were absorbed by the trees' shadows. We stopped briefly beneath the screen of branches, only the slightest sprinkling of moonlight penetrating the canopy above us, and we looked back towards the town where lanterns flashed and shouts travelled hot on the air. Whether a hue and cry had been raised by Father Oswald, John Stanton or the apple-man, I knew not, but the prospect of following us blindly into the darkness was too much for the townsfolk; the clamour died away and the lights disappeared one by one until we were left quite alone in the blackness.

'I ... I could not kill him, Rosamund,' I said, pushing my hood back over my shoulders, the darkness so thick beneath the trees that my voice seemed to exist as a separate entity. 'I thought I would have the boldness to take the knife from my belt and sink it into his heart, but I could not.'

'Because your own heart is too good, Alwin,' she said. 'You are strong, but you did not witness what that monstrous man did to my sister. I think a token of his blackness dwells yet in my own heart, Alwin, which cannot be got out until I set things right. Strength is a good dog, but Justice is a better one, and I will one day assign the justice to Roger de Marsh that he is due. Tonight, we were caught by surprise, but next time we meet him, I will be ready.'

Just as before when we sat above the little stream in the woods, Rosamund's words of justice sounded more akin to revenge, and I worried how matters would come to pass when that final confrontation happened. I wondered, if after all, I might find the strength to end de Marsh's life; not in an act of revenge, but as a means of preserving Rosamund's soul, for I loved her so dear that I could not let her carry the burden of murder and would rather condemn my own soul than see hers lost.

It was the call of a screech owl that cut my thread of thought; it soared down from the top of a pollard oak, carrying moonlight on its wings as it glided down from above us. And seeing a creature of the night come to life like that further served to endorse my discomfort at travelling through the darkness and had me think of contrasts.

Not long since, I was a farming man rendering my obedience to the cycles Nature dictated. Many a time, I lay awake beneath the rafters of the house at Crown Croft as the night passed by, listening to the nightingales, screech owls and vixens that sang their calls through the Whittaker woods. But our two worlds were distinctly separate and never the twain did meet. Suddenly, I had crossed over. Trees were still trees and land and sky were still down and up, but everything had changed and I was a different creature; a stranger in a new world, as opposite and different as night and day.

Rosamund was changed, too. The candles of vitality that dwelt behind her eyes had at last burnt themselves out and she slumped forward a little in her saddle as our ponies walked on through the night, Rosamund looking weary with both physical exhaustion and over-busy thoughts. Seeing how tired she was, I tried to let the moments pass by in silence as we rode on, but then a thought would enter my mind with such force that I was obliged to speak it out loud. I could not help but talk about Roger de Marsh, speculate on what circumstances would create such a devil of a man. I talked about his features, how they were regular and well-set, and that he should be considered handsome with his thick black head of hair and fine sable whiskers. But it was behind his eyes the evil lurked, I concluded; that was the source of his persuasive eloquence, which spoke unholy rhetoric that moved the blood and sent shivers down the spine.

'There is such darkness behind his narrow, pitiless eyes,' I reaffirmed. 'Did you see it, Rosamund?'

'Yes. Yes, I did.'

'And what dishonourable house he hails from, I cannot guess,' I went on. 'His father must surely be brutish, and Heaven help his siblings and scions.'

After that, I sank back into silence. Later, I asked Rosamund what new opinions she held of Roger de Marsh now she had a clear picture of the man in her mind, and a little further on I enquired what she had discovered in Father Oswald's satchel; but on each occasion, she gently declined to discuss the matters further and begged that we may defer all thinking until after we had refreshed ourselves with sleep.

So, on we travelled for many a mile, riding long past the mid of night before we finally stopped. Where previously moonbeams lit our path, clouds suddenly curtained the moon and stole away our sight, then a fine rain fell down about us and dusted our faces with a cobweb of moisture. With the light too dark to see beneath the trees, we adhered to a sheep-track that wound through copse and scrub, and in time it led us to the ruins of a homestead.

Perhaps its dereliction was a legacy of the plague, or perhaps its former occupants had been deceived with family secrets and had left to discover hidden truths, never to return. Whatever the reason for its abandonment, it was perfect for us to shelter until morning.

We tied the horses to a hitching post that had been set in the ground outside an old pentice, where the ponies might seek shelter from the rain if they pleased. I unpacked a candle and lighted it, then Rosamund and I carried our bags and saddles and took sanctuary beneath the eaves of the main farmhouse. Two of the walls had crumbled away and only half the thatch was left, but we were out of the rain, and the ground was dry beneath us.

How comforting it was to hold Rosamund in my arms as we lay there croodling beneath our cloaks. Too tired in our bodies for passion and lust, we each lay moulded to the other's curves. With a bond as tight as man and wife, and with fears and futures dancing about my mind, she was my life and breath that night. How strange that love can take so many forms; a honeyed eye, a gentle caress, passion of the bed and now such profound comfort as I had never known. Perhaps that was the greatest gift love had to give; the sense of not being alone.

I did not sleep well that night and a thousand moments passed by in wakeful silence as Rosamund slept exhausted in my arms. In that like manner the hours glided by, until the edge of the night became sharp against the blanching horizon and a distant cockerel throbbed out its daybreak chant. Safe in the knowledge we had trekked far and away from the beaten track, we gathered sticks and fallen thatch and lit a fire in the hearth of stones. Rosamund was pinched by the cold, even when the fire was ablaze. I asked if she was in good health and she replied that she was, but I suspected she was brooding on both past events and future fears; I did not blame her, and I too meditated on all that had happened since leaving Crown Croft and especially the vile nobleman who touched so many lives with his immorality.

My mind was still dominated by thoughts of Roger de Marsh as I checked on the horses and it was not until I returned to the warmth of the derelict parlour-room, that I consciously called to mind Father Oswald proclaiming my name as I rode away from the inn. Surely, he knew that his papers had been read and replaced and that I was the instigator of that dupery. A flush of heat rose across my chest and up around my neck as I recalled the deceit, the contrived wrong against a holy man; God's own delegate. Would that I might write my sin in dust, that it could be blown away and forgotten! How the pain smarted in my sad heart.

Suddenly, the whole enterprise seemed pointless. Since taking the risk to read his papers, so much had changed; we had the nobleman's name, and could expose Roger de Marsh's deeds to the local lord and his constables if we chose, or take time to plan Rosamund's justice, or simply await him at his family seat in Walsingham.

I sat down beside Rosamund, wondering whether I should raise the matter of Father Oswald's papers or not. It was one thing to look at a man's private notes and quite another to discuss what they contained, and by asking Rosamund to report to me what she discovered, it felt as though we were about to perpetrate the misdemeanour all over again.

At length, I said distractedly, 'Now that we have learned the nobleman's name, it seems as though we wasted our time with Father Oswald's documents after all. I assume there was nothing of significance in his papers,' I went on, adding, 'and with nothing there to help us then we have caused no harm.'

Rosamund flicked her eyes towards me, then quickly looked away; and such a sorrowful sigh she breathed as she did so. She bit down on her lower lip and initially, I supposed she, too, felt regret at the risk we had taken in reading the priest's documents, but her glumness persisted and only grew darker. I let it be for a moment or two, then could not help but ask, 'What exactly was in his bag, Rosamund?'

'His breviary, his penitential and a prayer-roll,' she said, monotone, flat. 'His psalter and ...'

She paused for the longest time and drew her fingers to her lips, brushed her forefinger along the skin of her mouth.

'What else?' I said, urgency growing in my voice, my eyes searching hers.

'There was a ... a folded parchment document bound with a flox silk ribbon. I ... I loosed the ribbon, unfolded the document and studied what was inked on its surface.'

'What was it?' I urged.

'It was writ in Latin,' she mumbled, casting her eyes downward, clasping her hands together, twining her fingers.

'Could you make out what it said?' I asked.

She nodded and said, 'It was a church record; a list of names and dates.'

She was silent for a while, before she softly asked, 'What was your mother's name, Alwin?'

'Margery,' I said. 'Why? What did it say?'

'It appears she was not from the shire of Derby, Alwin; she was from Walsingham. The name recorded was Margery of Walsingham Parva, if that is she. And tell me, Alwin, what year were you born?'

'The year the plague came on very violent; thirteen hundred and forty-nine, on the feast day of Saint Anne. Why?'

'I believe the document is a record of your birth and the name you were given.'

'What's wrong, Rosamund? I can see the look in your eyes, something's wrong. What name was I given?'

'Anne.'

'I am Anne of Whittaker?'

'No.'

'Then who am I?'

Rosamund's eyes were suddenly weaker and more spiritless than I had seen before, her lips slack and down-turned, as though she were about to speak by the Devil's proxy. A tear bulged in her right eye and, as she blotted it with the heel of her hand, she quietly and solemnly said, 'Alwin, your name is Anne de Marsh.'

CHAPTER ELEVEN

Mother used to say: 'Where we least think, there goeth the hare away,' and how true her words were, because of all the revelations I might have expected to discover in my life, to share kinship with the de Marsh family was not one of them. How sharp the stings of the blade when I spoke the name inside my head; one cut for Eleanor, one cut for the nuns and a final pierce to the flesh of my own heart. Only twice in my life had I heard the name spoken, but already those two occasions were linked, like some diabolical chain that shackled ill deeds to my soul and twined like a ligature, cutting a sore within me that could surely never be healed. So heavy was the blow, I could not move. My breathing was suspended for a moment, then started again in short gasps, and all I could do was fix my gaze, unblinking, and consider the implications.

'My mother must have been unwed,' I said, still staring forward to a vague point in the middle distance. 'My father is a de Marsh and I am of noble blood; a vile, poisonous, noble blood, which courses through my veins and renders me a cursed branch of their toxic family tree.'

In a reflex, I put my hands to my mouth, stemmed the flow of words, fearful of their sound and meaning, then I turned away from Rosamund. I walked forward, unsteady on my feet, and I reached out for the wall, leaned against it. In time, Rosamund followed my steps and placed her hand on my shoulder.

'I will not turn and look at you,' I said, my voice reedy with the suffering that rose up from my heart. 'You will see him in my eyes. You will see Roger de Marsh whenever you look at me and know his blood is inside my veins and ...'

'Alwin,' she said, in a loving voice. 'Nothing has changed. The blood in your veins has remained constant since the day you were born. You have shown no signs of violence or deceit. You are the finest, most gracious person I have ever met. The shame is all Roger de Marsh's; the pity he could not be more like you.'

At that, she dropped her hand to the top of my arm and applied a little pressure, had me turn around to face her. I could not say her eyes were any less loving than before, no more than I could say they had changed from blue to brown, but they were different, of that I was certain. And her look put me in mind of the manner in which I once saw a mother in Badeswell cast a loving glance at her son.

The boy was Johnnie of the cornfield – Alice's older brother. He died at the age of four and in his short life, he spent his days shuffling about on his polt-foot, suffered badly from the falling sickness and only ever spoke in his own, special language. Mother and I walked past Johnnie in Badeswell on one Ascension Day well-dressing, and I took note of the way his own mother looked at him. Her eyes were soft and sent out a sad, lingering look. I asked Mother why Johnnie was better loved than me, for that is how I supposed it must be, but Mother said it was the same amount of love any cherished soul received, just delivered in a different, more compacted way, so as to make up for the lad's deficiencies and help him deal with the burdens he did carry.

It was that same look I received from Rosamund as we stood in the dilapidated farm cot. I believed she loved me the same as before, but the density of her affection was concentrated, no doubt to help me withstand the new impairment that now deformed me. But the longer she cast her look upon me, the more I felt my insufficiency and, in the end, I was obliged to walk away from her.

I tended to the horses, rubbed them down with some old straw from the pentice, fed them forage and walked them to a trough filled with rainwater. All the time, I tried to angle my thoughts towards the job in hand, but everything I did raised a doubt. As I brushed loose hair from the ponies' backs, I was forced to consider matters that had never been brought under my eye before; I wondered if my hands looked like Mother's or were they more like a de Marsh's? I caught my reflection in the water vessel; did my eyes feature the maternal or paternal side of my ancestry? And who exactly was my father? I tried to hazard a guess at Roger's age: five-and-twenty? Seven-and-twenty? It was as my mind was running through those thoughts that Rosamund approached me. She walked slowly, barely making a sound, and she stopped some paces from me, ever considerate of my mood and feelings.

'He might only be a distant cousin,' she said, her tones possessed of much kind belief.

I took her words and held them tight against my heart, that they may be true, but my heart was a cold fellow that day and had me answer, 'But Rosamund, although he has not the age to be my father, he may be my half-brother, or uncle, and my own father might be a far worse example of a de Marsh than Roger ever could be.'

'Alwin,' she continued, 'you cannot build your life on foundations of supposition. You cannot guess. We must move forward together and, one by one, discover the truths and discard the lies, until doubts can plague you no more.'

I nodded my agreement. I knew she was right. Then we came together and embraced one another. The warmth of her arms about me was a comfort, but I sensed a certain stiffness and I could not tell if it hailed from me or her; it simply lay between us, narrow as a name, cold as a curse.

I felt very low in spirits as we pulled apart and set about packing up our bags. So lost in my mental anguish, I seemed to forfeit the power of speech and we continued on in a separate, silent way, as though postponement of facts and futures might reduce their potency and shape a different outcome. Gloom became my temper's condition and melancholia tinted all my thoughts, not least my speculation on Father Oswald and his role in my life's history.

As ever, the deeper I delved, the lower the depths became and I was no closer than I had ever been to discovering whether the priest was sinner or saint. I could not know whether he had held the knowledge of my ancestry for just a short moment or a whole lifetime. I could not measure if the document further defamed him or proved him worthy defender. I mused on the parity of innocence and ignorance, wondered what harm might come if I stayed my quest, accepted all I had learned, nursed the consequences and turned about to return to ... return to where?

It was that realisation of my displacement in the world, the feeling I belonged nowhere, that somehow gave me the strength to go on. I knew I could not live my life with just a day's provisions in my bag and the road below me. I had lost my mother, my home, my name, my very identity: but for every loss there is a gain, and since leaving Crown Croft I had found knowledge, clarity of eye and, above all, Rosamund Blackmere.

Time passed by as I stood and meditated, and when I returned to my senses, Rosamund had bundled up the bags, tacked the ponies and thrown earth on the fire to disguise its happening. At first, I wanted to tell her all my thoughts, have us deliberate on prospects and outcomes, but then I thought about the waters of the River Crown and how destructive they would have been if they had all rushed past in one mighty flood. Instead, they ran constant and measured, sometimes troubled, sometimes spare, but in the main they were steady. I decided that was how I must proceed. I would think about matters carefully inside my own head, be wary of how doubts and recollections could play their fallacious games, then once in a while I would talk to Rosamund, seek her opinion. But I would resist a deluge of conjecture, instead I would demonstrate strength of mind and, above all, I would strive to be worthy of Rosamund's love, despite my familial bane.

That is how we went on; we took our departure, followed the main route to the east, plying our measured course towards Walsingham, and we forged forward one step at a time, persistent and composed. Every once in a while, I brought a subject to the fore and we each gave our opinion on the facts we had thus far discovered. Then we fell into silence and flowed on in a thoughtful fashion.

From that point on, the landscape we traversed gradually changed. Where before the countryside had been a flatter version of my own Derbyshire dales and peaks, with clustered settlements of timber-framed cots and dwellings, suddenly the land did not adhere to the regular enclosure pattern I was used to. Open fields abounded, sometimes as many as eight or ten together, and many plots of land were hedged, unlike the familiar dry walls of Crown Croft. There seemed to be more of an emphasis on cattle-rearing and the few homesteads we did pass were styled in the fashion of longhouses, where the dwelling was spilt between byre and living space. The tracks and byways were different, too. With paucity of rocks with which to strengthen the surface, over the years the mud had quite worn away and we found ourselves riding in dips and hollows where footfalls had rubbed the lanes into a deep rut.

It was not long after midday when we arrived at another such longhouse, the thatch sparely laid on its single storey and the whole building dishevelled and uneven. At first, I thought it must be another plague house, forsaken of all dwellers a lifetime ago, but on closer inspection a narrow coil of smoke rose up from the apex of the roof and sundry fowls scratched in the dirt beside the front door.

With time enough for us to pass by and ride a good few hours more before dusk settled on us, we took the path at the back of the house that favoured our general direction. Behind the dwelling, the earth was set with cabbages and amongst those herbs, like a fay on a toadstool, sat a girl picking weeds.

The breeze was blowing gently in our faces as we approached her, so the sound of our arrival was scattered away from her ears and she neither started nor turned about. The girl was slight, an old straw hat on her head and a seedlip by her side into which she was placing the weeds. Rosamund quietly dismounted and walked towards her. I wondered if the child reminded her of Eleanor, for the girl was no older than twelve or thirteen. It was not until Rosamund's shadow fell over the child that she slewed round quite suddenly, as though someone had whispered in her ear, and she raised her face to Rosamund's, with both a frown and a question in her eyes.

'Are you come to nurse me?' the girl enquired, slowly raising herself as she spoke.

At first, I wondered why Rosamund did not reply. I supposed the wind had distorted the words and sent them beyond the compass of her hearing. Then, as the girl finally got to her feet, my eyes were drawn to her swollen belly, the distension so pronounced that I marvelled at her legs having the strength to hold her up. The girl was no bigger than a pollywig, but she was expecting a child of her own.

She stumbled as she turned and pressed her hands to the small of her back, as though by folding her arms behind her, it might counterbalance the weight of her abdomen and stop her from toppling forwards. She looked so strange; frail and undernourished but charged with carrying another life inside her.

Rosamund screwed round to front me briefly, a look of incredulity on her features, and fleetingly I speculated we were facing a phantom; the ghost of Eleanor being conjured before our eyes. Then the hex was broken by a man's voice, brittle and stern through the air behind us.

'Who art thou?' he called, loud and coarse. 'Who art thou to pollute this land and consort with my daughter?'

'We are pilgrims, sir, and mean you no mischief,' I said.

The man eyed me, still advancing, his galoshes and wooden pattens sinking deep into the mud each time he set his feet down, kicking spatters of earth and dung into the air as he approached me. His raiment was worn and patched, and from the tip of his sheepskin cloak to the base of his hose, flecks of dirt did daggle him, lending a sense of wildness to his appearance.

'Your crops grow well in this soil, sir,' I said, catching his eye for a moment. 'It is barley and corn that has ever thriven best on my own land,' I added.

I hoped my words might quell the man's hostility, but the effect was far better than I bargained. The scowl that had hitherto been etched across his face at once relaxed, and his troubled eye faded.

'Farming man are you, lad?' he asked, as though they were the first words he had spoken to me, the testy tone of before long since gone.

'I am,' I said. 'And it grieves me sore to be away from my acres and beasts, wondering at the work not being done in my absence.'

The man nodded, flitted his gaze about for a moment, then settled his eye on me and said, bowing his head, 'Diccon. Diccon of Westcott.'

'Alwin Whittaker,' I replied, 'and this is my wife, Rosamund.'

I felt a certain confidence and clarity return to me at the saying of the name I had lived beneath for so long, and the saying of my name brought with it recollections of the old homestead and the winding River Crown. It was at that moment, I first came to realise how similar I was to the old river; curving and carving its path through the valley, appearing to be constant and unchanging, but never truly the same from one moment to the next; carrying the past and forging a future, all in one endless sweep of motion.

'You will be seeking hospitality under my roof tonight, Alwin?' Diccon asked, a hint of brusqueness returning to his manner.

'We do not wish to inconvenience anyone,' I said. 'Perhaps if you might direct us to ...'

'You will not reach another settlement before nightfall on the east road,' he replied.

'Our needs are few,' I said. 'We seek only shelter and will not burden your wife with the wanting of a meal.'

'My wife is dead,' he said, plain and flat. 'She died last year, sudden and quick. Now it is just my daughter Agnes and me, but of course she is—'

At that, he slanted his look at the girl and his eyes spangled with wrath. At least, that is what I saw at first. But in an instant, I recognised his anger as simply a means to disguise his pain, and the longer I looked at him, the more I saw the hurt behind his eyes, the more I understood him. Tradition dictated his daughter was to blame and custom compelled all others to ostracise her, as though she were the only one ever to have sinned.

'Get you away, Agnes,' he said gently. 'Take yourself from the sight of these good people, they will not wish to associate with you.'

I wondered how many neighbours had shunned him and chastised him with hard hearts and weak minds, how many words his priest had used to list the sins, how many tears he had wept inwardly at a situation he could not control. I understood his reason, but could not relish his cruelty, for Agnes's face coloured violently at his words, before she collected herself, lowered her head, scuffed her way past Rosamund, Diccon and me and disappeared inside the cowshed.

'My wife and I do not think as others do, Diccon,' I said. 'Your daughter is very young and cannot be held accountable for any decisions she might have made. If we all truly believed children were capable of sound judgement, we would surely entrust them with all our chattels and have them manage the world's commerce. But we do not, because we know in our hearts it would be foolish.'

'And,' Rosamund added, 'Agnes must have been bred up with sound morals, because she trusted the man who did this to her. She did not see the Devil in him, because she knew only worthy expectation and could judge matters solely by the integrity with which she had been schooled.'

In my heart, I suspected Rosamund was talking about Eleanor, trying to explain away how matters had come about, but it did not matter whomsoever was the subject, because for ill or good, surely all children's mistakes are rooted in the world in which they are nurtured; the world their forebears have created.

Diccon's lips narrowed, his eyes became rheumy and he nodded briefly, then lowered his head and coughed, before he said, 'Best hitch your horses to that post and bring your bags inside the cottage. Come in, bide the night and good welcome to you.'

At that, he showed us into the heart of his home. The thatch was at a steep angle and the wattle and daub walls were very low. Even Rosamund was forced to lower her head as we entered through the doorway and, once inside, the light was scant and the odour was stale; the harsh perfume of animal dung and unclean bodies dominant in the air. The floor was trampled earth, no rushes, reeds or herbs to make it sweet, and the furnishings were spare indeed; a bench, a trestle table, a stool, a chest and two straw palliasses.

'My wife was a brewster,' Diccon said, following us inside, 'and did earn good purse from her trade. Now we are reduced to penury, but we do not starve and I will not have our guests stinted. I have a rabbit hanging in the byre,' he went on, 'if your wife might care to dress it for the pot?'

'Aye, sir,' Rosamund said. 'I shall cook up a fine stew.'

As soon as Diccon left us alone, Rosamund rushed to my side and whispered, 'Can it be that Roger de Marsh has been visiting this poor girl and punished her womb, filled her belly with a babe?'

'We have no real grounds to suggest such a thing,' I said, truly believing the words as they left my mouth, but already dogged by doubts as the sound of each syllable echoed in my ears.

'Agnes,' she went on, 'can be no older than …'

'We cannot know her age. She may look younger than her years,' I said. 'And we cannot speculate on her history. Perhaps at harvest she took too much ale or perry and did lie with a hayward and ...'

'Did you not take note of the hoof marks on the ground as we approached the cottage?'

'What hoof marks?'

'The mud was churned not by the cloven hooves of cattle, but by iron-shod horses; two by the appearance. You cannot have forgotten how tired de Marsh's mount looked, how hard he had ridden that night to have scarred his horse with his rowels. Who's to say he was not returning from here and ...'

'Enough!' I shouted. 'Enough!'

I turned as I yelled and strode briskly towards the doorway. I paused on the threshold, thought I might be able to explain myself to Rosamund, but found I could not. Once outside, I walked on until I came to a paddock fenced with willow withes and there I stopped and considered my thoughts.

Many years before, I had been wandering the Whittaker woods when a storm brewed up in the skies above me and sent down a thunder-dart that tore apart the head of an oak. There was such a crack, then a flash so bright that for a heartbeat I was blinded, and in that brief moment, I could feel the charge fizzing through my body, pushing up goose bumps and prickling the hairs on my head. Long after my sight returned and the storm had rolled away, I could still feel that tingle deep inside me, as though the tempest had left some of its force and anger within me.

That was how I felt about discovering I was a de Marsh; the lev-in-bolt had struck and passed on, but the pain and wrath lingered. At first, I had begun to contain it, visualised Father Oswald's scroll on which my real name was written and seen my ancestry in my mind's eye as ink-black, flat and, in that inert state, unable to cause me real harm. In that like manner I had been able to detach myself from its true implications, but with Rosamund bringing the matter so close to me by suggesting Roger had spread his poison to Diccon's and Agnes's lives, I suddenly felt the sharp sting of shame by association. As a boy, I had lived such an uncomplicated life; I told the truth and believed others returned the honour. But now I realised the truth was not as simple as I had once believed, for it is made of many layers and, knowing only one aspect, is as naïve as looking at one blade of barley and believing the whole world is covered in grass.

As quickly as the sense of shame had risen within me at being a de Marsh, so the feeling of guilt at my treatment of Rosamund came fast on its heels. Instead of demonstrating the strength of my character and proving my love for her, at the first time of asking, I had succumbed to the weakness my ancestry compelled.

I turned about, determined to say all my thoughts to Rosamund and have her know how I loved her, but as I started to retrace my steps towards the cottage, Agnes appeared from the cow-byre, her face streaked with tears, her shoulders low and her back arched forward, as though old age had slanted an early bias to her frame. Before I could reach her, she sank slowly to her knees, folding her arms around her belly as though nursing a great pain.

'Rosamund!' I cried. 'Rosamund, come quick!'

By the time I reached Agnes, Rosamund was out of the cottage and at once bade me help the child into the dwelling house. Diccon burst in soon after and, his face pale and drawn, he asked, 'Is the infant coming?'

'Yes,' Rosamund said. 'See? Your belly is smaller, Agnes. The babe has slipped lower, to make ready for entering the world.'

'Mistress Rosamund,' the girl wept, 'I did ... soil myself. Father, I am so sorry, I could not stop it.'

'You are not meant to stop it, my dear,' Rosamund said, calm and kind. 'It is your body dispelling its waste to make the birthing easier. It is a good thing; it means your body knows what to do, that you are ready and strong enough to bear all that must happen.'

'I prayed to Saint Dorothy and to Saint Margaret,' Agnes wept, 'but … will it hurt?' she asked, her voice timid and thin.

'You will be distracted by your labouring efforts, Agnes,' Rosamund said, 'and what discomfort there may be will be forgotten, just as your mother forgot her birthing pangs, as her own mother did before her.'

With Agnes lying prostrate on the straw mattress, Rosamund sent Diccon to fill water pails and bring as many rags as he could find, and she asked me to fetch wood for the fire. When I returned with an armful of hewn birch and a budget of dry twigs, Rosamund had cleaned Agnes and laid her travelling cloak over the girl to preserve her modesty.

'We must leave the women to it. It would not be seemly for us to stay,' Diccon said to me as he handed a bundle of rags to Rosamund, then turned to leave.

'Only because that is a custom, Diccon,' I said. 'But I wish to break with tradition and stay to support my wife. Will you not linger too, to give comfort to your daughter when she most needs it?'

Diccon cast his eyes at Agnes, then looked at Rosamund and me, before he gave a gentle nod of his head and took a seat in the shadows.

Nothing happened at first, then every once in a while, Agnes's face flushed up and the veins in her neck grew thick and blue. At times, she lay in apparent tranquillity, then of a sudden she became agitated and asked to be helped to her hands and knees that she might lower her head and ease her suffering. But in the main, Rosamund had her lie on her left side with her frame bent forwards; to relax the muscles, she told us, that would be needed to expel the infant when the time came.

Noon-spell blent to eventide, then the colours of night dropped dark about us and still the infant did not come. The periods of quiescence gradually became shorter and less frequent, and Agnes's agitation grew stronger and more continuous, until her cutting and grinding pains came every few minutes.

Many times, I had witnessed the birthing of lambs and marvelled at how quick and easy they came. One moment the ewe would pace and trample a nest in the grass, then once on her side, would expel her lambs as though they were peas from a pod. Never before had I seen such exertion as I witnessed from young Agnes on that night. With her cheeks waxing red, she switched her head from side to side and gnashed her teeth, and with her face contorted and beads of sweat strung above her brow, hour upon hour she strained and pushed and battled to deliver her babe, but as Nature was kind to the ewes and the lambs, she was less forgiving to Agnes, and the child's reserves of fortitude were very low by the time Rosamund announced that, at last, the head had presented.

Rosamund was kind with her words, but prudential in her encouragement, perhaps knowing greater hardship was still to come. And on it went, seemingly slower than time itself; moments of frantic effort with cries of anguish, the heat thrown out from Agnes's body hotter than blazing straw, followed by an age when nought could be heard but breathlessness and sobbing.

In all my days, I had never understood how close women came to death in their effort to give life. In my ignorance I had presumed the women who died in the birthing room were simply weak vessels, feeble creatures who had failed in their one duty to mankind. I had also been schooled by Father Oswald to believe that once in a generation, there came a hero; the like of King Alfred, Achilles and our own Black Prince. But the battle that raged in that longhouse was as noble, brave and courageous as any conflict fought between men, of that I was certain.

The longer the night went on, the closer the battle-lines were drawn, until between the silent babe – not dead and not yet fully alive, and Agnes – spent of all strength; life and death mingled together and became a suspended moment in time, the most anxious experience I had ever lived through.

Then, of a sudden, it was over. The babe slipped out and into our world, gave a sort of wet cough or a tiny sneeze, like the tip of an angel's wing had tickled its nose, and its little voice rang out, chiming its entrance with the loudest cry it could muster from its dainty, crinkled body. And what joyous music it sung to our ears. It was the most sovereign thing in the world!

Rosamund, still on her knees, took the babe in her arms, but said nothing. Diccon rose to his feet and I held my head in my hands. But none of us spoke, all of us so enfeebled by what we had witnessed. It was Agnes in the end, gifted with the strength of motherhood, that said, 'Is the babe halesome? And be it a boy or a girl?'

'She's a beautiful, healthy baby girl, Agnes,' Rosamund said and so saying, she swaddled the infant and lay it on Agnes's chest, then she went on to press her hands gently on Agnes's belly to dispel the last of the membranes and tissues left inside her. And as Rosamund busied herself rinsing and cleaning, so the infant employed herself taking suck from her mother's pap; and such joy the child took from setting her thirsty lip to that first beverage.

As I sat and watched, it came to me that I had witnessed a miracle that night, such a wonder as my eyes had never beheld, and I wondered why the paragon of childbirth could not be reason enough for men like Roger de Marsh to afford greater respect to all women, such a marvel it seemed to me.

So strange the night had passed with its nocturnal breath heavy on the daybreak, that I lost the measure of time and I suffered surprise when the cock began to crow and the shadows started to pale in the morning light. In turns, Diccon and I inspected the baby. He looked so awkward as his arms took up the child and rocked her, so gentle and blithe. He handed her to me and I cradled her, could not help but smile at her tiny nose and the watery blueness of her eyes; like she had come from another world, a purer one than ours, and was looking at us with a superior eye, as yet untainted by the sights we would one day have her see.

Not long after she was placed in my arms, her face coloured and wrinkled, and she let out a cry of anguish. With Agnes deep in slumber, I appealed to Rosamund and she took the child from me, loosed the swaddling, gently placed the tip of her little finger in the infant's mouth, and sang a sweet lay that lulled the babe into sleep. How clean and fresh was the innocent delight of that infant; she knew not of her father or her immoral conception; she was ignorant of Eleanor's death and the lies my mother had spoken; and the child's immaculate existence seemed to mellow past ill deeds, and I noted a sort of peace descend over Rosamund's features as she nursed the infant.

Perhaps in some way the bringing of new life had softened the sting of Eleanor's death, and given Rosamund courage to view the world anew, the stain of past wounds at last beginning to heal. I mused on that point as I watched Rosamund and at first took comfort from her contentment. Then demons of doubt, as ever, began to dance around my mind. If the arrival of new life and the glory of motherhood were such restorative conditions, then if Rosamund lived on as my wife, I could not give her what her soul and her body needed, as she would live a barren life alongside me and surely grow to resent it.

After that strange and wild night, a sort of slowness and peace descended over the longhouse. Agnes lay on the palliasse in deep slumber, Rosamund sat on the bench drifting in and out of gentle drowse with the babe asleep in her arms, and Diccon sat himself down on the bare floor, a tired but contented expression on his face. But although I could sense the tranquillity, I could not absorb it. My body ached with fatigue and my skull-bone throbbed with weariness, but however much I glued my eyes shut and wished for sleep to come, I remained restless and wide awake.

In the end, I surrendered to my body's persistence and quietly busied myself about the place. I fetched wood and built up the fire, picked a handful of cabbage leaves and cut them for the pot, then skinned the rabbit and jugged it over the fire in a brass cauldron. But just as before, I could not harness my mind to the matters I undertook; instead, visions of Father Oswald, Mother and Roger dominated my thoughts. Where before, I had considered my pilgrimage to Walsingham a promise to Mother, a solemn duty I was obliged to fulfil; suddenly, I had neither the patience to wait for answers to come to me, nor the forbearance to continue on to Walsingham. Unanswered questions raved so loudly inside my head, I could not grasp coherent replies, and just as moonlight can thicken a fog, so recent revelations deepened the mysteries of my life to such a pitch that I was blinded by my own ill judgement.

I became so vexed and impatient at not knowing who I was, at the uncertainties I presented to Rosamund, that I lost sight of all reason. In the watery light of early morning, I paced about the farmyard as though a process had begun that I could not stop, just like the birthing of Agnes's babe. Sense had me pause in thought, but Nature impelled me forward, goaded me to follow my instincts and see the matter through to the end. So, hot-headed and hasty, I saddled my horse in the cold morning light, certain I must ride alone back to the township and confront both Roger and Father Oswald; demand answers and discover my true history.

I was fastening the girth and straightening the stirrups, fumbling with a strap, when Diccon approached me carrying a pail of milk and two drinking vessels. He placed the bucket on the ground, filled both cups and handed one to me. I could neither ignore him nor explain myself to him, so I just stared down at the cup of milk and the pearls of air that bubbled on its surface. Diccon said nothing. He cast his eyes over my pony's saddle, then briefly looked at me and, in many ways, I was grateful for his muteness. He neither quizzed nor judged me, his arrival alone sufficient to inform me that he cared enough to be there. It is without doubt that Diccon's presence put me in delay and, if he had not come to me at that moment in time, in my confused and emotional state I would certainly have mounted my pony and ridden away to town. How gracious the gifts of chance that God sends us, for that deferment changed the bent of my fate, of that I am certain.

I drank two cups of the warm milk and Diccon talked sparingly, but with great favour, about his new granddaughter, how strong her lungs were, how blue her eyes; just like his wife's, he laughed. In those few short moments of pause, Rosamund came out of the cottage, stretched her arms, yawned and walked over to us.

'Both mother and child grow stronger with every heartbeat,' she said, apparently unaware of my foolhardy plans and sensitive state of mind.

'And all thanks to you, dear lady,' Diccon replied, a smile on his lips.

Just at that moment, a slant of sunlight fell across Rosamund and rendered her more beautiful than I had yet seen her, that honey-russet glint so lovely in her hair. Weary of wakefulness and tired of eye, she wore the respect Diccon bestowed upon her with great gentility. She continued to talk to Diccon about the baby and Agnes and I gazed at her, long and soft, and in that moment I loved her more than ever before. But the folly of great love is that it is shadowed by doubt, and the more I loved Rosamund, the greater I scrupled my own worthiness.

It was in that state of conflict that my eye was drawn to a movement farther up the lane that led to the cottage. The distance had dissolved itself in morning haze and through that milky light, a figure advanced. It was the white wimple that caught my eye first, then a woman with full figure and round face emerged, discarding the mist with every step she took.

'A visitor approaches, Diccon,' I said, anxious in my tone, searching the lane with my eyes for other figures, but the woman was alone.

A look of awkwardness bloomed ruddy on Diccon's cheeks and he said, 'It is my sister.'

With that, he took a step forward and received the woman with an oblique glance, a look of foreboding busying his features, his head slightly bowed as though bracing himself for hard words. But chastisement did not come. The woman's features softened into a smile. She was older than Diccon, well beyond the age of five-and-thirty, but her plumpness defended her skin against the mark of time and she looked healthy and hearty.

'Brother Diccon,' the dame said warmly as she neared him. 'At last, my husband did agree to let me come,' she went on. 'I shall stay for a week, make sure the girl is strong enough for what will come ahead. Your priest and neighbours may be virtuous and wise, Diccon, but their judgement of you and your daughter is severe; and not one of them is without sin, of that I am certain. God may guide us throughout our life, but it is surely family that gets us through one more day.' She took Diccon's hand in her own and went on, 'Now, how fares my niece?'

'Agnes ... and her daughter,' Diccon said, 'are both well, thanks to these good pilgrims who passed by our homestead yesterday.'

At that, Diccon cupped his sister's elbow in his hand, and turned towards Rosamund and me, saying our names to the matron as he fronted us, by way of introduction.

When pleasantries had been exchanged, we all crept quietly into the longhouse and gathered round the straw mattress, where Agnes lay in peaceful slumber with her babe in a wicker bowl at her side. At first, all our voices were issued in a whisper, but then Agnes awoke and set about talking with Diccon's sister. In time, with our words no longer spoken in a hush, a gentle conversation frothed and bubbled about the place, like new-poured milk.

Diccon's sister had many things to say and talked with fluency and charm; she had married well and she lived well, had four fine sons and enjoyed the respect of her neighbours. Her voice was pitched quite low, which rendered her tones pleasing to the ear, and her laugh was gravelly, as though she had just eaten mustard seeds. Once in a while, the upper lid of her right eye fell down of its own accord and was slow to open as though its health were disordered, but so pleasant was her conversation that the eyelid became an interesting quality rather than a distracting one.

Somehow, in that little room of wattle walls and earth floor surrounded by good people, I felt quite at ease. It put me in mind of when Alice of the cornfield and her mother and father would visit us at Crown Croft; that sense of kinship and safety that only others' conversation can supply. I thought back to the point in time when Diccon had unwittingly stopped me from making my rash departure and I wondered if there might be a chance, after all, of leaving matters as they were, letting sleeping dogs lie, as Mother used to say. Perhaps that was what God meant by His intervention and what Mother did ultimately wish; that the end of my journey was not so important as the journey itself, and that once I found satisfaction, I might develop the strength to let secrets lay hidden forever. It was as I turned those thoughts in my mind that Diccon's sister changed the bent of her speech.

'Of course,' she said, 'I was obliged to pass through the town on my way here. More loud and noisome it grows by the day, I am sure. There was such uproar at the inn on the night before last, so said the cheesemonger, that men from the manor were sent for.'

'Were matters settled?' I asked.

'Well, the men who caused the affray were military men and ...'

'How do you know that, sister?' Diccon asked.

'Well,' the lady went on, 'I know the bible tells us not to believe every tale, but the cheesemonger said it was so; he had spoken to an apple-woman whose brother was at the inn when the leader of the troops came riding into town. And of course, the road from town to here is always busy with wayfarers as they journey to the eastern counties, and our safety from cut-purses is augmented by walking together. So, I strolled with a pedlar of wooden spoons, walked a while with a poulterer and his wife returning from market, then I was passed by a small band of pilgrims; a master, a dame and a priest.

'The priest was gentle and kind, and did while away some moments in conversation with me. He was wary of the soldiers, he said, and had set out before dawn to find an alternative road to the east, to make certain he kept out of their way. I set them on a path not far from here, did bid them to follow the fringe of the forest for a mile or two before they would be obliged to join the main track again.'

Diccon's sister seemed to tire of talk about the town as quickly as she had raised it and went on to coo over her niece's baby, as the child gurgled and fidgeted in her mother's arms, and the happy, domestic scene continued as before. But I was no longer part of it. I was surrounded by spectres of the past, deeds and doubts, questions and words, all hovering about me like an army of ghosts; that unravelled riddle of Mother, Roger, Father Oswald and me.

It was then I realised once and for all there was no escape for me, until the last of my family's secrets had been uncovered. Whatever future I dreamed for myself, whatever path I took, I would always be dogged by a cursed fate that would ail my endeavours until the day I could finally vanquish it.

Rosamund had been watching me lost in my own enchantment, and when I looked at her, she was studying the effect of the dame's words in my eyes.

'Diccon, Agnes, good mistress,' she said. 'Master Whittaker and I must take our leave of you now.'

And with those words, she initiated the ritual of departure; kind phrases, glad faces, and half-hollow promises of return. At first Diccon pressed us to bide another night and take sleep to refresh ourselves, but I think he knew from before that I was keen to move on and set course for my journey's end.

The mists had cleared and the winds had risen by the time we rode away from the Westcott homestead. The westerly breeze was strong and buffeted us from behind, throwing up clouds of dead leaves about us, urging us onward, and the rush of its breath stifled our conversation and our words were spare. Whereas Rosamund had glowed with vitality with Agnes's babe in her arms, she now looked drawn again, and both her spirits and expression were dejected, as though her body were harbouring the beginnings of a distemper. As before, I asked if her health had been compromised, and she answered that all was well.

When we took to a woodland path and were sheltered from the gale, I rode my pony close to Rosamund, made up my mind to tell her how close I came to riding back to the township alone to confront de Marsh and Father Oswald. I would put an end to all doubts, and prove myself worthy of her love. But as I pulled rein alongside her, I looked down at her right hand and wished I had not. The pearl ring, that token of my love and constancy, which spoke of a bond to be broken only by death, was missing from her finger.

I drew a breath to quiz her, but could not bring myself to speak. What answers could there be? At best, she had lost it and did not care enough to have me help her find it. At worst, that circle of gold and sphere of nacre had become a torment to her – a symbol of her redundant womb, the de Marsh family and my blood-ties to Roger – to be treated with contempt and discarded at the first opportunity. Of course, her feelings would also control her demeanour and thus explain her despondency.

The realisation sent ice to the chambers of my heart. But it changed me in another way, too: it was at that point in time I finally understood that justice was indeed too good for Roger de Marsh; revenge was what was required after all.

Rosamund seemed oblivious to the consequences of her actions and she started to talk about Agnes and her baby. I could not hold my mind to all she said, so agitated and distracted I had become, but I know she spoke of a woman whom Agnes believed was supposed to nurse her through her birthing, just like Eleanor had disclosed. Apparently, the woman should come a week before full term, and was waiting at an inn at a settlement a mile or two along the north road.

'What do you think, Alwin?' Rosamund asked, as though nothing had changed. 'Should we adopt a detour and try to talk with the woman, see if she is indeed connected to Roger?'

'If it is not far from our intended course and if it helps ensnare de Marsh, then all the better,' I spat. 'Let us quiz her and bring the hour of de Marsh's death ever closer,' I concluded.

I do not think it was just the words I spoke that sounded alien, so much as the way I said them; my voice sounded different, cold and insensitive. It was clear my intentions were no longer a threat, but had become a solemn promise. Rosamund looked at me as though she were seeing someone else, and that is how I felt; as though a stranger were inside me, speaking words I did not mean. And the words themselves seemed to exist of their own volition, like some sort of prophecy.

How strange that in such a brief time, those words would prove to be true. Within a single turn of the sun and the moon, Roger de Marsh would be dead. But which one of us would become the cursed soul who would end his life and would carry shame, regret and guilt to the end of their days was in God's hands alone.

CHAPTER TWELVE

The weather closed fast about us that day. So grey the clouds and sombre the landscape that I could not tell when morn turned to noon or whether moonlight or sunlight lit our path. And the cold wind chafed our hands, our bare, ring-less hands, until our skin smarted red with soreness. So spiteful was the storm that it stole all our speech and was the sort of tempest where even God-fearing Christians would invite the Devil to take warmth by their hearth.

At last, we arrived at a hamlet; an untidy cluster of dwellings, barns and an inn, strewn alongside a mud-clotted lane. The inn was a quarter size of the hostelries to which we had afforded our custom in the towns, and looked as though the innkeeper had simply opened up his homestead to travellers on a whim and fallen into the trade by accident. There was no proper stabling for our mounts and no ostler to remove their tack, so we loosed their girths and left them hitched beneath a lean-to, which rattled its laths to the call of the wind and caused the horses to fidget.

On entering the inn, it was a relief to take shelter from the wind and to mute its wail, but for some moments after its bluster still rang in my ears, and my face felt both tender and numb, as though the blood had been blown deep beneath my skin. Rosamund's hair was disordered, her cheeks flushed and her eyes wind-wet, and all we could do was stand and let the calmness settle about us.

With the storm having deterred other travellers, we stood alone in that chill parlour, the only sign of life being the meagre flames that flapped in the hearth, stooping their tongues every time the wind sang its chant. We put down our bags and sat ourselves on a bench, then I called out for the innkeeper, but no one replied. I rose and walked about the room, wove my way between trestle tables and benches, listened for sounds of life, but all my ears heard was the wind agitating the shutters.

It was as I returned to Rosamund that the stairs to the right of her gave a creak and a woman descended, carrying an empty pottle-pot and a blanket. She was afflicted with a swelling to her face, and her jaw pouted out like a mastiff's, giving her a sullen expression. When at last she eyed us and spoke, it was clear she suffered from defective teeth.

'The wind is eager today,' she said, her words sounding wet as they passed from her lips. 'You will be looking to stay the night?' she added, treading the final stair and making her way towards a door behind the counter. 'Sixpence it will be, sir; for you, the lady, your supper, and the fodder for your ponies. There's a ready chamber at the top of the stairs to the right.'

'Aye, lady. It is a fair price,' I said. 'And are we to expect company from other travellers, do you suppose?'

'No more than is here already on a day like this. There's just a master and dame arrived on the east road four days since. My habit is not of a suspicious and mistaking kind, but mind how you talk with the wife; something dogs her step as though a demon's on her back.'

With that, the innkeeper's wife turned about and left through the counter door. I looked at Rosamund and drew a breath, ready to suggest our hostelry companions might indeed be the de Marsh agents, but Rosamund's face was blank, her eyes half-lidded, exhaustion marked deeply on her features, as though half her body were already locked in sleep. I felt great shame as I looked at her.

In my endeavours to rid myself of my own doubts and demons, I had not truly considered just how fatiguing our journey had been; I had not demonstrated a single virtue that might ever induce her to replace the pearl ring or consider me to be anyone but a de Marsh.

'Come, Rosamund,' I said, kind and gentle. 'You have lost hours of slumber, nursed Agnes and ridden long and hard, it is time for sleep to restore you.'

She nodded, but I believe her thoughts were already clouded by an advancing dreamscape. I helped her to her feet, slid my arm about her waist and set us to climbing the stairs. She leaned her weight against me and I was glad I had the bodily strength to support her. The feeling blushed warm inside me, made me feel good I had been bred up with physical power and could use it for such reward. How sad that Roger de Marsh never experienced such a blessing and could only use his might in such an abhorrent manner.

The bedchamber door was stiff at first then opened with a whine. I led Rosamund through the dimness, past the wooden chest on which had been placed a brass basin and a pitcher of water, and I sat her down on one of the two beds. The straw mattress was thin, the hemp cover torn in two places and the bed was strung with slack ropes that sank low as Rosamund lay down.

Not long after she slipped into slumber, there was a knock at the chamber door and the innkeeper's wife appeared with a lighted candle. I thanked her, took the light from her and placed it on the wooden chest. I sat on the bed next to Rosamund's, intending to watch over her and wake her when supper would be served. But sleep cares not whether you are a shepherd or a king. It takes you when it has a fancy and holds you fast till it is done with you.

I laid me down just for a moment and closed my eyes. I thought about Father Oswald and whether it was good or ill that, according to Diccon's sister, he avoided Roger de Marsh when he set out from the town. Did he fear the man as we all did? Or was he working in concert with him, that between them they may follow both roads to the east and leave no stone unturned?

It was from those musings that the image of Roger set itself in my mind and followed my wakeful thoughts as they slipped along their drowsy path to sleep. My dreams were disjointed and obscure; the man who inhabited them was featureless, no more than a dark shape, but somehow I knew it was Roger. My heart panted wildly and I could barely breathe. I had a blade in my hand and brandished it before him, drew it back to run him through. But he was already dying. Rosamund had fed him her elixir, condemned herself to a life of regret and there was nothing I could do to change it. The scene was so real and alarming of character that it caused a pain in my head. I tried to resist the images, change them, but my attempt to escape them was ineffectual, and in the end they faded to blackness, but in their dark mass, they pressed against me, the size of largeness itself, stealing my air and my life, pushing down on my breast and expelling the breath from my body. Then I tripped or fell or slipped over a cliff-edge, I could not tell which, and falling from a high place I suddenly awoke. Blear-eyed and confused, I looked about and Rosamund was sitting beside me.

'I am sorry,' I said, my mouth tasting dry, my words feeling sticky on my tongue. 'Did I wake you? You must try and rest and ...'

'Alwin,' she said. 'We have both slept for many a while and eventide is upon us.'

I looked past her face at the darkness beyond the candleflame and gradually came to my senses. The shutters no longer rattled and the still air was fragranced with wood smoke, boiled leeks and roast goose. The candle had burned low and the wick spat every once in a while as it sat in its pool of fat, sending mottled light about the room.

'We must hasten to supper,' I said. 'Lest we miss the opportunity to speak with the woman we seek.'

At the tail-end of my sentence, I damped down the volume of my voice, because in the room next door there was movement and a mumble of speech. A door opened then closed and footsteps sounded on the stairs, light of foot, soft of tread.

'Do you suppose it is she?' Rosamund whispered.

'Let us go down and see,' I said.

We quickly poured water into the brass pot and washed our hands and faces, and Rosamund tied up her hair in a coif, then we descended the stairs to the parlour-room. Where before, the room had been cheerless; the fire had since been fed and candles had been lighted about the place, bathing the whole room in a soft, amber glow, disguising the un-swept floor and the greasy trestle-tops, and raising the spirit of the place with its flickering warmth.

The woman who greeted us earlier was absent, but the innkeeper himself was setting down a trencher and a horn mug at a table as we descended the stairs. The woman to whom the supper dish was being served looked no older than Rosamund and, sitting quite alone with her eyes cast downwards and a chamlet cloak drawn tight about her shoulders, she seemed both afraid and forlorn in equal measure.

I tried to catch her eye as we made our way to a bench by the hearth, and Rosamund smiled at her as we passed, but the woman did not acknowledge either of us and continued to push her food about the trencher with her knife. At that, the innkeeper gave us a loud and hearty welcome, as though he wished to bring attention to the woman's ill humour and discourtesy, by exaggerating the disparity between his good cheer and her sullenness, but the woman did not react.

'I bid ye welcome, sir, lady,' he said to us and he shuffled his way to our table, his left shoulder somewhat enlarged and deformed, and his right foot slow to follow him. 'Anything I may do to please you, sir, then command it to me. Cedric is my name. Now, what will please your bellies? Stubble-goose or stock-fish? I believe I can guess which,' he laughed.

We thanked him for roasting up a goose and we went on to speak words of great pleasance to him for a moment or two before he went about his business. In time, his wife brought our supper from the cooking-shed, and a talbot-hound burst its way in through the front door and briefly trotted and nosed its way in a circuitous route around the parlour, before the innkeeper shouted and chased it back outside, and then we were left alone; just Rosamund, me and the woman in the chamlet cloak.

'The teeth of the gale were sharp today, mistress,' Rosamund said at length when we had eaten most of our meal, rising from her seat and walking towards the woman, but stopping by the hearth.

The woman gave a brief reply, no more than a mumble, and did not raise her eyes from her platter.

'But sometimes a brisk wind is good,' Rosamund went on. 'It blows away lies and exposes the truth.'

On hearing those words, the woman's eyes grew wide, she cast a sharp glance at us and in a heartbeat, she stood to her feet, knocking her drinking vessel over and spilling its contents as she did so. In a reflex, I stood, too, and in that strange, silent stand-off, we each eyed one another, feline and testy, as though hackles stood bristling on the backs of our necks. Then the woman made a sudden dash towards the stairs, but Rosamund pre-empted the move, stepped to the side and blocked the woman's path. I advanced and stood alongside Rosamund and for the first time looking directly into the woman's eyes, I saw the terror in her soul.

As I had learned already by that time in my life, and would go on to confirm again and again; both anger and violence are born of inward pain, and although their temporal defeat can be effected by superior power, they can only ever truly be cured by gentle words and gentle deeds. I compared the woman's eyes to Roger's and hers were not like his; she was not his willing agent; she feared and loathed him like the rest of us.

'We are not with Roger de Marsh,' I said, soft and reassuring. 'We are against him.'

With that, the woman's expression changed in an instant. Her features went slack, she breathed a long, heavy sigh, then took her seat on the bench again. But it was her eyes that were altered the most. Where before they were colourless and hard, at once they became hazel and soft tears glistered about them.

Rosamund and I slowly sat on the opposite bench, the trestle table between us and the woman, and Rosamund took the woman's hand in her own and reassured her with kind words. She went on to tell her about Eleanor and Agnes and I told her of the Winfeld Priory. When I had finished my tale, I made it clear we would not stop until Roger was brought to justice, but I did not tell the woman I was a de Marsh, nor did I speak of stabbings, elixirs or damnable revenge. The woman listened to our stories and then sat in thought, hesitating about whether she might tell all or nothing in return. At last, she took in a hearty draught of air and began.

'I dare not tell you my name,' she said in a low voice. 'My husband will not forgive me. But I will tell you the truth of why I am here and pray God it will be enough for it all to stop.' She paused at that and a tear bulged and burst, before she brushed it away with her hand. 'Roger de Marsh eternally seeks to create an abundance of progeny. He rides his black horse from the tip to the toe of this land, taking what he wants, sowing his seed wherever he pleases. And I ... I was born into one of the families that serves him, a family that has obeyed the de Marshes' bidding for five generations.'

'You are their midwives?' Rosamund said.

'Yes,' the woman nodded. 'Sometimes that is what you would call us, but other times there is a far darker word that describes what we do. My mother has taught me all she knows. She has knowledge of folk-herbs, the stars and planets, and words from Galen; there is no one better practised than our family at bringing forth a healthy child.'

'But the shame of birthing a base-born upsets you?' I asked.

'No, sir. I am grown used to it,' she said. She paused, bit her lower lip and cast her eyes downwards.

'Then it is the number of births you are forced to attend?' Rosamund tried, but the woman shook her head and still struggled to explain herself.

'Sometimes,' she eventually began, 'we are given ... different instructions and must attend to our masters' wishes if the child is not suitable.'

'How so?' Rosamund said.

'I cannot say,' the woman said and her words were already clotted with tears. 'This is the first time I have been sent out alone, without my mother ... forcing me to watch her ply her vile employment. I cannot live my life in such a manner,' she sobbed. 'I will not return to Walsingham. I have wed my sweeting in secret; he rests upstairs, and we are to set out for the country of Cymru tomorrow; a place where Roger de Marsh will not come for us.'

'And this is because you are forced to take the babes from their mothers at Roger's orders?' I asked.

The woman shook her head and screwed her eyes into a sort of frown, perhaps annoyed at having to speak the words, instead of avoiding them by her previous allusions.

'We are not commanded to take the selected babes away,' she said, 'we are ordered to ... murder them.'

'All of them?' Rosamund said, her voice rising in agitation. 'But how many can that ...'

'I cannot talk about it,' the woman cried. 'I have told you too much already. It is such a curse, such a curse! And if I do not take the life when I am told, the debt remains outstanding and I must make the kill at a later time. If I refuse, then my own life is forfeit.

'My mother lost track of just such a babe, a girl, many years ago,' the woman went on. 'The child had been selected as being dispensable by the de Marshes, but her own mother fled with her before

219

the deed could be done. My mother, afeard as we all are of the de Marshes, lied to her master; said the babe was disposed of and the matter was closed. She believed she had got away with it, then lately, only weeks since, her master discovered the babe did not die; now my mother is searching as we speak, as is Roger and his band of savages, trying to put an end to the poor soul's life. But my mother is not like me; she does not feel regret or sorrow. She takes pleasure from her work and I curse her soul for bringing me into such a life!'

A river of tears fell from the poor woman's eyes as she spoke and Rosamund was obliged to go to her side and cradle her head. In time, the sobs subsided and the woman dried her eyes on the corner of her cloak.

'Do you believe you can put an end to it?' she eventually asked me, a pleading tone to her voice, her blood-shot eyes searching my own for a sign of hope.

'My road is straight and clear,' I said, forthright and certain. 'Duty is my spur and I will not rest until this is over.'

'Roger de Marsh has a weakness in his left eye,' she said in a whisper, a cunning tone to her voice and a glint of would-be triumph in her sore eyes. 'Stand always a little to his left and it will bring you an advantage.'

'I thank you, mistress,' I said, 'for all you have disclosed. May God speed your journey and bless your marriage.'

She rose, bowed her head to each of us, then turned towards the stairs. With the woman's foot already on the first step, Rosamund suddenly screwed round and called after her.

'I know you cannot tell us your name, but what of your mother? What is your mother's name, that we might seek her out and quiz her?'

The woman stood in pause at that, as though doubt pulled her mind first one way then the other, leaving her undecided whether such a disclosure would be good or bad, until she abstained from replying altogether. Then she looked long at Rosamund, a change descended over her features and, as though disgorging a sour berry, she said:

'Her name is Goody. Goody Tanner.'

The woman turned about and ascended the stairs into the darkness, but her words lingered on behind her and once again, the hare did goeth away where least I did expect it! A strange sort of silence descended about us at hearing Goody's name again, and the air felt charged, as though the tempest had returned, but of course the storm was mute and raged only inside my own mind.

Such a welter of conjecture took lodging in my head that I could not speak, and it was not until the innkeeper's wife entered the parlour to clear away our dishes that I could return my mind to the present. I mumbled words of thanks to the good hostess, took up a rush-light and led Rosamund back to our bedchamber in haste. As soon as the door was fastened closed behind us, the words came tumbling out.

'It was Goody!' I said, breathless and urgent, frothed feelings scurrying about behind my ribs. 'Goody Tanner did murder Matilda and Adela. She mixed a herbal tincture and had her husband smear it on the pony's legs that it did bolt; she set flame to the bedchamber and had her husband pose as Father Oswald and push Adela into the mere. It is all so clear, Rosamund, all so clear! The girls were scions of a de Marsh and she had been tasked to kill them as babes, but something went wrong and …'

'She made mistakes at two or more birthings?' Rosamund said with doubt in her voice. 'With such high stakes?'

'What other explanation is there?'

'Perhaps she was indeed looking for the one infant that escaped her all those years ago; confounded at how the child could have vanished. She's been taking lives indiscriminately, to be certain of success. She must have found out the girl was from the shire of Derby and was heading to Walsingham with a band of pilgrims, but she did not know exactly which maiden to pursue. And of course, the real target was there all along, in plain sight. What better way to protect a girl from murderous hands than to disguise her as a boy? It is you Goody Tanner is searching for, Alwin, but she is too foolish and blind to see you.'

At that, I was forced to sit down on the bed, as though weakened by a strange malady. As a man, I had stood full square against harsh winds that blew and hard times that visited themselves upon Crown Croft. Time and again my physical strength had cast languor from my heart and fatigue from my brow. How uncomplicated life had been plying bodily power against God's elements; but now, the more I learned of duplicity and deceit, the weaker I felt, and how soon I had come to realise that emotional knowledge and sorrow ever travel on together. Of a sudden I could not deny; I missed the simplicity of being a simple, farming man.

'It must give you comfort, Alwin, to know now that your mother is vindicated, for what else was she to do with her most precious jewel?'

'Aye,' I nodded, 'she loved me right well.'

It is true, I did feel solace at knowing Mother's love was real, but just as a rainbow is tainted with grey clouds, so my recollections of Mother were tinged with thoughts of Father Oswald and the part he had played in my life, and the two thoughts quarrelled inside me.

'And what of Father Oswald, Rosamund?' I asked at length. 'How does he fit into all this?'

'I cannot say, for certain,' she said. 'But we cannot deny it was the priest that suggested you met with Goody and William at The Chequers.'

'Aye,' I conceded. 'But when he first sent me there, he said he had no knowledge of the pilgrims; he only knew the vague existence of the group because the abbot had told him.'

'But he carried the paper with your birth-date and name on it.'

'Perhaps he was withholding it to protect me?' I said, a flicker of defence rising within me.

'Or keeping it back to earn a higher purse,' she parried.

And so the night passed; moments of quiet agitation when thoughts were examined, then question after question trying to voice thoughts too deep to be expressed. Restless and fruitless rolled the hours, scant of hope and void of slumber, until midnight murmured darkness in my ears, silence became my language and all my cogitations centred around one image: Roger de Marsh. It was he who held the answers I craved and he whose forfeited life might redeem so many wrongs.

When morning came, I was still lost in my sea of dreams and could not place a time or situation to anchor me to reality. In my head, I drifted on past islands of recollection, washed by an undercurrent of anxiety and foreboding, until at last I remembered the storm, the inn and Goody's daughter. I opened my eyes and blinked at the daylight seeping in through the shutter-laths. Rosamund was asleep on my bed and our bodies were touching, but she had turned away from me in the night and her back was against me.

It was a peculiar feeling that infused my bones that morning and one I was not accustomed to. Haleness and hope were the birds of my dawn chorus; Mother used to say the sun could never fully rise till it sensed hope in waking eyes. But on that day, it was loathing and wrath that kindled my eyes and heated my brow; it was vitriol thoughts that flared up inside me, sun-hot and burning.

I rose, smoothed down my hair, washed my face and hands, then dressed and shod myself. With Rosamund still asleep, I walked with gentle tread and opened the shutters, let a broad, hard flank of unforgiving daylight into the room. I stood at the window and looked out at the lane littered with loose thatch and strewn with fallen branches and dead leaves.

The cottages looked even more dishevelled than before, with upturned milk pails lying at their feet, their wickets yawning open and rooves tousled. The skies beyond were still bruised with clouds, but where they thinned, the sun was just visible and had up-risen higher than I expected; it was far later in the day than I had imagined, long past terce and well into forenoon.

At first the day had no sound, as though the noises of daily life had been blown far away on the wind. Then a crow flittered from rooftop to rooftop, gathering loose straws, perking its feathers and sending out shrill cackles and caws, and through that plaguing noise, came the drumming of hooves and the cry of a man.

I leaned my body out of the window, cast my eyes towards the source of the sound and watched as a rider, distant and small at first, grew larger and louder as he approached the hostelry. His words were unclear and the measure of interval between him and the inn damped his voice, but it was obvious his cries were born of anguish, and the closer he came, the more distressed was his call.

I turned to wake Rosamund, but her eyes were already open and she was pushing herself into a seated position, her face turned towards the window, her head to one side, listening to the clattering hooves and the shouts.

'What's happening?' she said, swinging her legs to the floor and standing upright.

'A man approaches in distress. I cannot hear his words. Look,' I said, turning back to the scene outside. 'He's pulling rein.'

'He's coming here?' she said.

I nodded, cupped my hands around my mouth and issued a shout to the man as he dismounted.

'What ails you, sir?' I called.

He looked up, startled, confused, his eyes wide.

'They came ... to the ... church,' he gasped, breathless from fear or exertion I could not tell. 'A lord ... and a soldier, at the lychgate.'

'I am coming down,' I said, and at that, I turned, flung open the bedchamber door, raced down the stairs and into the parlour-room.

By the time I arrived, the man had sat himself down on a stool, swept the felt hat from his head and was nursing the cap in his hands, a vacant expression on his face. Cedric and his wife stood to his left, leaning slightly inwards towards the man, waiting for him to answer the questions they had asked. Rosamund arrived at my side, stopped and looked at me, then nodded her head, encouraged me to approach the man.

'You must have seen a fearful sight,' I began, approaching the man, pulling up a stool and sitting beside him. He nodded, but did not look up at me.

''Tis the wedding of my cousin; Thomas,' he said, still breathless, his eyes still cast downwards. 'At ten of the church clock this morning, they spoke their vows at the lychgate, the priest declared them wedded and all was such jollity—'

His voice trailed away and he wiped his hand beneath his nose.

'Sometimes, men do quarrel at the Bride Ales,' he began again, a frown on his brows, searching his thoughts for a reason, an explanation to justify what he had witnessed, 'but it was long before we were set to take sup. I cannot understand how ...'

'The soldiers stole your ale?' I tried. 'Started a brawl? Is someone injured?'

The man raised his eyes, stared at me, blinking.

'He did take her,' he said, tears in his eyes and tears in his voice. 'The lord on his black horse did take the bride away.'

'To where?' I said. 'Where is she?'

'He took her away into the woods. We have no horse fast enough to catch him, so Thomas set himself to running. The other soldier stayed; he has set sword to three men and their lives are ebbing. I rode as hard as I might, hoping travellers hereabouts at the inn would be great in number and riding swift horses, but ... now I do not know.'

'If I take the east road, will I come to the church?' I said.

'Aye, but what can you do, lad?' the man said, a look of disbelief in his eyes.

I turned to Cedric and said, 'Do you have weaponry? A poniard or a sword and buckler?'

'Our guest is right, lad,' Cedric said. 'You cannot stand alone against men such as these!'

'This noble lord and me; we have history,' I said, my voice pitched low and the words discharged through gritted teeth. 'He may have greater strength, but I have unconquerable will. I shall take him to task, or be damned if I do not.'

I do not believe it was my choice of words that persuaded Cedric to give me his grandfather's sword, I rather think it was the look in my eye. Fresh from my nightmares of Roger, I still carried a powerful attitude of loathing, which in turn lent me false courage. I could almost sense Roger nearby and the feeling made my heart race and my fingers twitch, as though already I had the sword in my hand and was about to pierce his heart.

Cedric shuffled with haste into the back room and reappeared moments later with a roll of hemp matting. He lay the package on a table, unbound it and lifted out a single-handed sword with a wheel pommel. The blade was battle-scarred, speckled with rust spots, but the edge was sharp and the tip had been hewn to a fine point. Cedric passed the weapon to me and I took it in my right hand, waved it through the air in the shape of a serpent to gauge the weight and feel of it; it was lighter than I expected and the hilt sat well in my hand.

'How much do you want for it?' I said.

'Nothing, lad. My hands are too knotted to hold it and my heart has not the stamina to take a man's life.'

Those last words put me in pause, brought dreams and reality closer to me, and the prospect of some distant, emotionless triumph was suddenly transformed into a joyless, tragic present.

Lost in my inward turmoil, I failed to observe the condition of the terrified messenger. Rosamund noticed the first signs of his haleness starting to fail and she rushed past me and reached the man just as he began to slump backwards. Undue strain must have enfeebled his constitution, blood drained away from his skin, and blisters of sweat appeared on his face and neck. Rosamund had the innkeeper's wife fetch water and wine; water was dashed on the man's face to wake him, and the wine was scalded with a poker to warm it, before it was fed to the man as he came to his senses.

It was as Cedric and his wife attended to the man's needs that I first came to understand just how easy and safe it would feel to hold on to tradition. When it suited me to blame custom for creating false and biased images of men and women, I was quite content to do so. But there, standing in that parlour-room with a weapon of murder grasped in my hand, I was suddenly compelled to hide behind the habits of antiquity, just as Cedric had done so. He was a man, stocky and strong, but he was also a cripple and therefore tradition dictated he should not be a fighting man. And in that moment of jeopardy, just like so many others before him, he chose to use tradition to his advantage and withdraw himself from conflict. But why could he not be a man-at-arms and set out to avenge the stolen bride? He could walk, he could hold a sword, he was capable of sinking the blade deep into another man's flesh. And so was his wife, and Rosamund, and me.

Perhaps we all grasp onto strands of tradition, to deflect our own shortcomings and fears; and that is how divided tribes are formed. How easy it would be to plead I was just a farmer. I could ride out to the local manor house, raise a hue and cry; send a parcel of manly men to see to the brutal business of bringing Roger to book, and no one would judge me for it. Rosamund and the innkeeper's wife could busy themselves in nursing the messenger, and no one would pronounce them cowards for not riding after Roger with a glaive and a buckler in their hands.

I suspected Rosamund was guiding her thoughts along the same path. She stepped back from the man, as though the Devil were tempting her, and she glanced her eye at me, in which I read trepidation and fear, but also defiance, bravery and a determination to enter a new field of enterprise and break with tradition, whatever the consequences.

'Come, Rosamund,' I said. 'We must make haste.'

She nodded and said, 'I will fetch the bags. Ready the ponies and I will meet you outside.'

Her parting glance at me was tender indeed, and I could only hope it was a sign she could see past the de Marsh blood that ran through me, and know how well I loved her in my heart.

'You cannot take a woman with you!' Cedric called, when I had taken the silver from the purse on my belt, paid the reckoning and taken up the sword.

In my mind, an answer rapidly formed itself, because I knew Rosamund and I had stepped outside the bounds of tradition, and no longer fitted into the simple tribe of our sex that our ancestors had formed a thousand years ago. Rosamund and I were not women; Rosamund was Rosamund, and I? I was Alwin of Whittaker.

I never did reply to Cedric. I was consumed by such urgency and ran so fast, that my language seemed to lag far behind me. I ran as though the Devil spurred my flanks and in no time at all, the ponies were unhitched and ready to ride. Rosamund appeared soon after, the bags in her hand, and she mounted her pony before I had stepped into the stirrup.

She kicked on first, but I soon caught up and we rode on side by side. The horses were lively and spry; we rode with long stirrups, and pulled and dropped their heads with soft reins, to have them gallop at their best pace, but with an even stride.

Time and distance were strange creatures that day, and I could no longer judge the measure of them, for the landscape was unchanging and the daylight cast neither colour nor shadow about us. So, on we rushed, riding from nowhere to somewhere with both an urgent dread and an unstoppable desire to meet up with our future fate and at last have it pass over and leave us be.

Eventually, the lie of the land changed and as the track rose upwards on an incline, we came to the church, sitting exposed on its hilltop, girdled by a copse of naked trees, solitary and forlorn in its oneness. We drew rein, slowed our pace as we approached the lychgate and looked at a sorry scene.

Weaving our way through discarded posy-knots and lost shoes, it was clear that much gore had been spilled. The ground, rubbed bare by generations of good Christians' feet, was motley where patches of blood had been shed, and here and there lay hay-forks and axes, their hafts and heads stained red.

Two men sat slumped against a wall and moans and sobs drifted out of the open church door, to where the injured had been taken. Then from behind us, footsteps sounded and a man and woman appeared from beneath the trees; he with rolled-down hose, mud-spattered boots and a bag filled with acorns, as though he had been fetched from his work with haste; she red-cheeked and breathless.

'Which path did the lord ride?' I shouted, my horse throwing his head back and champing at the bit, believing I did bid him take up his gallop again. 'Where did he take her?'

The woman looked up at me as she scurried past, but she eyed me in a strained and troubled manner, the trauma of the day's events making her doubt every image she saw. I repeated my questions and at last, she paused, then pointed with a quivering finger towards a narrow path that led northwards.

'The lord rode that way,' she said. 'And his sergeant, who took a gash to the belly, went eastwards. He will not get far.'

With a kick and a shout, we urged our horses on the north road and took to the path at full gallop. We thundered through a tunnel of ash trees, heedless of tree-roots and rose-briers, and in time broke out onto open pasture cropped low by grazing sheep. The ground was firmer on the grassland and we streaked along at a tidy pace, until some four miles onward, Rosamund called out for us to halt, reining her pony up sharp and severe. It took twenty paces for me to slow to a stop, and twenty more to retrace my steps and return to Rosamund.

As I drew level with her, she dismounted and, labouring to draw breath, she simply pointed to a mound of rags discarded by a rustic, heaped in a pile beside a fallen tree. I slipped down from my saddle and followed her steps until she paused, then she ran on. By the time I caught up with her, she was kneeling by the raggedy heap, but matters were not as I first thought. The garments were not carelessly discarded, neither were they the tattered raiment of a rustic.

Rosamund gently lifted the jacket; so smartly it had been stitched, with buttonholes neater than even Mother could have sewn, the brown woollen outer-jacket lined with linen, and a small pewter badge lovingly stitched on the front. It was the type of coat a wife might make for her husband to wear for church, or a bride might make for her groom on their wedding day.

I looked long at the jacket and sorrow rose in my throat and in that moment of sadness, I failed at first to see what the jacket had been covering. But as Rosamund's weeping grew louder, I stooped alongside her and saw the body that the coat had overlaid. I did not need my eyes to linger long, for it was clear the woman had suffered the same fate as the Winfeld nuns; her body had been defiled and her life had been stolen by a single gash along the breadth of her neck that had bled, then clotted and now hung like the Devil's rosary beneath her chin.

'God damn the man,' Rosamund said. 'God damn the man!' she repeated, before sobs stole her breath and stemmed her words.

I believed every syllable she voiced. There was surely nothing left but for God to take Roger's soul and send it to Hell and Damnation; and the sooner his spirit and mortal flesh were parted, the better the world would be. With that attitude of intent, I clenched my teeth, compressed my lips and carefully laid Thomas's jacket over the body of his new wife, that she might somehow sense his arms about her.

'Stay with her, Rosamund,' I said. 'I shall go on alone.'

I turned to catch up the reins of my horse, but without looking back, I knew Rosamund would not let me go on in solitude. As I mounted my horse, so Rosamund climbed into her saddle and followed after me, solemn and quiet as a shadow, and on we travelled along a track sure to lead only to more sorrow and regret, but unable to stay our feet.

The further we rode, the more snagged became the path and the denser the trees. But a rider must have gone on before us, treading down undergrowth and snapping branches as he went, because a narrow adit had been forged through the foliage. Riding in single file, we pressed onward, the woodland swallowing all sounds except the noise of our forward progress; the swish of trampled herbage, the jingle of tack, the creak of leather, hoof-falls and laboured breaths. The path seemed endless, until at last a new noise sounded ahead of us.

Someone approached on horseback. A dark form appeared up ahead, then suddenly took shape as it burst through the over-hanging branches, and Roger's black stallion galloped headlong towards us, its head held high in the air with foaming nostrils stretched wide and the fibres of its mane cast outwards by its speed of passage. It skewed to the right then, seeing us in its black eye, it halted and reared, stamping the ground, whinnying and snorting. But it was rider-less and Roger was nowhere to be seen.

How different his horse looked without the man himself astride its back; the saddle, scarlet belly band and furniture were unchanged, but the horse suddenly lost its threat of terror and was just another beast of burden, frightened of the world and its demons, just like the rest of us.

'We should go on foot,' I said to Rosamund. 'Roger must have been unseated.'

'Or perhaps he has heard our approach and lies in wait for us,' she countered.

'Aye,' I conceded. 'We must take care.'

We slithered down from our saddles in silence and I took Cedric's sword from my belt, clasped it tight in my right hand and took up the reins in my left. I glanced over my shoulder at Rosamund; she was following on behind, but she walked with her head bowed forward, and fumbled with an ampulla as she strung it about her waist. So, on we stalked, each with our chosen weapons to hand, striding closer to that obligatory point in time where triumph and regret would brand an indelible mark on one of our souls forever.

The thicket was snarled with bindweed and bramble and we moved at a slow pace, until at length the path widened to a clearing, and there in the centre of the glade, lying impotent and helpless, was the nobleman, Roger de Marsh.

The sight of him stopped me in my tracks, then I dropped my pony's reins and walked forwards alone. Roger heard the yielding of dry bracken and leaf-litter beneath my tread, and he moved his head towards me, but his Flanders cape was wound about his neck and he could not raise his shoulders from the ground.

'Who's there?' he called, angry, sharp.

I did not answer but took another step forward. Roger moved his right arm, tried to push himself up from the ground, but fell back and issued a cry of anguish. I took another pace onward and, at fewer than twenty feet from where he lay, I saw for the first time what ailed him.

His left shinbone was barked to the bone, which in turn was rent in two; the lower part of his leg lay inert and glistened with raw and disorganised flesh around it. His left arm, too, was rendered dysfunctional; it jutted at a sharp angle and curved outwards at the elbow.

I glanced back along the path and saw in my mind's eye how events had come to pass. There was a low-slung, thickened branch, snapped off at its base, that must hitherto have grown over the left-hand side of the path. Roger, with his impaired vision, could not have seen it and had been swept from his saddle when the tree-limb checked his onward progress and pushed him violently to the ground, where he had fallen to the measure of his height.

I looked at Rosamund and she, too, was tracing her eyes along the path, from the fringe of trees to the shorn scrub where Roger lay. How strange the feeling I carried in my heart at that moment; haunted by dreams of brave combat and the glory of fair triumph, but confronted with an entirely different prospect; a broken man, too weak either to raise his head or utter any words of contrition, even if they ever did form themselves on his lips.

I stood for an age, rooted and indecisive, turning the sword's hilt in my hand over and again, as though the weapon had become the agent of my heart and would not endorse the killing. Rosamund broke the stasis when she took a step past me, the flask of tincture unloosed from her waist and held tight in her trembling hands. I strode after her, caught her arm and stayed her purpose, and we looked at each other with troubled eyes, a primal intuition whispering in our ears to leave matters be and save our souls.

And in that distracted manner, neither of us saw the man approach. He walked with gentle tread, ghostlike and forlorn, his eyes blank, his mouth agape. He shouted no oaths and carried no weapon, but on he trod until he stood over Roger, then stared at him, unblinking.

If I knew then what I know now, I would have run to the man and taken him away from that glade, even if I had been compelled to render him unconscious by the force of my fist. I would have told him that vengeance belongs to God alone, because only He has the strength to bear it for all time to come. But I had not reckoned on how tainted a man's heart grows, once it has been pierced to the core.

The man looked down on Roger and said, simple and timid, 'My name is Thomas Shepherd. You killed my wife.'

As Thomas lifted the rock, raised it above his head and dashed it down on Roger's face, I was still too far away to intervene. In panic, I dropped my sword and could only cry out as I ran forward. Thomas did not hear. All his senses were centred on Roger, and in a heartbeat, he elevated the rock again, succumbing to the violent blood within him, and he brought it crashing down on Roger's head, never flinching from the intent of his purpose.

As I reached the two men, I glanced down at Roger and was stopped in my tracks by the horror of what I saw. His body twisted and writhed, but only a muffled noise rose from his throat. Just once, Roger mustered the strength to raise his right arm, but there was no surrender to his appeal from Thomas, no forgiveness, no pity.

After the third blow had been effected, Thomas turned to face me in a sort of reflex, and I do not believe he recognised me as a human; he must surely already have been living in Hell. His eyes grew wider and with the snarl of an injured animal, he greeted me with a punch to my stomach. It winded me and I could do no more than slump to the ground. Rosamund came to me, half lifted me, but I could not stand, and we were forced to watch, helpless and horrified, as the interminable murder lurched on.

All my life, Father Oswald had told me stories of heroic men who had been victorious in battle. He painted scenes with his words of glory and virtue, where warriors slew savage invaders and defended the hallowed lands of Albion, thus bequeathing their names to the annals of time, sepulchred in nimbus and revered as saints. But Father Oswald never spoke of how hard it was to die suddenly in violent combat; how brutal that passage between life and death.

Time and again, Thomas lifted and plunged that boulder downward, the face of the rock dyed scarlet with the colour of his vengeance. A low croaking sound came every once in a while from Roger's torso, and his body jerked in spasms, his heels pushed deep into the topsoil, but he made no vocal murmurs, for the flesh of his face was quite deranged.

On it went, brutal and endless, until at last Roger was silent, his body both featureless and soulless. In truth, I could not feel glad at his death. It was more vicious, long and cruel than I thought a man could suffer. Instead, my thoughts lingered on Thomas. Slumped on his knees, I believe he was more lost than Roger.

Where before Thomas was the victim, to be supported by his neighbours and friends, a law-abiding man whose suffering and sorrow would forever be respected; suddenly, he had become the perpetrator of a frenzied murder. And the realisation of that terrible burden was already clear on Thomas's face. His eyes spoke of the dupery with which Roger had ensnared him; Thomas had been tempted by the seduction of revenge, induced to show the baseness of man's nature and would spend the rest of his life lamenting in regret, tainted forever with the curse of Roger de Marsh.

CHAPTER THIRTEEN

An uneasy quietude fell about the glade at the moment Roger's soul was parted from his body; no motion but the moving of time, the woods silent and the air itself brittle and fear-smitten. No birds carolled, no leaves dropped and the breeze, chill and invisible, plied its ghostly path first one way then the other, casting its eye between visions of the next world and ours, then melting its substance away until the day was left in perfect stillness.

In time, I was able to rise to my feet. Rosamund stood alongside me and I took her hand in mine, somehow unable to stand alone and face in solitude what might come after. I knew not what to do, how to be, or what to say. For a lingering moment, I thought nothing would ever change; Roger's hideous corpse would lie reposed in that glade forever, Thomas would kneel at his side with blood on his face and arms, with thicker, darker clots gloving his hands, and Rosamund and I would look at that scene for eternity, until our skin blanched and our jaws slackened.

Then Thomas began to weep and the hex was broken. The noise that issued from his lips was nothing more than a breathy murmur, but the sound seemed to come straight from the centre of him, and it reached out to me and I heard it so clearly. I believed his heart must surely be rent in two, knowing it could never be conjoined again, but searching only for forgiveness, that it might bridge its wound and have the strength to move forward and live in a world of contrition.

For the first time, Thomas blinked his eyes, moved his head and looked around. His gaze fell first to his hands and he lifted his palms upwards, stared with disbelief at the glistening blood that coated his fingers. Then he travelled his eyes further and set them to looking at Roger. He frowned as though not understanding what he saw.

The sight drew a fearsome, grim expression from Thomas, a gesture of anguish descended over his face, and with his eyes staring, his outstretched arm touched the cadaver's shoulder. Thomas scrambled to his feet at that, and jumped backwards, his hands trembling violently. His cheeks flushed up and he held his breath, fighting to contain some inner voice that bore no earthly sound, then he let loose a piercing cry, before falling to his knees and sobbing with the thickened voice of a lost man.

There have been few times in my life that at a point of crisis my thoughts have remained untangled. But whenever such a crux did occur, it was neither thought nor reason that lent me clarity of eye; it was feeling, pure feeling. More than ever before, at that moment when Thomas could find no refuge from his agony, I felt compelled to offer comfort devoid of condemnation, like a mother to a wayward child.

I gently loosed my hand from Rosamund's and hastened towards him, a swell of gentle compassion rising within my breast. He turned and stood as I reached him and threw out his arms, unable any longer to withstand the despair on his own, searching my eyes for humanity. And with the highest of reverence I offered him my pity. I took him in my arms and soothed away the madness and the murder from within him, and his brokenness endowed my wholeness, made me feel more human than I had ever done before; and by understanding, I forgave him, for they are surely one and the same?

We stood there for a while and a while, then as though Saint Swithin himself walked among us, it began to rain, the whole sky giving itself up to crying and the drops falling clean and whole-some upon us. Rosamund laid her hand on my shoulder by way of appeal and, releasing Thomas from my embrace, I fronted her. For a moment, she looked at me lovingly, like she knew me better than I knew myself, then she nodded to the right and there, beneath the thicket of trees through which we had earlier emerged, a line of villagers and wedding guests appeared.

Under darkling skies and with solemn steps the men approached us in silence. The group fragmented as it neared us; two of the older men, with shovels and picks in their hands, dropped their weapons and went to Thomas, then finding he was still afflicted with torment, they walked him to a tree stump some yards away and had him sit down. The rest of the men, some seven or eight, circled Roger's corpse, some mumbling oaths and spitting gobs of phlegm at him, others viewing him with hard, pitiless eyes, as though he were nothing but a mortling.

In time, one of the men broke away and came to Rosamund and me. I supposed, by his grey whiskers and weathered skin, that he was a village elder come to ask us what our eyes had witnessed, that he may tell the story to their lord or his steward, to a constable and his tithing men, or perhaps their priest. But instead, he looked at us with stern eyes.

'The man ... the creature that lies dead in this glade,' he began, his voice low and hoarse, 'did debauch and set blade to my young-est daughter, Joanna. She lies as dead as he, up yonder.' His voice broke at that and he was obliged to pause and take a breath, before he said, 'You both good Christians?'

'Aye, sir,' I said. 'We are pilgrims.'

'Then you will have heard your priest say eye for eye, tooth for tooth and life for life?'

'Aye,' I nodded.

'Then you will also agree that my ... son-in-law, Thomas, has done God's will here today, and that the matter therefore be closed?'

His words put me in thought. I looked at Rosamund and she nodded, then my eyes were drawn back to Roger and the other villagers. Where before they stood slightly apart from the body, now two or three of them moved closer and kicked at the torso with violence. Some tore away trophies – one of Roger's mid-calf leather boots, his decorated leather purse, the brooch from his cape and his eating knife – and they waved the spoils in the air and issued shouts of triumph.

The remainder of the men began to clear away vegetation from the side of Roger, and dug their shovels and spades in the ground. The burden was indeed too much for Thomas to bear. He could never have withstood the scrutiny of his lord or priest, on top of all he had seen and done on his wedding day. So, the matter in hand, and indeed Roger himself, must at once be laid to rest and never spoken of again. Thomas's kith and kin were more than willing to create a secret confederacy, which might condemn them all, but would surely dilute the taint of guilt and bear Thomas up, that he may yet live a worthy life. And in our own way, Rosamund and I were already part of that brotherhood. We had plotted and dreamed, carried swords and poisons, and chased Roger de Marsh to his death. At length, I nodded to the old man.

'Today, we saw nothing,' I said. 'We know nothing, and are just two pilgrims plying our course to the east.'

The old man bowed his head to Rosamund, then clapped his hand to my shoulder, before he turned about and joined his brethren. Rosamund and I rounded up our horses from the hem of the forest, where they stood together cropping the autumn grass. We stood a while and watched the men at their labour. The ground they worked yielded softly and in no time at all a grave was dug. With contempt and irreverence, Roger's body was kicked into the hole, the earth cast over it, then the tussocks and sods replaced, and with the rain washing away all stains of his lifeblood, it was as though he had never truly lived at all and was always just a demon to be mocked and despised.

Rosamund and I took our departure in silence and retraced our steps, the shock of the day still ringing loud in my ears, waves of contemplation resonating deep within my thoughts. With Roger gone, my false ideas of justice and revenge also died with him. The abhorrence of his ill deeds had brewed a kind of daring swagger beneath my skin, which had frothed and fermented and carried me forward with impetus. Suddenly I felt empty and futile, like a skep with no bees. All I could see ahead was the blackness of darkness and the certainty of doubt; I still did not know who my father was, or whether he was dead or alive; and I could not be sure whether, in Rosamund's eyes, Roger's final act of brutality and subsequent death had distanced me from or brought me closer to the de Marsh clan.

From then on, the weather and turn of the season began to influence our journey more than ever before. The quick-sailing clouds and sharp showers gave way to a mantle of grey, which sent down diagonal rain and made runnels and puddles and clotted the mud. Mornings were late to rise and eventide was early to bed, the compacted day in-between filled with heavy travel, water-logged and drear.

Certain that knowledge was advantageous, and still feeling cheated that Roger had gone to his grave without being quizzed, I determined to seek out his sergeant and learn all we could from him, compromised as he was with his wound. I supposed, with him nursing an injury, we would catch up with him in no time at all. But the weather slowed our progress and any tracks we might have followed were washed away. At a crossroads we noticed a discarded rag, soaked in fresh blood, and further along the track a bloodied jerkin had been abandoned at the roadside. Those clues encouraged us, but still we seemed no closer to catching up with the man. We enquired about him as we passed through settlements and when we met wayfarers, but folks in those parts did not esteem discourse with strangers and we learned very little from them.

Two days we cut a path through the rain, the first night arriving drenched at a lonesome farm cot, the second night taking refuge in a barn. Both mornings when Rosamund awoke she was less vital than the night before and her face was pale, her appetite eroded. Sometimes, she seemed to wilt down in the saddle when first we set off, but as the day went on, she gained better strength. Three times, I asked her if it were better we returned to Maud's, that I might leave her there and go on to Walsingham alone, but she would not be said. We barely talked at all apart from that, the bride's murder and Roger's death filling my mind with sombre reveries; thoughts and recollections too dark for words. And so fast and hard the days passed, that as soon as we found a bed for the night, I fell into chasms of dreamless slumber.

On the third day after Roger's death, we arrived at a cluster of dwellings strung low in the fens. As had become my habit, I asked a rustic what name the place took and whether or not a military man had passed that way before us: 'This settlement is called Walpole St Peter,' was his reply. 'Many travellers journey this route; I cannot recall whether or not a soldier was amongst them,' he added, glib and evasive. 'But I suppose you will be seeking lodgings at the convent a little further along this road?' he went on. 'Perhaps they will know more than I do on the matter.'

With that the man went on his way and a mile beyond, as evening descended about us, we came across the convent. Tired and cold, we sought harbourage and were offered accommodation for the night. It was not lost on me that a short time before, I had journeyed to just such a holy house of God and been witness to the foulness of humankind. At first I could not face the prospect of looking at the nuns; seeing the serenity of their faces, the orderliness of their wimples and habits, but knowing all the time how easily their chastity and reverence could be defiled; how exposed and vulnerable they were; how inexpectant and defenceless all women were.

The convent was comprised of five buildings joined by a series of slypes and once we had entered through the gatehouse and were beyond the almonry, the porter accompanied Rosamund, took her to be received in the parlour alongside the prioress's lodge, and I was directed to the stables and granary on the left.

The stabling was divided into eight trevisses, four stalls on each side; a Scotch Galloway pony, a mule and two milch cows were tethered on the left, and on the right, were three empty stalls and a bay gelding. I divested our ponies of their saddle and tack and tied them together either side of a hay-rack. The bay horse partitioned on the right whickered and pawed its hoof on the ground, seeming uneasy as though it had eaten dusty chaff and suffered from the fret. I stepped around the dividing screen to inspect it closer and saw how hard its rider had ridden it; its withers were rubbed bare from the saddle, its flanks sore chafed and its right forefoot was unshod, the hoof itself grown brittle and cracked.

I left the stables in haste and with more than a pensive mind. As soon as my eyes met Rosamund's, she rose to greet me from her bench in the parlour-room, her features taut.

'Alwin, the prioress has confirmed they have a visitor,' she said, her voice hurried and low.

'I know. I have just seen his horse,' I said.

'The man's name is Gilbert Longspere,' she went on. 'The prioress said he arrived stricken with a grave distemper of the belly. Poison has set itself beneath his skin where the point of a blade did puncture it. I have told the prioress I am a practiser of folk-herbs and she has gone to ask Gilbert if he accedes to my ministering and ...'

Her sentence was abridged by the opening of a door, and a wimpled lady in the habit of her order entered the room.

'Master Whittaker,' she said, bowing her head, welcoming and genteel. 'Your wife has offered to attend to our patient. He is hot

with fever and ailing fast. He wishes to accept your wife's physicking, so will you both come through?'

We followed the old nun through a series of passageways that
threaded first past the refectory, then the chapter-house, until at
last we arrived at the infirmary. Six beds were set out, three against
each of the longest walls, all dressed with pillows, sheets and blankets, but only two occupied with invalids. An old man lay dormant
and pale in the first bed on the left, and Roger's sergeant, Gilbert
Longspere, was prostrate in the central sick-bed on our right. The
windows were shuttered and a weak, bilious light pulsed out from
the six candles that had been placed around the room, a thick, pungent odour rising about us, warm and stale in my nostrils.

'Master Longspere,' the holy sister said as she approached him.
'These are the good pilgrims that have knowledge of physic and
might aid your distemper.' Then turning to Rosamund, she said, 'We
have tinctures and dried herbs in our store and I am happy to place
them at your disposal.' Then, in a lower, less friendly tone, she added,
'Of course, I must remind you the chanting of spells is forbidden.'

The prioress then left us, with a promise to return in person
within the hour, and a pledge to send a novice to fetch us any
required supplies from the store. As soon as she had gone, Rosam-
und, in her goodness, attended to Gilbert.

I could not reckon how she managed to overcome her loathing
of the man. She surely suspected his involvement in matters concerning Eleanor, and she knew for certain he was party to both the
Winfeld massacre and the kidnapping of the bride. It was only later
in my life, I came to understand that the most virtuous decisions we
make are born out of the soul's bias towards doing the right thing.

Gilbert was lying flat on his back with his feet drawn up, his
body very still, his eyes closed and his teeth clenched together.
Rosamund perched herself on the edge of the bed and laid her
hand softly on his brow that she may gauge his body's heat, but I

suspected she knew full well his blood was up; his face was scarlet and beads of sweat were strung across his brow. The touch of her hand roused him and his eyes flickered open, then he moved his head along the pillow to see her better and, even though his movement was slight, it jarred his belly and he let out a wail.

'I need to move the sheets, Master Longspere,' Rosamund said. 'I must see the wound to know what herbs may heal it.'

'Do what you must,' he said, his words conjoined, issued in one breath.

Rosamund peeled back the blanket and sheet, and a putrid, stinking smell rose up. Gilbert's belly was enlarged and dark stains coloured the left-hand side of his shift. Rosamund raised a portion of his shirt and beneath was a gash where the flesh remained parted, perhaps a wound effected by a shovel or an axe. The outer flaps of skin were deep red, his whole belly pink and swollen, but even in the dimly lit infirmary, it was clear the centre of the wound was black where the tissues beneath his skin had become mortified. Whereas the sick flesh around the puncture caused Gilbert distress whenever he moved, when Rosamund touched her fingers to the black mass in the centre, he did not flinch. It was clear that a dreadful malady had set itself inside him and, when Rosamund turned to look at me, I knew there must be very little she could do.

As Rosamund replaced the covers, I stepped closer to the bed but said nothing, and Gilbert closed his eyes, his breaths coming short and fast.

'There was so much I thought we might talk to him about,' I whispered in Rosamund's ear. 'So many answers we might have discovered.'

My voice seemed to stimulate Gilbert, his eyes snapped open and he stared first at Rosamund then at me. He blinked in quick succession, his eyelids red and sore, the orbs beneath bulbous and bloodshot, then he fixed his gaze on me.

'I know you,' he said, his voice rasping and low.

'I was at the Winfeld Priory,' I said, plain and flat.

At that, Gilbert lowered his eyes and he swallowed hard. He was silent for a moment, deep in ponder, then he eyed Rosamund.

'And you,' he said. 'You were outside the town, riding with your brother. Are you the one they all search for; the girl that Sir Hugo de Marsh does seek?'

'Who is Sir Hugo?' I said, my voice suddenly loud and blunt. 'And why does he seek … this woman?'

'I suppose he fears the girl for the man she might marry and the army she might raise; that they will take away all the de Marsh riches. He also suspects he will be blamed by her for the death of her uncle; his own brother.'

'How did news of Roger's death reach you so soon?' I said.

Gilbert looked at me blankly, seemed to fumble for his thoughts, before saying, 'Roger is dead?'

Before I could reply, Gilbert's demeanour became more restless. He shivered and a thin coating of sweat broke out over his face, then despite his pains obviously being increased by the merest movement of his body, he rolled to the right of the bed and tried to raise his head. The action aggravated his discomfort and through a long, low moan, he spewed a fother of vomit, the issue black and foul in its odour, until at last he lay spent and inert. I leaned over him and lifted his shoulders and head, that he may find some comfort from his pillow, and Rosamund took the hem of the sheet and wiped the evacuation from his lips.

His breathing was so shallow, I was convinced his ghost was surely about to leave him, but with his eyes still closed, he heaved a fragile sigh and whispered close to my ear, 'I am not long for this world, lad. What I told you before; it is not the whole truth. It is all so intricate and I do not have the time. Take this woman to Walsingham Parva. Ask for Jacob Fenland and tell him I sent you. See the de Marsh treasure for yourselves. It will answer all her questions.'

With that, his strength deserted him and his breath became sticky and laboured. His expression was pinched and ghastly, and where before heat rayed out from his body; now an invisible cloud, cold and damp, seemed to hover over him. In time, his rasping breaths diminished to nought and at last he was dead.

Rosamund slowly pulled the sheet over Gilbert's head and we stood in silence for some moments, sombre and respectful. But inside my own head, questions were asking themselves, loud and irreverent, and at last I could contain them no longer.

'My father could well be this man called Sir Hugo de Marsh,' I said, the name sounding awkward and bitter on my tongue. 'But what of his fear of blame for the death of his brother? Were there once three brothers?'

'Alwin,' she said. 'We cannot know until we finish our journey. And you know as well as I, that when folks are close to death, they become delirious; they lose themselves in a fog of what has gone before and cannot tell good from evil, or right from wrong.'

'And what of the dread that their children will turn against them and steal the de Marsh treasure?' I said. 'It does not make sense; why create such an abundance of progeny if you then fear them and wish them murdered at birth? If Eleanor's son had lived, would the de Marshes have judged him imperfect and had him slaughtered? Is Agnes's daughter on the list to live or the list to die? Why did Roger not simply marry and be satisfied with the children his wife did bear him? I cannot make sense of it!'

'There must be something we do not yet understand, Alwin,' Rosamund said. 'We can only go on, as Gilbert Longspere said, and look for answers in Walsingham, perhaps then ...'

Any further words Rosamund was about to speak were interrupted by footsteps, and a young novice appeared in the doorway.

She bowed her head and with soft tread she approached us, then meekly said, 'I have come to fetch herbs and honey from the stores.'

'I am afraid physic is no longer needed for Master Longspere,' Rosamund said.

The holy sister stepped to one side, sheepish and shy, and looked over at the bed where Gilbert's body lay, then said, 'I must go and ... I must fetch—'

She left her broken words behind, disappeared through the infirmary door in haste and returned minutes later with the prioress and another nun. The two older women lifted the sheet, inspected the body and spoke hushed words to one another, then turned to Rosamund and me.

'It is a pity none of us could save him,' the prioress said, 'but a kindness and a blessing his soul now rests at the mercy of God.'

I am certain her words were meant as a comfort, but I shivered a little as she spoke them, keenly recalling his debauchery, wondering what a sorry song his soul would chant when at last it met its maker.

We stayed in the infirmary for a few moments longer and the prioress thanked us for our intentions and time, then she asked the novice to show us to our sleeping quarters.

'You must sleep in separate dormitories, I am afraid,' she said as we turned to go. 'A priest stayed with us last night, a good and kind man. He told us of a terrible outrage that happened some weeks ago at a priory in another shire. He counselled us to segregate our guests to guard them against temptation and lewdness, and he said it is better to have all the men together in case we come under attack.'

'What was the cleric's name?' I asked.

'Father Oswald of Giolgrave,' the prioress replied.

So, that was how Gilbert Longspere managed to guide his horse to a priory with an infirmary, despite the fatal wound in his belly;

he was accompanied by that ever-loyal servant of the de Marshes: Father Oswald. Knowing the soldier was beyond the cure of physic, the priest had left the man to die alone with his torments, and taken to the road to hasten back to his lord and master, Sir Hugo.

It was a dark and hostile hatred I cherished in my bosom as I thought of Father Oswald. All the residual belief and love I had once held in my heart for him, at last raged itself into nothing but grudge and malice. I took my feelings of animosity with me as we walked to the dormitory and, barely bidding a coherent word of goodnight to Rosamund, I nursed them all night long.

If I had been a better person, I would have cast out such worth-less musings, and instead broken the convent's precept by running to Rosamund, taking her in my arms and voicing my love for her. Then I would have had us ride away, back to Maud's cottage, the place where all life's blisses had entered my heart, and the wisdom of true happiness had brought me to pure felicity. But instead, I succumbed to a fitful sleep and, with the undiluted poisons of anger and contempt exciting the pipes beneath my skin, I awoke next morning dull-headed and morose.

We set off at first light, but the sun never fully rose, it simply glowed weak and grey from behind granite clouds that stood like rocks and towers about us. The rain held off, but the wind blew chill and damp in our faces, made every step forward an effort, and the ground was shot through with flint, which gave the ponies an uneasy step and set my joints to grating. I found the low, flat district wholly unpleasant. There was far too much sky and horizon for my liking and I could not see how the rustics worked such listless land.

In time, we came to a road that was better surfaced, where rocks had been cleared and the mud was trodden down to a rind. There we were able to travel on at a hand-gallop and cover the ground much faster. We shifted along at a brisk pace for half a mile before we were obliged to slow when the track skewed to the right.

Rosamund and I then trotted our ponies side by side, that we may better see between the trees that now grew in abundance alongside the track, for the road had narrowed, the daylight had darkled, and thoughts of ambush grew large in my mind. A breath of late morning mist still hovered above the trace where the breeze had been hindered, and the path before us seemed suspended in the air, hanging between the elements like a future memory.

However much I tried to concentrate on the present moment, see what was passing under my eyes, I could not help but think of Father Oswald; and his image wholly dominated my thoughts. How strange it was to think of his familiar features; his eyes that had known me since I was a babe, his arms that had rocked me, lifted me when I fell, guided me. In my mind, his face was twined so tightly with recollections of Crown Croft that I could not disentangle one from the other. Feelings of childhood contentment, of warmth and safety, blushed hot behind my ribs like steam. But how quickly those happy vapours condensed in the cold recollection of his betrayal.

I searched inside my head for the words I might use when that future confrontation finally arrived, but my questions and accusations all deserted me and I was left alone with the image of the man whom once I thought loved me best. Where I used to see a rainbow; only storm-clouds did exist, and with exaltation lost from the love I once held dear for him, nothing was left to me but the sense of disillusionment, as though my childhood had been but a dream. That odious taint of betrayal would surely dog me for all my days and steal away every pure recollection I had of Crown Croft, Mother and my happy childhood, because the truth was that not only had I lived in a world of lies, but also I had been bred up to believe them. Perhaps that was what smarted most; I was nothing better than a fool.

I have no clear recollection of the final leg of our journey that took us to Walsingham, save for taking directions from a native of that shire, who had us follow a river called Stiffkey, until we were delivered to a place he referred to as the milking ground; a rich, fertile meadow, where the grass grew in such abundance on the chalk soil that a multitude of dairy kine were left to graze its pastures all the year round.

As to what conversation I held with Rosamund as we rode those final miles, I cannot know. I only remember feeling torturous pangs of self-reproach, disbelief that I had not been able to see reality, and a cold realisation that in being blind to the truth about my past, how could I ever truly know my self? I felt so lonely as we entered the parish of Walsingham Parva; there was no sense of glory or elation at reaching my journey's end; no feeling of triumph. My curiosity had waned and my overarching mood was one of resentment and loss.

Whereas before I had single-mindedly forged a path towards discovery, with more than a relish for enlightenment; suddenly, I wanted it all to stop. I was no longer propelling myself forwards, but instead was being drawn ever-deeper into a world and a family I despised. I had supposed the wisdom I gained would be a gentle light that would banish all my shadows of doubt and shine warmly on a future perfect day. But instead, I was caught in a tempest and each new revelation was a thunder-dart, flashing hot and destructive. But just as a cloudburst cannot pass until it has spent its wrath, I knew I had no choice but to weather the storm and push onward to brighter horizons.

I did not voice my feelings to Rosamund and I offered no comfort, but neither did I seek it, for as a blacksmith cuts himself on a blade he has sharpened, he cannot curse the metal that has torn him; he must take his share of the blame for his own lack of vigilance.

We entered the village of Walsingham Parva not long after noon, but the onset of eventide seemed to set in early that day. The landscape faded fast through the greying of dusk, and evening dews broke out in cold sweats all about us on grass stems and spider-webs. Sounds were muffled by low-slung mists, which hovered uncertain above the ground, but every once in a while a corbie would crow in consternation at the premature approach of darkness, and the cawing sounded to me like a curfew marking the end of a very long day.

Few folks were stirring out of doors as we rode on, then at last a group approached us, walking barefoot on the road back towards Houghton St Giles. I asked if they knew of Jacob Fenland; they said they were not local, but instead were pilgrims returning from the Holy House, walking the Holy Mile back to the Slipper Chapel to collect their shoes. After that, we saw no other, and came to the end of the village, where I was obliged to dismount, retrace our steps and knock at the cottage doors one at a time.

Most shutters had been closed up against the dying day and my appeals remained unanswered, but eventually a door was opened to me, behind which stood a woman so advanced in years, I had never before seen the like. Her white hair was brittle, unkempt and absent altogether on the pate of her head. She stepped forward gingerly and leaned to the right, raising her eyes to meet mine, but she was afflicted with a stiffness in her neck and, being so small of stature, she could only see as high as my chest. I stooped, that she might see my face, to which her eyes squinted and she brushed her fingers over the white bristles on her chin.

Pulling her shawl about her frame with hands that were knotted and blue with age, she sucked her gums for a moment then croaked, 'Who knocks at the door of Mary Warren?'

Her voice was shrill but weak, and after speaking her name, her body fairly shook with the fret of coughing.

'I seek a man,' I said, 'named Jacob Fenland.'

She cupped her hand about her left ear and had me repeat his name, then she looked at me, her eyes pink and pale, blinking like a bird.

'What business do you have with him, lad?' she rasped.

'Roger de Marsh is dead and his sergeant, Gilbert Lon—'

'Roger de Marsh is dead, you say? Well, I shall not grieve his passing. It is only Edward de Marsh that will be remembered kindly around these parts.'

'Who is Edward de Marsh?' I said.

'He died nigh on twenty years ago. The best bred of all three brothers, perfect gentle he was, not a blot nor a falsehood on him. They say the good die first and it was surely true of the de Marshes when Edward went, God bless his soul. So, the youngest has gone now, has he? Well, only to be expected. Dance to the Devil's tune and you are nothing but his slave.'

'You seem to know the de Marsh family well,' I said, crouching lower still to have the old woman see the integrity in my eyes. 'How did Edward die?'

She looked long at me, her pale eyes moistened with tears, an uncertain expression drawn deep in the wrinkles of her skin. I have heard tell of a type of idiocy that afflicts ancients, where intellect and sensibility are compromised and life's events serve only to confuse and agitate. I wondered if Mary Warren was just such a passive being, whose great age had left her isolated in a sea of ponderings and memories, of dreams and imagined reality. She looked towards me, but not at me, as though stranded between two worlds, and I suspected she had deviated far from sense.

'You say you are looking for The Keeper?' she said at length, her eyes blinking fast again.

I shook my head and drew a breath in annoyance, ready to explain once more the purpose of my enquiry, but she seemed to gather herself and in a moment of lucidity, she said:

'Jacob Fenland lives beyond the dell and the lower mead. Take the path to the north, turn right at the broad oak, and his cot sits low in the gully. Prepare yourself, lad, for what you are about to see; it is both a shrine and a treasure, for sure, but one to Lucifer and not Our Lady.'

With that she turned about, closed her door to me and was gone.

I returned to the ponies and Rosamund. She was sitting low in the saddle, her travelling cloak gathered tight about her. I told her of the old gammer and her confused recollection of the de Marshes, how she had named Edward as the third brother, then I explained how in a moment of clarity the dame had discharged the directions that would lead us to Jacob Fenland's cottage. It took only a brief moment to tell Rosamund what had been said, and I finished speaking by the time I mounted my horse and slipped my right foot into the stirrup. I do not believe I even looked at Rosamund as I spoke, so easily drawn I had become into that dark and cloying sphere the de Marshes had been so clever in creating.

I always regretted my weakness at succumbing to their lure. One look at Rosamund would have told tales of her weariness; the paleness of her skin, the dullness of her eye. But being so obsessed with Roger, Hugo and Edward – engrossed with myself – I had neither the wit to take pause and see what was before me, nor cherish what I already had.

If time were a river and knowledge was a flood; how soon a deluge would carry me away. With more force than the waters of the Crown, the revelations I was about to discover would come at me as hard and fast as a storm-surge; and yes, the flood plains would be in richer plight thereafter and a calmness would come where the troubled waters once were. But at what cost? What cost?

CHAPTER FOURTEEN

The path we followed on that dreary afternoon twisted and snaked its way through tracts of scrubland where nothing but nettles, hawthorn and rose-brier grew. On the lands of Crown Croft, many paths had been created over time by travellers' footfalls, sheep-hooves, and the night-time explorations of deer. In the beginning, the vegetation was trodden down, which in turn exposed earth that was churned first to mud, then baked hard in the summer sun, until a firm crust paved the way ever more. But each and every one of those familiar routes trodden out by feet was virtually a straight line; a linear means of travelling from copse to mead, fell to dingle, or from treviss to paddock. A direct route to enable efficiency in both time and speed. The path to Jacob Fenland's cottage was different indeed. It was not well trod and it meandered first one way then the other, as though the few beings choosing to use it doubted where and why they were going, and surely considered the prospect of turning back.

In time, we descended into a lonely bower, threaded and laced with leafless bracts of dog-rose, the surrounding tree-limbs skeletal in their bareness, scratching at one another with each breath of wind that passed through them. The ground, littered with fallen twigs, was strangely pungent with rot and decay, and the further we went, the closer the trees were drawn together.

The lane dropped lower still, mists rising up around us from a stagnant rill, and at the base of the slope, in the mould-scented half-light, stood a wooden hut, shadows growing thicker about it, its thatch dull with moss. Neither rabbit, fox nor badger did we see, and all the birds had either fallen mute or flown away, and the land was devoid of any living creature.

'Master Fenland?' I called out. 'Jacob Fenland?'

My voice was not a shout, but it still tore the fragile air for a heartbeat, then fell stricken amongst the dying herbage. Nothing stirred, the bleak cottage stood brown and drear in its hollow, the woods around it pressing in on all sides, and with no lights within and not even a wisp of smoke about the roof, it seemed as though time itself stood still. Then something moved, barely discernible. Slow and deliberate, a dark shape shifted against the blacker darkness and made its way towards us from behind the hut. As the form approached us, a deep cowl was drawn back, revealing a pale head with wisps of grey hair that rose and fell like mist as the man strode onwards. He stopped some ten paces from us, eyed us, but said nothing.

'Are you Jacob Fenland?' I asked, my voice more subdued than before.

He nodded his head once, in a strange, exaggerated manner, but remained silent.

'A man named Gilbert Longspere did send us,' I went on, 'and an old woman, Mary Warren, told us where we might find you. We have many questions, Master Fenland, and believe that you ...'

At that, he held up the palm of his right hand to stem the flow of my words, then he beckoned us to follow him, turned about and led us down and down to the door of his cottage. He lifted the latch and we followed him into a single room, illumined by a lantern hung on a wall bracket. With darkness growing thicker by the heartbeat and the shutters closed tight, the sallow light had not been visible to us outside, and at first I welcomed the sight of it, but the quivering flame only lit up the darkness about it, made the air feel clammy against my skin and brought neither warmth nor hope to the interior of the cottage.

I tried again to engage Jacob Fenland in conversation, but the man was distracted, shuffling from one corner of the room to the other, carefully moving slats of wood from one workbench to the next, like a shepherd with his lambs. It was clear by the amount of wood-shavings and sawdust on the floor that Jacob was some sort of carpenter; partially made boxes – measuring half an ell by a foot – were stacked here and there both on stools and on the floor, and the tools of his trade were hung on nails around the walls.

At the third time of asking, I began to feel impatience at Jacob's reluctance to talk, and that, together with his strange mannerisms and vacant eyes, had me wonder if he were afflicted with chaos of the mind and a derangement of intellect. Then Rosamund, who had been studying the man, leaned in to me and whispered:

'Alwin, I suspect this man is a mute.'

Her voice was so light I could only just hear her words, but they travelled loud enough to Jacob's ears; he turned around to face us, nodding his head, a liveliness to his eyes that was absent a moment before. Perhaps, in God's wisdom, He had enhanced Jacob's remaining faculties, given him stronger eyes that could see in the darkness, and ears that could sense quiet sounds, to make up for the absence of his voice.

After that, I surrendered my desire to quiz the man, and stood in the silence of his world as he unhooked the lantern from its bracket, signalled us to follow him and led us out of the cottage into the night. In single file we aped his tread, ducked beneath low branches and splashed through hidden runnels. But as innocuous as the path was, the absence of immediate danger only served to magnify the fear of what lay ahead.

No more than a hundred paces from Jacob's front door, we arrived at what appeared to be a gate cut into the hillside. Hawthorn and brier grew in abundance around it and in the unlikely event of a traveller finding his way to such a place, he would have passed it by, quite unaware of its presence, so well disguised it was. But with the lantern-beam cutting the darkness, piercing the gloom with its yellow blade of light, a gate was just visible.

Jacob fumbled beneath his cloak and at length drew out a key, which he wriggled in the lock, then on hearing the latch bite, he opened the door. Thrusting the lantern into my right hand, he then stood to one side and pointed into the yawning mouth of the cavity, gesturing for me to enter. Snared by tendrils of rose-brier and snagged by twining doubts, I stepped over the threshold and entered the darkness beyond. I took no more than three steps, then turned to make sure I was not alone, searching the shadows behind me for Rosamund and Jacob. But the man, the keeper of that secret cavern, had gone away into the night and left us on our own.

'Should we follow him in retreat?' I said, raising the lantern to throw light on Rosamund's face.

'We have come so far,' she said, her voice tired, her eyes slow-blinking. 'There must surely be answers here, somewhere.'

I turned and lifted the lantern as high as I might, sending splashes of light over the walls, drawing images of rocks and hewn earth from out of the blackness. The cavern began to narrow at a point some twelve yards into the hillside and instead of irregular patterns of minerals and mud, the walls at once became straight-sided and uniform.

I took a step forward, squinting through the dimness, and said, 'What do you suppose this place is?'

'I cannot say,' Rosamund answered. 'I have never seen the like.'

Slowly, we advanced towards the tapered end of the vault and through the vagueness, stacks of wooden boxes took shape in the lantern's glow; small chests akin to the unfinished ones in Jacob's hut. From floor to ceiling they were stored, side by side, one atop the other, in great multitude, perhaps as many as twelve in height, in regular columns as far as the torch-light would show. Both sides of the underground chamber were a reflection of the opposite wall; chest upon chest, row after row. We walked past a dozen, a score, a hundred, and as the passageway thinned, so we walked nearer to them.

'They are numbered,' Rosamund said, pausing and inspecting one closer. 'Could be a codex, perhaps a date?'

'It must be their treasure,' I said. 'The fabled de Marsh riches that Sir Hugo so fears will be stolen from him, that drive him to wantonness and murder. Useless trinkets and baubles hoarded for generations, bloating his greed and feeding his dreams with dreams of more. How I loathe the man and all he stands for.'

I pressed on at a faster rate as I spoke, my pace increasing to match the growing agitation inside me. Then, as the passageway narrowed even further, I noticed one of Jacob's treasure chests on the ground before us, blocking our path. In the wall to the left, a socket had been dug in the earth, ready to receive the box of plunder; perhaps our approach had disturbed his sensitive hearing and he had left the box there to investigate the noise.

'What do you suppose it will contain?' I asked Rosamund, contemptuous in my tone. 'Gold? Pearls?'

I knelt beside the chest, placed the lantern on the ground, drew my eating knife from my belt and eased the blade beneath the lid. Stiff at first, the nails that held it down would not come loose. But I persevered, eventually able to slip my fingers under the cover and prise it from its body.

The smell hit my senses first; a peculiarly offensive odour, fetid and bitter and sickly, unlike any other, never to be forgotten. In that heartbeat of realisation when I caught the rancid flavour of the air in the back of my throat, I wished I could have stopped the final twist of my wrist that rendered the lid free, because the sight within I could already guess, and would haunt me to my dying day.

The infant had been laid on her back, the sleep of death too deep to let me rouse her, her body unencumbered by raiment. In life, such freedom from clothing would have lent ample play to her limbs, drawn a gurgle from her lips. But her spirit had long since left her body and her remains were grey and still. Her white face was pitched at a slight angle, the look of a seraph about her features, her lidded eyes surely questioning the brevity and small-ness of the world she had been forced to inhabit, which marked her death a doubly deeper crime. With her legs drawn up towards her chest and her tiny fists still clenched tight, it seemed as though life had been stolen from her before her first lungful of air had been taken, and that she would linger, bracing herself evermore for the rush of inward breath that would never come.

The slightness of her little corpse sent such a stimulus to my heart, quite stole my breath away and had my pulse beat quick. She seemed far too young and innocent to have been sent to her death. She should surely be warm in loving arms, swaddled at her mother's breast, not lying alone in a dark box. Not even a remnant of woollen cloth in which to lap her, not so much as a flower placed in the cas-ket with her to remind her that she was once human and did dwell on God's earth alongside other humans. The de Marshes were the only hosts she ever knew; and they murdered their most precious guest. The pity of it punched my soul with cold knuckles and called forth a heat of pity from me, which wept itself out from my eyes as I crouched over her, staring, unable either to understand or forgive.

In time, I looked up at Rosamund. Her face was wet with tear-shed, a pinched look and frown darkening her features. Her eyes were not on the casket but were searching the other boxes that lined the walls.

'They surely cannot all be ...' I said in a half-whisper, following her gaze, counting the number of boxes in my mind.

I gently replaced the lid on the tiny casket, rose to my feet, then walked back a few paces. I eyed the column of boxes, selected one at waist height, then slowly eased it from its earthy nook. Just as before, I loosed the cover and removed the lid; again, a tiny infantile form lay inside, and again the child was a girl.

I looked at Rosamund, but neither of us spoke, then at last she said, 'We have to examine more.'

'Why?' I said, horrified.

'Do you not see, Alwin? I suspect they are all girls; it is the female line that the de Marshes destroy.'

'Dear God,' I said, searching for reasons to disagree, but I had no reason to gainsay her, because the concept was both vicious and cruel, and in full keeping with the de Marshes' character. 'But how could they do such a thing?' I said, already knowing I asked a question neither of us could answer.

My thoughts were cut short by a noise coming from the entrance to the sepulchre, the sound of knocking on the gate, a frantic hammering. I took up the lantern in my right hand and pushed its light-beam back along the passageway. The door was still swinging open and, standing just inside the threshold, was Jacob Fenland.

He was banging some sort of cudgel on the slats of the door, hopping from one foot to the other in obvious agitation, and a gravelly grunt was coming from his throat, his hitherto absent voice seemingly caught in his windpipe. I raced towards him, Rosamund following hard on my heels. When I reached him, each and every one of my body's sinews was trembling beneath my skin and at first I could not speak.

Jacob stopped his clamour as soon as he saw me running towards him, but his eyes remained wide, and that strange, rasping hawk still rose from his throat. He took my arm and pulled me outside, then pointed to the ridge of the hill which we had previously descended towards his hut; there were torch lights flashing at the top of the slope, the sound of men, horses and barking hounds.

'How do we escape them?' I said.

He pointed through the scattered moonlight, the moon herself fallen low on the horizon, her face coloured up with a russet tinge; with anger or pity, I could not know. A narrow path coiled down the slanting land and wove its way towards the outline of a manor house on the opposite side of the shallow valley, and Jacob gestured for us to follow the track. Mother always told me never to trust a drunken man or a wild fool, and deep inside I sensed it was a trap; nevertheless, I was somehow compelled to go on, like blacksmiths' shavings to a loadstone, ever drawn forward against all will and reason.

Before we left, I fronted Jacob, raised the lantern to cast light into his eyes and asked him coldly, 'Does every one of your tiny coffins contain a baby girl?'

He drew his hands up, slowly nodded, and placed a palm on each side of his head, as though the pain held therein might burst out and cause him harm. A moan burst forth from his lips, then descended into a series of whimpers. His eyes seemed to bulge in their sockets, tears fell down his face and a string of phlegm dripped from his nose.

Initially, I wondered whether Sir Hugo or his father had chosen Jacob Fenland for the special job they required of him simply because he was dumb and could never say the truth of what they demanded. Latterly, I supposed the horror of his occupation had indeed deranged his mind and had him swallow down his speech, that words could never paint a picture of what he had seen and done. In the end, I could not help myself; I had to ask.

'If you have a voice, Jacob Fenland,' I said, forfeiting all lenity, 'then why in God's name could you not use it to denounce your masters?'

I made to turn away from the wretched man, inexpectant of any coherent answer, but he caught the sleeve of my coat and had me face him again. He knelt on one knee to be certain the lantern-light played fully on his face, then with his earth-caked fingers and blackened nails, he opened his mouth wide and pulled his lips outwards. I glanced into his mouth, more to pacify the poor imbecile than born of any real interest in what he had to show me. His teeth, I supposed, were normal for a man of his age; some diseased, some dead, several dropped away, but others quite sound. But it was not his dental rack that had me stare wide-eyed into his gape; it was the absence of his tongue. Where that strip of flesh should have been, there was merely the root of it at the back of his throat, blackened and uneven where a blade had cut it from him a long time ago.

'The de Marshes did this to you?' I said, and Jacob nodded, closing his mouth but holding my gaze.

You would suppose his eyes would have been a mixture of bitterness and contrition, resentment for the heinous injury inflicted upon him and repentance for the work he had been forced to do, but instead his eyes spoke of shame. And it was that same look of shame that I had seen in the eyes of Goody's daughter and in the dying orbs of Gilbert Longspere.

So, that was how the de Marshes wielded their power. Rich and urbane, they flaunted their wealth full specious and gaudy, with Flanders capes, Turkish cloth and scarlet belly bands. Just as Roger, debonair and noble, had flattered me – a mere farming boy – by asking me to navigate a woodland path for him and speak a falsehood on his behalf to gain entry to the Winfeld Priory, so he had engendered within me a sense of shame. It took but a moment to do, but once done, I unwittingly crossed a line and in so doing, lost a portion of my liberty, for part of me would always have been under Roger's power. Then feeling isolated and guilt-ridden,

I believed I was the only one to have been gulled in such a manner and, if I had not been able to speak out to Rosamund, then Roger would have succeeded.

What a clever trap to have been set! We are all schooled to respect our lords and betters; gold has a powerful tongue and speaks with firm authority. Jacob was no different to me or Goody's daughter, to Eleanor or Agnes; all of us bred up to be respectful of monied power, flattered by the patronage of our elders and betters, isolated in our guilt, our tongues silenced by shame. The de Marsh strategy was perfect indeed! But perhaps there was another power, too. The power of knowing the truth and telling it, of no longer being ashamed of our shame. Let the ignominy and disgrace belong to the de Marshes, have God decide their fate, knowing that of all the serpents in Hell, it is Dishonour to fellow humans that surely bites the keenest.

Looking at Jacob Fenland, thinking also of Eleanor, Agnes, Matilda, Adela, the tiny corpses in the cavern, and of Mother, too, I was provoked by a deep glow inside me, hot and sudden, the onset of a feverish hatred of all that the de Marshes stood for. And knowing that so many had suffered at their hands, the number of their victims grew wide and expansive in my mind, and as God is my witness, I swear I could sense a wave of endorsement emanating from each and every one of them, centring on me, dilating inside me with a surge and a swell. If by confronting Sir Hugo I would forfeit my own life, then so be it. I had no choice. Duty and destiny are one and the same, and I had been bred up to fulfil both at that precise moment in time, I was certain.

'It is me they want to stop, Rosamund,' I said, turning my head to view the path I must navigate. Then fronting her again, 'Save yourself, stay hidden. Pray let me go on alone.'

She shook her head, pushed past me and began to descend the narrow path ahead of me, but a finger of bramble ensnared her skirt and sent her tumbling to the ground. I dropped the lantern, raced to her side and helped her to her feet, and evermore I was glad for that brief moment, as it was tender indeed. Once back on her feet, I could not help but draw her to me, caress my lips on her forehead, not knowing back then just how long that intimate gesture would have to last me; nothing touches the whole heart as deeply as a remembered kiss.

The moment was broken by the baying of a dog in the distance, which invoked an urgent moan from Jacob and had me release Rosamund from my embrace. I left the lantern lying in the leaves where it had fallen, as it would only have drawn attention to us. Instead, the moon's silver eye lit our path, blinking between ragged clouds and shimmering her broken light along the track, just enough to see by.

'I will prove myself worthy of you, Rosamund Blackmere,' I called over my shoulder as we scrambled down that slope. 'One day the pearl ring will again adorn your finger, I swear by the saints.'

I think Rosamund replied, but I could not tell what she said, as there were stray shouts and barks carried loud on the wind that distorted her speech, and from further behind, someone called my name. Father Oswald's voice was unmistakable and it jarred in my ears, served only to compel me to a faster pace. I supposed the remaining soldiers from Roger's band of militia men had caught up with the priest and were travelling as one swarm, with their stings primed, back to the nest from whence they came.

On we raced down the path, so steep and wearying, pushing on through matted boughs and branches thrown out in every direction, scurrying onwards into the moon-dappled darkness. The footpath was braided with ivy and brambles, catching and tripping our every step, and that tangled track seemed relentless in its endeavours to snare us. But on we tore, with moonbeams glancing through the tree-branches and chill vapours rising as we neared the belly of the vale. We finally reached level ground and directed our steps towards the manor house that we had seen from the opposite slope.

At first, the light was in our favour, but the moon, she was tired that night, she faded by degrees and in a heartbeat, shadows haunted the hillside and the only light came from cressets that had been flamed on the entrance to the outer bailey wall of the manor. On reaching the gate, I banged my fists against that oaken portal, loud enough to wake the Devil himself. In time, a latch was lifted and a face and a lantern appeared. Breathless as we were, I further exaggerated the effects of exhaustion and the guard softened his hostility towards us, took Rosamund's arm to steady her and asked me what the matter was.

'I am a loyal servant … of Roger de Marsh,' I began, my sentence divided into two by my gasps of air. 'Gilbert Longspere is dead and my lord and master is gravely wounded. I have a message for Sir Hugo de Marsh and no other. You must take us to him, sir, and without delay.'

The man paused for a moment and eyed me, brushed his hand over the whiskers on his chin.

'By the saints, man,' I said. 'If my master's haleness is compromised by your hesitation, by God he shall learn of it and you will pay the price of his wrath!'

The prospect of Roger's anger was a powerful stimulus and the man at once turned about and led us across a darkened courtyard, the ground uneven with cobbles and straw. The day's work having finished at dusk, the stables, granary and workshops were all silent and the servants must all have been in bed. There was only a talbot-hound chained to a stake in the ground. The dog grumbled but did not raise a bark.

We followed the man up a covered, wooden stairway and, passing through a doorway, we arrived at a room that was part of the hall but had been screened off, the rafters of the timbered roof high above us, a chill air seeping into the wide space and causing the sweating candles to bend their flames.

'Wait here,' the man said and he disappeared behind the partition, then returned a moment later. 'Sir Hugo will see you,' he said. 'What is your name?'

'Alwin,' I said, proud to say it. 'Alwin of Whittaker.'

We were led beneath a thick, woollen curtain and into the manor's hall. How different it was to the house at Crown Croft; there were no soft lines of plasterwork, no sweet-rushed floor or smells of pottage, no lavender hung from the rafters. Instead, it was all hard edges and dark shadows, boars' heads and antlers. The air was cold but stale. A fire had been set in the central hearth and orange flames licked upwards, sending speckles of light onto the weapons of chase and battle that adorned the walls, but little heat radiated out and the air smelled of sweat and rot.

At the end of the hall, a line of trestle tables and benches were set out with spoons, trenchers and horn mugs, but the tables were in deep shadow and, where jollity should have been, with frothed tankards overflowing; instead the room was cupped with silence, cold and still. An old lymehound lay prostrate at the side of the hearth, raised its head as we entered, then resumed its sleep, and beyond the dog, sitting in a chair of burnished oak with carvings upon it, was the man I supposed was Sir Hugo de Marsh. The servant who had accompanied us thus far, announced his lord's name, spoke my name by way of introduction, bowed his head very low to his master, then left us.

I supposed Sir Hugo must once have been an active man, perhaps even handsome in his youthful years, but time had stolen the hair from his head, and the flesh on his bones had grown thick and slack, giving his dew-lapped cheeks the look of an old hound. His plump right hand grasped the knob of a stick, but his grip was weak, his thumb red and swollen, the skin raised and wet with pus. He sat with his left leg propped on a stool, his bare foot enlarged, the ball of his great toe swollen and skinless. His wounds were corrupt and did stink and I questioned the soundness of his flesh; even his face was infected with a crop of pimples.

He eyed me for a moment, cast a lingering look at Rosamund, then turned back to me and said, 'Well, boy?'

With eyes devoid of all humanity, he looked at me, and with a hand that would not cast a crumb to a beggar, he gestured for me to step closer.

'Margery's daughter,' I said, advancing, 'has come to confront you and hold you accountable for all your sins. I have seen the bodies in the sepulchre and I have spoken with Goody Tanner's daughter; I know it is wilful murder and has been done for generations.'

He looked at Rosamund, studied her deliberately from tip to toe, then turned back to me and said, 'And you are the stripling come to slay me on my daughter's behalf?' His voice was mocking, insincere, forever on the cusp of ridicule.

Over time, I had wondered what marked the de Marshes out as victors. It did not seem to be their stature – although Roger was tall and lithe, he was not thick-set. And it was not their elevated intellect, as mistakes had been made by both brothers, which had led me to that very moment of confrontation. With Hugo's gaze upon me, an unappealing glint in his eyes, I could not help but suppose it was their ability to recognise frailty and doubt in their opponents. They knew their vindictiveness was keener than any other's.

Initially, Hugo stared hard and cold into my eyes with well-practised threat. I endured his look with discomfort, but was able to deflect his ire with a hardened look all of my own making. Thoughts of his despicable deeds rose in my mind and conjured such a loathing for the man, that killing him seemed to be nothing but a blessing. He seemed to sense I was different; I had the look of a mad dog in my eye and would surely bite him to gain my own reward. Unnerved, he lowered his gaze, fidgeted in his seat.

'No cause to be hasty in these matters, lad,' he said at length, smooth and debonair, sounding just like Roger.

But my blood was up and the time for talk was over. Outside in the courtyard, a coil of sound rose up and fumed through the shuttered windows; men's voices, whickering horses, hooves and dog-barks. I drew the sword from my belt, the hilt chill and damp against the palm of my hand, and I raised the blade, compassed the tip towards Hugo.

Footsteps thumped up the stairs, fists were banged on wood and shouts grew louder. I took a step forward, my legs strangely steady, my arm unwavering. My heart throbbed hard beneath my ribs, but not in a flighty way, in a sure and steady manner, filling the pipes beneath my skin with some inner strength.

Hugo blinked his eyes fast, then dared to cast his gaze at me. He knew the end was coming. I drew the sword backwards, the pommel brushing my hip as I did so, ready to thrust it forward and repay the debt of revenge for so many that had fallen at his hand. But in the shortest of moments, I was stopped in my tracks by a noise, a voice.

'No, Alwin!' came the cry.

As a reflex, I spun a quarter turn, backed towards Rosamund, then flicked my eyes in the direction of the curtained partition. I expected to see five, six militia men, perhaps more. But, standing alone, unarmed and breathless, was Father Oswald. His eyes looked back at me, unblinking, and I have to admit there was brazen honesty in his deceit – he looked sorry for all that had gone before. But he made no attempt to deny or explain.

With conviction I withheld the vitriol that danced on the tip of my tongue and instead, I stared deep within his soul and said through gritted teeth, 'Why?'

A moment passed in silence. I shook my head, looked upwards, appealing to the heavens, then settled my eyes back on him. 'Why?' I repeated.

At that, the priest did something I did not expect, something I had not seen him do before; his lips trembled and tears fell from his eyes.

'Your tears are not a worthy tribute,' I seethed. 'The past is gone and can never be restored. You are nothing to me.'

I thought those words would ease the pain with which I was afflicted, but of course, the sting of issuing them would never truly leave me. Father Oswald at last drew a breath and I wondered how he might explain himself. But in the end, it was Hugo who spoke first. I flinched, but it was not his voice that startled me; it was the name he carried on his tongue. A single word, spoken with both certainty and doubt, with belief and incredulity:

'Edward?' he said, staring long and hard at Father Oswald, as a man might look at a phantom, his heart daunted by what he saw.

The word grazed me at first and did not penetrate. Then I thought about its implications; could Edward have merely disappeared and was not dead? Were Father Oswald and Edward de Marsh one and the same? The name hung in the air, scorching white-hot, damping all other noises. The hairs on my head prickled against my scalp and a rushing sound filled my ears. I could do nothing but stare at the priest, not with the hatred I had latterly cultured in my heart, but with a look of abject confusion. He returned my questioning expression with a look of kindness, of repentance and apology.

'Hugo,' he said, turning to his petitioner, calm and measured. 'More than eighteen years have passed since last I set eyes on you, brother,' he went on. 'Time has not been kind to you. Your looks are gone, your soldiers have deserted you, and your body yields to a ponderous disease.'

'My soldiers are with Roger,' Hugo parried. 'He is injured, but …'

'Roger is dead, you fool,' Father Oswald said.

'So were you, Edward, so were you. And it did not serve to deter me in my endeavours.'

'What endeavours?' Father Oswald asked, irritation colouring his tone.

'To secure a male heir for the de Marsh riches, of course, as well you know. Even you cannot hold me responsible for the curse our family carries; a hundred pointless females for every boy that is born; and every boy a worse cripple than the one before; weak, withered and dead before they learn to walk.'

'Do you know how many boxes Jacob Fenland has in the de Marsh sepulchre?' Father Oswald said.

'As many as is needed,' was Hugo's retort.

Never before had I witnessed such contempt in Father Oswald's eyes. If his look alone could have ended his brother's life, then Hugo would have fallen down dead in an instant. But instead, Hugo seemed to absorb his brother's hatred, used it to give him strength.

'Does it hurt, Edward,' Hugo began, smooth and sly, 'that Margery loved me best?'

'She never loved you, Hugo,' Father Oswald answered, sure and certain. 'She was young, naïve, and you beguiled her, like you did so many others.'

'She loved me well enough to lie with me, before our wedding vows were taken.'

'And she hated you well enough,' Father Oswald spat, 'when I showed her the family sepulchre.'

'Just because she hated the family curse,' Hugo said, 'did not mean she loved you. What were you? Fifteen? Sixteen? Your voice was still pitched high like a girl's, if I remember right. You were nothing more than a love-lorn whelp.'

'I was not love-lorn,' Father Oswald protested. 'Love was never lost to me; I loved Margery all these long years, and I love her daughter yet.'

'So how has it come about that Margery sent word to me? Said she forgave me. Sought out a pedlar on the Icknield road a month since, paid him to bring a message to me: my daughter did live.'

'She forgave you, Hugo,' Father Oswald said, 'because she was a good Christian. And she told you of your daughter, because the child grew up and became the greatest treasure that Margery ever knew. She wanted you to see the light, to understand that the de Marsh family curse should have been seen as a blessing. All life is precious, Hugo, both sexes are gifts from God. If only you and Roger could have had faith and embraced those feminine virtues that were such a mystery to you. It would have made you better men.'

'Feminine virtues! What rot! A virtue was it, that had the midwife lie to me for eighteen years? The woman swore on her life that the girl-child had been ... dealt with. Then Margery's message arrives and I am obliged to send the woman out to right her wrong, and to dispatch Roger to search villages, convents and all manner of dwellings to ensure the matter is resolved. So, do not talk to me of feminine virtues, Edward. The Church has addled your mind,' Hugo scoffed. 'You are acting on emotion instead of reason.'

'Think upon what I say, Hugo,' the priest began again. 'What if the dominant beings in our society treated young men in the manner they treat women? To be docile, virtuous, obedient, indolent and weak? Never to challenge teachings or authority? Never to question? Never to disagree? What sort of men would we cultivate?'

'You are deranged, brother,' Hugo said, his voice dark and low. 'Next, you will be suggesting we breed up females to become horsemen, soldiers or farmers!'

I suppose in my mind, I had always imagined a glorious moment of triumph when at last I confronted my father, nimbly stepping forward to reveal my true identity, like a character from one of Mother's stories, watching the moment of understanding and regret dilating in his eyes, as I stood over him with an air of superiority. But, as is habitual in life, matters did not turn out as I had foreseen. As I write down these words and you read them, the sequence of events and their passing might seem cumbersome and slow, but in reality the whole affair was over in the blink of an eye and left me breathless and reeling.

It began with a hand touching my right arm. I had moved away from Hugo when Father Oswald entered the hall, but inched forward, sword in hand, as the two men exchanged words. Rosamund had shadowed my advancement and she was right beside me when she reached out and placed her hand on my arm. I turned to her and her skin was ashen, the accumulation of a week's weariness descending on her features in an instant. In a moment, she staggered and leaned her weight against me. Her eyes rolled upwards in their sockets, as though she were sinking or falling at speed. Then her body crumpled, then folded and she fell forwards to the ground. It all came about so quickly that I could not take up the weight of her before she fell. She melted through my arms and was prostrate in a moment. I remember dropping my sword, tumbling to my knees, calling out her name.

Then the light changed. The shadows became deeper, darker, as though the candles had been snuffed and the fire had died; but they were still lit. I blinked and looked up. Sir Hugo, his corpulent body somehow grown larger still, had managed to rise from his seat and had drawn a dagger from his belt.

Menacing and grotesque, he loomed above me, stealing the light, deepening the darkness about me, as though the moon had closed her eye forever and the stars had all withdrawn their glint. I did not take my eyes from his face as I fumbled to find my sword, but the man's gaze was not fixed on me; his wrath was centred on

Rosamund, and I realised he had not guessed. He still believed she was his daughter; he had not the depth of humanity in his being to recognise his own kin.

He lurched to the left as he took a step forward and raised the dagger high above his head, a hideous grimace torn across his face from ear to ear, despicable thoughts rising in his mind, the prospect of that final conquest stealing all reason from him.

At last that fatal sword was in my hand, one deadly strike but a heartbeat away. I drew the blade back, clenched my teeth, closed my eyes and thrust that shaft of cold steel out before me with such force that I toppled forward in its wake. But I misjudged the reach and the sword never met with any resistance, it neither pierced Hugo's flesh, grazed his skin nor stopped his malicious intent. And unable to halt my forward motion, I fell through the air and landed heavily, hitting my head on a hearthstone as I tumbled.

It was during that motion of declension and slump that I saw a flash of metal in the tail of my right eye. I dismissed it at first as a burst of fanned flame from the fire or indeed the glister of my own sword as I pushed it into the darkness, but I know now that it was a glaive.

The moment Father Oswald understood Hugo's intent, he fetched down the weapon from its hanger on the wall and, as I groped for my sword on the floor, Father Oswald launched the glaive like a spear and felled Hugo in an instant. By the time I scrambled to my feet, Rosamund's hands and lips were moving by small degrees as she came out of her swoon, and Hugo was couched on the ground, his legs and arms in sprawl, the weapon of chase from his own collection embedded deep in the left side of his chest, his dagger fallen from his grasp, lying unused and inert at his side.

CHAPTER FIFTEEN

'Are you all right, Alwin?' Father Oswald asked, rushing to my side and helping me to my feet.

'Aye, Father,' was all I could say.

I went to Rosamund, raised her so she might sit on a bench against the wall. Then the curtain moved at the far end of the hall and five men entered, cautious and silent, eyeing the scene. The first man I did not recognise, but the other four were all part of Roger's band of militia men, the ones that had shouted in support of Ilbert and then lay slumped in innocent inebriation as Roger, John Stanton and the handful of evildoers committed their heinous crimes. How forlorn they had looked when last I saw them, the goodness of their masculinity lost to them under the sway of Roger's power and impiety. What courage they must have gathered from within themselves to see at last that good men and evil men are two different creatures, and the latter when challenged in unity by the former are nothing but weak, sexless cowards.

'Henry Warren?' Father Oswald said, approaching the man at the head of the group. 'You are still steward, I see.'

'Yes, sir,' the man replied, lowering his head.

'You know me, Henry?' the priest went on.

'I do, sir. And it is with gladness that I am here to see you return.'

'For those of you who do not know me well,' Father Oswald continued, 'I am Edward de Marsh, last surviving son of Sir William de Marsh. I have lived in exile from my family these past eighteen years and have grown close to God and the teachings of Jesu Christ, Our Saviour. My brothers, my father and his father before him, all brought evil into your world. But those times are gone. The Psalm of David says: 'Fret not thyself because of evildoers, neither be thou envious against the workers of iniquity. For they shall soon be cut down like the grass, and wither as the green herb. Trust in the Lord and do good; so shalt thou dwell in the land, and verily thou shalt be fed.

'A village elder with whom I have lately communed has told me that Roger de Marsh brought death to his own body by a fall from his horse. And as you see with your own eyes, Hugo lies deceased in this hall. Roger has been laid to rest in an unmarked grave and Hugo will be buried on de Marsh land, but not beneath hallowed turf or on consecrated ground. I will not say mass for him. A pit shall be dug outside the sepulchre, that his spirit may pass by all the souls in that sacred tomb and be judged for his deeds before he finally meets his Maker and is cast out of Heaven for all time. Leave us now, good men. Much work is to begin tomorrow.'

At that, the steward and militia men each gave Sir Edward a low bow and left the room. I stared at Father Oswald; the priest, the cleric, the nobleman, the father-figure. At once he was both stranger and friend, both familiar but unknown to me. I looked deep into his eyes and saw truth and integrity, wholeness and understanding. But there was also the shadow of self-imposed destruction, a fragility I had not seen before, and at once I recognised the burden of taking a life, just as I had witnessed it in Thomas's eyes.

The moment Father Oswald had thrown the glaive and rent Hugo's heart asunder, he had condemned himself to a lifetime of repentance and regret, and I came to understand that when death is imposed in the name of Good, as a last bastion against Evil, it is more often than not invoked by men, and in so doing, a certain tenderness that existed inside them in their younger years, is lost to them forever, because unless they harden their hearts, they will not survive. In short, the burgeoning tradition of manly men is born again when such a responsibility is taken on, and so the wheel turns.

As I turned those thoughts about my mind, I walked towards Father Oswald, gently looped my arms about his neck and drew him to me. His tears did not come straight away, but in time his shoulders trembled and soft weeping sounds came from his lips.

'Forgive yourself, Father,' I whispered. 'For you have not sinned.'

We stayed in tight embrace for some moments more, but then a sound entered my ears, a wet sound, constricted, bloated, desperate. I released my arms and turned about, my eyes darting this way and that, trying to identify the source. Then, Hugo's body moved, just a fraction, and it was clear he was not yet dead. It was more out of curiosity than care that I stepped towards him. Father Oswald followed after me and we both looked down at Hugo's contorted features, as faint breaths rasped in his throat. As though he knew he had an audience, his eyelids suddenly snapped open, his eyes wide and black. He moved his eyes first one way then the other, but whether he saw this world or the next was moot.

'If you still have vision in your eyes, Hugo,' Father Oswald began, his voice not unkind, 'then look upon your daughter. This is she.'

Hugo's eyes flicked askance, centred on me for a heartbeat, then moved on.

'She is brave and strong,' the cleric continued. 'She has been bred up with great physical power and works a plough harder than any man I know. She has sense and reason, tenderness and feeling and owns wisdom beyond her years. She is your daughter, Hugo, a child that any father should be proud of. But you were always too blind to see that. Any one of Roger's or your children could have been just such a specimen as Alwin, here; and that is the reality of the family curse, Hugo. Not a propensity to produce innumerable girls, but the inability to see their potential.'

I can never know what thoughts turned inside Hugo's mind as his life slipped away from him. With his lips forbidden to speak and his body broken, I can only describe what tales his eyes told. I wish I could say I saw repentance and humility, regret and understanding, but I did not witness those virtues. Instead, I saw confusion and humiliation; a sudden and profound realisation that he had never truly understood the world in which he lived and was therefore never master of it after all.

In the end, Hugo's death was quiet and insignificant; as though in bravado his mouth twitched into a simper, then his irises grew dark and wide, his eyes slowly closed and a final, faint breath passed over his lips and he was gone.

I turned about and looked at Rosamund sitting on the bench. How weary she was, all colour drained from her face, a pinched look about her eyes. As I observed her exhausted condition, for the first time I also became aware of my own state of tiredness. Somehow, the compulsion of discovering hidden truths had lent me a certain strength of endurance, which at once began to fade. A strange species of headache started to attack my skull bone, commencing on the crown of my head, throbbing, drumming, like the beating of a small mallet. A pain, keen and piercing, crept over my scalp, made my eyeballs feel tender.

Father Oswald marked the sudden change in my demeanour, he took my elbow and led me to the bench to sit alongside Rosamund. I looked at him searchingly and could only think of gaining his pardon.

'I wronged you, Father,' I said. 'I dishonoured you with doubt. I believed you had drowned Adela and ...'

'You trusted your own eyes, Alwin, and that is not a sin,' the cleric gently parried. 'You were duped by William Tanner and his wife, as were we all. I have already sent men to find them. They will not evade justice this time.'

I cannot recall the detail of what happened next. I heard more voices, but they were oddly both distant and near, alternately muffled then clear. I leaned back, let my eyelids fall over my eyes, then I heard a woman's voice – could it be Mother's ghost? Surely not. Soft words. Mumbles. The air moved, I moved, warm darkness enveloped me and—

When I awoke, the blankets on the bed on which I lay, were neatly drawn over me, as though I had not moved an inch since first the pillow had touched my head. A candle was aflame somewhere in the room, but I could not see exactly where; there was a yellow glow about the space and a shadowy figure in the dimness.

'Rosamund?' I asked, sitting myself upright as I spoke, blinking fatigue from my eyes.

'It is Father Oswald, Alwin.'

'How long have I slept?'

'A full night and day.'

'And Rosamund?'

At that, the shape of Father Oswald rose, gradually defined itself in the scant light, then showed me the face of Edward de Marsh. He sat himself down gently on the mattress, and the bed sank a little under his weight, the blankets growing tighter against my legs.

'Damosel Blackmere,' he began, 'suffers from lassitude. Her bodily strength is not so robust as yours, Alwin.'

'How does she fare since last I saw her? Is she ill?'

'No, no. She must rest, that is all. A servant is attending to her. She will be well cared for.'

'I shall go to her …' I made to peel back the blankets, but Father Oswald gainsaid me.

'Best to let her sleep, Alwin,' he said.

I nodded and the room was silent for many a moment, before Father Oswald remarked, 'You are grown attached to her?'

'Yes,' I said, at once shy and thoughtful.

'And is she ... fond of you, in return?'

I thought upon those words for a while and a while and I reflected on the Rosamund I had first met; our awkward exchanges; the fire behind her words and her eyes; her courage and beliefs. Then I mused on our intimacies. How alive I became in her arms! How softly her kiss touched the core of my heart. But latterly I suspected a cooling of her ardour towards me. Of late, there had been a scarcity of words between us and we had barely spoken of our feelings or of each other. All had been about the de Marshes and the discovery of untold truths. We had become mere travelling companions, two disparate people treading the same path at the same moment in time. Then I pictured the pearl ring, its absence from Rosamund's finger the representation of so many fears and failings; my inability to provide her with the maternal contentment I witnessed when she held Agnes's baby, my fractured standing in the world, my de Marsh kinship.

'Tell me how you feel, Alwin,' Father Oswald said, gentle, coaxing.

'I ... I gave her a ring to wear, but she does not ... it is not on her—'

The pain of confronting the only truth that really mattered to me, was an agony indeed. That terrible realisation of rejection, of spurned love, was greater than any loss I had yet encountered, and would surely become the keenest sorrow of my life. For an age I could do nothing but suffer the torture of my inward woe.

'What shall I do, Father?' I said at length, my voice clogged, my eyes wet and smarting.

It was some time before Father Oswald replied and when he did so, his voice was low, his words delivered slowly, as though he bore news of some terrible tragedy.

'You are very special, Alwin, and in my experience, you are unique. Before we can expect the world to understand us, we must learn to understand ourselves. We must simplify our own complexities, that we may see the world through lucid eyes and begin to understand the limit of what we can expect.'

He paused at that, placed the palm of his right hand on the back of his neck and rubbed the skin, as though the thought of what he might say next caused him physical discomfort.

'Hugo was right, Alwin. Your mother was in love with him and not with me. She did grow to ... care for me as the years passed, but I always loved her more, and that ... imbalance is a burden indeed, Alwin. If you have been stricken with a yearning for Rosamund Blackmere, my counsel would be to take yourself away and develop more balance in your feelings, before you decide to commit yourself to a lifetime of idolatry. Rosamund may indeed have a care for you, but one day soon she will sense the lack of a child in her life and—'

To hear my inner doubts at last spoken out loud by another rebuked my soul with keenness and had me shrink into myself. What before was speculation and fancy, at once entered into the world as a reality and I knew at last that my fears were true: it was not simply that I was a de Marsh, it was indeed more than that. I could never make a child lie inside Rosamund and she would always know that, and always feel the sorrow of it when she looked at me; that was indeed the source of her reticence. I knew then, I could never surrender the knowledge of that truth.

'And the world,' Father Oswald went on, 'may not be so easy to deceive as you grow older and the whiskers on your chin never come, and the curves of your flesh tell tales of your sex. I am ... so sorry, Alwin. At the time, it seemed the only way; you were so vulnerable and we were desperate to protect you.

'At first Margery and I hid you away from the world, fearful that Hugo would seek you out and end your life, because you were not the male heir the de Marshes sought so desperately. But then we struck on the plan to endow you with strength to protect yourself if ever Hugo found you out. Of course, your grandfather never knew the whole truth; he yet believes you are a fine young man, I am certain. But he despises you for being illegitimate, for being a de Marsh, and Margery believed every one of his empty threats.

'Some traditions and beliefs are difficult to overcome, Alwin. It is not always easy to winnow truth from lies, when that which is false is told from every tongue that surrounds you. Even after all these years, I cannot say in earnest that I am wholly persuaded by the veracity of the de Marsh curse.'

'What do you mean?' I said.

'I know that my grandfather and father took maidens to bed in their scores, yet struggled to produce healthy male heirs. I also know that when Hugo was fifteen, he was ordered by our father to secure himself a son. Inside wedlock, outside wedlock; maids or matrons. Hugo was told there were no rules; as long as a son was produced.'

'And were you tasked the same?' I said.

'No. No, I was not,' the priest said, shaking his head. 'My father viewed me as a tainted youth; the weakness in my haunch bones together with my love for the written word had him see me as a runt. It was Hugo he pressed to produce a strong and manly heir. But it was five girl-childs Hugo's harlots did deliver him, but by then I am not certain Hugo cared. It was as though he had only ever been educated in vice and debauchery; a way of living that carried an endorsement from his own father and rendered him unable to curtail his vile habits.

'Roger was but a stripling when I left, but it seems he too was swayed by his father's and brother's will; and far worse did the bloodlust and madness afflict him. But who is to say that their willingness to be corrupted was not the root of the curse? What if Hugo had ignored our father's wishes and instead married a fair maid for love? My brothers were weak, Alwin; and surely all such weakness is wickedness? And they both enjoyed that wickedness too much to look at their world with an objective eye. So, do you see, Alwin? Do you understand why Margery and I had to do what we did?'

'Aye, Father,' I said, meekly.

'And we had to be convincing. I had to teach you what men are taught to believe; that women are born subordinate to the race of men. Now that you are grown and I know you so well, I doubt all that I thought I knew and ...'

'Do you regret who I am, Father?'

'No, no, Alwin. I just wish the world knew you as I do. I wish that I could hear God's thoughts upon you.'

'Does He not speak to you of me?'

'In matters such as this, God will give guidance only to you, Alwin.'

'But how will I know what He wants of me?'

At that, Father Oswald lowered his head, as though thought upon thought built up in his mind and rendered his eyes heavy. Then after a while, he looked at me; the thought he had conceived, so holy and good that it put a smile in his eyes.

'You must seek hallows, Alwin,' he said, declarative and certain, as though he truly spoke the will of God. 'You must become a true pilgrim; take the holy waters, kiss the relics, pray to the saints.'

'I must leave Rosamund and you?'

'You must visit the holy shrines of all England. There is much for you to learn.'

At that, the same feelings I experienced when Mother first told me I must leave Crown Croft came flooding back to me; that terrible prospect of inhabiting a land wholly different to the one upon which my soul had been nourished, but also knowing in my heart that Father Oswald was the dearest and most learned man I knew and that there must be no alternative to what he preached.

With close-lipped forbearance I anchored my will to the tide of his resolution, let time and silence wash over me. But I could not willingly accept my fate. Twice I asked Father Oswald if there could be another way; twice more I said resolutely I could not go. But in my heart, I knew my life was no longer what it had been before; that gleam, that spark of certainty had died away, and my protests against the priest's recommendations were as futile as denying either my present circumstances or my existence on this earth.

'It may not be what you want,' Father Oswald finally said, 'but it is what God has willed.'

Many moments passed as I considered those words and many moments more before I was able to ask the final dread question that burned in my mind.

'When shall I go?' I said.

'Time passes quickly and is lost to us,' Father Oswald said, his voice no more than a whisper. 'If you have the strength, then go soon and forge new and better thoughts, not the ones Margery and I tried in vain to inculcate in you; go tomorrow, Alwin. Go while God's will is so clear in my heart.'

'Tomorrow?' I echoed, the prospect of such sudden change pulling me up sharp, sending a pinch to my belly. A thousand questions about such a journey flooded my mind, but a thousand more posed problems if I stayed. 'What about Rosamund?' I said. 'How shall I tell her? And who will protect her and provide for her?'

'Go at first light, Alwin. I will tell her after you have gone. I will see that she is looked after.'

'And what about Crown Croft and Grandfather?'

'I will send a messenger, and hire men to work the land until you return. And however much your grandfather said he would not tolerate a de Marsh on his lands, I do not believe he ever truly wished you harm.'

'So, I will one day return to Crown Croft?'

'The land at Crown Croft is in your blood, Alwin. When the plague came and took Margery's brother, her mother and many of her cousins; Margery and I persuaded your grandfather to take over the derelict lands that your Uncle Whittaker and his grandfather had left when they died. If it is your wish to return to Crown Croft when God and the saints have shown you your path in life, then let it be so.'

'I wish it with all my heart,' I declared, and tears rose up and clogged my eyes. 'And tomorrow is so soon, Father! How can I muster the strength?'

'God will give you the strength, Alwin. Think about what we have discussed, take sleep, then I will wake you at first light.'

With that, Father Oswald took up the candle and left the room, left me in the dark to fathom what I might. For so many weeks, I had imagined my return to Crown Croft at some point in the future, a time and place conjured by my own fancy, where Grandfather had forgotten his wrath and Mother had not lost her life. But in my dreams and fantasies, Rosamund was always by my side with that look of love that I had once seen in her eyes.

At that moment, lying alone in the darkness with my senses deadened, a heavy heart and a stiffness having settled on my soul, I began to understand just how wide the chasm was between my dreams and actuality, and that however much I invoked visions of impossibilities, even God himself surely could not make them come true.

So, it was a strange and long night that passed as I lay alone in the bedchamber inside the house of my forebears. For so long I had travelled a road that I believed would lead me to answers. But the future had played me for a fool, for there was a time not long since when the present was a bliss to me, and now those moments of happiness were in the past, a place I could not go. And all that was left were ambiguous answers to questions I had not asked, and a future as uncertain as ever it was.

I slept in fits and awoke every so often with a sense of sadness and ill-being, and at times a feeling of despair. I moored my mind to images of Mother, recalling the stories she used to tell me: one in particular about the sea; a huge expanse of water, a thousand times the breadth of the River Crown, she said, with wind-waves so large they could carry a ship on their backs and dash it to pieces in an instant. It felt as though I were adrift out to sea as I lay there that night, suspended in a wasteland of dark water, life rolling and eternal about me, throwing me this way and that on the whim of its tide.

One moment I was certain Father Oswald was wrong, that there must be another way. Then I considered the pearl ring and how Rosamund's womb would never quicken with life. Repeatedly I gainsaid myself; convinced myself I must go to Rosamund. But the possibility of hearing rebuttal from her own lips checked my steps and made me cling to the vanity of ignorance; better never to know than to discover the certainty of a painful truth. So, on my mind drifted, sea-sick and weary, until at last I anchored my thoughts to God, just as Father Oswald had counselled, for I was certain no other might save me.

Father Oswald woke me early in the morning-tide and, startled from my slumber, I succumbed to a fit of weeping that had built within me during the night. A deluge of tears rose up from my heart and flowed from my eyes. I could not say exactly why or rank one reason above another; they were tears born of many woes and even after they dried, they never fully went away. In the midst of my effusion, I lost my resolve and again begged my plea to Father Oswald that there must be another way.

With kind eyes and gentle words, he said, 'Alwin, you know as well as I do that the hardest part of riding a spirited horse is getting in the saddle. Once you have taken the first step on your journey, the next will be easier. You will grow stronger in your mind, see more of the world and better understand your place in it. God will show you the way. Have faith.'

He stayed with me while I composed myself, all the time talking to me about the marvels I would see, the relics I would touch, the saints who would bless me. He told me he had arranged for two travelling companions to accompany me on my journey: Geoffrey Kempe and his wife Elizabeth; trusted servants of the de Marshes whom Father Oswald had known when he was a boy.

He spoke of gold coins he would give to me, and a fresh horse from the stables. But some strange sensation had afflicted me during the night that I could not shake off, and it had my mind drift away from the moment in which I existed. I could neither attach feelings nor emotions to Father Oswald's words. I could feel neither excitement nor trepidation, neither sorrow nor fear. My heart still throbbed its beat, but it stopped sending out sentiments, as though there were a disturbance of balance between me and the world about me.

In time, I asked after Rosamund, and Father Oswald informed me she was still asleep and that it would be better if I left before she awoke.

'You mean I really am to leave without telling her?' I asked, a painful kick from my heart jarring my ribs.

'I will explain everything to her, Alwin. She may not understand at first, but it is better this way, I am certain.'

I nodded, as though I understood, but I was merely agreeing to duty, taking the first step on the road that would bring me closer to God. But instead of feeling righteous and good, I felt a numb sort of sadness wash through my mind, and the thought of doing anything other than lie down and sleep seemed a burden indeed.

The cleric then left me and, with slowness of movement and dullness of vitality, I rose up and dressed in clean tunic and chausses. I can only describe what happened from then on as akin to being a captive, chained to the undulating motion of time, drawn forward against my will and reason, but unable to muster the strength to break free. And with the subsequent depression in my spirits, also came aches in my skull-bone; the sense that a weight was pressing on my head and causing pains behind my eyes. Either living in a dream, or perhaps dreaming whilst awake, a sort of stupor entered my body, and both my thoughts and senses became distorted.

I recall Father Oswald returning to my chamber and walking with me to the courtyard. He talked to me, I am certain, but I did not retain a single word or instruction he voiced. Everything became fleeting and insubstantial to me. I am sure I ate before the journey began, but I cannot remember doing so. A route must have been discussed, but everything held such weak remembrance to me that it was as though I had grown the mind of a caddis-fly and existed in each separate grain of time, then died and was reborn in the next moment with no recollection of what had passed a heartbeat before.

At last, two people were presented to me; the Kempes. Then baggage and bags were packed and horses were saddled, all perfunctory and impassive. The Kempes rode on before me and I found myself hesitating, turning my horse round in a circle, waiting for something, anything, to snatch me from that dream and return reality to my heart. But nothing passed. There was no intervention from God, no double-sun or earthquake. In point of fact, the day was empty, windless, a drear day with blunt shadows, devoid of all season.

At length, I turned my horse about and set my face outward on the road to the south, all flavour of life pressed out of me. Then, as I followed the track away from the manor, having trotted some hundred or so yards along the lane, I heard a shout from behind me. It was a woman's voice, piercing and distressed, issuing an inconsolable cry of woe.

'No! Alwin, no!' came the words soon after, then they died away and the voice returned to its pitiful lament.

The sound of Rosamund's suffering caused a sharp, stabbing pain in the flesh of my heart, each word carrying its own blade and cutting me deeply, and that was the last time for many a while that my heart told my head of its private opinion; for a long time after, there was a rift between the two organs and the one always distrusted the other.

I pulled rein, but could not look back, and the words and the manner in which they were delivered were a thorn in my eye and I could only speak out loud to distract myself from the agony: 'I will suffer your will with meekness, Father Oswald,' I said. 'I know you must be right and I must let God and the saints guide me.'

Then, quite forgetting myself, I screwed round a quarter turn in the saddle, and looked back over my shoulder. Rosamund had fallen to her knees and was weeping as Father Oswald cupped his hands beneath her elbows. Sensing my gaze, she suddenly looked up and that parting glance set a splinter in my heart that I carry to this day. I pray time might one day remove its sting.

The rending of my heart was complete, its chambers sore and disturbed with anxiety, and the intolerable chill of wintertime suddenly descended about me. I clucked to the horse and made effort to continue on my journey, but tristful was my mood as I rode away. Ever after my heart deplored that baneful day and I do not believe I was ever quite the same again.

It is so hard to chronicle those following weeks. My cares waxed cold thereafter, I recked not where I roamed and my recollections are disordered. I remember Geoffrey Kempe and his wife acting gentle and kind towards me, but with a sense of uncertainty, as you might look at a stranger's dog, not knowing whether it holds peace or fury in its bones.

I always felt as though Elizabeth were a little wary of me and might have slept more soundly if I had been secured with a good chain, in some safe place and watched carefully. But although I had not the heart to be good friends with them, we travelled on as adequate companions; I suppose, as I think back, I was silent and sullen for the most part, as I was at war with myself and battling with the world to find my place in it.

In time, our days fell into a rhythm. We rose at prime, dined in the forenoon and took supper an hour before vespers. Fifteen miles we travelled in a day and took shelter and meat from good Christian folk along the way, weaving a path from Bromholme to Ely, from the Guesten Hall at Worcester, to Hailes and Winchcombe, then down and down until we arrived at the shrine of St Thomas Becket in Canterbury.

That is how my life went on; daily rising with the sun and journeying to the next holy place and the next, from mountain to mead and from frith to forest, travelling enough miles to fill the measure of the day, believing that if there were a right way to live life, then God would have me come at it.

At each of the holy shrines, I put up a prayer to God and the saints. I bought a fragment of the rood and a phial of holy oil, and at Canterbury I bought a flask containing the blood of Saint Thomas. The Kempes told me I must be loved by God and would have a good life and death on account of me always giving a generous tribute of coins to the priests at the shrines.

But I felt nothing. To touch my hand to a reliquary or look at a relic was no better than brushing my fingers over a tree branch or watching a bird. I did not feel closer to God and I did not feel blessed by the saints. In point of fact, I disliked the commotion at the shrines. Hordes of folk would assemble in great number, push out their elbow-points and jostle for space, lose command of themselves, always blowing their whistles as we waited for the high priests to open up the holy site. Tricksters and cut-purses abounded, manners were lost, language was coarse and a multitude of savage folk gathered as you would not believe. There was such a rush forward at Winchester that an old woman was hiked underfoot. No salve could be her helping and her body was broken at the hip, then she was carried away and I heard after that she died. It seemed to me that some of the priests found excitation in the affrays and were guilty of stimulating turmoil by delaying the opening of their doors.

In time, frosts slowed our progress, snow trimmed the collars and cuffs of all the ashes and elms thereabouts, and we were obliged to bide in Whitchurch until the season mended. It was the longest and hardest time of sorrow I had yet known. The good people of that vicinity were very welcoming, had us join them in their mummery and wassail, but although Christmas, with its carolling and cheer, might have soothed a heart less hurt than mine, it only served to show me sadness.

I found little pleasure in merrymaking, slighted the festival and the season, and was always keen to take to my bed at sunset. As often as I could, I sat solitary in my room, bleak outside and bare within, or I walked alone through the streets at dusk beneath declining light and glancing sleet.

Hapless I existed from one day to the next, dragged reluctantly to the rattle and whip of daily life. And at night time, I lay awake for many a while ever nursing that secret wound in my heart because somehow the sadness gave me a depth of feeling I did not experience during daylight hours, and love, loss and Rosamund each forfeited their individuality and merged into one sacred recollection that comforted me like no other relic. Yes, the agony of lost love caused me suffering, but somehow I could not let myself forget.

By Plough Monday, the weather changed its face again and exceptional high winds whipped over the lands. Then a strange star appeared in the sky in the evening and an earthquake shook the lands thereabouts. The denizens of that borough never told their fears direct to our faces, but it was clear we were no longer welcome amongst them and we were obliged to recommence our journey the following Friday.

Within the week, we arrived in the town of Plymouth – a port so busy it seemed that all the hulks of the ocean were moored in its harbour. Geoffrey sought out and secured hospitality for us at the house of his distant cousin and we were granted a comfortable bed and honours of the table for as long as we might wish to stay. The Kempes made plans for us to strike out again when the weather improved; to wend a passage up the western borders of England, then across to the holy shrine of Godric of Finchale at Durham, before returning to Walsingham. With my weakened will and no firm future set before me, I agreed to their plan, believing with full faith that God deemed it right.

I wonder to this day how long I might have ranged the counties of England searching for the light of God if it had not been for the malady that struck me down. Two nights before the sickness came on, Geoffrey had spent the day walking about the town, collecting up provisions for our journey northward. The following day, at suppertime, his colour had all but drained away and at first, I supposed the meal he had taken did not accord to his complexion. But then he was struck down with sickness. He took to his bed and Elizabeth did minister comforts, until she too was stricken with the distemper.

My hosts said I must leave; make my way to the abbey that lay some twelve miles out of town and stay there until the sickness passed over. I therefore set out alone the following morning but began to suffer from muscular weakness and could only ride on at a very slow pace. Within the hour, my guts were in ill-humour; a feeling of biliousness, nausea, and I also developed a severe ache in my head. By early afternoon, my body began to shiver and I could think only of dismounting and laying me down to sleep.

My pony must have wandered away from the beaten track, and the onset of eventide caught me at a forest of trees. The breeze dropped low, the clouds grew thick and beneath the sightless sun and the wordless winds in my disordered mind I supposed God had brought me back to the Whittaker woods. I could do no more than sit down on the turf. Then I slept, and my thoughts were stolen away from me.

They told me afterwards that the man who found me was an anchorite, a gentle man who had withdrawn himself from daily life to live among the woodland animals. Local legend had him made of such meekness that once a throstlecock nested in the palm of his hand and he did not move until the last chick had fledged. They say he lifted me in his arms, lay me gently upon my pony's back and took me to the abbey, where holy sisters nursed me. Of course, it was only afterwards during my convalescence that these facts were told to me, because amidst the raging of the malady I was quite lost in my mind.

Inside my head, I thought my journey was continuing; not the physical one, but a spiritual one. How strange that God was not there at the holy sites, or churches and shrines I had visited: not once had I felt His presence. But there in my sick-bed, so far away from my self and my home, He began to teach me. Silent and blind His lessons came to me, a shaft of daylight finding its way into the darkness, and at last I understood.

CHAPTER SIXTEEN

My whole life I had been taught of God's power and creation; manifold and great his blessings, wondrous his miracles. From that, I supposed his strength was all of a physical kind: creating light, water and land, making herbs and trees, fish and fowl, Adam and Eve. But there in my sick-bed, I came to realise that God's light was not simply the sun, the moon, a candle or a lantern; it was the virtue of each and every one of us understanding our own selves and shining a light on the truths within us.

So, as the fever raved on the outside of me, on the inside I walked within my secret mind, witnessed the light of understanding for the first time, and the holy torch of veracity burned within me. I had no more questions to ask of the saints or God. I no longer sought answers. I finally accepted everything as it was.

The first truth was, I loved Rosamund Blackmere right well – I loved her better than my life. It mattered not whether she loved me or not, because I was in thrall to her and would always be so. The second truth was, I loved the lands at Crown Croft; the river, the pasture, the meads and the woods. How I longed for farm smells, croft smells, odours deep and earthy, sharp and sweet, air loaded with the fragrance of summertime or yesterday or just a transient moment. The third truth was, I was born a girl, but brought up as a boy and must live my life in acceptance of past events.

Father Oswald was right, too. To become a pilgrim had indeed shown the wisdom of God to me, but not by paying tributes at shrines, touching my fingers to a remnant of Saint Peter's shroud or looking at a flask containing the captured breath of Christ. Pilgrimage had not guided me to enlightenment through relics, but it had led me to the truth. It was not by wandering England's shires and feeling foreign and out of place that would bring me contentment, wearing out my life with travel and postponements; it was by seeking out Rosamund and returning to the county of my upbringing; being unashamed of the manner in which God had made me. And in that moment, I believed the shire of my childhood sent for me, like a nest calling back a flown fledgling.

Since leaving Rosamund, I had viewed love and pain as one and the same, and as one dropped on my heart, so the other landed soon after. Then I had ceased to conjure feelings of love altogether, afraid the pain would come and spite me. But that doctrine had only brought me misery, and in all honesty, I had drunk deep of life's sorrows and supped my cup of solitude to the dregs. In truth, my life lacked the things I loved best and I was all the poorer for it, so from then on, I roved freely in my mind, no longer afeard of the haunt of her I loved so deeply.

There, rendered inert by physical malady, all my energies centred on thoughts of happier times, and whereas before I thought only of the agonies of rejection and parting, suddenly I was able to unfurl gentle pictures of Rosamund in the folds of my memory; walking side by side through woodland glades spangled with cheerful sunlight; sleeping long beyond forenoon with bodies mingled in soft repose; exchanging words and smiles whilst lost in each other's eyes.

All those things did happen in times past and should be cherished, not spurned, I understood that now. I went on to dream that I might seek her out, forgive her for not wearing the pearl ring and explain to her how I left her for the right reasons.

Mother used to say that to recognise the existence of a problem was the first step to solving it and she was right, so I allowed myself to dream some more. I spoke Rosamund's name out loud, wishing she might somehow hear me, and like wind-whispers through the trees, I heard her voice inside my head and it conjured that same special pleasure within me that it had always done before. My mind wrought images of her in my head and, glowing with the pleasure of them, I lost myself in both pictures of the past and hopes for the future.

The nuns who nursed me asked afterwards what the significance of the name 'Rosamund' was, because upon my speaking that word out loud, my condition began to improve. I told them it was one who was dearer to me than all others, but could say no more than that, for surely words are but a shadow to reality?

The following week, I was moved from the cell in which I had been nursed to a bed in the hall alongside other invalids. How strange that a plague came on so violent as I entered the world, and a pestilence also infected me in such a faraway county, as though I had been born all over again.

Thereafter, the sisters fed me up with rye bread, milk and pottage and they said lessons and prayers to me at mealtimes. In a fortnight, I was able to take myself to the chapel and attend prayers and mass, thereby bringing further cure to my body. Within a month, health and vigour returned to my bones and I was ready to strike northward. I sent word to the Kempes that I was setting out alone to hurry myself back home and that I was grateful for their previous companionship.

On the first morning of my homeward journey, I was impatient to make good ground and I hastened on my path from dawn until dusk. But my body became fatigued and I was forced to ride at a slower pace. I accepted God's will and took the opportunity to enjoy the countryside through which I traversed. On my journey southwards, I had barely taken time to look about me, so busy had I been bustling from one shrine to the next, mired in sad thoughts and purblind to all of it.

My voyage northwards, however, was different indeed. The colours of the counties about me burned bright as a painted window; ingots of gold beamed down from the March sun, drew colours from the trackside flowers and lighted the roads on which I travelled, which ran gilt through the hills, pressing me homewards through the passage of time, until at last I stepped on the hallowed turf of Derbyshire, half a year since first I had left.

Sweet and benign the weather was on that feast day of Saint Patrick and I was wonderful glad in my heart to be closer to home. From then on, the miles were swallowed up and the house at Crown Croft moved steadily closer to me, at last its ice-sharp image appearing suddenly as I rounded that final curve.

Hot ran the blood beneath my skin as I stood and stared at the sight of it; the mead starred with daisies and buttercups; grass stalks paying homage to the southerly wind. The sight of it fairly stole my breath away. Buffeted forward by a favouring breeze, I walked onwards to the old house and beautiful it looked with the sun refulgent about it. Unchanged and honest it stood with such a constancy of heart as only a true-love might have.

Faithful to his word, Father Oswald had hired the wainage necessary for the cultivation and care of the land, and the beasts and crops were all in good plight. The house itself was empty, but the furnishings were just as ever they were, as though I were expected home at any time and had simply spent the morning in the lower meadow or walking the pigs in the Whittaker woods.

In time, I heard men's voices outside and I went to speak to them. Through common discourse, I discovered that they were two labouring men returning to their hired homes in Giolgrave. Each man was being paid three pennies a day to work the land at Crown Croft, they said. When I asked after Father Oswald, I was told that although he hired the men, soon after he left on important business in Walsingham and that it was a Father Ralph who lately gave the men their coinage. I also learned that Grandfather had died some weeks since and that a neighbour's wife was suffering from scrofula.

The men went on their way and I was left alone with my thoughts, a strange brew of sad thoughts and pleasant thoughts, of past recollections and a realisation that time's pigment colours all things, leaves its mark on all of us for ill or good, and that the only neutral thing we truly own, is the present moment in which we exist.

I stayed two nights in the old house, but my legs knew, as surely as my mind did, that my own pilgrimage was not yet done. Once again packing baggage and bag, I set forth alongside the majestic Crown, the water glinting and anxious in the morning sun and the riverbanks burnished with marsh-marigolds. Sweet and fair the spring was that year; ripe and rich the harvest would be! And as the sun shone its light from dawn till dusk, so my mind filled the measure of its days with happy meditations on Rosamund.

I wondered how time might have marked her since all the months had died away between us, and I prayed that my image might dwell beneath the candles of her eyes and that she might sometimes think of me. Repeatedly, I imagined the moment of our future reunion. In point of fact, I thought of it so often and deeply that it might already have happened. I could turn my mind to no other thought and in that like manner I made my way eastwards.

I heaved many a gentle sigh as I plied my course on those familiar roads and tracks, with a multitude of vivid images, recollections and precious thoughts at once filling my mind and stirring my heart. I passed the turning to the Winfeld Priory and was forced to pull rein, a sense of terror bringing tremors to my knee-pans, cold sweat to my skin and painful emotion to my mind. Further on, the house where Matilda had perished showed no signs of the inferno that had raged and scorched and stolen her life, but it still conjured blackened memories for me and I was obliged to turn my eye from its newly built façade and have my pony pass it by with a fleet foot. And the lake that held Adela beneath its skin was smooth and flat, benign and blue; but I rode by cautious and mim, and I kept my gaze firmly fixed on the land.

Soon, I began to thread my way between a path of oaks that had deep-struck roots and branches in full spray, weaving my way through pied shadows beneath the trees. The sun did dight herself in gossamer clouds as I approached the little cottage and the light thereabouts fell a shade darker, greyer, as I put my hand to the door latch.

I pushed the door open. Maud was not there and must have been absent for many a while, for although the inside of the little house was just as I remembered, the roof had grown heavy with moss those past months and some of the thatch had fallen in and strewed the floor. Dust and dead leaves lay dormant on the bed, and woodland creatures had left fur and feathers behind where they had slept away the winter. What once was a place of warmth and love, had become cold and decayed; and in such short a while. How cruel that time can mar the world so freely, but how kind that memory can fix and make amends.

I left the woods with a keener sense of reality than my mind had held since setting out on the final leg of my journey, and I began to perceive that dream-desires might yet be blighted wishes, and that hope and expectation were but distant cousins. All along, I had supposed Rosamund still lived on under the protection of Father Oswald at the manor house in Walsingham. But what if she had left? What if I could never find her?

From then on, woes and cares fell heavy on my heart and I cannot recall any detail from that moment on until the day I neared the county of the de Marsh manor. By the time that particular day arrived, I was desperate keen to see Rosamund; that much I do recall. So, I awoke before dawn, looked out of the inn's window and watched as the sun cast its seed of light on the morning and bloomed into a blazing spring day.

I set off with vim and vigour and rode along a track where halesome herbs and flowers grew in abundance, and primmies and pasque flowers turned their faces to the morning sun. It was one of those perfect days in the season when spring tints begin to grow bold and golden, and Coppers and Brimstones birth themselves out, shimmer their wings in the breeze, then take the westerly winds and soar towards the heavens.

When I gained the village of Walsingham Parva, the sun was noon-day high, an endless slope of light inclining from sky to land, and the de Marsh manor house at the foot of the lane stood luminous between a tract of woodland and a field of pasture that rippled under the breeze. The colours of springtime extended all about me, the birds sent their voices to the treetops and a swell of excitement seemed to tingle in the air, but somehow, I had not the pluck to venture further.

Having given no thought to what I might actually say to Rosamund, I dithered and dallied, then rode on through a meadow, retreated to the margins of the forest and took cover beneath the thatch of leaves. I dismounted, hitched my horse to a low branch and then I wandered on a little through a clearing, a mist of purple orchids growing plentiful in the belly of the brake, all with their blooms in full blow, careless and perfect.

I decided to pick a nosegay of flowers for Rosamund and, kneeling, I suddenly heard voices coming from the track that led towards the manor. One voice I knew in an instant, the sound talismanic to my ears and making pleasure flower inside me. Stimulated by Rosamund's tones, I scrambled to my feet.

Two women walked close together, one holding a swaddled infant in her arms, the child making sounds of distress and fatigue. I crept towards the lane but kept myself hidden and, stopping to conceal myself behind the bole of an oak, I observed the women in silence.

In time, they drew level with me and I was better able to see Rosamund. Suddenly she was there, more comely and fair than even my memory had painted. She strolled alongside the girl with the infant, carrying herself jimply as ever she did, her beauty only ripened and rounded by the passing of time. For a moment, she was scarce a cubit's length from me and outstretched arms might have fetched her to me, so close she passed, and her proximity made me catch my breath. Hot shone the sun through that freckled canopy and hot raced the blood in my heart.

I stood perfectly still and watched her, but I must have leaned my weight to one side by a small degree because a twig snapped beneath my left foot and sent its brittle sound through the air. Her companion did not react, but Rosamund perked her glance in my direction. I jerked my head behind the tree trunk and gathered my cloak tight about me, both wishing she might notice me and hoping she might not.

Then she passed on by, went down the lane towards the manor and I followed her with my eyes. In time, I slid out from behind the tree and watched as Rosamund chatted with her confidante until they both went inside the bailey gate and were gone.

The thing that rooted my feet and muted my tongue was that Rosamund's appearance was so different to when I last looked upon her. From the day I met her to the morning I left, her haleness seemed gradually to decline. How pale she was upon rising, how weak and dispirited she was on the last leg of our journey together. Yet, how vital and glowing she looked alongside her companion. And all that had changed was that I was no longer in her life. Father Oswald had been right after all; it was better I went away from Rosamund; if not for me, better for her.

The pain of that thought burned smartly and all I could do was stare at the ground. My mind fell still and eventually I started to walk back to my horse. Up the track I went, away from the house, still clutching the posy-knot of orchid stems tight in my hand, tears of dew spangling molten in the heart of every bloom.

I cannot say exactly how many steps I took; but after a while I heard Rosamund's voice in my head. I stopped. A soft wind blew and the flowers in my hand sighed out their fragrance. Then the voice came again and it was not in my head. Always enchanted by the spell she cast, I turned about and there she stood, dappled with a tracery of leaves, absorbing the shadow of the elm tree above her.

For a moment she was still, the polarised play of sunlight and shadow shimmering around her, then she stepped out of the shade and at once was held fast in the noon-day sun. With the wings of my heart flapping beneath my ribs, I took a step forward, then another, advancing with urgent restraint. At first, she inclined her head towards the ground, then at last I captured the vagrancy of her eye and when finally we stood just inches apart, all that was missing from my life was suddenly there before me; that sense of private familiarity I shared with no other. I knew at last that peace and gladness stood before me.

We could only speak with our eyes to begin with and I was so joyous that my heart became afraid, then Rosamund blushed a smile in its totality, her eyes, cheeks, lips; all parts to the whole, an absolute smile and no less.

'Come, let us walk together,' she said, and linking her arm through the crook of my own, she led me deeper into the woods.

How mixed my feelings were as we strolled between the trees; joy at her presence, regret at my long absence, and sorrow for remembrance of the manner in which I left her.

'I have travelled many miles,' I said at length, trying to make my tone blithe and merry, 'and seen much of the country these past months.'

'Aye,' she replied, but the smile had gone from her voice and her features became over-clouded. 'Many a long while has passed since the day you left—'

Hearing her speak that sentence out loud, and with such pity behind the words, had a sudden and keen effect on me, as though time itself had not passed in the centre of my heart; the agony of leaving her returned, hot and stinging. At that, we stopped and faced each other, I let the posy of flowers fall to the ground and in turn took Rosamund's hands in my own, suddenly feeling lost and guilty and defensive and raw.

'I ... I could not ... give you ... a child,' I said, my voice weak and broken. 'That is why I left.'

She looked away from me and frowned, her eyes dark and her features suspended, as though the words I had spoken were in a foreign tongue and she must translate them to make sense of them. Then she returned her gaze to me, her eyes offering up that violet stare that I remembered so well.

'But,' she said, quiet and soft, with misted eyes, 'I ... I did not wish for a child. I wanted only you.'

'I thought I had lost your favour,' I said, my words hurried, my features rigid.

'Because I was a little less vigorous and more thoughtful?' she said.

'Aye,' I nodded.

'But, Alwin,' she said, 'it was contentment that stayed my tongue. For the first time in my life I had a glad heart and a loving eye. I did not need to fight battles any more because I had a quiet mind and doubtless love. And my body was weary, Alwin. I was so tired and ...'

'But when you did not wear the pearl ring, I thought ...'

'I always wore the ring,' she said, her voice urgent, confused. 'I wear it still to this day.'

She wiped the tears from her cheek, then with wet fingers she took up the chain she always wore around her neck and there, from beneath her gown, hidden and safe, she drew out the pearl ring.

'It was too precious,' she went on, 'to wear on my finger, so I placed it next to my heart. I thought you saw; I thought you knew.'

I blinked my eyes and flashes of memory scorched through my mind. How selfish and blind I had been! What little attention I had paid to Rosamund all those months ago during the final miles we had travelled together. I had barely looked at her. Obsessed with the de Marshes and concerned only with myself, I had not cared to open my eyes nor even pay her the respect of discussing the matter of the ring. Had she tried to tell me about the ring as we ran down the slope towards Sir Hugo's lair? No doubt she had, but I was too far gone to listen.

How righteous I had felt only yesterday when planning my magnanimity towards her, but how sightless I still was; only able to use the light of God to view my own world, when instead I should have used it to light another's. At once I felt tears rising and ready to spill out from my eyes, but how selfish it would have been to let them loose. I stemmed the flow with the back of my hand, looked her full in the eyes, then drew her towards me.

At first she wept, then at last a sort of peace enveloped her, and there, after so many months had severed us, we embraced one another, the cords of love still entangling both our hearts.

'You come to me in my dreams,' she whispered, her words still tinctured by tears.

'And you to mine,' I said. 'And though I was far away, my heart's bliss never left you.'

'I will always love you, Alwin,' she said in return, with more tenderness than I could have wished for. 'Till the end of my days I will love you with all my heart, but ...'

That last word she spoke, though short and quick, carried sadness with it and a long silence followed. We stepped a little away from one another, our fingers still entwined, the gossamer touch of soft fingertips maintaining our connection. Then a voice called out from behind us and Rosamund dropped my hands.

'Damosel?' came the cry. 'Damosel Blackmere?'

'It is Isabella,' Rosamund said. 'She is a servant that Father Oswald hired to attend my needs.'

A young woman appeared through the trees, weaving her way first one way then the other, looking up towards us every once in a while, to ensure she still advanced in our direction. Breathless she arrived, nursing a scratch on her left hand where rose-brier had snagged her. She looked at me with a frown, then fronted

Rosamund with a vacant expression, all recollection of her message apparently lost somewhere in the woods.

'Well, Isabella?' Rosamund asked.

'Oh, yes,' the girl said, casting another distracted glance in my direction. 'Peregrine will not settle, Damosel. I believe only his mother might give him peace and I bid you attend him as soon as ever you might.'

I suppose in everyone's life, a multitude of factors dictates the passage we take; God's will; the Dog Star; the Fates of others; and indeed Time itself. All those aspects and more had had a hand in my own life and the longer I lived, the more complex my journey became. But I had already begun to understand that only two things might deflect the pain of unexpected events; patience and hope, for no other virtues were surely closer to peace.

Inwardly, on realising that Rosamund had a child, my heart stuttered in little contractions as though it silently sobbed, but externally I kept my features taut and I did not succumb to weeping. Instead of shining the light of truth on myself and exposing my own wants, I directed its beam on Rosamund and at once felt a fragment of the joy she must have experienced when becoming a mother; I genuinely felt delighted for her.

For several moments I was lost in my own thoughts, a sort of pulsation agitating my mind, stirring up rights and wrongs, hopes and disappointments. And from the world outside my head I heard only wisps of conversation as Rosamund sent Isabella back to the house. Then Rosamund and I were alone again, facing each other, and the love-light in her eyes burned fierce as she looked up at me.

'About my child, my boy,' she began, her voice treading uneasily, trying to find the right path.

'I am ... glad,' I managed to say.

'Do you not see, Alwin? I was ... already carrying the child when I met you,' she said, the tone of her voice now tinged with distress.

I paused for an age, hearing her words, knowing what they meant, but unable to understand their implication. 'What can you mean?' I eventually said. 'What are you saying?' I asked with greater urgency, all answers to her statement evading me; did she always love another? Was she wed before we met?

'I made the mistake of trying to reason with Roger de Marsh,' she said quietly. 'Just before Eleanor gave birth, I had her tell me their trysting place and I went there one eventide. But I made the mistake of believing he was a man, when in fact he was a fiend, more dreadful than any fables do tell. He saw me there in the twilight; a woman, alone. His eyes were so dark; two tones darker than any other blackness about me. A savage hunter, and his prey was woman. He did not seem to hear my voice and I do not believe he saw me as a human. He … took me with great violence and left me there in the dead of night. I never told Eleanor and I did not know the child was coming. My menses did not stint at first and …'

'Your child is the son of Roger de Marsh?' I said. I did not intend to colour my words with any bias, but Rosamund flinched a little as I spoke them, as though I had pronounced a great severity and abandoned all charity. But how wrong her reaction was. Surely our worlds had grown closer and our bonds of kinship become tighter? 'Then he is my cousin,' I declared, warm and loving.

'Oh, Alwin,' she breathed.

At that, I forgot all cares and propriety, and I quenched my lips in the bliss of her kiss, and when her mouth touched mine, she took me to a place beyond my eye, beyond my intellect and outside my understanding, to a pathway for my heart only. In all the months of our parting, I had not truly understood just how much the kiss of her lip had left a mark on my soul. But when the kiss was done, the world rushed back to me. Questions and complexities whirled around my mind, and how I might navigate my way through them was beyond my ken.

Then Rosamund said the words that put everything right; two questions she asked, with such love and yearning in her eyes as might only happen once in a hundred lifetimes.

'Will you always love me?' she said.

I nodded and whispered, 'A chain of links binds both our hearts. I think we both know that.'

'And will you hold my hand when I am dying?'

'It is an unhoped promise I pledge to you, here and now, as God is my witness.'

And with those words and looks, we did bind ourselves to a vow more sacred than any litany chanted since the beginning of time, and a sense of peace came over us as though we had caught a glimpse of the end and must simply guide our steps towards it.

At last we stirred ourselves, unhitched my pony, and made our way to the bailey gate. Rosamund led me across the courtyard, up the stairs, and on into the hall where last I had seen Hugo lying dead on the floor. Beyond the hall, she walked through a doorway, then turned and beckoned me to follow.

At the far end of that withdrawing-room, another screened doorway stood on the right and from that chamber threaded a ribbon of joyful noise, that wove its way through all my apprehension and fear, through both my ignorance and bias. And the music of that infant's voice made my heart into a bird that flapped gently behind my ribs. How sweet the child's visage when I laid my eyes upon his face! How new and fresh he looked, clean of all blot and stain, not yet a month in this world.

Isabella, who had been watching the boy, rose from her bench and left the room. With his mother's arms about the babe, he cooed and gurgled, lifted his blue eyes to hers.

'Alwin,' Rosamund said, turning to me. 'This is Peregrine. Our boy, Peregrine.'

Then she passed his little frame to me; I took him in my arms; and I took him to my heart. On that, our first meeting, he was so lusty and strong. But within a week and a day of my return, Peregrine developed a fever, his sweet soprano tones became hoarse and his breathing was so laborious to him that I was certain he would suffocate. The fierceness and suddenness of his ringing cough sent shivers to my heart, and all our lives stood still as his battle with life and death raged on before our eyes.

Rosamund called on all her knowledge of herbs and healing, brewed a tincture and had Peregrine inhale the vapours in his sleep. At first, he seemed to breathe with more ease, but in time the symptoms returned and hour by hour his haleness decayed, and with a thousand pities we watched over him.

Deprived of sleep and eroded by anxiety, I lived on in a sort of stupor; a stifled misery from which I could find no relief. It was as though a cold, grey cloud had settled beneath my skin; as though I would always live my life at the end of the day when nothing more could be achieved. In desperation, I sent the steward and a man to ride out, find Maud and bring her to us. In like manner I sent a farm boy, with the most mettlesome horse in the de Marsh stables, to seek out Father Oswald at the abbey where he was presently discharging the duties of his office.

Three days passed. Four days and a night. Then on the fifth morning, Father Oswald rode into the courtyard and how gladsome it was to set eyes on the dear cleric! With neither time nor reason to dwell on the past, all of us centred our prayers on Peregrine. And as Father Oswald spoke holy words and performed holy rites, at length Maud came to us and set about mixing her potions.

But a day and a night onwards and the boy seemed to be slipping away from us. He left off taking his mother's milk, and his shallow, fitful sleeps became deeper, quieter. There was a moment in the mid of the night, when Isabella and Maud were gone to the kitchens and Father Oswald was at prayer in the chapel, when a profound silence entered the chamber and lay itself over Peregrine, Rosamund and me. After all the prayers, after all the herbal elixirs; just silence was left. I had not heard such quietness since last I slept at peace beneath the rafters of the house at Crown Croft.

I let the hush wash over me; let it grow from more to more; made it mine. And in that moment of silent clarity, the saint of all trusty truths came into my mind and I knew at once there was only one thing that would be the curing of Peregrine; there was but one patch of land in the world that might heal him; a place where peonies and gromwell grew; where the scent of honeysuckle and lavender wound upwards through the windows all summer long; where dabchicks and moor-fowls oared themselves through the waters of the Crown, and widgeon and coot were ever busy about the river's brink.

'Rosamund,' I whispered, never more certain of anything that had gone before. 'We must go home. We must take Peregrine to Crown Croft.'

'But Alwin,' she protested, 'he is so frail. He might not live if we go.'

'He will surely die if we stay,' I said.

For more than a moment, each of our pair of eyes stared at the other, a gentle shock rippling between us. Her assent was then sudden and clear. She looked at me in a way she had never done so before, as though some fundamental truth were visible to her, not through her eyes but in the chambers of her heart; the embodiment of a wish so sincere that belief had finally invoked its happening. She gently folded her arms about my neck and drew me to her and I knew in that moment that what I wished for was possible; because it seemed to be possible and we both believed it.

When first we told Maud of our plans, she cast out all prudence and distrust and told us we were right; unequivocally right. Father Oswald also said yea to us, and told us that Saint Peter believes we must all hope to the end. From goblins' hour to daybreak, we packed bags and provisions and by the time the sun was up-risen, we were on our way home; Maud, Father Oswald, Rosamund, Peregrine and me.

At first, the child's demeanour did not change. But after a mile or so, he wriggled his little swaddled body and opened his eyes, the air and the light appearing to stimulate him. That night, Father Oswald gained us harbourage at a lord's house; introducing himself as Sir Edward de Marsh; taking full advantage of his noble birth. In our bedchamber, as Rosamund rocked her son in her arms, the boy gave voice and she put him to pap. He took only a meagre sup, but it was surely enough to sustain him. Then in the mid of the night, he took more. By morning, I swear the grey tint of his skin had faded and a sort of glow had returned to his cheeks.

On we travelled. Day by day drawing closer to Crown Croft. Hour by hour, Peregrine gaining his vitality. At last we found ourselves on a familiar woodland track, where deer bruise their path through the saplings. We followed the cleft alley through the oaks and elms, the southerly breeze gently buffeting us forward. Eventually the trees fell away, we crested the brow of a hill then descended a slope of heather-dappled moorland, until we came upon open turf that shimmered with tender-bladed grass stems.

By the time we reached the crossroads, the skies had reached that pink-blue flush of eventide. The sun drew long shadows on the ground and the evening breathed soft dew on the air. The days of my journeying were far behind me now, and undulating pasture rose and fell beneath me as we advanced homeward. That familiar landscape was always pleasing to my eye, its calming curves always able to smooth the frown from my brow.

Finally, I saw our journey's end; the homestead's silhouette enveloped in a crease of sky. The house at Crown Croft when seen at a distance was nothing more than the suggestion of either a hunched old woman or elderly man, its stooping thatch buffeted by the storms of times past, the texture of its wattle walls wrapped close as a cape about its frame. With timeless timbers and ageless plaster, it welcomed us all, induced us to step over its threshold and live our lives within the comfort of its walls.

So, at last, my dearest wish came true; I took Rosamund Blackmere home to the house at Crown Croft and gave blithe welcome to her and our boy, and there we lived content in our own felicity.

Maud, driven out of her woodland cottage by bigots and slander, stayed on with us till the day she died some years later. Father Oswald disposed of the manor house in Walsingham, gave half its worth to the church and let the rest be put aside for Peregrine and the upkeep of Crown Croft. The dear priest took up his old lodgings in Giolgrave and was a fine mentor to Peregrine.

But over the years, I could not help but notice the cleric was a changed man. At last, he told me he could not reconcile himself to the pangs of remorse that haunted his departed years. He lamented in regret that he had severed my cares for Rosamund and sent me away. He believed he had blighted my life; but I told him that was never so. And he could not forgive himself for Hugo's death, although what else he could have done in that awful moment, I cannot wonder.

In the end, he took his own counsel and journeyed on a long pilgrimage. Not only did he visit the holy sites of all England, but also he travelled to the shrines in Zeeland, Santiago de Compostela and the Holy Lands. Myriad countries he roamed, countless shrines and relics he venerated, but when he returned many years later, he said he still carried shame in his heart for decisions he made as a younger man. He said all that was left, was for him to pray for the peace that my pardon might bring, and hope through Christ he would find mercy and forgiveness. So, he went away from us for the last time, took holy orders and devoted his last years of life to prayers and contemplation. I never saw him in person again and he died an old man in his fifty-fourth year, but I still see him in my dreams as a younger man and my love for him will never die.

From the moment Peregrine was carried over the threshold, a sense of vitality returned to the house at Crown Croft, a feeling of safety, hope and promise. It was with such fondness I looked upon the lad; I was so proud to be his kith and kin. Each day he grew stronger. The meadows gave him health, the sun gave him vigour and the love of his mother was the best physic of all. Each year his height was stinted at first, then a rush towards the sky come summer; just like the barley.

By the time he was seventeen, he was tall and well-favoured in his looks. In time he took himself a sweeting, was wed to her and she gave him two fine boys and a girl. His sons and daughter now play in the garden where the peonies and gromwell grow. They ride their ponies through the meadow with its grasses tawny and sere from the summer sun, and they paddle their feet in the River Crown, where dabchicks and moorfowls oar themselves through the water.

So, Rosamund and I spent our days in peace, surrounded by our family, ever in love with one another, our lives breathing a long farewell to the bygone age of our youth. With Father Oswald's endorsement of our union, the neighbours thereabouts accepted us in their fold and never doubted that Rosamund and I were man and wife, or that Peregrine was my son. Or if they did harbour any scruples, they neither voiced nor demonstrated them to my knowledge.

But the weeds of time grow thick on passing years, a cycle of suns and moons rises and falls; each season passing faster and our bodies growing slower and softly sinking until the past conjoins with the present.

In Yuletide last year, Rosamund took ill and seemed to advance suddenly into the winter of her years. Day after day she lay in bed, unable to rise, her silvered hair loose about her shoulders as though snow had frosted her pillow. With her family all about her and her hand held fast in mine, my final promise of true-love's pledge was at last fulfilled. Her ultimate breath was exhaled and where once was the flow of life, came the ebb of ever after. The turn of the seasons had taken their toll on her and the stillness of eternal peace finally settled on the woman I had loved so dear.

Those who wear Time's furrows on their brows know that life does not stop when half your heart dies, but the strength of your pulse is slower and weaker. My hair is no more than white wisps and my skin is so weathered that it could belong either to a master or a dame, and Time itself might have forgotten which. The house at Crown Croft might ring for future generations with the sound of life and love; but my own part in it is drawing to a close, for an ending of all things must be.

The doorsill at the old house is never without the gentle tread of footfalls; each and every pedlar, traveller and pilgrim is invited in by Peregrine, and as they sit by the hearth, he tells them stories of his happy life on the land with his kith and kin. He is the kindest and gentlest of all men, who lives a calm life in contentment and is truly master of himself.

There is no person that can describe or imagine the joy of closing the circle, of bringing goodness and right to the place of its belonging, and I hereby charge God, Mother, Father Oswald and Rosamund Blackmere with being most just and benevolent in gifting this privilege to me.

I pledged to tell the legend of my life and I hope its telling has not been unprofitable to any soul as might have read it. Some folks will say it was extraordinary, some will say it could not be true; but, as God is my witness, that was the way of its happening.

AUTHOR'S NOTE

There are many sources from which I have drawn inspiration for *Requiem for a Knave*; museums, priories, documented eye-witness accounts from the period and contemporaneous literature and poetry. Some of the many books which helped me along the way include: *The Time Traveller's Guide to Medieval England* by Ian Mortimer (2009), *The Witches' Ointment* by Thomas Hatsis (2015), *A Medieval Miscellany* edited by Judith Herrin (1999), *A History of Everyday Things in England 1066 - 1499* by Marjorie and CHB Quennell, *Medieval English Lyrics* edited by Theodore Silverstein (1971), *They Saw It Happen – An Anthology of Eye-witness Accounts of Events in British History 55 B.C. – A.D 1485*, compiled by W. O. Hassall (1973), *The Book of Margery Kempe*, translated by Anthony Bale (2015), *Revelations of Divine Love* by Julian of Norwich, translated by Elizabeth Spearing (1998), *Mothers, Mystics and Merrymakers* by Sarah Hopper (2006), *Life in the Middle Ages* by Martyn Whittock (2017), *Medieval Life* by Andrew Langley (2002), *Piers the Ploughman* by William Langland translated by J F Goodridge (1970), *Medieval English Verse* translated by Brian Stone (1964).

It would also be remiss of me not to pay respectful remembrance to the sixty nuns who in the autumn of 1379, according to the contemporary chronicler Thomas Walsingham's *Historia Anglicana*, were mercilessly raped and murdered by Sir John Arundel and his detachment of soldiers.

ACKNOWLEDGEMENTS

Following what has transpired to be rather a challenging year, I cannot thank family and friends enough for their unstinting support: Janet Carlin, Caroline Lee, Brian Lee, James Underhill, Jayne Underhill, Fiona Keohane-Gaskill, Michael Keohane, Angela Keohane, Janet Lampitt, Ray Lampitt, Graham Richards, Ann Richards and Betty Blount.

I owe a huge debt of gratitude to my brilliant agent, Laura Macdougall at United Agents, and I offer my profound thanks to my editor at Hodder & Stoughton, the wonderful Melissa Cox.

Special thanks also to Lily Cooper, Katharine Delves, Will Speed and everybody else at Hodder who has worked on the book.

I've also really appreciated the support and encouragement I received from authors in the writing community for which I am deeply grateful, including: Kaite Welsh, Ruth Hogan, Louise Welsh, Zoe Strachan, Sara Collins, Imogen Hermes-Gowar and Sophie Ward.

Finally, for her patience, humour, support and love, I offer heartfelt thanks to my partner, Shirl. All that I am, I owe to her.